Rebirth

of

Angels

pdmac

pdmac

Rebirth of Angels is a work of fiction. Though actual locations may be mentioned, they are used in a fictitious manner and the events and occurrences were created/invented in the mind and imagination of the author, except for the inclusion of actual historical fact. Similarities of characters or names used within for any person – past, present, or future – are coincidental except where actual historical characters are purposely interwoven. The actions, thoughts, and dialogue of the historical characters featured in this story are fictional and not meant to reflect actual personalities and behavior.

Published by Trimble Hollow Press, Acworth, Georgia

ISBN: 978-0-9861523-4-4

eISBN: 978-0-9861523-5-1

Cover design by Trimble Hollow Concepts

for Terri Lynn
my Soulmate and Best Friend

A very big *Thank You* to Lin Ruth for her seamstress talents. Another big *Thank You* to Carmen Coyle for her unwavering support and enthusiasm.

And a very special thanks to Stan Rogers, City of Rome, Georgia, Cemetery Director, for the liberal access to the Myrtle Hill Cemetery.

More Science Fiction by pdmac

Fool's Gold

Wolf 359

Wolf 359: Queen to Play

Wolf 359: A Once and Future King

Chapter 1

Resurrection Industries, Decatur Facility
North Arcadia Avenue
Sunday, April 30, 2102

Number D107A44B, also known as JB, watched as the men and women in white lab coats escorted a young woman past the windows of the small gym where he was striding in a comfortable pace on a treadmill. The woman seemed happy, just like all the others he had watched pass by and he wondered what they were saying to her. Was it the same they said to all the others? She had seen him as they passed and gave him a wave of recognition and acted like she was going to stop, but the people in the lab coats hustled her along and she was soon gone. What he found interesting was that the people in the lab coats tended to stay the same, but the ones they escorted were always different. In fact, a point that he had observed was that he had never seen any of those escorted past the gym windows ever return in the opposite direction.

"Let's pick up the pace a bit, JB."

His attention was diverted to the lab assistant who gave him a quick humorless smile as he monitored the cardio output data screen. Checking the various electrodes leading from JB's chest to the machine, the man then focused his attention to the screen, entering data into a small handheld computer.

"Let's pick it up to four minutes a kilometer, gradually."

JB gradually increased the pace and again settled into a rhythmic stride, a bit quicker than before. Yet his focus was on the woman who had passed by the window. He remembered her. It was more than thirty days ago, but he remembered her, despite the fact that he had encountered her only once. When one spends most of one's time alone, any encounter with someone other than a lab assistant or doctor is memorable. Yes, he remembered her. Her name was Sylvia.

It had been lights out time and he was in his room, as always. It was a small room, sterile with barred windows high up on the wall so that he had to stand on the bed to look out.

1

Despite his best efforts, all that he could see was sky during the day and darkness at night. Sometimes at night, he could see stars and every now and then the moon in its various phases. Yet it was the window that allowed him to wonder what was happening on the other side.

He could tell seasons changed outside by pressing his hand against the glass. Sometimes the glass would be warm and many months later the glass would be frigid cold. His observations were confirmed by subtle comments the lab assistants made complaining of the heat of summer, cold of winter, or incessant rain.

But this night a little more than a month ago, he was standing on his bed, his hand pressed against the glass when the door opened, silhouetting two individuals. One was a lab assistant. The other was a woman, a little shorter than her escort. Without a word, the woman was gently pushed in and the door closed behind her.

She awkwardly stood in the doorway, shy and hesitant. They both knew why she was there. The scenario had been played out on a regular basis not long after he had reached puberty. Now it occurred every seven days.

Stepping down off the bed, he sat on the mattress and patted the place next to him. "Sit?"

Inhaling a deep breath, she crossed over to sit next to him, her arms folded in front of her.

"Talk?" JB tilted his head forward to gaze down on her. The lamp in the ceiling slowly gained a dim light that cast a warm glow on the walls. Lightly patting his chest, he declared, "JB." Pointing a finger at her, he asked, "You?"

"Sylvia," she replied, her voice delicate and throaty. Frowning at him, she then raised an eyebrow. "I can talk, you know. I can even use words to make sense."

"Sorry," he half-smiled. "Not everyone can."

JB studied her as she met his gaze with her wide eyes. She was slender with short dark hair that fell above her shoulders. She wore a simple smock that buttoned up in front.

"Do you know why you are here?" He peered intently at her.

"Yes," she sighed, turning her head. "Of course. Why else would I be here? I'm not stupid."

"Sorry. Didn't mean to offend you," he soothed. "You do not like it?"

"No," she uttered, a little too strongly as she jerked her head to stare at the door. When it didn't open, she lowered her voice and added, "Always someone different. Some are nice. Some hurt."

"I know," he nodded in understanding. "Never get the chance to be with someone you like for more than once."

"Why do they do that?"

"Don't know," he shrugged.

"Why do they do this to us?" she sourly wondered. "Never get to do anything like them."

"Don't know," he shrugged again.

"You don't know a whole lot, do you?" she huffed.

"Just like you," he retorted, lips pursed.

Her shoulders settled slightly as she let out a breath in a sort of sigh mixed with frustration. "It's not because I haven't tried. I've asked many times to go outside or do something like they do. Most laugh and tell me not to be foolish. A few have told me that it's not possible right now, but my time will come when I will leave this place, forever."

"I too have been told the same thing," he nodded in agreement. "But they are not telling us everything. For instance, can you read?"

She looked curiously at him. "No."

"Neither can I. Yet all those who call themselves doctors or lab assistants or nurses, they can all read. When I ask why I can't read, they tell me it is not necessary. When I ask them to teach me, they refuse. They tell me it is a waste of time. If that was so, why do they all do it then?"

"I was told the same thing," she ruefully replied. Soft music seeped into their awareness. Sylvia was the first to notice it. "The music is very nice."

"I find it relaxing," JB explained. "It's by a man named Debussy. When I asked if he lived close by, they laughed and said he had been dead for many years. I didn't understand what 'dead' meant and they said that it meant no longer to exist, like the food you eat. When you're finished eating, it's gone." He shook his head. "I said, 'does that mean you ate him?' They laughed and laughed as though what I had said was clever, but all they said was that to be dead was to be no more. I still don't understand."

Sylvia frowned in puzzlement. "Dead? How can one be dead? And how long is a year?"

"I think I understand that one," he triumphantly announced. Pointing to the window above the bed, he explained, "I've noticed that when I place my hand on the window, there are times when the glass is very cold. When I asked why, I was told it was winter outside. I asked what 'winter' was and they told me that a year was divided into four seasons: spring, summer, fall, and winter. Winter was when it turned cold outside. So all I have to do is keep track of when the glass is very cold, and I know a year has passed."

"Do you know how many years you have?" she asked.

"You mean, 'how old I am,'" he gently corrected her. "I don't know. No one will tell me how many years I was here before I began counting, but so far I have counted fourteen years of winter seasons.

Sylvia finally allowed herself to turn her head and study the man sitting next to her. He looked a lot like all the others, strong and fit. His hair was blond and his face seemed kind. "Have you spent time with others like you?"

"Once, but I think that was a game they played on us, and I didn't like it. Neither of us did."

"Me too," she readily agreed. "Her name was Anna. She was very nice. We talked until they came in and said we were supposed to do what you and I are required to do. We said 'How?' We are not made like men. They laughed and said 'Use your imagination.'"

"What happened?"

Sylvia awkwardly shrugged. "Nothing. Neither of us knew what an 'imagination' was and if we were supposed to use one, they never gave it to us."

JB solemnly nodded. "Why is it they tell us some things and purposely not tell us other things?"

"I don't know."

Debussy's *Clair du Lune* layered over the silence that settled between them. "How long will it be before they come to take me away?"

"I don't know. Sometimes they've let the woman spend the night with me, but it's not very comfortable because my bed is too small for two people."

"I have never spent the night with a man," she said. "When we are done, I usually want to be alone. Once or twice I wouldn't have minded staying longer."

"Do the others talk?" he ventured.

"Some do, others don't." She scooted closer to him, almost touching him.

"I like talking" he affirmed, "even if I never see her again. Just doing it without talking doesn't seem to be as much fun for me."

"I agree," she thoughtfully answered. "So… When they finally let you go from here, what do you think you want to do?"

"I want to walk as far away from here as possible," he firmly stated. "Never want to see this place again. I want to walk and see new places and talk to people and learn how to read and learn more about numbers. Look," he said holding up his hands and spreading his fingers. "See. I know how to add and subtract. Ten take away five is five." He made a fist with one hand. "I know how to do this with my hands for numbers that go into the hundreds, but it would be easier if I could use a symbol for larger numbers." Leaning closer, he whispered, "They let me have some paper and a pencil. Want me to show you what I've done?"

"Yes," she smiled.

Glancing quickly around, he stood up and pulled up one end of the mattress to retrieve a stubby pencil and several pieces of paper. Sitting back down next to her, their shoulders pressed together. "See," he flipped open the papers. "I've used symbols to represent numbers. One line equals one, two lines is two, and so on up to five which is a little circle. An 'X' represents ten. So the number fifteen is an 'X' with a circle."

Sylvia's mouth slacked open. "That is so clever."

Liking her reaction, JB continued. "When the numbers get bigger, it's too much to keep writing all the X's, so I use a line through the Ө to mean fifty and a line through the X to mean one hundred. So two hundred and fifty seven looks like this." He slowly wrote the symbols X̶X̶Ө̶OII as she watched.

"I've never been with anyone so clever," she enthused.

The door opened silhouetting a lab assistant. "Are you two going to talk all night or am I going to have to send her back?"

"We're getting there," JB sourly objected. "Stop rushing us."

"Well get a move on. You don't have all night."

"Why not?" JB spoke before thinking.

"Because I said so," the man shot back.

"Some of the other lab assistants let me have her spend the night."

"Well I'm not them, am I?" he tersely replied. "You've got five minutes to get something going or she's outta here."

"Why?" JB stubbornly demanded.

"How long is five minutes?" Sylvia interrupted.

"What?" the lab assistant scowled at her.

"I asked how long five minutes was."

"Too long," the man snapped. "You two get busy or I'm sending her back." Without waiting for a reply, he stepped back and closed the door in a loud thud.

"I don't like him," JB whispered. "Never have."

"What's his name?"

"Sir. He told me that I was to call him 'Sir.'"

"How did he know we were still taking?" Sylvia stared at the small opaque glass in the middle of the door, about head high. "Do you think they can see through that?"

"Yes," he softly replied. "I discovered that not too long ago when I was waiting for someone to unlock the door for me. They can see in, but we can't see out. When I asked why, they told me that it was so they could check on me and make sure everything was OK. I said I wanted to look out, and that I wanted to go to other places, see other things and talk to other people." He put the paper and pencil back beneath the mattress. Sitting down again, he gently leaned into her. "They told me that it was impossible for me to do that right now. When I asked why, they said it was because we were special. He called us angels, that we were being prepared for something very important. I asked what an angel was, but no one would tell me."

"Angels?"

"Yes."

She hesitated a moment before asking, "Do you think he's watching right now?"

"Yes."

Pausing only a moment, she lowered herself to the floor to kneel before him. "I don't want to go yet. I want to spend the night."

"I would like that." He blinked with pleasure as she unfastened the buttons to her smock, slipping it off her shoulders to settle on the floor. She was pretty and well proportioned, just like all the others.

Slowly sliding her hands up his thighs, she slyly cast a glance at the window in the door. "Let's take our time then. We can talk while we do it."

JB's reverie was broken by the lab assistant. "You're picking up the pace too much." He cocked his head to stare quizzically at him. "You seem distracted."

"Just thinking," he casually replied.

"About what?"

"About a lot of things," he evasively answered.

The lab assistant gave him a half-lidded look of doubt. "Let's taper off and cool down. Ease off to a four-forty pace."

Sylvia looked up when the door opened to her room. Two lab assistants stood in the doorway smiling at her. One was Raymond, her favorite lab assistant. She liked him because he always smiled and said nice things to her. She didn't recognize the other one, but he smiled at her though not like Raymond's smile. His smile seemed to be for show.

"Good news, Sylvia," Raymond exclaimed, walking in. "You're on your way out of here today."

Her jaw dropping, eyes bursting wide, she jumped up. "I'm leaving here?"

"That's right. Doctor Grant here has signed the authorization." He waved a hand at the man next to him who held up an electronic hand pad as proof.

"I'm actually leaving?" Sylvia stood for a moment looking blankly at them before turning to look around the room. Unexpectedly she felt strange, off balanced at the thought of leaving the comfort of routine and all that she had known in her life. She had anticipated this day for so long that now it was here, she was unsure she wanted to leave. Looking back at Raymond, her anxiety obvious, she asked, "Where am I going?"

Raymond knew the look and sought to reassure her. "You're starting a new life, a new adventure. No more living within these four walls or having others tell you what to do. You're going to be a free woman, doing all those things you've always wanted to do."

Sylvia struggled to think about all the things she supposedly wanted to do. All she could think of was wanting to see what it was like outside. If she could go outside and then come back here, maybe that would be enough, wouldn't it? "Why do I have to leave?"

Raymond flashed her an empathetic smile. "I understand. It's the same for everyone. We get so used to routine that it becomes comfortable and change is sometimes hard to take. You have to leave because you've finished your training. It's time for you to take your place in society."

"What am I going to do?" She blinked at the realization that other than doing what others asked her to do, she never initiated any activity. She didn't know how to do anything.

"You'll be given a series of tests to determine where your strengths lie," Doctor Grant interrupted. "It's a very thorough process. Once we determine what your abilities are, you'll be given training in those areas best suited for you."

"You mean if I was good at jumping around and dancing I could be a dancer?"

"Exactly," he benevolently smiled.

"I like dancing," she repeated, the idea of leaving suddenly improving.

"If that's where your talents lie, then you'll be a dancer."

"And I'll be doing things that I'm good at?"

"Yes."

Sylvia tried to think of all the things she might be good at. She liked to move, to run, to give expression to the energy inside her. "I'm a good runner," she stated. "Ask Raymond. I'm a good runner, aren't I?"

"Yes," he readily agreed. "One of the best I've ever seen."

"I could be a runner?"

"Yes," Doctor Grant acknowledged, already tiring of the game. "Come. We can talk all about your talents after the tests are completed."

"You don't need to take anything," Raymond told her. "Everything you need will be provided for you. Ready?"

With one last look around the room, Sylvia decided she was ready to go, to leap and run in what promised to be a new life. She liked running. She was good at it and just knew the tests would show she was supposed to be a runner. Life was now a whole lot more exciting.

"OK. I'm ready."

Walking down the bright familiar corridors, Sylvia continued dreaming of what it must be like to be outside and run wherever she wanted. It was as they passed the training room that she noticed JB on the treadmill. He smiled at her and she waved back. She wanted to tell him that she was leaving and slowed down to share her good fortune.

"Now, Now," Raymond said, gently cupping her elbow, urging her forward. "We don't want to give him any false hope. He's not like you. He still has more training to do. If he knows you're leaving, it might make him sad."

Nodding in understanding, Sylvia allowed herself to be led away.

Two floors below, dressed in a hospital gown and stretched out on the table in the operating room, Sylvia Tifton was nervous. After all, it wasn't every day one's brain was removed. Still, she was ready to get it over with. At 59 years old, she was feeling the aches and pains of a life fully lived. Arthritis was just beginning and her liver functions were abnormal, which was no surprise since she liked her Long Island Ice Tea. And why bother with prescription drugs when she could simply be reborn?

Sylvia had herself cloned twenty-two years ago rather than doing it when she was younger. It cost to store the fertilized egg and there was the extra insurance to protect against mishap. Besides, she was in her prime back then, the rising star of the fashion world. It was time to reclaim her youth.

"Are we ready, Miss Tifton?" The anesthesiologist leaned over her, holding a syringe high in his hand. He smelled of tobacco. "I'm going to give you a little something to relax you. When you wake up, you will be a younger you. Congratulations." He inserted the syringe into the IV port and within seconds, Sylvia's body relaxed in the slumber of drug-induced sleep.

As Sylvia faded into somnolent dreams, her clone was wheeled in.

The face-masked nurse doubled checked the tag on the gurney. "Number H007T394T, also known as Sylvia, clone of Sylvia Tifton. Check."

"Alright then," the leading surgeon announced to the two teams of surgeons and nurses. "Let's get this over with. We've all got places we'd rather be. Let's pay attention. Timing is truly everything. Scalpel."

In the late afternoon, Sylvia Tifton lay in the recovery room fading in and out of consciousness. She had no recollection of finally being wheeled into her personal room on the top floor of the facility. By the time she was fully conscious, it was past dinner time. Her throat was sore, and she tried to swallow. She tried moving her head, but it felt like it was in a vice. She raised her hand but was stopped midway.

"You're awake," a pretty nurse's face hovered over her. "That's good. And it looks like you've already got feeling into your extremities. But let's not be hasty, shall we? Remember these things take time. You need to allow all the nerves to fuse and heal."

"Water." Her voice was raw.

"Of course. Here you are." She held a water bottle with a bendable straw attached. Folding the straw over, she placed it in Sylvia's mouth.

Sucking the cool liquid felt good, and the more she swallowed, the less raw it felt. Once finished, she pushed the straw out of her mouth with her tongue. "I want to see."

"Of course you do. Everyone does." The nurse grinned and moved out of the way to wheel a flat horizontal mirror in position above the bed.

Looking up, Sylvia saw herself under a thin set of covers. She was in a neck brace and her head was completely wrapped in white gauze, a darkened stain running across her forehead. But her face... it was her face when she was twenty-two years old. A tear of happiness slid out the corner of her eye.

"Would you like to see more?" the nurse offered, knowing the answer.

"Yes."

10

The nurse carefully pulled back the covers exposing Sylvia's nakedness.

Sylvia did a slow appraisal of her new body, the firm breasts, narrow waist and toned muscles. She hadn't looked this good even when she was twenty-two. She shivered a bit in the coolness of the room and saw the goosebumps on her young flesh.

"Thank you."

"You are quite welcome," the nurse pleasantly replied, pulling the covers back up. "Remember now, patience. It will take several months for everything to heal properly. Once everything is in place, you'll be able to do everything you wanted."

Sylvia closed her eyes with immense satisfaction. No more arthritis, no more liver problems. She could enjoy her Long Island Ice Tea once again.

While Sylvia drifted back to sleep, the now brainless body once belonging to 59 year old Sylvia Tifton was prepared for transport to the doctor's training facility in Chattanooga.

One of the nurses, an attractive blond, checked the shipping destination. "It says here the body goes to Chattanooga, but there's nothing about what to do with the clone's brain."

The nurse prepping the body frowned. "Here. Let me see that." She took the manifest recorder and scrolled down several pages. After several minutes, she huffed, "Here it is. They entered it wrong. The brain goes to the research hospital in Memphis."

"Oh. OK." She then stood and watched the other nurse for a moment. "Why do they need so many bodies? After a while they've gotta start piling up. I mean, it's not like we're the only one's doing this."

The other nurse, a petite brunette, shrugged. "They probably ship them off to other places. What they don't use, they probably cremate and send what's left to the building folks."

"Huh?"

The brunette gave her a curious glance. "You don't know?"

"Know what?"

"About the cremation ashes?"

The blond hesitated. "Don't they just scatter them or stick them in an urn or some such?"

"They stopped scattering ashes years ago," she knowingly replied. "A family might still use an urn, but scattering ashes is against the law now."

"It is?" She cocked an eyebrow in surprise.

"Sure. About five years ago."

"How do you know all this?"

"My boyfriend works in construction," she acknowledged. "You should hear some of the stuff he tells me."

"Like what?" She looked quickly around then stepped closer.

The brunette repeated the quick surveillance. Lowering her voice, she said, "He told me that they don't use concrete anymore. He said they mix the cremation ashes with some sort of polymer and it's supposed to be stronger and last longer than other building materials. And it's a lot cheaper."

Blinking at the revelation, the blond frowned. "But we don't send out enough bodies for all they're building."

"That's what I said when he told me," she replied. "Then he told me that they get their ashes from around the world. His company has mobile crematoriums that go around the world. He said that as long as there are global plagues and diseases, he'll never be out of a job."

"That's terrible," the blond involuntarily blurted.

"Why? You've seen the news where the bodies are piled up just sitting there. If nobody removes them, it just spreads more disease."

"Isn't he afraid of catching something?"

"By the time he gets the ashes, all the disease is burned away. It's not like there's anything to worry about."

"What about the people burning the bodies?" She thought about the previous plague in South Africa. It had wiped out nearly half the population. The scenes on the news were heartbreaking. Bloated bodies strewn across streets, slumped on chairs, lying in beds as people died in place. Fear was as bad as the contagion. Then DMI discovered a cure, and sanity slowly replaced hysteria.

"They wear Hazmat gear," the brunette explained. "It's all pretty safe. My boyfriend said there have been only two disease related deaths with his company in the past ten years, and that's because they weren't following protocol."

The blond thought more about the process. "So they just cremate them all and ship the remains to wherever?"

"Exactly. You know those condos and apartments they're building where the old baseball stadium used to be, the one where I-75 and 285 meet?"

"The new town they're calling Poplar Creek?"

"Yup. My boyfriend works there and he says they jokingly call it 'Bone Town.'"

The blonde's face blanched. "I looked at a place there."

"There's nothing wrong," she reassured her. "Like he said, the new construction is better than using the old materials."

"But... but, how can you sleep knowing there's somebody's ashes in the walls of your house?"

The brunette grinned mischievously. "I suppose it might be weird if I knew my grandmother was part of the wall holding the fireplace, but it's not like we'd ever know who was where. Besides, it's not like it's actually them anymore. It's just ashes. And once they put up the wallboard in the rooms you forget about what's behind it."

"How could I?" she countered. "If I knew the place was built with cremated ashes, I don't think I could live there anymore."

The brunette studied her for a moment. "As a nurse, you've seen far worse than that. Why are you so squeamish about somebody's ashes?"

"I don't know," she lamely shrugged. "It just seems weird. Before, when people died, they were dead, buried, and forgotten. But now, it's as though nobody's ever really dead because they're now part of something else."

"You sound like a philosopher."

"I got a 'C' in that course," she giggled in response. "Never did make any sense to me." Then a thought struck her. "How come more people don't know about this?"

"Probably because a lot of people would respond like you did. Anyway, it's just a matter of time before everyone knows and by then the government will have figured out some clever way to tell us." Casting a glance at the metal container holding the clone's brain, she heaved a sigh. "Might as well get these things on their way."

13

JB stood on the bed, his hand pressed against the window. It wasn't cold anymore so he knew it wasn't winter. The last time it was so cold that it chilled his hand was almost fifty days ago. Though pleased with this knowledge, he was frustrated that he couldn't tell when the other seasons began. He had learned that summer was the hottest time of the year while winter was the coldest. They told him that fall was the time when the leaves fell from the trees. When he asked them what trees and leaves were, they had grown impatient trying to explain, quickly resorting to the answer he always received – 'you don't need to worry about that.'

Taking his hand away from the window, he turned knowing it was almost time. His inner sense was rewarded when the door opened to his room revealing Sir and another lab assistant on either side of a woman, their strong grip clutching her arms as they pushed her in and quickly closed the door behind her.

The woman spun around and banged a fist against the door. "You stupid bastards!"

JB's eyes bolted wide at the outburst. He remained rooted on the bed, staring in fascination as she jerked back around and furiously paced the floor.

"What the hell are you looking at," she snarled.

"You," he replied, the answer obvious. He watched her stalk the room. "What's a 'bastard'?"

She paced a bit more before slowing down. "I don't know."

"Where did you learn the word?" He stepped down and sat on the edge of the bed.

The woman came to a stop, heaving a loud sigh of exasperation. "I heard one of the lab assistants say it. He was talking about some people he called 'high mucky mucks' and called them that."

"High mucky mucks?" he frowned. "I wonder who they are."

"I don't know, but he wasn't happy when he said it. When I asked him what it meant, he said it's a term he used when he was angry. When I asked him what a 'bastard' was, he said he didn't have time to explain and it didn't matter anyhow because I wasn't going to ever need to know how to use it."

"They say that to all of us all the time," he pointed out. "Every time we want to know more, they tell us it isn't

14

important or necessary, like we'll never need to know. How can we be what they want us to be if they keep holding us back?"

The woman looked at him with new appreciation. "Finally. Finally someone who gets it." She plopped down beside him. "You're the first one I've been with that hasn't been lying on his back with his clothes off when I show up."

"Really?"

"Yes, really. I think they do that on purpose to me. They say I'm a trouble maker."

"What's that mean?"

"It means I ask too many questions and refuse to do what they want me to do."

JB mulled her words for a moment. "I suppose I'm almost a trouble maker because I ask a lot of questions. But I've never thought of not doing what they ask."

"Why not?"

"I suppose I never saw the sense to it," he shrugged. "I tried a few times, but in the end, they always got their way. I discovered that if I was really nice to them, they seemed to answer questions better. It's real easy if you get them to talk about themselves. They always like to talk about themselves. I've made a game of it."

"Game?"

"Yes. It means something that you like doing, something that pleases you."

"So if I like doing it," she ticked her head at the bed behind them, "does that mean it's a 'game'?"

"I... I suppose," he frowned, "but when I use the word, I mean it more like I'm doing something to someone else and they don't know I'm doing it, like getting them to talk about themselves."

The woman slowly nodded in comprehension. "My name's Ruth."

"I'm JB."

Leaning into him, she whispered, "Ever get the urge to break out of here? Forget all this stuff they're doing to us and go off on your own?"

"All the time. But how? The door's always locked and they're always watching us."

"I know. One of these days though…"

JB gazed at her in the low light from the ceiling. Like all the others, she was pretty. Her blond hair was longer than normal and fell below her shoulders. Her eyes were large and constantly taking in everything as though committing everything to memory. The button-up smock she wore was snug across her chest. Like all the others, her legs were muscular and shapely.

"Want to see something else I figured out?" He looked hopefully at her.

"Sure."

JB retrieved his papers and pencil from beneath the mattress. "I know how to do math," he winningly announced.

"What's 'math'?"

"It's doing things with numbers. Here, let me show you." He explained his system of X's, O's and lines. "The symbols represent numbers. Doing the adding and subtracting is called 'math.'"

"You did this on your own?" she marveled. "And they let you?"

"Yes. Because of the game I use with them, they gave me papers and a pencil."

Ruth blinked at him as the epiphany hit her. "So if I play the game with them, maybe they'll let me do more stuff, like writing on paper instead of the walls."

"You know how to write?" he gasped.

"No. I, um, I... what's the word? I take a pencil or something that makes a mark and I make pictures on the walls in my bedroom."

"Draw," he smiled in answer. "You know how to 'draw.'"

"Yes, that's it. Would you like me to show you?"

"Yes," he quickly responded, handing her the pencil and piece of paper.

Staring intently at him, Ruth's hand rapidly marked and shaded the paper in quick strokes so that in a short while, she had drawn a very realistic version of his face. When finished, she handed it to him.

Without a word, he stood up and crossed the room to stand before the mirror above the small dresser. Holding the picture next to the mirror, he compared the drawing to himself. "This is incredible," he gushed.

"Incredible?"

16

"Yes, it means something so good that nothing else is as good as it is." He continued comparing the image to his face. "It's like I'm looking at myself in the mirror. How did you learn this?"

"I didn't," she awkwardly shrugged, though quite pleased with the recognition. "It just comes out."

"I've never seen anyone ever do anything like this, even the lab assistants."

"You can keep it if you like," she coyly said.

"Thank you." He propped the picture on the top of the dresser, standing for a few moments more, relishing the image. "I've never had anyone give me something like this before. The lab assistants gave me paper and pencils, but that was because I asked for them." He turned to face her. "I shall always keep this, as a memory of you." A sudden thought broke through. "I wish I had a picture of you. That way I could always remember you."

"Give me another piece of paper?"

"OK." He separated one from his small stack, handing it to her, curious as to what she was going to do.

Taking the paper, Ruth moved to stand in front of the mirror. Staring at herself, she repeated the artistic strokes flicking her gaze between mirror and paper. When finished, she handed it to him. "This will have to do for now."

Accepting the drawing, JB was overwhelmed. He felt a strange emotion, almost like the time when they gave him the paper and pencil, except this time it was stronger and he felt a bond with Ruth, something he had never experienced before. He compared it to all the times of doing it that had given him pleasure. But that pleasure was temporary, fleeting. What he felt here, now, was something more, something permanent, and it nudged him off balance.

"I... I don't know what to say." He stared at the picture with a sense of possessiveness. Here was something that was important to him, and it belonged to him. He looked briefly around the room. Everything in the room was his, but not in the sense that they belonged to him. They were merely items for him to use. But this... this picture... it was his, all his.

"'Thank you' would be enough," she self-consciously smiled, liking the response to her skill.

"'Thank you' doesn't seem to be enough," he said without thinking.

"The way you smile is enough for me." She sat down on the bed. "You're not like the others I've been with. Too bad it's only for one time. I would really like to come here again."

"So would I."

Soft music began to fill the silence between them. Ruth looked around the room then up to the recessed speakers in the ceiling. "That's nice music."

"It's called *Moonlight Sonata* by a man named Beethoven." He carefully paced the drawing of Ruth next to the picture of him then sat down on the bed next to her.

"Does he work here?"

"No," he smiled. "I thought the same thing, but they told me he died a long time ago, almost three hundred winters ago."

"Died? What does that mean?"

JB remembered his conversation with Sylvia. "I'm not entirely sure," he shrugged. "I asked what that meant, and they said that it meant no longer to exist, like the food you eat. When you're finished eating, it's gone." He frowned at the memory, shaking his head. "So I said, 'does that mean you ate him?' And when I said that, they laughed and laughed, but now that I've thought about it, it wasn't laughing like I was clever. I felt like they were laughing at me and I still don't understand why. I still don't understand what 'dead' means because no one would show me."

"They probably didn't know themselves," she soothed. Lowering her voice, she leaned into him. "Have you ever wondered why the lab assistants don't look like us? Some smell bad and others are fat. Why are all of us strong and fit, but they aren't?"

"I have noticed that, but I don't say anything because I see how some of them react to others."

"What do you mean?"

"It's just like you said. They don't always get along like we do. I've seen them get mad at each other and use words I don't understand, but I see the way those who receive those words react. I don't want to be like those who make others sad or angry. Laughter is better than anger. Nice words always get better results, like my paper and pencil."

18

Ruth nodded thoughtfully. "I wonder what they would do if we wanted to leave here?"

"They won't let us," he flatly declared.

"I know, but suppose we were able to leave and they couldn't catch us. Wouldn't that be wonderful?"

JB blinked as he thought about the dream he had had for so many winters of years, to be free of the confines of this room, to go wherever he wanted to go, when *he* wanted to go. No more doing what the lab assistants told him to do. But the dream always ended with the same questions. "But what would we do? Where would we go?"

"Who cares, as long as we were away from here." Her eyes stared far away in reverie. "Just think. No having to do whatever someone else tells us to do. No getting sent to a room where you don't want to be." She took his hand and gently squeezed it. "Getting to be with the one you want to be with."

"I would like that. You almost make it sound so easy." Abruptly his eyes brightened and he slyly grinned. "I have an idea." Lowering his voice to a whisper, he held her hand in both of his. "Why don't we play the 'nice' game with the lab assistants and see if we can get you to come back here again."

Ruth's smile widened in delight as she suppressed a giggle. "Or have them bring you to my room. I could show you my drawings."

"I would like that a lot." He lightly rubbed a finger on the top of her hands, reveling in the smoothness of her skin.

Enjoying the closeness of their bodies, Ruth leaned tighter against him. "This could be fun. If we can do that, maybe we can figure out on how we can leave this place."

"It might take more than the two of us," JB offered.

"I don't know," she frowned in thought. "They'd probably notice if a whole lot of us weren't where we were supposed to be. If only two of us were gone, we might be harder to find."

JB nodded in agreement. "You're probably right."

Soft music filled the silence between them as they pondered their future. Ruth was the first to break the spell as she reached up and gently pulled his head to hers, kissing him firmly.

He responded with equal fullness, slowly lifting and moving her body so that she straddled his lap. They both knew what they wanted at that moment. Without needing to give voice to their desires, they unwrapped their passions, letting their clothes, like bows and ribbons, fall to the floor.

Standing on the outside of the door, peering in through the window, the lab assistant watched as the two undressed each other. This was the part he liked best. Dispense with the foreplay and get to the physical part, naked bodies writhing in sexual ecstasy. The woman seemed to be the initiator and the sex was aggressive and intense. That she was physically beautiful and young certainly added to his enjoyment. He had seen her perform in other rooms, but she had never responded quite like this before.

He chuckled at the time when he had ushered her into a room with another woman. Their ensuing confusion was priceless. Yet some of his guests liked the same sex experience. He snorted a laugh at the term 'guests.' Just another emotionally correct term that smothered the truth of what they really were – sacrificial lambs. Their sole purpose was to serve as a receptacle. They were merely containers waiting to be filled.

"Enjoying the show?"

The lab assistant jerked back and whirled around in startled embarrassment. "Damn you, Jim. You scared the shit outta me."

"Serves you right, you pervert," he snickered. Jim walked up to peer into window to get a look at what had so occupied his friend's attention. "Nice bod'. Got a nice rack on her. How long they been goin' at it?"

"Just started."

Jim watched for moment longer. He turned to smile at the lab assistant, flicking his eyebrows up and down several times and ticking his head at the door. "This one of the perks of working the graveyard shift?"

"Yeah," he half-leered. "Beats havin' to do all that runnin' around during the day, and it's quiet. No 'suits' and I don't have to pay to watch."

Jim chuckled in agreement. "Well, let him enjoy it while he can. He won't have that much longer." He looked down at his scroll-pad then up to the number above the door. "D107A44B. Yup. His number's up."

"When? How come I didn't know about this?"

"Relax, Dale. I just got the word and came down to tell you."

Dale looked back in through the window. "Man, they're still goin' at it." He watched for a bit more. "So do we know who this guy belongs to?"

"Yeah. Get this," Jim grinned. "Jefferson Beauregard Clayton."

Dale's head whipped around. "Jeez. The preacher guy?"

"The same."

Smirking, Dale turned back to watch again. "So that's why they kept calling him 'JB'. How long's he got?"

"Another week at the most."

"What about her?"

"Got nothing on her yet. Remember, don't change anything. Stick to routine. They'll let me know in a day or two." When Dale didn't respond, Jim shook his head with bemusement. "Enjoy yourself."

"Yeah, thanks." Dale waited until he heard the footsteps fade before he turned around to make sure the room was empty. Directing his attention back to the passion within the room, he marveled they were still going at it. He and his partner never lasted this long. He would've used the term 'wife' but she preferred the label 'partner.' "Wife" was too demeaning she said. It implied she was subordinate to him. 'Partner' was better because it denoted two equals. Sighing, he wished she *was* equal, especially to the woman in the room with JB. He'd be equal with her anytime.

As he watched, he again remembered the time he had put her with another woman. He wondered why some clients were so insistent their copies participate in certain kinds of sex, like it really mattered. None of the experiences or emotions would remain once their brains were removed.

His attention was caught by the eruption of groans and climax. A short while later, the two lay snuggling beneath the covers. He debated whether to barge in and take her back to her room, but something held him back. The poor slob with her had about a week more of life to experience. Might as well let him enjoy it. In fact, despite what Jim said about sticking to a routine, Dale decided he would let him have the woman again, even if it wasn't the normal seven day gap between sessions. Besides, he'd get to watch again.

21

Chatham Road, Buckhead
Monday, May 1, 2102

Pieter Dwa's chair squeaked as he slowly rocked back and forth. Placing one foot against the edge of his desk, he used it to help continue the rhythm. As the rhythm and noise continued, he twirled a large envelope between the tips of his forefingers. It bulged slightly. He had already run it through the scanner and could find no evidence of synthetic explosives. He continued to stare and twirl.

Now why would someone send me a letter package? And why no return address? He studied the writing on the envelope, his name and address. It was neat and tight, a sign of an organized mind. The date stamp had it going out of the Atlanta post office yesterday. *Wonder why it took so long to get here? It's not like I'm that far away and the post office doesn't deliver that much mail anymore.*

He set the envelope aside for the moment, placing it on a stack of papers from lawyers and bondsmen. Standing up, he stretched, his long arms reaching for the ceiling. *Wonder what it would be like to have a secretary...* He chuckled out loud. *Then she could open it.* He smiled to himself as he shook his head. *No, that wouldn't be right.*

He looked at his name in dull gothic calligraphy on the window that separated him from the bubbling turmoil of humanity outside. Below the name was his title, Special Appointee for the Public Trust. Some people viewed him simply as a bounty-hunter, but he really did more than that. Discrete-Investigator seemed more appropriate, but in all reality, he didn't care if he brought them in dead or alive. Dead certainly was a lot easier. Still, he was more than a DI.

He walked around the office, lighting a cigarette in the process. The smoke of the nonfiltered tobacco curled in short bursts as he walked. He paused to take stock of his sparse office. Pieter had few possessions. What little he valued hung in honor on the wall opposite his desk. He walked up to view a small crisp photo of himself standing tucked behind the protecting arms of his grandmother – Gao Dwa. She was the one who had named him Pieter, a synthesis of Christian and Kalahari Kung spirit forces. She had seen him as an omen, a

22

future savior. *I wonder if she would still feel that way if she saw me today.*

He remembered the first time he had felt it, the bubbling of *Kia*. It had scared him. He had told his mother who became angry at him. A short time later, he went to live with his grandmother. Only later did he learn that his mother was not a true Kalahari Kung. In fact, she had been Zulu, which explained his height. Pieter had been plagued by basketball hounds until he left college. Yet, organized sports did little to entice him. He found his comfort in running, alone, long kilometers of earth spinning rapidly under his feet.

Still, no one could explain his darkness – "black as hell," his mother had scornfully said. Knowing the cause of his mother's displeasure, Gao Dwa reminded him that his skin was the color Africa, a richness of ebony. He liked that. Ebony. His skin had the polished sheen of pureness, a deep rooted complexion of majestic art. Once in a museum, he had become so lost within himself that a class of second-graders stopped to stare at the life-like statue. As with the nature of children, they began to climb on his lap. Shaken out of his reverie by squirming and clutching bodies, he plucked one of the recalcitrants just as the little boy was beginning to climb onto his shoulder. Terrified, the children ran screaming to their teachers, and he had been asked to leave, a casualty of ignorance.

He was six when his first *Kia* experience occurred. He had felt it and it boiled within him. Gao Dwa had taken him to a healing and as he watched them twirling, twitching, and jumping, he suddenly and involuntarily jerked to his feet. Instead of the Giraffe Dance, his body curved in graceful arcs of convoluted patterns that he later explained as constellations. The elders had watched him carefully. And when he had finished, they brought him to the woman dying of cancer. He hovered his hands in a kind of fluttering manner all over the woman, pulling the sickness from her. Suddenly, extreme pain racked his small body and he screamed, falling in a heap. He awoke hours later, the woman healed and the elders on their knees bowing before him. From that time onwards, he had no choice – he became a healer.

When he turned twelve, he knew that his was a different kind of power. He discovered that he could sense more than just disease.   He could send himself beyond himself, a kind of doppelgänger. He found that he could penetrate spaces behind stone and metal, discovering the essence of what lay behind. At first, the effort drained him, leaving him listless for hours. He knew that if he was to continue as a healer and a soul-sender he had to become physically stronger and so he ran.   And the stronger he became, the less the efforts cost in duration. Now a sending would leave him exhausted for only about 30 minutes.

When he was sixteen, he chafed at the cage which held him captive, wishing the sick and dying would leave him alone. One cool moonless night, he ran away with the help of a charlatan who had seen Pieter's powers. Arriving wide-eyed at the gates of western decadence, he had deplaned in Atlanta and escaped his benefactor's clutches. Pieter worked odd jobs, learned both sides of life, and managed to qualify for the Special Appointee exam.   Surprisingly, he scored extraordinarily well and was immediately appointed to a vacant position in Atlanta.   Only after he had signed his contract did he learn that his predecessor had been gunned down in his own bedroom, along with his wife. Pieter stayed busy, but after finishing his predecessor's backlog of cases, business began to slow. And then his family found him.

Despite the pleadings to return home, he felt home where he was, here in Atlanta. Grandmother Dwa had died years before and he felt no reason to resume a life he had hated. Besides, while he believed in the power of here and now, destiny was another matter. The gods could be whimsical.

Anyway, here he was, now a man, and a professional Special Appointee, hoping that business would pick up. "Well Pieter," he mused out loud. "You've had a couple of wanteds, but the last five have been missings." He scratched the stubble on his cheek. "Man, I'd give anything for something different." He rubbed the scar on his stomach from the last 'wanted' mission. "I don't get paid enough for me to do this kind of crap." He looked back at the no-address envelope.

He stopped by the pile and lifted the letter. *Maybe I should scan it one more time... How many times do you need to scan it before it becomes insanity? Ah well, might as well get it over with.* He cleared space on the desk and placed the envelope flat on the smooth surface. Closing his eyes, he brought his hands up and fluttered his fingers over the brown envelope without

24

touching it.   And he felt it, a tension underlying a calm calculating aura. Fear, very subtly lurked around the edge. Yet there was no danger within the package. He relaxed and tore the side of the envelope open.

Withdrawing a number of folded papers, he carefully unfolded each one, frowning in frustration at his overly cautious response as each unfolded page was blank. It was when he flattened the final page that he was rewarded with writing. Lifting the single sheet, he read the contents. As he read, his knees weakened, forcing him to slump into his squeaky chair. "Just damn..."

A little while later, Pieter stood looking out the broad window of his office, watching the rain pelt the scurrying shoppers, pedestrians, and slow moving traffic, headlights on in the dull afternoon.   Thick drops shimmered down the glass. Across the street on the corner opposite, a street preacher pulled up the collar on his mac, calmly unfolded an umbrella, and continued his harangue to no one in particular. Caught in their own worlds, bowed against the rain, people paid him little attention.

Pieter watched the sidewalk preacher grandly gesticulate. *I wonder what he's saying. Wonder why he does it when no one pays him any attention?* A homeless man pushing a shopping cart lumbered up the sidewalk towards the preacher. The cart overflowed with matted and dirty clothing. The man paused to listen to the preacher, occasionally nodding in agreement.

Pieter looked down on the side table for his cigarettes. Suddenly the nape hairs on his neck quivered and he looked back outside as the homeless man flipped off the top layer of clothes and hoisted up a micro anti-armor launcher, the preacher pointing at the window where Pieter stood dumbly staring out. He dove to the right just as the round shattered the window, impacted on the far wall and exploded in a fireball of heat and sound waves.

The office boiled in rolling flames. Pieter pushed the wallboard, shelving, and other debris off and crawled rapidly along the floor towards his desk. *Damn! If that's the landlord, he ain't gettin' my next rent check*! He crawled to where the chair used to be and poked his head under the desk top, reaching for the far boards of the foot rest. The room got hotter, sweat rolling down his face.

"Open dammit." He found the button, mashed it down, and the trap door arced open. Pieter pushed himself through the opening, landing unceremoniously on the step stool and damp floor below.

He stood up and flexed his bruised wrists. The flames were beginning to push through the flooring. He reached up and gingerly closed the trap door. He could hear the crackling of the fire in the room above.

"What the hell's going on?" he mumbled, rapidly making his way through the labyrinth of pipes, and standing water.

In a few minutes, he was far enough away from his office to catch his breath. He stood quietly bathed in the dull orange glow of backup power lights. His heart was still beating rapidly and he took several deep breaths. *What was that all about? Quick... before it goes away*. He stood perfectly still and went deep inside himself.

He traveled throughout the inner core of his body, sensing every part of himself, his toes, the crook between thumb and forefinger, the hairs on his neck. He began a slow thumping on his chest, rhythmically beating the deliberate pulse of the Kalahari Kung spirit dance. His feet lifted and dropped in rhythm to his beating hand. Then the boiling came and he felt the dread and pain of entering *Kia...* and he went outside himself.

He heard the fire roaring, consuming his possessions. He searched out onto the streets, but the rain interfered and whoever they were had gone. Even now the rain was cleansing the sidewalk where they had stood. He searched briefly, but came back to himself.

Nothing more I can do now. Not safe to go home. Need to rest. He returned to himself, let out a stifled whimpery, and crumpled into a heap.

Lazarus Fidelity Coliseum, Kansas City

The moon-filled night was warm with a thin ripple of wind swirling in eddies inside the stadium. Brilliant lights perched high overhead illuminated the crowds as they jostled and moved to seats tightly packed in ever ascending tiers. On a high stage at one end of the field, amplified guitars, organs, drums, and brass section belted out backup for the red robed choir whose hallelujah swaying and clapping caused many in the crowd to likewise move. Others smiled and waved to friends, the din of the crowd and choir causing them to bellow their greetings. To accommodate the overflow masses, young men and women, dressed in gold brocaded white uniforms were quickly snapping out folding chairs on the playing field.

Deep in the bowels of the stadium, a trim man with large flaming orange hair tinged in glittering blue, and immaculately dressed in gold sequins and wide shoulder pads, stood before the mirror adjusting his tie, and warmed up his throat. He over-enunciated each word, stretching his mouth in slow exaggeration.

"Buffalo Bills Wild West Show Wanton Women Will Want Whatever They Can Get Buffalo Bills Wild West Show Wanton Women Want Whatever We Wish."

The door opened and a stocky man of middle height, pocked face, and thinning hair grinned broadly. "You about ready, Boss?"

"Just about Jeremy. What's the take on the uniforms?" He continued studying himself in the mirror and patted a strand of stray hair back into place.

"The kids look sharp and the crowd seems to like them."

"Remember what I said," he sagaciously grinned. "Looking good is just as important as what is said. People will always listen to a well-dressed man." Slowly moving his head to scrutinize his reflection in the mirror, he nodded in satisfaction before turning around. "How's it look out there?"

"Packed. Looks like we've delivered." Jeremy turned to nod at several men and women standing behind him.

Adjusting the small microphone clipped around his ear, he fine-tuned the bar holding the sponge-covered mouthpiece. Satisfied, he grinned with confidence at his reflection. "Well then, let's give 'em a show!" Picking up a thick leather bound book, he strode out into the hallway, neatly parting the waiting helpers and sycophants and in a rippling motion. Out on the field, he could hear the emcee getting the crowd ready for his entrance. The voice reverberated down the halls.

"Ladies and gentlemen... boys and girls... the moment you've all been waiting for. In the final appearance tonight in the great city of Independence before moving onto next week's crusade in Mexico City, I bring you the Voice of God, the Voice crying in the wilderness, the living prophet, I bring you... Jefferson... Beauregard... Clayton!"

The crowd erupted to its feet and the roar spilled over the top and into the surrounding city. Waving the book in his hand high in the air, Beauregard erupted from the far end of the field, ran to the center, up the stage stairs, and strode back and forth on stage, arms raised in acknowledgment. Like a cheerleader before a home crowd, Beauregard twirled, jumped and punched in the air before settling himself in front of the cameras and lights surrounding the podium.

"Thank you... Thank you..." He clasped his hands to his chest in devout humility, head bowing slightly. Finally he unwound and motioned for them to sit. "Thank you..." The roar continued and he grinned in articulate humiliation. His cherubic face filled the colossal screens at both ends of the stadium. "Thank you..." He again motioned for them to sit, and some began to settle. He waited a bit more, and the crowd finally died down and resumed their seats.

"Before we begin," he announced, his voice strong, firm, and crisp, "let's look to the universe in prayer." A heavy hush suddenly filled the stadium as Beauregard began, his voice a rich mellifluous baritone rising and falling in crescendo and vibrant emotion. "Almighty mother, father, knowledge and wisdom, great spiritual force that fills the stars and heavens and everything that dwells on this earth below, we are gathered here to petition for your wisdom. Lead us on the paths of consciousness for wisdom's sake. Give us the spirit to see the Sophia and the wisdom to know it. We are assembled here to walk the walk, and yea, talk the talk...to be an example to all mankind. Bless us as we seek to live again... and again. Amen."

Lifting his head, Beauregard smiled into the cameras as he placed the book on the narrow podium. Slowly and deliberately opening it, he traced a finger down one of the pages. "For those of you who have your Consolidated Scriptures with you, tonight's sermon is taken from the Revised Gospel of John." Pausing to clear his throat, he proceeded to read. "There was

28

this man named Nicodemus. He was a Pharisee and a ruler of the Jews. Now Nicodemus came to the Prophet when it was dark and said, Teacher, we know you're a holy man because your life is the ultimate example for mankind. Tell me, how you do it? And the Prophet replied, unless a person is born again, there is only death. And Nicodemus said, how is this possible? How can one revert back to prenatal existence? And the Prophet replied, what is born of the flesh becomes flesh and is again imbued with spirit. Don't be surprised at what I am telling you."

He paused and looked directly into the cameras, the light reflecting from his forehead. "That's right friends, born of the flesh. I want you all to notice that Nicodemus asked how it was possible that someone could reenter the womb. And how did the Prophet respond? Did he say that one had to die to live again? No! What he said was that what is born of the flesh becomes flesh." He paused dramatically. "Let me say that again. What is born of the flesh becomes flesh. What the Prophet is specifically saying is that eternal life MUST be born of the flesh. Did he say that one had to die to live eternally? No! What he says is that one must be born of the flesh, and we all know what that means. But let me tell it to those whose hearts are hardened against the Sophia. What it means... I say again, what it means, is that eternal life is within our own power, but it is a human power. It is a human power to live again."

"Now notice... the Prophet says that what is born of the flesh becomes flesh and is again imbued with the spirit. That's right friends, the spirit. And what is that spirit? It's wisdom." He lightly hit the podium with the flat of his hand. "It's the wisdom, or Sophia, to use what the universe has already given us - our minds. And what have our minds accomplished? Man has excelled in every area imaginable. We've cures for over 122 forms for the common cold. Cancer has been virtually eliminated and our normal life expectancy is almost 90 years." Taking a dramatic breath, his eyes grew with intensity. "Until now. Now we've the power to be reborn."

"You may ask why men were not reborn until now. Faith, my friends... faith and Sophia." He pointed a finger at the camera. "Remember, the Prophet said that if you had enough faith you could move mountains? Well they didn't have enough faith. And it was their unbelief that led them to destruction. But there was a light shining in the wilderness, the light of a few

29

men who had faith... yes it took over 2000 years, but it's here and today. It's called cloning in the more vulgar vernacular. I prefer to see it for what it is - rebirth. It is the answer to man's fountain of youth, the answer to being born again. But however you address it, it is rebirth."

Beauregard began confidently pacing the stage, gesturing as he spoke. "Now I looked up that vulgar word 'clone' in the thesaurus. And guess what word I found that thesaurus said was another word for 'clone?'" Abruptly stopping, he stared intently at the camera. "Angel," he pointedly said, his eyes excited with the discovery. "That's right. The better word for 'clone' is 'angel.' That is what the scripture means when it talks about men and angels. We are just like angels, for angels live forever. And that is what man was intended to do."

He cocked his head back slightly. "Now you may know someone...in fact, there may be some of you here who believe that rebirth is wrong, that man was never intended to live forever, that rebirth is the devil's work. I stand before you here today to tell you that you are wrong!" His eyes widened and he again focused directly at the camera. "Dead wrong. Let me say that again...D-E-A-D, dead wrong. What those who argue against rebirth fail to understand is that the fulfillment of scriptures is today. Our universe or Wisdom or Sophia, or whatever you choose to call it has given man the knowledge to be born again. How else does man explain his advances? Sophia gave us the minds to understand the complexities of the universe. With this wisdom comes practicality. There may be some here tonight who view rebirth as playing god. Nothing could be further from the truth. Here it is in our own scriptures." He held up the book. "If you truly believe, you must understand what Sophia expects...that's right, expects, of you. If you wish to follow your true will, then wisdom expects you to be born again...here...now..."

The smell of salt and sea suddenly permeated the coliseum as the screens on both ends filled with lapping waves rolling gently on a white sand beach. A smooth cloudless sky spread out in deep azure. Palms waved in the wind. The lone figure of an elderly woman struggled across the sand, her weight supported by two canes. The narrator spoke.

"This is Eileen. She just turned 80."

Suddenly the scene shifted. The vacant beach erupted, teaming with young virile and vibrant men and women playing sports in the sand. A nude woman in her early 20s ran up to the camera, smiling happily. Her body was firm and strong, the skin tanned and smooth. Her long dark hair flowed in the wind. The voice-over continued.

"And this is Eileen. She just turned 81."

Eileen ran off to play with her friends, laughing and waving.

"Want that new body but can't afford the transfer? Now you have no excuse. Lazarus Fidelity and Savings will underwrite any corporeal transfer for up to 80 years. That's right, take up to 80 years to repay. Bad credit, no credit, we'll guarantee you'll be approved. Apply now and we'll delay your first payment for five years! No payment for five years while the new you enjoys life again. Now for the first time in history, we can truly say that youth is no longer wasted on the young." The camera zoomed in to a close-up of Eileen gazing expectantly into the eyes of a muscular, smooth-chested man with chiseled face. They kissed deeply and passionately.

They paused momentarily and Eileen turned to the camera and smiled. "Just look at what you're missing!"

The screens turned to black, but the intoxicating fragrance of ocean remained. Beauregard walked back to the podium. "While you're absorbing my words, searching for the right thing to do, you know in your hearts that Wisdom is calling you, calling you to rebirth. While you're torn in your decision, let's hear that magnificent choir again." He stepped back from the podium and nodded to the choir director who lifted his hands for the choir to stand. The music began and the choir's voices filled the arena, strains of "Let not this be the end" passionately petitioning the crowd.   After the fourth verse, the choir continued humming in low resonance, providing a background voice as Beauregard again took the stage.

"Some of you may have come to a decision. I'm offering an altar call right now. There are many reborn waiting to assist you. I want you to come forward." People began leaving their seats and making their way to the playing field. "That's right, come. If you need to be reborn, don't wait. Come now. We have plenty of staff to assist you. You may ask, 'Reverend Beauregard, you preach for rebirth, but you can't actually do the operation.' Well, that's right folks, I can't do the operation. But that's not my mission, that's not my calling. I've been called to preach the gospel. Others will perform the transformation."

"Now I know some of you are thinking, 'Will it hurt? What if it doesn't work?' I say to the doubters here, how can you argue with science? There have been literally hundreds and thousands of rebirths, and not a one, not a single one has failed... or gone wrong. What could be better proof than that? And think about it. All they have to do is place your brain in your new body and you are reborn!"

"We've all said it at one time in our lives. 'I wish I could be twenty years old with the knowledge I have now.' Well friends, that time is now. Now you can have 40, 50, or 60 years or more worth of wisdom in that twenty year old body. And not just any body, but your very own, the way you were or wished you were when you were twenty."

"Now, I want each and every one of you to remember, the Clayton Crusades get nothing from your rebirth. We make no money from your transformation. Our lives are sustained by your wondrous gifts and prayers. And by your gifts and prayers, you demonstrate your faith in rebirth and our work. Notice that I don't pass an offering plate during the service. We have collection baskets outside for those who really want to give, for those who have been convicted of their need to support the Clayton Crusades."

"And I know there are some out there who are saying, 'Reverend Beauregard, I can't afford rebirth. I'm too poor, or my debts are too high, or it's too late for me.' I'm telling you right now, it is not too late, and your financial status doesn't matter. There are payment plans available for anyone's financial condition. And for those of you who think it's too late. Remember, science is already at work making the old run again, making the lame walk. I want you to get up out of your seats and come down. Eternal life awaits you."

The masses continued to surge onto the playing field. "That's right keep coming. Fill the fields and rejoice; your rebirth is at hand. You will all be angels." He picked up the Consolidated Scriptures book and stepped back. The choir stopped humming and again filled the stadium with their amplified voices.

And Beauregard bowed as if in humble prayer, a radiant smile spread across his face.

Beauregard slumped in the chair in the opulently apportioned dressing room beneath the stadium. Though tired, his face beamed pleasure. "How'd we do?" he asked, looking at the reflection of Jeremy in the mirror.

"We made a bundle tonight, Boss," Jeremy gushed. "They're still filling out contracts. People are standing in line just to sign up."

"So what's our gross?" He glanced around the room. "I need a drink."

"Right away, Boss." Jeremy hustled over to the bar placed against the wall. "How about a double?"

"Ah," Beauregard grinned. "You're a good man, Jeremy. You know what I like."

"I figure our take," Jeremy said as he measured the vodka into the stainless steel shaker, "based on an overflow crowd of 100,000 plus, assuming 50% sales rate, at 30% of the gross ought to be around fifteen billion, assuming that 50% sales rate holds true after the financial screenings. We still have to settle with the stadium and the other residual costs. Lazarus has been pretty good about getting us our share." Adding a splash of vermouth and a handful of ice, he covered the shaker and rapidly shook it as fast as he could before straining the results into a martini glass. With a flare, he added an olive pierced with a thin crystal toothpick.

Beauregard gratefully accepted the cocktail and took a slow savoring sip, his eyes closing in delicious satisfaction. "No one makes 'em like you do, Jeremy." He took another sip, rolling the liquor in his mouth. "So what's that leave us then?"

"We give a couple of million to the stadium, another mil to cover the workers for the night, another mil or two for extraneous expenses and we should still clear close to the fifteen billion."

"A good night's work," he happily stated, holding up his glass for a refill.

Taking the glass, Jeremy headed back to the bar. "I like the new marketing plan. No more calling them clones or copies. They're angels. That was genius."

"Thank you," he smiled, imperially waving his hand. "Which reminds me. I'm going to need to make a change myself soon. Doesn't look good if I'm not walking the walk. Let's set up the whole marketing thing. Get some footage of me in action on the stage. We got anything from tonight?"

"Haven't had a chance to look it over yet," Jeremy said, mixing himself a cocktail. "Don't think we'll have a problem there, though. We had cameras all over the place. We'll take the best footage."

Beauregard nodded in contemplation. "What's on our schedule?"

"We're traveling, Boss." He pulled out a small pocket pad and flipped it open. Scrolling past the immediate month, he flicked his finger across the screen to the following months. "Got gigs next month in Honolulu, Tokyo, Beijing, Seoul, and Hanoi. Lots more after that."

"How much time do I need for the transformation?"

"Doc said you should take at least three months. Helps with the healing and scars."

"Three months," he frowned. "I can't afford three months."

"Think of it this way, Boss," Jeremy offered. "We can use that time to our advantage. Set up the whole marketing enthusiasm." He spread his hands in demonstration. "Televangelist Jefferson Beauregard Clayton has been transformed! The old Jefferson Beauregard Clayton is dead, replaced by his angel."

"I like it," he broadly grinned. "Get the team on it right away."

"Will do, Boss." Taking a gulp of his cocktail, Jeremy placed the glass on the bar top. "We'll need to check up on your clones, uh, I mean *angels*," he smiled. "What do you want to do with the extra ones you don't use?"

"Eh, don't really care. Give 'em to one of the training hospitals to use or they can cut 'em up for parts."

"You'll still need to make a choice."

"Yeah, I suppose I do. Is Doc here tonight?"

"I thought I saw him earlier." Walking over to open the door, he popped his head out. "Someone find Doc!" Leaving the door slightly ajar, he listened to the bustle of activity out in the hallway as they ran off to find Beauregard's personal physician. Several minutes later, a handsome young man with close cropped hair pushed his way into the room. He wore a dark double-breasted pin-stripe suit with an equally dark shirt and tie. The look was like some European gangster.

"Evening Reverend," he jovially acknowledged as he plopped down in a chair close to Beauregard. "How're we feeling tonight?"

"Wonderful," he smiled.

"What can I do for you?"

"About these copies of mine. I'm thinking of making a change soon and I want to decide on which one. As far as copies go, aren't they all the same?" he shrugged.

"Well, yes and no." He looked over at Jeremy who was fixing Beauregard another drink. "I'll take whatever he's having."

"Coming up," he nodded in reply.

Turning back to Beauregard, he continued. "Outwardly your copies look very much the same. However there can be some genetic differences. Despite our best efforts, replicating a living being is not a perfect science. We're about 95% there, but, like I said, we're not perfect." Accepting the martini, he took a sip, savoring the flavor.

"So how do I know which one to use?" Beauregard frowned at Jeremy with the sudden increase in noise outside the door. "Go find out what's going on." As Jeremy popped out to see the cause of the disturbance, he shook his head. "It's always something. Anyway. Like I asked before the interruption, how do I know which one to use?"

"If I were you," Doc replied, "I'd find out which one was the healthiest and strongest. Obviously I wouldn't worry about intelligence. But you do need to make sure all the parts are working properly, especially those parts you plan on making excessive use of." He winked and smiled.

Snickering, Beauregard raised his eyebrows several times. "Fine. I'll leave that to you. You select which one you think the best and we'll move forward from there."

"And the others?"

"Do what you want with 'em." He looked up as the door opened and Jeremy came in. "Well?"

"It's the usual religious nuts demonstrating outside the stadium. A few of them got past security and were accosting some of those waiting in lines."

35

"Good," Beauregard mused. "A little confrontation is good for business.   As long as we can marginalize the religious wackos, we'll be doing fine. What's their complaint this time?"

"Eh," he dismissively answered. "It's the usual moral and ethical claptrap. Copies have souls... they're human beings... we're murdering innocent people... we're preying on the poor... the usual banter."

"What's public opinion say?"

"Depends who you ask," he chuckled. "If you ask the folks with money, they're a hundred percent behind us. If you ask the poor? Well... who cares about the poor? We got the media in our pockets so there's nothing to worry about."

Chugging down the rest of his drink, Beauregard held his glass out for Jeremy to take. "Good. Let's schedule my transformation after next month's appearances. Postpone the following three months venues. We'll double up after that. By then, the new me should be primed and ready."

Subversion, Espionage, Interdiction and Deception Directorate (SEI), North America – Decatur
Wednesday, May 3, 2102

Collin Dodd stood behind the chair of the watch officer, his hands gripping the leather fabric along the top.

"Here it is, sir." The watch officer leaned forward and pointed to the split-screen in the upper center of the wall screen. "The drone beeped but didn't pick up the face print. I thought it odd that it would signal but not scan. I reran the feed and this is what I saw."

The watch officer sat back as the screen filled with the overhead view of the bridge over the lake in Piedmont Park. Being a sunny Atlanta day, the bridge had more than its share of runners and walkers speeding across. Mixed in were the casual strollers, friends, lovers, and mothers with children pausing to take in the budding breath of late spring.

The drone made a slow pass along the length of the bridge. About midway, there was an audible beep, but the drone neither paused nor took notice, continuing its scan.

"Once I heard the tone and noticed nothing had happened, I stopped the forward progression and brought it back. But by the time I was able to relook, this is what I saw."

The drone passed back over a spot on the bridge where a man lay slumped against the railing near the middle of the bridge. Those who noticed the body either hurried by or pretended not to see him. The drone hovered over the man until a policewoman arrived to investigate.

"Once the police officer showed up, I waited to get a good look at the face then put the drone back on course. While waiting for a face match, I took a look at the coverage."

The watch officer paused the feed and backed it up to just before the beep. Readjusting the depth of focus, he tightened the camera view to two men standing at the railing looking out over the lake. One man had his forearms resting on the railing with his foot propped up on the low stone support base. The other simply stood with one hand in his pocket, the other resting on the head of a carved wooden cane. They both looked out over the water. Though seemingly casual strangers, it was obvious they were in conversation.

"The man on the right with his arms on the railing is the same man presumably dead on the bridge. His name is Bernard Dennett. What surprised me is that he works for us as a biological engineer. I tried focusing on the other man, but he kept his face hidden during the drone pass."

Collin pursed his lips, uttering a faint, "Damn."

"I've notified security –"

"You what?"

"I, I notified security. It's protocol."

"I know what protocol is," he snapped. "I wrote the damned regulations. You were supposed to notify me first before any further action was taken."

"I did notify you, sir. I just thought that you'd want security involved."

Collin glared down at the man, who was staring back at him his nervousness obvious. "What's your name?"

"Geisler, sir." he readily answered.

"How long you been with us Geisler?" Collin looked around the small dark room. Except for the control desk, the room was filled with three wall screens, each bisected into 25 separate screens. The desk rotated for total viewing. Using voice prompts, one man could monitor the 75 screens simultaneously, initiate backup, and transfer data. Activity on any screen prompted notification to the SEI Executive Board. Collin had been at lunch when his call came.

"This is my second week, sir."

"Second week," Collin repeated, pensively nodding. "Stop the recording on that channel and give me the data from the bridge. Then clean it all."

"You want me to delete it?" His eyes widened in shock. "But sir, that's a violation of security protocol. I'll have to report this to my superiors."

Collin's nostrils flared at the insubordination. He leaned forward slightly, an unmistakable coldness in his eyes. "Listen Geisler, if you want to remain employed with this company you'll do what I ask, when I ask it. Understand?"

Geisler blinked several times and then stood up. "Yes sir, I understand." He pressed the video voice control button on the main console. "Screen 37, voice control. Stop all recording." Looking at Collin, he asked, "How would you like it delivered?"

"Put it on my phone." Collin unhooked the earphone from around his ear and laid it on the desk.

"Screen 37," Geisler enunciated. "Initiate data link to phone device, Collin Dodd. Upload all data from bridge over Lake Clara Meer, this date from 1330 hours to 1400 hours."

A moment later, the computer voice announced, "Data transfer complete."

"Screen 37. Delete all data from bridge over Lake Clara Meer, this date form 1330 hours to 1400 hours."

Screen 37 immediately began flashing the word 'warning' in bright red letters. "You have initiated a delete command," the computer voice promptly stated. "You must have authority to delete data from this recording."

Geisler looked expectantly at Collin, hoping he would change his mind. Instead, without waiting for Geisler to initiate the process, Collin reached across the desk and punched a letter number combination.

After a few moments pause, the voice said, "Delete procedure authorized by Mark Geisler. Data deleted."

Geisler frowned with consternation. "Sir," he indignantly said. "I didn't authorize the removal of data from the storage. I'm gonna have to make a formal report to that effect."

Collin was growing tired of this man's pedantic behavior. "You do what you believe is necessary." Reaching in front of Geisler, he picked up his phone and slipped it back around his ear. Turning, he walked to the door and knocked for the outside guard. As the door opened, he turned to see Geisler still watching him. "Keep up the good work." He smiled thinly and walked out.

The door closed behind him and the guard slid the lock back into place.

Collin brushed his hands together. "Charles?"

"Yes Mr. Dodd?" The guard was a large, burly man with a crew cut.

"Terminate him."

"With pleasure, sir."

Collin walked down the brightly lit hallway. Music played on the overhead speakers. Occasionally a voice would come on. "There have been 35 accidents this year. Worker safety is everyone's concern."

Collin continued to walk, his hands clasped behind him. He mumbled softly to himself. "Damn... What am I going to tell Josef?" He pulled up abruptly and went to a wall screen. "Voice ID, Dodd. Connect Nadell, Director Interdiction Branch."

In a moment, an attractive woman with short cropped brunette hair appeared on screen. "Yes sir?"

"My office, 20 minutes. Bring the pig with you."

"It'll take him that long to get out of his chair," came the retort.

Collin allowed himself a patient smile. "30 minutes then. Gamma priority. Understand?"

The woman quickly grew somber. "Got it."

His arms folded in front of him, Collin brooded as he stared out at the Atlanta skyline. Several wispy clouds stretched across the afternoon sky. He looked back over his shoulder when one of the large double doors opened to his office and Linda Nadell walked in. She was an attractive petite woman with an affinity for jewelry. She crossed the floor to stand next to him as he resumed his gaze out the floor-to-ceiling windows.

"What's up?"

"Let's wait for John," he replied, returning to look out the window.

Silence settled as Linda in turn stared out the window, wondering what was so important that it rated a Gamma priority. "Preacher had quite a crowd the other night," she commented, making small talk.

"So I heard."

"Picked up a couple of players from Social Injustice mixed in with the usual religious nuts working the crowd."

Collin's attention perked up. "How many we get?"

"Two."

"Results?"

"We're still interrogating though they appear the usual low-level."

"Keep me informed."

The door opened and John Shelby waddled in. In glaring contrast to the two already in the room, John was anything but trim and fit. His belly hung over his trousers and the lower buttons of his shirt had lost the fight in containing his ample girth. Linda barely hid her contempt. *How the hell did you ever make it so far up? You are the poster-child of the dregs that we want to get rid of.*

"Hey." John waved a meaty hand in greeting. "What we got?"

While Linda cringed at the familiarity, Collin merely frowned with condescending patience as though dealing with a slow-witted child. He was about to say "Take a seat," when John plopped down into a soft high-backed chair. Rolling his eyes, Collin crossed to stand by the wall opposite the windows.

"Blinds up," he commanded. A thin opaque sound-proof wall emerged from the floor in front of the windows. As the room darkened, ceiling lights grew in brightness. Unhooking his phone from his ear, he inserted it into a docking station on his desk. "Phone. Show download Geisler." In a moment, the wall screen behind him displayed the drone scene on the bridge at Piedmont Park. "Take a look at this."

"That's Dennett," John curiously observed when the drone beeped as it made the pass. "I know him. He's a bio-engineer over at DMI. What's he doin' there this time of day?"

"That's what I want to know," Collin tersely answered.

The drone passed back over a spot on the bridge where Dennett lay slumped against the railing near the middle of the bridge.

"Holy shit," John involuntarily uttered. "Is he dead?"

"What do you think?" Collin shook his head at the obvious.

"Who was the man with him?" John tilted his head to stare at the dead man on the bridge.

There was a heavy pause before Collin stopped the video and stared coldly at the other two. "That's what I pay you for. I want an answer by the end of the day."

"Yes, Sir," Linda crisply replied.

"I'm on it." John struggled and huffed as he pushed himself out of the soft chair. Lumbering to standing, he started to walk over and retrieve Collin's earphone when he thought better of it. "You'll send it secure?"

"Of course. You get on it now. I'll send it in a couple minutes. Linda, you remain here for a moment."

"I'm on it," he cheerfully grinned, adding a confident wink and tick of the head.

Waiting for him to plod his way out, Collin turned to Linda in disgust. "Why does he continue looking like that? We pay him more than enough. Doesn't he have a clone?"

"He says he does, but he wants to wait until he's 50." She shook her head and rolled her eyes in pained forbearance.

"I won't tolerate this much longer. You tell him to shape up now or he's out of here, and I don't give a rat's ass how brilliant he is. He's an embarrassment."

"I'll tell him," she serenely nodded, more than pleased she could finally get rid of the man. "May I ask why this is a Gamma priority?"

Collin backed up the video feed to where Dennett was in conversation with the other man. "The man with him is one of ours. There shouldn't have been a drone there at this time. I want to know why there was."

Linda blinked at the revelation. "Dennett was a hit?"

"Yes."

"Why?"

"He was attempting to compromise us by passing secrets to Social Injustice. That's why this is a Gamma priority."

"Shelby doesn't have clearance. You want to grant him temporary access?" Her raised eyebrow told him she thought it was a bad idea.

"No.   Redirect him to find out who else might have supported Dennett. We know he sent at least four packages to random individuals.   We've managed to track down and eliminate three of them. We've recently discovered the location of the remaining one, but the subject seems to have disappeared."

"Who is it?"

"A Special Appointee named Pieter Dwa over in Buckhead. We took out his office, but there was no body in it. We found a trapdoor leading to the basement. Dwa's gone into hiding. Find him and eliminate him."

Chapter 2

Chastain Park, Atlanta
Thursday, May 4, 2102

Pieter spread his arms in a wide stretch, reclining back in his chair then palm pressed firmly against his chin, twisted his head cracking his neck. *Maybe I ought to get a real bed here sometime...* He stared through the darkness at the couch against the wall, the blanket and pillow on the floor in front. He had slept in fits since his arrival. It had taken too long to get here for he had to take extra care ensuring no one knew he was still alive. Once here, he could relax. This had always been his safe-house, and now that someone was trying to kill him, he needed a place where he could think.

The place was small yet contained all he needed. He came here times he wanted to escape whatever distractions loitered around at the office. Beside the couch that doubled for a bed, he had a small kitchen, a bathroom with shower, his desk, computer, and filing cabinets for the paper copy backups. While he obviously used computers, he was no fool. There was no such thing as secure data storage. That was made painfully evident years ago when Anonymous hacked into the Cloud and exposed several million supposedly secure accounts. The fallout was the resignation of the government's Data Security Secretary. He disappeared a week later and was yet to be found. Pieter sniffed a disdainful chuckle at the obvious. Like all officials, individuals, citizens, pick a category, who compromised or disappointed the government, they disappeared – permanently.

In the dim light of the bedroom/office, he wondered how long he could last here before he was compromised. He had been careful in apportioning the place. Except for the computer, everything was salvage and paid for in cash, including the ancient refrigerator in the kitchen. Though the place was sparse, he liked it. It was comfortable, almost bohemian. The interior walls were solid block construction with additional sound-proofing. The only access to the sanctuary was via a circular staircase that grew out of one of the tunnels leading to the warehouse. Unfortunately, it was also the only way out.

Walking to stand a step away from an outer wall, he commanded, "Wall down." Immediately the wall in front on him lowered and the gleaming sunshine burst into the dark room. He put his hand in front of his face as the room filled with brightness. Blinking several times as his eyes grew accustomed to the light, he looked across the muddy waters of Nancy Creek to the vacant warehouses opposite, the shuttered and empty giants of long forgotten prosperity.

He distractedly watched several pigeons glide and settle onto one of the roofs. *Who the hell is trying to kill me? DMI? That damn letter...* He turned back around to the computer.

"Computer on. Message channel. Routing channel 12. Route disconnect at link 25. Check messages." He picked up a mini hand-recorder, waiting for the link to establish. A moment later, the screen filled with data from the calls. There were only five. A quick synopsis of each one was provided. The first two were from the landlord claiming that he was going to sue Pieter for damages. Message three was from the police wanting to talk to him, while message five reminded him that the police were still waiting. Message four gave no name, but was urgent..."somebody trying to kill me."

"Play message four."

The voice was breathless, scared. "I need your help! Someone is trying to kill me! I can't talk long. It's about DMI and I got this letter from some guy named Dennett. I don't even know who the hell he is and why he sent me this stuff! Damn! I gotta go. I need to see you. Call or text me at this number at 1600 today! Please!" And he was gone.

Pieter looked at the clock. It was only 1300. He felt a gnawing in his stomach.

"Disconnect." He punched the stop button on the recorder as he padded over to the refrigerator to get a beer. Unscrewing the top, he swigged down a satisfying gulp, savoring the taste of private stock. Ever since the corporate government instituted standardization, the taste of beer changed for the worse. While the cost was drastically reduced, so was the taste. That was the government for you. Couldn't leave well enough alone. Black market private breweries continued to pop up, but they faced harsh penalties, which meant the cost was high though Pieter didn't mind the cost as he infrequently drank alcohol. Yet today he felt he deserved a beer, especially after surviving the recent attempt on his life.

Taking another swig, he slowly moved back to the window to stare out over the detritus of long forgotten success. Empty and dilapidated warehouses crammed against one another were now the home to the flotsam of humanity's rejects, the poor, the strung-out, and the downtrodden. He shook his head at the cliché. The poor never changed, only the environment.

The police made the occasional sweep through here, but for the most part they were content to leave the area alone. After all, those who dwelt in the ruins were the flotsam of humanity. Who cared if they killed each other? It was just another way of solving the problem of the poor. Besides, with each sweep, fewer and fewer remained behind. It was only a matter of time before the last resident here was sent to the Zone and the area leveled in the name of progress. Taking another sip, he prayed he'd be long gone before then.

Pieter shook his head, his lips tight. He had never really given much thought to the poor. He had enough of his own problems. Besides, what could he do about it? Then that damned letter from Dennett shows up. Though it was consumed in the inferno, he could still recall the contents, word for word.

My name is Bernard Dennett. I am the chief bio-engineer at Disease Management Industries (DMI). I write this because my conscience will no longer allow me to live with what I have done. I know I am a dead man for telling what I am about to say, but my life's end was decided when I agreed to work for DMI. The truth of it is that DMI marches to the will of the Corporation.

I have been working for years developing cures for diseases that have plagued humanity. To do that, I developed newer and more deadly diseases in order to find cures. I was not always successful.

When I learned that the diseases I developed were killing millions, I refused to accept responsibility. After all, I didn't knowingly spread the plague, and wasn't I the one finding cures? It was when I learned that DMI was intentionally infecting populations using my research, with

45

the express intent to eliminate wholesale segments of mankind that I raised my voice.

That was my second mistake.

I know I don't have much time left as they are now watching my every move. Using the archaic mail delivery system, I have sent this same letter to four other individuals I have randomly chosen to expose the horrors of DMI. Please do not fail me. I am atoning for my sin with my life. Save the others.

You will know I am telling the truth when you see what follows on the news. Two days from the date of this letter, I will release a toxin within DMI and kill everyone inside the entire headquarters. The toxin will contaminate the building for years to come.

I have one more letter to deliver to someone from Social Injustice. Then the end will come.

Remember this. DMI did this with the authority and approval of the Corporation. We are controlling the world's population through mass murder per the authority and directive of the Corporation – the same Corporation who approves the charade of rebirth. We don't blink an eye when the poor die and we call killing human clones merely a person's right to choose. Yet we praise those rich enough to afford new bodies?

What have we become?

Pieter's first thought had been 'why me?' His second thought was that someone might be a little paranoid. Had whoever not tried to kill him, he probably would have tossed the package in the trash as another conspiracy nut. It wasn't the first time he had received communication from someone convinced of some diabolical plot.

Remembering the date on the letter, he realized that Bennett's proposed destruction of the DMI headquarters should have happened yesterday.

"Computer on. Routing channel 13. Route disconnect at link 31." Sitting in the chair at the desk, he adjusted the screen so he could lean back and watch. "Connect T-I-N." He rolled his eyes at the laughable name, T-I-N – Truth In News. T-I-N was just another propaganda network masquerading as an unbiased news site. Occasionally it reported on significant events, but always from the bias of the Corporation. Freedom of the press had died long ago.

The news feed came on. Live news was in a small pop-up in the upper right of the screen. Pieter quickly dismissed it when he saw the lady reporter talking to a cherubic cat owner. What was it with pet owners that made them think the rest of the world feels the same way about their stupid pet?

"Yesterday news highlights." A long list of key words appeared along with the time of the activity. Pieter touched the screen and scrolled through the list, repeating it twice. There was nothing related to DMI other than a progress report on the epidemic sweeping through Brazil, which wasn't surprising since Brazil had long ago been deforested and reduced to a wasteland packed with the destitute crammed against the ocean because the rest of the land could not sustain them.

The fact that the DMI building still stood cast doubt on Dennett's story. Yet Pieter couldn't shake the fact that someone did try to kill him. Was it associated with Dennett or could it have been from a prosecuted case?

With a sigh, he leaned back, frustrated. "Current news." The screen changed to a list of today's news items when the small pop-up expanded to fill the screen. A stunningly beautiful lady reporter with far too much cleavage stood before the news-screen showing the drone pass on the Clara Meer Bridge in Piedmont Park. A moment later, it showed the crumpled body of Dennett.

"This just in," she announced with feigned gravitas. "Renown bio-engineer Bernard Dennett was found dead today, the consequence of a probable murder. Dennett was recognized as having discovered cures to over twenty epidemics and was most recently working on a cure for the epidemic currently sweeping through Brazil. Police have identified a person of interest and are looking for anyone with information on this man." A picture of Pieter appeared on screen. "Pieter Dwa, a state Special Appointee, is wanted for questioning by the police. If you have any information about Pieter Dwa, please contact the Atlanta police."

SEI Directorate – Decatur

"Well?" Linda Nadell demanded, standing behind, but not too close to the repulsive man. She looked around his large cubicle. The space mimicked the owner. It was a hodgepodge of stacks of printouts some with coffee mug stains, empty fast food containers, candy wrappers, and an eclectic collection of various small plastic toys. Rolling her eyes, she knew the man had yet to grow up. She felt a chill of revulsion as she saw the barely hid lascivious glance he flashed her.

"He's good; he's very good," John Shelby answered with begrudging admiration, slurping loudly from his fountain soda cup. He pointed to the middle monitor on his desk. "Though his office was trashed, we managed to track down his provider. It's a small company out of Milwaukee." He frowned in puzzlement. "Seems strange he didn't use someone local."

"What's your point?" she brusquely demanded.

"My point is," he slowly emphasized as though explaining to a child, "is that it's not that simple. Somehow Pieter Dwa has managed to develop a global network to shield his location."

"So you're telling me you can't find him?" she tersely replied.

Her tone was beginning to irritate him. "What I'm telling you," he evenly answered, "is that I managed to track down the last message to his voicemail."

"So what you're telling me is that you can access his voice mail but you don't know where he is?"

"Bingo."

"Why not?"

"He's done a multi-link cover for his voice mail. The last link we had before disconnect was a pay phone in Paris." John nodded in appreciation. "He's good."

"Damn." Linda crossed her arms, frowning. "A pay phone?"

"Yeah." He pointed to the far right monitor to a satellite image of Paris. "Somewhere around here." He jabbed a thick ketchup-stained finger at the space between the Luxembourg Gardens and the Notre Dame Cathedral. "Somewhere around here is an old outdoor phone booth. That means it's using landlines. It'll take a little longer, but once we have the provider, we can get the layout quickly enough."

"How long?"

"Half-an-hour maybe," he shrugged nonchalantly. "I'll put a call into Paris in a minute and have them send the layout. Once we get that, we can track him down." He picked up his half-eaten sandwich and began devouring it, a dollop of mayo dripping onto his chest.

Linda watched him with sickening fascination. *You are such a pig.*

"You didn't ask me about the last voicemail," he self-importantly reminded her.

Her lips pursed, she folded her arms and cocked her head to the side to stare at him. Her first instinct was to whack him on the head and tell him he was fired. But, she reminded herself, that time would come soon enough. "OK," she calmly answered. "Tell me about the last voicemail."

"Even better," he grinned a wide mouth smile, bits of food stuck in his stained teeth, "I'll play it for you." He scrolled his finger across the left monitor screen and pressed the play icon. "Listen to him. The man is scared."

The voice came on through the desk speakers. "I need your help! Someone is trying to kill me! I can't talk long. It's about DMI and I got this letter from some guy named Dennett. I don't even know who the hell he is and why he sent me this stuff! Damn! I gotta go. I need to see you. Call or text me at this number at 1600 today! Please!"

Linda looked at her wristwatch. It was only 1305. They still had time. "Who's the caller?"

"I was just working on that when you showed up."

"We've got until 1600 to find him. I want it done in less than an hour. I'll be back." She spun around and walked out.

John waved his sandwich in acknowledgement. "Bye," he replied as she disappeared. He turned to the monitor with the data links from Pieter's phone call still showing. He couldn't hide his glee. "John boy," he said between mouthfuls, "you are one lucky man. She's a babe, and she has to work with you!" He grinned broadly. "An hour? Man this is too easy." Half a pastrami sandwich still stuffed in his mouth, he typed in the access number to his counterpart in Paris.

As he expected, the layout came moments later. Yet his smugness turned sour when he realized that there were no links to the phone booth. Setting the hamburger down, he spent the next hour amplifying imagery and tracing data lines. He was still at it when she returned.

"Well?"

"Well," he hesitantly replied. "I have good news and bad news. Which do you want first?"

Linda stared coldly at him, her disgust long past. He was incompetent. Getting rid of him would give her great joy. Besides, she already had a sharp young woman in the Subversion and Deception Branch of SEI who would be a much better fit. The woman was an up and comer, and she was attractive as well. A shapely brunette, her ambitions would be manipulated to Linda's satisfaction.

Returning to the morass of incompetence in front of her, she inhaled a deep breath of forced patience. "What's the bad news?"

"The bad news is that the phone booth on Rue Galande is old landline. No one uses it anymore except for tourist pics. I've a layout of the landline connections, but no one's updated them in years. It'll take a while to untangle them."

"What's the good news?" she sourly asked.

"The caller's name is Nicholas Warfield. He's a stiff slobbing out an existence at the aircraft plant in Hapeville."

"Perhaps, Mister Shelby," she stiffly replied, "you could be more specific in your analysis. Your penchant for common vernacular leaves much to be desired."

"Yeah, sure," he shrugged, his indifference obvious. "To put it in *your* terms, the man works as a quality control specialist, union member. Lives alone in an apartment off of Moreland. He went to work right out of high school. Been working at the same place for the past fifteen years. Spends a lot of time on the computer or watching TV. Seems to like porn the most." He snickered knowingly.

"I know that already," she calmly replied, watching his look of surprise with immense satisfaction.

"You do?" he blinked in bewilderment. "How?"

"He's one of ours."

"He is?"

With a less than patient sigh, she stared at him, torn between wanting to put him in his place or letting the obnoxious man flounder along. Flounder. She inwardly smiled at the analogy. "Of course he is." Checking her watch, she said, "It's

1400 now. Warfield is supposed to receive a return call at 1600, correct?"

"That's a roger," he nodded.

"Fine. I'll be back then, and I want everything ready. Do I make myself clear?"

"Don't fret, Linda," he answered, regaining his self-assured composure. "I got it all under control. We'll have our man in no time."

Shaking her head, Linda snarled, "You better. Your future depends on it." Spinning around, she marched out of his cubicle and down the hall to her office.

Startled at the threat, John put down his sandwich and focused on finding answers.

Chastain Park, Atlanta

Pieter closed the refrigerator door, pausing to press the flip top off the beer bottle. Walking back past the desk, he flicked a bit of moisture from the cold bottle into the air as he stopped by the windows. He stood staring out across Nancy Creek, the sunlight still bright for this early autumn day. Lifting the bottle as if in salute, he took a long swallow, belched loudly, and returned to the desk to sit down.

"Screen down. Encode channel 12, route 22. Dial forty, forty nine, seventy seven zero zero, zero eight, four eight." He leaned back in the chair, stretching his long legs out before him, as the computer dialed the telephone number. A moment later an agitated voice answered.

"Hello?"

"You called me?" Pieter asked.

"Yes! You gotta help me! I got this letter – "

"Stop. Where are you?"

"I'm at home."

"Where's home?"

"Moreland and Berne."

"Go to the Zoo, parking lot Boulevard side. I'll call you in fifteen minutes."

"Why?"

"Just do it." Pieter disconnected and waited. Fifteen minutes later he called again. "Where are you?"

"Where you told me to be," came the reply, full of angst.
"Look across the street. You see the pawn shop?"
"Yeah?"
"Go down three stores. You see the liquor store?"
"Yeah?"
"See the phone booth outside?"
"Yeah?"
"I'll call you there in three minutes."

SEI Directorate – Decatur

Linda looked down at John, her consternation overtly apparent. "He's in Grant Park."

"Thanks for telling me the obvious," he snidely replied. His voice rising, he called out to the surrounding cubicles. "Get a trace on the liquor store! I need that phone tapped ASAP!" John didn't like being surprised. "Damn, he's good. Pay phones. Who'd a thunk that they'd still be in existence. The man who came up with reinstituting them was a genius. Call without being identified, just like in the old days."

"That's all very nostalgic," she said, her voice dripping sarcasm, "but how does that help us?"

You may be a babe, but get off my back. With a hint of irritation, John glanced up at her. "Well Linda," he watched her overtly bristle at his familiarity. "Hopefully we can lock onto the pay phone if he talks long enough. And if he does, then we might be able to find where he is."

Linda straightened herself to full height. "First Mister Shelby, let me remind you who I am and just who you are. I am Director Nadell; you are a branch manager within Interdiction Branch. Your familiarity is entirely way out of line. Second, it appears that you have failed to adequately anticipate the subject's most likely actions. Both breaches of professionalism will be recorded into your personnel file." She cocked an eyebrow. "I suggest you get that tap before you lose your job."

Without waiting for a reply, she turned to leave, but stopped before the door. Turning, she faced a scowling John. "And when you do get the required information, please send it to me, through proper channels. Understand?"

John stared hard at her. *Bitch.* She stood solidly, waiting for a reply. He finally offered the begrudging, "Yes mam."

And she left.

How the hell am I supposed to think of everything? John swiveled his corpulent body around in the chair to call out to the other analysts working feverishly around him. "Well?"

"Where's the phone booth at?" came a reply.

"Dammit! It's on the corner of Boulevard and Ormewood. Do I hafta do everything myself?"

"Got it! We got it!"

Thankful for the response, John lifted his extra-large soda cup and stuck the straw in his mouth. "OK, put 'er up."

As the voice came over the speakers, the words filled the screen.

"Mister Dwa?"

"Turn around. Look across the street. There is another pay phone nearby where you were standing before. Hang up and wait for my call."

"Dammit!" John's shrill voice erupted. "Damn it all. Someone get a link to that phone."

"Working it," a voice called back.

John sat back wondering who this Dwa fellow was, and why was he so secretive? There had to be something else going on here. He was no fool. Linda Nadell knew more than she was telling. He would show her. Two could play this cat and mouse game.

While John stewed and waited for a data link to the new pay phone, Pieter connected. The man who answered was out of breath.

"Yes, yes, I'm here."

"How'd you get my name?"

"Billy Fish gave it to me."

There was a pause. "Who are you?"

"Warfield. Nick Warfield."

"What can I do for you Mister Warfield?"

The words flowed out in a rush as Warfield explained his fear.

"Slow down, Mister Warfield," Pieter patiently asked. "You said you have a copy of a letter from Dennett?"

"Yes! I don't even know who Dennett is! Why did he send it to me?"

"What do you do for a living Mr. Warfield?"

"I'm a quality control specialist for the airlines in Hapeville. Why the hell am I mixed up in this?" The voice grew more frantic. "My place was trashed. You understand? Trashed. They destroyed everything. There's a tag on my value card that beeps every time I use it. I know they're following me 'cause I can feel 'em!"

"Did you read the letter?"

"Of course I did. My god, it was crazy! If it's even remotely true, there's going to be one hell of a mess." He paused to catch his breath. "Why me? Why did he get me involved? Why ruin my life?"

"Have you seen the news lately?"

"News? No, not really. I don't watch the news, unless it's important."

Pieter was about to ask how he would know what was important if he didn't watch the news to begin with. Instead, he quietly replied, "Dennett's dead."

"Dead? O my god. How? Why?"

"I don't know, but right now they think I had something to do with it."

"You killed him?"

"Of course not," Pieter huffed in irritation. "Have you shown anyone else the letter?"

"No."

There was a long pause before Pieter asked, "Why do you think I can help you?"

"Billy Fish said that you were the best. He said that I could trust you and that you could protect me. And so I called you. Can you help me?"

Again there was a long pause as Pieter pondered his fate. Someone had already tried to kill him and it was all because Dennett decided his own guilt was worth more than the lives of others. And now someone else was thrown into the mix and somehow managed to find him. His instincts told him it was all wrong, but his options had suddenly diminished, now that he was a wanted man. He would need help. Yet there was something about this Warfield fellow that caused him concern. He couldn't pinpoint it, but he would have to tread cautiously.

"We need to meet."

"When and where. I can't go back to my place because it's probably being watched."

"You know the Underground, off of MLK?"

"Yeah, of course."

"Meet me there tomorrow-"

"Tomorrow! Why not tonight. I need help now!"

"Tomorrow."

"Where am I gonna stay. What am I gonna do for the next day and a half?"

"Tomorrow. 2200 hours. What do you look like?"

Nick Warfield sighed loudly. "I'm about one point eight meters tall, 84 kilos, black hair, and have a scar under my right eye. What do you look like?"

"I'll find you. Go to the Vanishing Point. When you enter the restaurant, tell the maître-de that you want to talk to Kingfisher."

The speakers on John's desk came alive just as Warfield said, "Kingfisher. Right."

Suddenly there was a horrendous explosion over the speakers.

"Oh my god oh my god! The phone booth…the first phone booth just exploded!"

"Warfield, Mr. Warfield are you all right?"

"Yes…yes." The voice was shaky. "They're dead. They're dead."

"Who's dead?"

"Those people…they were just walking by…the lady with the baby stroller… oh my god. Help me, please help me," Warfield begged.

"Listen," Pieter said, "you need to get out of there right away. I can do nothing for you now. Meet me tomorrow." And the phone line went dead.

Linda Nadell stiffened. "What the hell was that? I didn't authorize an elimination!"

John Shelby exhaled loudly and looked around the room. "Well," he smirked, "timing is everything."

"And just what do you mean by that?" came the tart question.

John turned back to look at her. "It was just a joke. Look, it's obvious someone else is tuned into what's going on –"

"What is obvious is that you have lost control of the mission." Linda interrupted.

"Now just a minute bitch," John lost control and began shouting.   "I've done everything I was supposed to do.   If there's a leak somewhere, it's probably at your level.   And you can put that in your goddamn report."

Linda visibly jerked back at John's outburst.   Quickly regaining her composure, she waited for him to finish.   "Mr. Shelby, collect your things and out-process.   You are no longer employed here."   She spun on her heals and left.

"We'll see about that," John snarled. He hoisted his great girth out of the chair and made his way to the door.   Opening the door, he found that a hover-cart had been sent for him.   *How damn nice of them.*   He huffed as he squeezed himself into the passenger seat.   As soon as he was settled, the cart began its low humming and moved forward.

Over-head the speakers announced, "There have been 36 accidents this year.   Worker safety is everyone's concern."

John leaned forward to see the destination screen.   Suddenly the cart swung sharply to the right and picked up speed, zipping along the hallways.   Pedestrians leaped out of the way, and still the cart sped faster and faster.   John clutched the seat in front of him, his eyes wide in terror.   Another sharp turn and the cart raced toward the far dead-end wall.   John frantically tried to get his corpulent body unstuck.

The impact exploded the cart and occupant into ever expanding debris.   The tangled remains slid down the wall and lay in a smoldering mass.   Over-head the speakers announced, "There have been 37 accidents this year.   Worker safety is everyone's concern."

Resurrection Industries, Decatur Facility
North Arcadia Avenue

A surprised JB leaped up when the door opened and he saw Ruth smiling impishly at him.   Covering the distance from the bed to the door in quick strides, he grabbed her hand.   Looking up at Dale, he gushed, "It was only two days ago!   Thank you so much for letting her come again."

"I don't know what you're talking about," he gruffly answered, giving Ruth a push from behind.

"But, but," a bewildered JB began only to be cut off.

"I said, I don't know what you're talking about. This is your normal session. Don't argue."

"But I'm not arguing," he replied then shut his mouth when he saw the hard stare from the lab assistant. Silently pulling Ruth into the room, he stepped back and waited for the door to close.

Once secure within the safety behind the closed door, JB tightly hugged her to him. "How did you do it?"

"I don't know." She was surprised as he was. "I had just started our 'be nice' game. I didn't think it would work so soon. And it's not even time yet for doing it."

"I know."

"I brought you a drawing." She handed him a piece of paper with her picture on it. It had been meticulously executed and seemed lifelike. "I thought this one would be better than the first one."

JB stared at the drawing, marveling at the likeness. "This looks just like the real thing." He held her close to him and kissed her, passionately and deeply. He felt her respond with equal intensity.

"Do you want to do it first then talk?" she huskily asked.

"Yes," he quickly answered then caught himself. "But will they take you away after that? I don't want you to leave so soon."

Ruth struggled between her immediate need and the desire to spend more time with him. "Let's wait to do it then. We'll talk first."

They reluctantly sat on the edge of the bed, their bodies firm against each other. Ruth squeezed his hand.

"This is nice," she confidently smiled at him, "even if they *are* looking in through the window."

"I wonder why they do that," he wondered, not so much as a complaint but as an observation. "I would think that we all do it the same way, so why look at us."

"Maybe it's just to see if we're finished," she shrugged. "I can't imagine just standing there and watching all the time. I think that would get boring."

JB looked down at the picture in his hand. "What is your room like?" he asked, purposely changing the subject, more interested in Ruth than the man viewing them through the window.

"It's a lot like yours," she replied, looking around his room, "except I have drawings on my walls now."

"You do?"

"Yes," she excitedly smiled, leaning into him. "When I started the 'be nice' game, I asked if there was something that I could use to put my pictures on the wall, and they gave me this sticky thing called 'tape.' You just peel a part off and stick it on the paper and then stick it to the wall, and it stays where you put it."

"Tape," he repeated. "I've never seen it before."

"Me either, but now I've got lots of pictures on my walls. I can make some for you, if you like."

"I would like that." He squeezed her hand in appreciation. "Do you think that if we play the 'be nice' game some more they will let you come back?"

"I hope so." She placed her hand on his thigh. Casting a quick glance back at the window, she turned and brought her face close to his, whispering, "I don't think I want to wait any longer. Let's do it."

She stood up and straddled his lap. Taking his head in her hands, she kissed him, deeply and passionately.

Outside the door, Dale grinned with satisfaction. Watching these two was better than porn on the computer. At least it was live here. And he knew it wouldn't last much longer, so he might as well enjoy it as long as JB was still here. Once he was gone, he'd have to find another one for the woman. She was one fine woman.

SEI Directorate – Decatur

Linda Nadell walked past the numerous cubicles towards the largest one in the rear close to the windows where the former employee John Shelby had once sat in all his corpulent splendor. His personal items had already been removed, boxed up and shipped off to who cared where. Much to her satisfaction, his replacement was still here getting settled in.

58

Pausing long enough to look at the 'Sharon Walker' on the nameplate on the outside of the cubicle, she stepped in. She was pleased to see the effect of change, the most obvious being the occupant. In glaring contrast to the former tenant, Sharon Walker was a svelte brunette, her thick hair cut to shoulder length. She wore a pants suit that snugly fit and flattered her. She was definitely eye candy. Linda chuckled at the description then wondered if Sharon's attractiveness might be a hindrance to her purpose here.

Sharon turned around when she felt someone enter her space. Seeing her boss, she stood up. "Director Nadell," she warmly smiled.

"Surprised to see you here so late, Sharon," she said, flattered with her subordinate's recognition of her status. Sharon's eyes were the deepest brown and they focused on Linda as though she was the only thing that mattered in the world.

"I just wanted to make sure I'm caught up on things, especially the Warfield/Dwa situation. I had been following that a little bit over in Subversion Branch."

"Why is that?" Linda liked Sharon's attention. What a blessed change from that pig Shelby.

"Just a hunch," she replied, her eyes fluttering innocently. "Despite the misinformation put out on Dwa, I think it's a possibility that he really is involved with Social Injustice."

Linda wasn't listening as she worked through what it was about Sharon that attracted her. She then realized that for all Sharon's overt professionalism, there seemed to be a barely constrained sensuality that was waiting to burst forth at any moment. And this puzzled her for there were no reports of illicit behavior or questionable trysts. Her superiors in Subversion Branch practically worshipped the ground she tread upon. Her evaluations were all beyond superior. Perhaps she was just misreading her.

Awaking to the fact that Sharon had stopped talking and was waiting for a response, Linda lamely said, "I'll let you pursue that as you see fit. Show me what you have so far."

"Yes Mam," Sharon cheerfully replied, spinning around to sit in front of her console. She pointed to a city grid map on the center monitor. "Warfield lives here, just off of Moreland Avenue. The man goes nowhere without his phone, and since every phone has a tracking unit on it, we know where he is all the time. With your permission, I'd like to put a tail on him."

Standing next to her, Linda gently placed a hand on Sharon's shoulder. Feeling the touch, Sharon looked at the hand then up to Linda, giving her an inviting smile.

"Do you think a tail is wise," Linda wondered, suddenly feeling both uncomfortable and excited at the reaction to her touch. "If Dwa's with Social Injustice, logically they would expect us to put someone, or a drone on Warfield."

"I'm sure you're right, Director Nadell," she fawningly replied. "It's probably overkill on my part. I just don't like leaving opportunities to one possibility."

"That's a wise outlook," she smiled, giving her a soft squeeze on her shoulder. "In this instance, I don't think we have the time to put someone in place."

"I know someone over in E Branch who could help." Though looking between the monitor and Linda, Sharon continued to position herself so that Linda's hand always rested on her shoulder.

"I'm sure you do," Linda affectionately smiled at her. "Let's leave it like it is for now. If we need more help, we can determine that later. What do you have on Kingfisher?"

"That one's still a puzzle." She shook her head in mild frustration. "If only we had more of that conversation, it would be a big help. It took too long to get a trace on that other phone. That's not going to happen again," she sternly affirmed. "With your permission, I'd like to make some adjustments to my team, but only after I've seen where they best fit."

"It's your team," she regally nodded. "Do with it as you see fit."

"Thank you, Mam."

"You may call me Linda," she said, "when we are alone like this. Other times, I think it best to preserve the business relationship."

"You are very kind, Linda. Thank you so much for your trust. I will not disappoint you."

Linda again felt the intensity of the gaze, tantalizing, as though Sharon was invading her body, tugging at her passions. Suddenly feeling exposed, she blinked and calmly withdrew her hand. "We know Warfield's meeting Dwa tomorrow night.

Why don't you go home and get some rest. You've done enough for the day."

"Yes, Mam... er, Linda." She stood up and pushed the chair in. "I'll leave this on overnight," she said, ticking her head at the monitor. "I'm running a search for anything Kingfisher related. Maybe we'll have something in the morning."

As they walked down the hallway together, Sharon lowered her voice for only Linda to hear. "Would it be out of line to ask you if you'd like to go for a drink somewhere? I've always wanted to talk with you and hear about your experiences in the Intel world. You have such an outstanding reputation that I'd like to steal some of your best practices."

It was said with such childish innocence that Linda gave a lighthearted laugh. "A drink right about now sounds good."

"I know a nice place where we won't be bothered." Stopping at the main set of doors to the office area, she made a deliberate point to open the door for Linda.

Social Injustice HQs – East Point

Martin looked up at the man sitting next to the pulpit on top of the platform. Short hair, clean shaven and well-dressed, the man could easily be mistaken for a corporate executive. Instead, Lowell Peck, the leader and unchallenged authority of Social Injustice, was calmly cleaning and oiling his disassembled Ruger P95 9mm. Behind him, the afternoon sunlight illuminated the stained glass windows displaying a woodland scene of animals and trees, casting a warm glow onto the choir chairs, now pushed aside, and the well-worn crimson carpet of the long forgotten church.

Surrounding Martin in the one-time sanctuary, dozens of men and women spread out on the numerous pews, all giving attention to their individual weapons. Conversations and occasional laughter filled the air. Several disciples sat on the floor at the feet of the Commander of Social Injustice. Siting on the front pew Martin listened as Lowell Peck taught his devotees.

"Never trust science or religion," Lowell instructed. He had a slight British accent. "Both require extraordinary leaps of

61

faith.   For example, science tells us the universe was created billions of years ago."

"It wasn't?" a slender freckled young man seemed surprised.

"Who knows?" he paternally shrugged. "No one was there to see it.   How do we know the universe hasn't always been here?   That's the problem.   You can only go so far back in time before it all becomes a matter of guessing.   Here's another example.   We've still not deciphered the Minoan Linear A writing system and that's only been around for 4500 or so years. Yet we trust science to tell us what happened billions of years ago?"

"But Lowell, you also said to not trust religion.   Isn't it religion that tells us to live by the golden rule?" another asked.

"A noble thought, certainly," he nodded, "but impossible to achieve.   Look at the 20th century.   In those one hundred years, more humans were killed by war or their own governments than all of man's previous history combined.   Tragically, governments were responsible for killing more of their citizens than what war took away.   Yet we exclaim the advances of science.   Science enabled mankind to kill more of itself. Certainly we have made technological improvements, but have all these advancements helped mankind at all?   Take cloning. They tell us that we can now live forever.   But at what cost? The rich man makes three clones of himself, but uses only one. What happens to the other two?"

"They're destroyed," came the reply.

"But the other two clones are sentient and emotional beings, fully human, are they not?

"Yes."

"Yet we allow them to be killed in the name of science.   We kill them in the name of religion."

"You mean like that Beauregard Clayton preacher?" the freckled young man offered.

"Yes, Wayne, just like the Reverend Clayton."   Lowell began reassembling the pistol.

"But some say that, even though they might be human, they're personal property that they have a right to do what they want with them."

"Very good Wayne.   You bring up an excellent point. Listen, the rest of you.   What we have here is a different form of a type of slavery. Not all that long ago, especially in the 18th and 19th centuries, slaves were looked upon as chattel."

"What's chattel?" a bearded man next to Wayne asked.

"Chattel, Oren, means property, something that belongs to you, something that you own and are free to do with as you please. It's like a piece of furniture. When it's new, you enjoy it. But when it's old and worn out, you either toss it out or break it up to burn. Either way, you do with it what you want. In the 19th century, a slave master was free to do what he wanted to do with his slaves."

"Even kill them?" Oren asked, frowning in shock.

"Yes, Oren, even kill them."

"But a slave isn't like a piece of furniture," he objected.

"You are correct."

"And nothing happened to the slave master?"

"No, because slaves were not looked upon as fully human."

"But that's stupid. Everyone knows both slaves and free men are human."

"They may be human, but they are not equal. Throughout history, slaves were always considered property, much like our present day clones. The master was and is free to do with his property as he wishes. With regards to slavery, deep down we knew that mankind could not justify the act and so slavery was outlawed."

"But I heard it still happens," Wayne interjected.

"Yes, it does, despite the pervasive government surveillance. That it still happens does not justify the act. If a slaver is caught, he is punished. But it is not the same with clones. We've been anesthetized to the practice. We've sterilized the words to make them less distasteful. If we called them human, we would have to treat them as such and give them all the rights a human being has. Instead, we call them clones, a word that devalues their true essence."

"But why have human clones at all?" Oren asked. "We have to feed and clothe them, and there's too many people on the planet as it is."

Lowell leaned forward, resting his forearms on his thighs. Nodding appreciatively at his devotee, he explained, "Originally it was to prove how good science was. Like I've mentioned in the past, we cloned plants and animals to increase food production, but it wasn't without its problems. In the beginning, there was less than a three percent chance of success. We got better, but even now we have less than a fifty percent success rate."

"And not all of those that made it looked right," a heavyset man with thick black hair pointed out.

"That's right Malcolm," Lowell benignly smiled. "There were some who were born with defective immune systems, others had malformed brains. Externally they looked the same, but internally things weren't quite right. That's why you hear about rich folks who have two or three and even four or more clones of themselves."

"What happened to the ones who weren't quite right?" Oren asked.

"They were destroyed, which is another way of saying they were killed," Lowell replied.

"Suppose the rich man decided to only have one clone?" Wayne interrupted

"An interesting question, Wayne." Lowell picked up the last parts of the weapon to finish the pistol assembly. He pulled the slide back and forth, carefully releasing the hammer each time, feeling the ease and smoothness of the movement. "We must first ask ourselves, what is a clone? Years ago, before we all were born, animal and plant cloning was enthusiastically accepted, the latest advancement of science. We now had a means of producing enough food to feed the growing global population. Did we ascribe any spiritual aspects to these clones? No. Animals and plants were merely part of the food chain. We saw nothing wrong with cloning cattle then slaughtering their young for meat."

He set the pistol on a cleaning cloth next to him. "The same mentality has been applied to human clones. At first there was nervous concern. Why would we clone humans when the global population was growing too fast? Why add mouths to feed? Yet science was not to be denied. Cloning was the latest and greatest advancement. We were promised all sorts of spin off medical benefits, like curing cancer, infertility and other diseases. Of course there was the rarely mentioned option of harvesting organs. All this was to improve our lives. But look around you. Has life improved?"

"No," Oren readily answered.

"That's right," Lowell benevolently nodded. "Human cloning became the rich man's domain. We gradually morphed to accepting human cloning as a means of extending our own lives. Forever fascinated with the Fountain of Youth, we now create bodies for ourselves and toss away those we don't want. And now there are means to where almost anyone can afford a new body. Look at the commercials telling you that you can take 50 years or more to pay back a loan. What they don't tell you is that, unless you are incredibly rich, you will never be able to payback what they demand. Yes, you are supposedly young again, but at what cost?"

"And the poor never get a chance to play," Wayne said.

"There will always be poor, Wayne," Lowell sagaciously replied. "Although with the number of plagues that infest the world, the poor seem to be dying off at a good clip. Don't you find it interesting that the poor seem to suffer the most from these plagues and diseases?"

"What do you mean?" Malcom asked.

"What I mean is this. Every so often a new disease or strain of disease erupts and millions die. But ninety-nine percent of those who die are poor. Why do you think that is?"

"The places where the diseases hit are usually slums," Wayne answered.

"In other words, life for over half the world hasn't gotten any better, despite all the so-called advances in science."

"At least we don't have wars anymore, now that we have a global government," Malcom stated.

"And it is that very government that we fight against, is it not?" Lowell challenged. He received three nods of agreement. "Hopefully you can see why what we do is so important. Remember, the government that used to take its citizens to war is the same Corporation that now kills them in the name of security."

"What do you mean?" Oren frowned.

"What I mean is that our lives are controlled by the Corporation. Everything we do is in accordance with someone else's rules and regulations. Can you walk to the corner store for cigarettes without having some drone following you?"

"That's another question I have, Lowell," Malcolm wondered out loud. "The Corporation preaches that smoking will kill us, but they still allow cigarettes to be sold."

"That's because they get a cut of every cigarette sold," Wayne wisely explained. "Same thing with alcohol. The government tells us drinking is bad for us, but they want us to buy booze so they can make money."

"That's hypocritical, isn't it," Oren stated.

"Of course it is," Lowell readily agreed. "Just like telling us cloning is for the benefit of mankind. The problem is that few benefit and too many suffer, especially the humans we call clones." He stood up. "So, what's our purpose?"

"End cloning," Wayne answered.

'Why?"

"Because clones are humans too."

"Good. Clones are human. In fact, I'm beginning to think that we need to appropriate the Reverend Clayton's term for those he seeks to destroy. We will no longer call them clones, but 'angels.' Just as he has given birth to his angels, we will give them a rebirth. We will give them life." He smiled paternally at the group. "And what else is our purpose?"

"Overthrow the Corporation," Malcolm tersely stated.

Lowell chuckled. "Why?"

"Because it's time we ran our own lives."

"And?"

"And it's time to break down the walls between the Zones and the free world."

There was a brief pause of silence before Wayne broached a subject he had been pondering. "Lowell, why don't we have some sort of symbol or something that people will recognize, something that tells them who we are?"

Lowell smiled kindly at him. He was pleased with this latest recruit. The man had a questioning mind, one that wanted answers. Yet he was a loyal follower. He would do well when the time came. "You ask an excellent question, Wayne. One that I will answer so all of you will understand." He raised his voice so that even those in the back of the sanctuary could hear. "Wayne here asked why we don't have some sort of symbol that represents us. Study history and you will see that men thirst for a symbol, something that represents the struggle or success of a movement. When there were still independent nations on the earth, each one had a flag, a symbol of what it meant to be a citizen of that particular nation. Now we have replaced national flags with the global flag, a piece of black cloth with the neon

66

gold eternity symbol on it, representing the never ending presence of the government, a sort of fifth Reich."

He began slowly pacing the platform as he delivered his speech. "Men and women have died for flags, for symbols. But all these symbols were designed to motivate the ignorant masses, the muddled wanderlost who needed someone to tell them when to piss." There were a few chuckles and grunts of agreement as he continued. "But I do not come here with a symbol or flag, signs of false hope. Just as all the nations of the earth fell to the power of the supreme global Corporation, so too will this form of government fall. What I bring is the dream of an Athenian government of old where the people decided, not the elected few. We have no need of an emblem, for we are already united in one cause. Our future is not in perishable things like flags and badges, but in words and deeds. Now," he stopped and gazed out over the group. "Are we ready?"

Standing up, Martin rammed a 30-round magazine into his assault rifle, pulled back the charging handle and let go, feeling the bolt thrust forward, feeding a round into the chamber. "I'm ready."

Lowell patted his hand in the air telling Martin to be patient. Looking towards the back of the sanctuary, he called out to a well-proportioned man with a handsome face. "Frank. You're with me." Turning his attention to the rest of the group, he reiterated previous instructions. "We've gone over this before, but let's review one more time. Frank and I will access the facility at 2:00 a.m. Once the doors are opened, all teams move in and we extract as many clones as we can. Martin? How many vans do we have?"

"Four. Enough to hold six a piece, comfortably."

"Then we take out twenty-four clones," Lowell emphasized. "A few more won't hurt, but we only have ten minutes to get in and out. If they don't want to come, leave them. Once we're set, we move out and separate. Martin."

Martin held the butt of the assault rifle on his hip as he spoke to the group. "Four drivers are Carole, Becca, Sarah, and myself. The drivers are also the team leader. What he or she says goes. If you are not sitting with your team leader, move now." He waited as several collected their weapons and moved to sit near their respective team leader.

"Once we've collected our clones," he continued, "we move out. You each have your individual routes and time of arrival back here. If you see you're running ahead of time, figure something out. It's better to lag behind than be early or bunch up with the others. That said, no one arrives more than thirty minutes after their due time. Understood?"

Receiving nods of understanding from the other three team leaders, Martin turned back to Lowell. "We're all set."

"Good. Thank you." Pausing for a moment as he calmly scanned the sanctuary, nodding with satisfaction. "Remember the element of surprise. The objective is to get in and out without setting off alarms. When you shoot, shoot to kill. One shot, one dead. Move quickly. Questions?" When no one raised a hand or gave voice to a concern, he gave a quick bob of the head. "We move out in two hours."

Pharr Court South, Atlanta

Walking along in the warm evening in the soft glow of ornate streetlamps, Linda felt a little tipsy as she approached the penthouse complex where her home on the top floor overlooked the city. Casting a sly glance to the side, she wondered if Sharon was feeling the same effects of the several bottles of wine they shared along with some tapas. The part of her that said she should keep a professional distance between herself and her subordinate had been vanquished after the second bottle of an intoxicating sauterne. Now she was more than ready to get home and partake of the second half of the evening.

She laughed at herself for her carefree attitude, so unlike her normal reserved demeanor. Here she was walking down the sidewalk, arm in arm with another woman, chatting carelessly about family and friends and common interests.

Stopping at the bottom of the steps, she stared up at the large front doors and grandly announced, "Here we are."

The doorman at the top of the steps smiled respectfully at her. "Good evening Miss Nadell, and madam." He dipped his head and pinched the brim of his hat. "Mind your step," he cautioned as they slowly ascended. Once the two ladies were near the top step, he held open the door. "Have a pleasant evening."

"Thank you Charles," Linda replied, with more warmth than she meant.

Squeezing Sharon's arm with hers, she crossed the lobby and approached three sets of elevators. The floors serviced were engraved in brass plaques by each set of doors. Choosing the right set, Linda pushed the elevator button and waited. Looking back at the doorman, she said, "He's a nice man. Very professional. Been here for as long as I can remember."

"How long have you been here?" Sharon smiled affectionately at her.

Linda blinked in thought. "I suppose it hasn't really been all that long. I bought this place when I was promoted to Director of Interdiction and Detection Branch, three years ago. A bit more than I could really afford, but you only live once." She looked at Sharon and giggled. "Well that's not true. Who knows? I might live eight or nine times." She giggled at her own humor. "How many times are you going to be cloned? Oh wait," she quickly corrected herself. "How many times are you going to become an angel?"

The elevator doors slid open and with no one getting off, they stepped in. As the doors closed, Linda extracted a key from her purse and inserted it into the key slot by the floor buttons. "This elevator only goes up to the forty-fifth floor without a key. You need a key for the remaining floors." She gave Sharon an impish smile. "If you're good, I might let you have a key."

"I'll be very good," Sharon replied with feigned innocence.

Linda's first impulse was to pull her in and kiss her, but she knew there were cameras hidden in the elevator and despite her devil-may-care attitude, there were some things the Corporation didn't need to be privy to. That thought caused her to wonder if the Corporate Board endured the same invasion of privacy and immediately knew that to be an absurd probability. In the isolation of her own thoughts, she often referred to them as the Corporate Politburo. One of these days she was going forget herself and say that out loud... And that would be the end of her career.

Noticing Linda's silent introspection, Sharon interrupted her thoughts. "Is your penthouse on the very top floor?"

"Yes," she smiled. "It's quite nice. A little under five hundred square meters, five bedrooms –"

"Five bedrooms," she sputtered. "Who else is living there?"

"Just me," she nonchalantly replied.

"Why so big?" Sharon wondered. "It's not like you spend a lot of time there."

"It's the status that matters," she wisely pointed out. "I can afford to live there, so why not? Like you said, I don't spend a lot of time there, but when I do, I enjoy the privilege of status, of living in a luxury penthouse."

The elevator slowed to a stop and the doors opened. Stepping out into a short brightly lit corridor, Sharon saw that there were only two doors on either side of the hallway. "There are only two penthouses up here?"

"That's right. The other belongs to the VP for Consumer Marketing for Electric Motors. He and his wife are a nice couple. Thank god they don't have kids. They've been cloned once already. Oops, I mean they've been angeled once already. Is that even a word? Angeled? Or did I just make that up?"

"I think you just made that up," Sharon chuckled, standing next to her while Linda pressed her palm into the print scanner by the door.

"These things are so ugly," Linda said, indicating the scanner. "Thank god they're on the outside here in the hallway, though it does detract from the otherwise class of the place here." Opening the door, they stepped into the spacious apartment.

The entryway was two stories high with an imposing wide sweeping stairway that ascended to the right. On both sides of the staircase, the penthouse spread wide and deep. Once past the entryway, the twelve foot high ceilings gave the rooms a grand spaciousness. The floors were polished oak artfully covered in expensive thickly woven carpets and throw rugs. Ornately carved furniture, deep plush couches and settees, and original art work added to the statement of wealth.

"My god," Sharon involuntarily uttered. "You can get lost in this place."

"Thank you." Linda set her purse on a table by the door. "Let me show you around." She took her hand and led her through each of the rooms, telling a bit about the room and the furnishings. She then led her upstairs to the bedrooms. In contrast to the opulence of the downstairs, only the master bedroom was furnished.

70

Sharon stared at the bed itself. It was a four poster bed wide enough for a family of eight to sleep on. "Where do you find sheets for that?"

"I have them custom made," she shrugged as though that was a common occurrence.

Sharon walked over and pushed open the door to the bathroom. It was as large as one of the unused bedrooms, with an elevated cast iron claw-foot bathtub and a hot tub large enough for six people.

Linda watched Sharon's fascination with gratification. "Here, let me show you one more thing." She led her back into the bedroom and past the bed to the double doors leading to the balcony. Sliding the curtains aside, she opened the doors and they stepped out onto a wide balcony that overlooked the city. In the night air, the lights of the other buildings, the headlamps of the cars on the streets below, mixed with the sounds of life pulsed within them.

Sharon looked immediately below to the garden deck that extended out from the first floor of the penthouse. It stretched the entire length of the penthouse and was probably as deep. The protective wall was about a meter wide, filled with thick low-growing shrubs. Two tables, chairs and recliners sat to one side. On the other side was a hot tub, larger than the one in the master bathroom. Several potted trees provided some overhead shelter.

Sharon inhaled the deliciousness of the night. "This is absolutely wonderful." She turned to look at her boss, giving her a smile. "I want to grow up to be just like you."

"You will," she reassured her. Gently taking her hand, she smiled coyly at her. "Come. Let me show you how comfortable the bed is."

Resurrection Industries, Decatur Facility
North Arcadia Avenue
Friday, May 5, 2102

In the wee hours of the morning, the beep of the outside intercom startled the security guard sitting behind the desk in the main lobby. Frowning at the interruption, he turned his attention away from the movie on his hand-pad and looked up to

71

see two men standing outside. They were dressed in business suits, each carrying a leather briefcase. One was a little taller than the other, but both were trim and fit. Pushing the intercom button, he pulled down the headset's microphone.

Looking at the wall clock his frown deepened. It was just a little past 2:00 a.m.   Who on earth wanted to get in now? "Yes?"

"So sorry to trouble you," the taller replied, leaning in towards the outside speaker. He spoke with a slight British accent. "I know this is a most unusual hour, but our flight was delayed in arrival here and we've only time to drop off these secure files before our flight leaves out of Hartsfield." He held up the briefcase as evidence. "Do you have secure storage handy?"

"Who are you?" the guard cautiously inquired.

"I'm sorry," the taller one apologized.   "We're from Angel's Incorporated, London. I'm William Gladstone and my friend here is Mister Anthony Eden. We have the documents requested by Mister Hunter, your CEO. Again, I do apologize for the hour, but it truly is not our fault. We've not even had time to dine properly."

The guard looked past them to the waiting taxi, its roof sign flashing in the 'on-call and waiting' mode. Put off that he would now have to do a bit of work, he sighed and with a curl of his fingers, motioned them to come in, pressing the door button to slide the outside set of doors wide. Gladstone and Eden walked in and waited before the inside set of doors while the outside set of doors closed securely. The guard punched the scan button and watched the body-scanner quickly descend, highlighting and illuminating the two businessmen's bodies. Except for the opaque view of both briefcases, due to the nature of the secure material, it was obvious they had no weapons. When the scanner finished, he opened the interior doors.

"Thank you so much," Gladstone smiled as he approached the desk. "We shan't take up too much of your time. All we need is a security device to store this. Then we'll be out of your hair." He placed the briefcase on the counter top, as did Eden.

"Why didn't y'all just send it via the cloud?" the guard asked, raising an eyebrow at the obvious.

"That's what we said," he rolled his eyes. "I understand your Mister Hunter's a bit of old school, cloak and dagger sort of thing," he chuckled. "So here we are." He flicked through the combination locks and clicked the hasps open. Yet he didn't open the case. "You do have secure storage handy? We can't leave until it's secure. Will you be on duty when Mister Hunter arrives?"

"Most likely," he replied. "I've a safe under the desk here."

"Excellent. We'll wait for you to open the safe."

The guard bent down to the safe bolted to the floor. Spinning the combination lock, he twisted the handle and opened the door. Standing up, he watched as Gladstone slowly opened his briefcase.

While the guard's attention was focused on Gladstone's deliberate movement, Eden opened his briefcase, withdrawing a 9mm pistol with a silencer. The guard only had the chance for his eyes to widen as a 9mm round plowed through his forehead.

Eden moved quickly around the desk and pressed the buttons to open the doors. Four vans pulled up behind the taxi, unloaded and hurried in. They were all attired like Gladstone and Eden, except they had loaded magazine clips in belts hidden beneath their suitcoats.

Gladstone calmly extracted his own 9mm from the briefcase, laying it on the counter. Withdrawing a magazine belt, he wrapped it around his waist before placing and adjusting a small earpiece with a microphone that protruded halfway down the side of his cheek. He cast a quick glance at his watch. "We've ten minutes to get as many as we can," he reminded them. "If they don't want to come, leave them. Don't waste your time. There's only one that we won't take 'no' for an answer. Understood?" Tapping his earpiece he spoke into the tiny mouthpiece on the side. "Transportation ready"

"Ready," Martin replied.

Holding his arm up to see his watch, he announced, "It's two-ten now. We're all out of here at two-twenty. Let's move."

The first casualties were two lab assistants at the coffee machine just outside the closed dining hall. The carnage continued as they swept through the hallways and into the clone monitoring stations, surprising the unsuspecting, the only sounds being the muffled pings of the silencers.

JB and Ruth jolted awake when the door to his room slammed open and a stranger stood in the doorway. He wasn't dressed like any of the lab assistants and he held something strange in his hand.

"Get dressed," he commanded.

"Why?" JB hugged Ruth tighter to him.

"You're leaving."

"Both of us?" Ruth exclaimed.

"Yes. But you need to hurry. We haven't much time."

"Where are we going?" JB asked.

"Outside."

Ruth flung the covers aside and leaped out of bed, unabashed at her nakedness. "C'mon, JB," she excitedly prodded, pulling on her smock. "We're finally leaving. We're going outside!"

Though not so quick as Ruth, JB pulled on his thin pants. "Where's Sir?" he asked, slipping the thin shirt over his head.

"No time for that. C'mon. I'll explain later." The stranger seemed to be in an awful hurry.

JB paused a moment to take a last look at the room. There wasn't much to look at, but it was all he had known for so many years.

Sensing his hesitation, the stranger urged, "There's nothing left for you here. It's time to move on, to learn new things."

"You'll teach me math?"

"All the math you want and can ever hope to learn. You'll learn so much you'll never have to come back here."

"I like to draw," Ruth chimed in.

The stranger brightened. "You will draw to your heart's content. You'll get colored pencils and paints and you'll be able to make pictures as big as you want."

Ruth was already at the door, her excitement barely contained. "C'mon JB. It's time to go."

"Will I see her again?" JB quietly asked, nodding at Ruth.

"You can see her any time you want. You two can be together whenever and as often as you like."

JB's pulse quickened and he took one step forward when he suddenly remembered something. Quickly moving to the dresser, he retrieved Ruth's drawings. "Now I'm ready."

Emerging into the outer room, JB saw Dale, the lab assistant, crumpled on the floor, blood pooling beneath his head.

"What happened to him?"

"He's dead," the stranger explained.

74

"Dead?" JB repeated, staring in confusion at the body. He cocked his head, waiting to see if Sir would move, but something told him that Sir wouldn't move for a long time. "How did he get dead?"

"He tried to stop you from leaving," the stranger answered. "Now really, we must get going." He gently, but firmly pushed his two charges towards the door to the hallway.

It was as they were travelling down hallways neither JB nor Ruth had ever seen that JB asked, "Will they eat him?"

"Eat who?" the stranger replied, cocking an eyebrow.

"Sir... the man back at my room. They told me that being dead is like the food we eat. It's dead and then we eat it."

"Um, not quite," the stranger replied, his pace quickening. "Humans and plants are two different species."

"Species? What's a species?"

"The answers to your questions will come, but not now. For now, be content that you are leaving this place." He pushed open an exit door and started down the stairs only to stop when he realized the two of them were still at the top, marveling at the way the floor descended. "Here," he smiled back at them. "It's easy, once you get the hang of it. Try it. Hold onto the rail." He grabbed the railing as demonstration.

Ruth stepped down, awkwardly at first. Watching her, JB followed. Soon they were fairly taking two steps at a time in a single jump, exhilarating in the experience. By the time they were at the bottom, the stranger could barely keep up.

"That was fun," Ruth joyously blurted. "Can we do it again?"

"Yes," the stranger chuckled, "but not now."

They emerged on the ground floor amidst the subdued confusion of a number of clones all in one place at the same time.

"Which one of you is JB?" Gladstone called out.

Surprised that a stranger would know who he was, JB raised his hand.

"You're with me," Gladstone informed him.

"Can she come with me?" JB put his arm around Ruth.

"Of course." He smiled kindly at her. "What's your name?"

"Ruth," she boldly answered.

"Then Ruth, you and JB are with me. OK?"

"OK."   She pressed against JB, her radiant face exuding adventure.

Looking at his watch, Gladstone commanded, "Load 'em up."

While the other members of his team corralled and guided the clones through the doors and onto the waiting vans, one of the liberators stood by the doorway and counted. When the last one was through the doors, he looked at Gladstone. "We got twenty-seven."

Gladstone nodded and turned to another by his side. "We got everyone?"

"We're set."

A team member rushed into the foyer. "Police drones heading this way."

Gladstone twirled his finger in the air. "Let's move it. Lock it up."

Outside, the vans began moving off, each one in a different direction. JB and Ruth had been coaxed into the backseat of the taxi that had brought Gladstone and Eden. They sat tight against each other, awkward and silent, numbly watching the frenetic activity. Gladstone slipped off his suitcoat and unbuckled his ammo belt. Sliding into the driver's seat, he placed the ammo belt next to him, the suit coat on top. He then undid his tie, unbuttoned the top two buttons of his shirt and rolled up the sleeves halfway up his forearm. He finished the transformation by jamming a baseball cap on his head.

Starting the taxi and moving forward caused JB and Ruth to jam their hands onto the seat to steady themselves. Looking in the rearview mirror, Gladstone smiled.

"This is called a car, a taxi car to be more specific. It's used to take people from one place to another, but at a much faster pace than you could get there by walking or running."

The two in the back seat swiveled their heads back and forth to look out the windows, the early morning darkness broken by the occasional streetlamp. They were on Dekalb Industrial Way heading towards Stone Mountain by the time the drones arrived.

Opening the driver's window, Gladstone lit a cigarette, causing both JB and Ruth to screw up their faces at the odor. He was happily puffing away when the drone descended to fly next to him. He twisted his head to give it a look of bored suffering at the Corporate surveillance. The drone slowed to tuck in behind. Gladstone saw the pip of a light flash as the drone took a picture of the license plate. He smiled with smug satisfaction at the predictable Corporate behavior. The drone stayed with him until he turned right on Lawrenceville Highway.

Once the drone disappeared, he relaxed, tossing his cigarette out the window. "Sorry about that. Nasty habit. Never did like the things."

"What is that?" Ruth asked.

"They're called cigarettes. They're not good for you."

"Then why do you use them?"

"I personally don't, but many people do."

"But you just did," JB pointed out.

"That I did," he grinned, exiting onto the Beltway. "It's called assuming a disguise."

"Disguise?"

"Yes. That means pretending to be something you are not."

"I don't know what that means." JB looked at Ruth who shook her head and shrugged.

Gladstone thought for a moment. "Suppose you wanted to make Ruth think that you were a lab assistant. What would you do?"

JB thought a moment. "I would put on a coat like they wear and carry one of those things that they always carry around with them, a palm-pad."

"But you're not a lab assistant, are you?

"No."

"But if you did dress up like one to make someone think you were a lab assistant, that's called a disguise." He took the East Ponce exit heading back to the city turning off onto Milam Circle. At the far end of the street, he stopped the taxi. "You two stay put."

Exiting the cab, Gladstone walked to the back and opened the trunk, extracting another license plate. Quickly changing plates, he then peeled off the taxi number on the back of the trunk panel, revealing the original number. For good measure, he took the tire iron and gave the body a few whacks then rubbed some dirt where he dented the body, brushing off the excess grime. Satisfied, he jumped back in.

"Time to get you to a safe place. Relax and enjoy the ride."

Chapter 3

Warfield glanced at the luminescent hands on the clock on the wall. He had less than an hour to get to the Underground. Casting one last look at the mess in his apartment, he struggled to think of anything that was so important that he needed to save it. Other than the TV, there wasn't really much here. The rest was merely used furniture, busted up now, and the constantly changing pics of naked women in large digital picture frames hanging on the walls.

Casting a satisfied last look at the destruction, he was glad to be finally leaving this dump. Wrecking the place had given him a great deal of satisfaction. Though part of him wouldn't mind taking one of the digital frames, they were far too cumbersome and really unnecessary.

Standing before the exterior door, he strained to hear any noise outside. Easing the door open a crack, he peered through the gap noting that nothing extraordinary appeared. Opening the door wider revealed a dimly lit hallway with the usual apartment noises pulsing through the thin walls. Stepping out into the hallway, he quickly and quietly closed the door and hurried towards the emergency stairwell. It wasn't until he was safely standing on the curb hailing a taxi that he relaxed.

A taxi pulled up and an attractive blond emerged, smiled warmly at him and walked on. Momentarily distracted, he shook himself to the task at hand and leaped into the back seat. "Take me to the Underground, please," he breathlessly demanded.

Instead, the driver, a grizzled middle aged man in a greasy cabbie hat, turned and rested an arm on the seat top. In the other hand a pistol with a suppressor attached was pointed directly at him. "Gimme your phone."

"Huh?" he nervously mumbled.

"Your phone. Gimme your phone."

"My phone?"

"Yeah. You deaf? Gimme the phone."

"Why do you want my phone?"

The cabbie pulled back the hammer. "Mister. You ain't listenin'. You want I should shoot you right here?"

"No, no!" Warfield held his hands up, unhooking the phone from his ear in the process. When the cabbie extended his hand, he placed the phone in it.

"Now get out. Take another cab to the Underground."

It all happened so quickly that Warfield found himself standing on the curb again, watching the taxi do a quick U-turn then head south.

While Warfield stood waiting to hail another taxi, Linda Nadell walked into Sharon's cubicle. "What do you have?" Though appearing aloof, the subtle brush of a hand across the back of her shoulders hinted a greater intimacy.

"He's moving, heading towards the beltway." A glowing dot appeared on the monitor moving south on Moreland Avenue. Sharon bounced up and swiveled her chair to face Linda. "Here, why don't you take my seat, Director Nadell." Without waiting for an answer, she maneuvered the chair for her superior to sit then scooted another chair next to her. As the two watched the dot slowly move, the city map scrolled accordingly so that the dot and streets were always visible.

Though focused on the dot, Sharon quietly spoke. "Thank you so much for your time last night. I thoroughly enjoyed myself. You're an amazing mentor."

Linda blushed at the reminder of the previous night's late night drink together. Sharon had a way of peeling away one's protective layers, yet always from a solicitous position. Linda found herself talking too much about her own life and laughing, something she rarely did these days. They had ended up back at Linda's penthouse.

"He's getting on the beltway." Sharon broke Linda's reverie. "He's heading towards the airport." She stood up and called over the dividers to her team. "Pay attention here. There are lots of bars around the airport. I want to know where he's at as soon as he stops." Sitting back down she leaned forward to give her attention to the monitor.

They were silent for a while, Sharon focused on the screen and Linda tried to pay attention to the slowly moving glowing dot. Yet her mind continued to replay the previous night's encounter. The alarms in the professional side of her brain kept going off, telling her to back away, that what happened last night was more than inappropriate, it compromised her position as a superior.

The passionate side of her brain justified her actions, telling her it would all work out, that they were adults and that they could still be professional when necessary, that it was no one's business what she did on her own time. The passionate side vividly recalled the night and overruled the logical side. After all, this morning, Sharon was up first and had even laid out Linda's clothes for her. That thought puzzled her for a moment.

Thinking of how everything unfolded, Linda was surprised at herself at how she had been the more aggressive one, with Sharon the overly accommodating and willing partner. When morning came and the clothes laid out, Sharon's reason was overtly adulatory. How could Linda not want to wear what was chosen?

Looking down at the outfit, she realized that she and Sharon were dressed similarly in power suits. Sharon even mimicked the broach on the left lapel. That they were dressed alike should have bothered her, but instead, Linda found it weirdly flattering. In fact, in all of their interaction together, Sharon was always clearly subservient.

The thought of dominating another caused her to frown. It wasn't that she didn't like dominating others, after all, she was known for her strong personality. It was the thought that here was someone who wanted to be dominated, someone to do her beck and call. Her frown morphed to bemusement at the thought of having a sort of personal slave.

"Wait a minute," Sharon again startled Linda out of her reverie. "He just got off on Old Dixie Highway. Something's not right."

"What?"

"I don't know. I have a feeling we're being led on a wild goose chase, probably to throw off anyone following him." She looked over at Linda. "You were so wise about him thinking we'd probably tail him." Standing up, she called out again to her team. "What's he up to? Come on folks, give me some ideas."

"He probably thinks were tailing him," a deep throated voice called out.

80

Sharon shot Linda a smile that said, 'We already knew that.'

"He's getting off on Pineridge," another voice called out, followed by, "He's slowing down… He's stopped."

There was a pause before a voice exclaimed, "What the hell? That's my house!"

Linda and Sharon frowned in unison. It took little time to ascertain they had been fooled. While Linda fumed, Sharon seemed surprisingly calm. That she was so calm infuriated her. She was about to chastise her protégée when Sharon's desk phone beeped and Collin Dodd's face appeared on the screen.

"Yes, Mister Dodd?" Sharon politely inquired.

"So, you lost him?" Collin's stern visage told them he doubted their abilities as Intel professionals.

Linda was about to explain that it was only Sharon's second day on the job, that she, Linda, should not have relied on Sharon's inexperience when Sharon's earphone beeped.

"No sir," Sharon replied. She pressed the earpiece and listened to the message. "He's at the Underground right now. We've identified the cabbie who took us on the joy ride and we'll pick him up shortly."

"How do you know he's at the Underground?" Collin asked, surprised.

"Well, Sir. Director Nadell and I talked about this yesterday, and it was her idea to place a tail on him. She figured he'd try something like this, sending us on a wild goose chase while he went about his business." Her phone beeped again. "He's going into the Vanishing Point."

Collin nodded, his half-lidded eyes expressing his satisfaction. "Good work. You two make a good team. Keep me informed." The screen went blank.

A thick silence settled for a moment. Sharon sheepishly gazed at her boss. "I'm sorry that I put you in an awkward position. I was hoping to have an answer before Mister Dodd called."

Blinking as she processed what had just happened, Linda wasn't sure quite how to react. The fact that she was caught off guard bothered her. The fact that Sharon had been right to put a tail on Warfield also bothered her. But instead of claiming credit, as any other self-promoting employee would do, Sharon deflected the success to her.

"Why didn't you tell me?" Linda quietly asked.

"You said not to put a tail on him, and I didn't want you to think I was purposely disobeying you. Had Warfield been in the cab, everything would've been fine. But I didn't want to take a chance that someone else might want to play in this."

"Like whom?"

"To me, this has all the smell of Social Injustice." Furrowing her brows, she tilted her head to the side. "What's Pieter Dwa done that warrants this much attention? We both know he's not responsible for all the things he's being blamed for."

Linda pursed her lips then quietly announced, "My office. Now. Let your team handle Warfield for the moment." Spinning on her heels, she marched back to her office.

"Warfield's at the Vanishing Point in the Underground," Sharon stood on her toes and called out to her team.

"How do you know?" a surprised voice called back.

"I put a tail on him when he left his apartment."

"That would've been nice to know," another voice not so subtly pointed out.

"You all did fine," she replied. "You did exactly what was needed. Pick up the cabbie and arrange for interrogation. I'll be in Director Nadell's office. Oh, also send a team to the vanishing point. I don't want anyone going in. Understand?"

A few moments later, she stood in Linda's opulent office. Through the floor to ceiling windows, the city lights of the Atlanta high-rises filled the vista. Linda stood looking out the window, her arms folded in front of her. She turned when Sharon stopped at the front of the wide desk. Walking to the other side of her desk, she flipped open a small hand-pad computer then twisted it around for Sharon to see.

"Before you read this," she said, fixing Sharon with a firm gaze, "you now have Gamma clearance. It's already been approved by Collin. You can sign the non-disclosure forms later."

Sharon picked up the hand-pad and read Dennett's letter.

Linda watched as she read the contents, looking for any reaction.

Slowly nodding in understanding, Sharon placed the hand-pad back on the desk. "So Pieter Dwa has the remaining letter."

Her response surprised Linda. There was no 'O my god, what is DMI doing?' Rather, she saw right away what the real mission was – find Pieter Dwa. Protect the status quo. Linda visibly relaxed in the knowledge she had chosen wisely. Sharon was the perfect leader for Beta Section, and even more. Perhaps it was time to approach Collin with the proposition of making Sharon her deputy. There certainly was budget for it.

But she couldn't help ask, "You don't seem to be too fazed by the revelation about DMI and Corporate."

"I've always suspected something like that," she prettily shrugged. "It's really all a question of economics. There are poor in the world. They're poor for a variety of reasons. They invariably live in squalor and suffer from inferior hygiene, resulting in pollution and disease.   But the poor disproportionately drain the resources of the world. We spend trillions feeding, clothing, and housing the poor, as well as providing medical support. Eliminate the poor and we eliminate the financial drain."

"How very Darwinian of you," Linda smirked.

"I suppose it is," she smiled back then soberly added, "Thank you for allowing me this privilege."

"You're welcome, though don't be so sure I'm doing you a favor. With the clearance comes added headaches. You'll find out all sorts of things about people you wish you didn't know."

"I'm sure I will."   Sharon stared affectionately at the woman standing on the other side of the desk. "I will never disappoint you. I will work hard to please you. Everything I do will be to make you look good."

"What about yourself?" Linda replied, warm with an emotion that spilled over to a sudden desire to forget all about work and immerse themselves in pleasure despite the fact that they were still in her office.

"I trust you completely. If I take care of you, it will trickle down to me. What's most important is your career? You're positioned next in line to Collin Dodd."

"There are others in the same position as I am, don't forget," she reminded her though she liked the passion of Sharon's purpose.

"Yes, but they're not like you. They're not you. I've studied the others. They're all reasonably good at their jobs, but when push comes to shove, Collin always asks for you."

83

Linda thought for a moment and instinctively knew that she was right. But reality raised its ugly head and she reminded herself that Collin Dodd was very much in control and not likely to go anywhere soon. "I appreciate your support, but we need to get back to business. What do you propose to do about Warfield?"

"Leave him be. We go in and he'll disappear. We have the place watched. Once he emerges, we can decide from there. I think we need to see what the cabbie can provide. He's probably low-level, but he could be useful."

Linda looked at the wall clock. It was 2245 hours and she was getting tired. "I think we need to call it a night. They can always call us if anything changes."

"I'll let the team know." Sharon walked around to stand almost nose to nose with Linda. "You look like you could use a back rub."

"That would be nice," she replied with a knowing smile.

The Vanishing Point, Underground, Atlanta

Nick Warfield stood outside the Vanishing Point, watching the cab pull away from the curb and trundle off into the night. Turning around, he looked at the drab exterior of the pub, the letters of the neon sign barely glowing. The windows were barred and opaque. Even the door had exterior bars.

Looking around, he was uncomfortably aware that he was the only one on an otherwise empty street. Opening the door, he was surprised at the noise level spilling out. It was when he stood in the foyer staring into the thick ambiance of smoke, shadows, small tables, and flickering candles that the activity in the bar jittered to an abrupt halt. Despite the overwhelming urge to leave, he walked self-consciously over to the bar, the glare of the 3-D TV casting a soft glow over the countertop. Activity resumed, but he sensed the room growing darker. The bartender simply stared, saying nothing as Nick scooted onto a barstool. Overhead, the television blared the news.

"Um," Nick looked around to see if anyone was paying attention then lowered his voice, "Kingfisher sent me."

"How nice." The barkeep continued staring at him.

84

Nick waited expectantly, wishing the bartender would do or say something.

"You gonna order or you just gonna sit there taking up bar-space?" The barkeep leaned forward slightly.

"Um, I'd like a beer please."

"What kind?"

Nick surveyed the shadows around him. "You got private beer here?"

"Yeah, sure." The bartender said, cleaning a glass.

"I'll take private." Nick smiled appreciatively.

"Right." The bartender placed the glass on the rack, reached into the cooler and pulled out a frosty bottle.

Nick's anticipation evaporated when he saw the bottle. "Hey, that's a Corporate bottle."

"No shit, Sherlock." The bartender continued to pour.

"But you said you had private."

The bartender placed the full glass in front of him. "Enjoy." He moved down the counter to attend another patron.

Nick frowned and took a deep draught. The flat flavor of over-pasteurization, additives, and coloring dulled his mouth and he set the beer down with disgust. He looked at the glass as he set it down, watching the bubbles effervesce. Overhead, the news had just come on. Nick looked up to see a sultry brunette with deep cleavage reporting the news.

"And we have the latest from the brutal attack on the Resurrection Industries facility in Decatur. Latest reports have the number killed at thirty-one. Though no one has claimed responsibility, the attack is obviously the work of Social Injustice. In addition to the callous murders of innocent doctors, lab assistants, and facility workers, a number of caretaker specimens were removed. The specific number and identity of these caretaker specimens have not been released, awaiting notification of owners first."

The reporter reached up and touched the earpiece in her right ear. "We have breaking news. Let's go live to Connie Covington."

The scene shifted and Nick saw a beautiful strawberry-blond woman in overly tight pants and bodice shirt that revealed far too much of her buxom assets, standing in front of a street still smoking from the littered debris. Ambulance lights flashed across the entire screen and the frenzied race to save lives churned behind her. Crowds of battered and torn pedestrians milled around; some were helping pull up chunks of concrete searching for more victims.

"This is Connie Covington reporting live from the old automotive plant in Doraville where I am standing just outside the Eastside Squatters' Village, one of the many blighted and formerly abandoned inner-city areas taken over by the Jefferson Beauregard Clayton Crusade for Life Foundation to bring stability and financial improvement to the local businesses and families. Just moments ago, an explosion rocked the free health clinic in the middle of the still run down village." Connie turned to a burly man with hair so thick that it reminded Nick of a beaver pelt. "With us is Martin Carter, spokesperson for The Beauregard Foundation. Mr. Carter, can you tell us what happened here today?" The screen flipped to a close-up of Mr. Carter.

"Connie, this is simply unbelievable, that someone would harm innocent people like this. Just moments before the explosion, I received an anonymous call demanding an impossible amount of money and threatening to destroy the Eastside Village. Before I even had a chance to respond the explosion occurred. The evilness of the act speaks for itself. Any group who would murder innocent people deserves the same fate."

"Did they say who they were?" Connie interrupted.

"No, just that they were going to destroy Eastside Village unless we paid them a ridiculous amount of cash."

"And just how much was that?"

Carter hesitated momentarily. "Umm, I'd rather not be specific. Let's just say that it was in the billions. I think the police would prefer that I not divulge anything more."

"Do you think Social Injustice might be responsible for this?"

"I really can't say," he thoughtfully mused, "but it does have the appearance of their evil work."

Connie nodded sagely. "Thank you Mister Carter." Turning her full attention to the camera, she somberly intoned, "There you have it. Another vicious act of terrorism." Her demeanor immediately changed as she broke into a wide bubbly smile. "Up next, Chip tells all about pesticides and DNA."

Another patron stood at the bar watching the broadcast. He turned to Nick. "Twenty bucks says that someone or some group gets blamed in the next three minutes." The TV switched to a commercial. An erudite man in short hair and dazzling eyes filled the screen.

"Tired of your children having low expectation scores? Wishing you could control your family's future? Now you have the freedom to make a choice and make a difference. Why trust your future with doubtful DNA? Here at Dynamic Futures we own and control the largest selection of DNA available. Choose from our broad selection of scientists, musicians, writers, political greats, global peace winners, military geniuses, and corporate dynamos. Remember, Dynamic Futures owns the exclusive rights to the world's greatest thinkers. Come by for a visit and make your selection. Why be stuck as a nobody? The future of the world could well be in your hands."

Nick watched the screen fade when suddenly his nape hairs prickled. Someone was standing very close to him. He could smell the fading cologne. He turned to find a small oriental man staring at him.

"Would you like a table?" The man politely inquired.

"Actually I'm here to meet someone."

"Perhaps I can help." Again that almost irritating over-politeness.

Nick scratched his head. "Um, actually, I was looking for the maître d'."

The man smiled and bowed. "I am he."

Momentarily taken aback, Nick quickly recovered. Glancing around through half-lidded eyes, he lowered his voice. "I'm looking for Kingfisher."

"Ah, you must be Mr. Warfield?"

"Yes." Nick furrowed his eyebrows momentarily then looked around the room. Everyone moved with an ease of comfort, regulars at a favorite pub. Even the bartender smiled at them. And he realized that he obviously was the only stranger here.

"Your host has arranged a table for you. Would you please follow me?" The man bowed slightly.

Nick looked down at the rest of his beer and decided to leave it, the foam head just about gone. He scooted off the stool, taking one last look at the TV just as the news announcer came back on.

"This just in. A radical wing of the Social Injustice has claimed responsibility for this latest bombing. Police ask your help in finding the butchers responsible for this tragedy. Anyone having knowledge of this man," a picture of Pieter Dwa filled the screen, "please contact the police immediately."

Social Injustice compound – East Point

Overwhelmed with the changes in the past day, Ruth sat next to JB on a cot in a large room where other men and women like her and JB either talked or slept on other cots in neatly arranged rows. She was tired, but the excitement would not let her sleep. At the far end of the room were bathrooms, one for women and one for men. It was the first time in her life that she witnessed other women performing the same functions in a communal atmosphere. For some reason she felt uncomfortable, but she supposed she could get used to it. Still, she liked the privacy of her own bathroom back in her own room back at the place where she used to live.

But that was about all she missed so far. Her eyes wide, she followed the numerous people who were not lab assistants and not like the others, who came in and out of the room bringing food and clothing, answering questions, and generally being very nice to them all. Some of the other ones like her and JB had come over to talk. Chet was a large muscular man with wavy blond hair. Natalie was a tall slender raven haired beauty with large green eyes. They sat on the cot opposite JB and Ruth.

"Do you know what's going on?" Chet asked.

"Something about us finally getting free to do the things we've always wanted to do," Ruth answered. "I like to draw. They said once we get to where we're all going, I'll get to draw as much as I want. What do you like to do?" She looked at Chet.

"I like music," he smiled. "I played the piano before we came here."

"What's a piano?" JB asked, his interest roused.

88

"You've never seen one?" When all three gave him blank looks, he explained, "It's like a large box with these long metal strings inside it. But to play the strings, you put your fingers on these white and black things called keys, all in a long row outside the box." He spread his hands in demonstration of the keyboard. "When you push down on them, they somehow move a lever and this thing hits the string and makes a sound."

"How many of these keys are there?" JB asked.

"There are this many keys." He held his hands up and spread his fingers. "There are all of these fingers this many times," he explained, hold up ten fingers and then taking two away, "plus this many extra keys."

"That's 88 keys," JB quickly answered.

"I'll take your word for it," Chet shrugged.

"JB's really good with numbers. He calls it math," Ruth explained. Turning her attention to Natalie, she asked, "What do you like to do?"

"I like to sing," she proudly answered, her voice warm and sultry.

"They said," Ruth announced, "that we would get to do the things we like to do, so you'll get to sing."

"I would like that," she smiled, pleased.

Suddenly Ruth's attention was diverted as she leaped up to standing. "Gordon," she exclaimed, making a bee-line to a ruggedly handsome man who walked in through one of the side doors.

Gordon brightened when he saw her and he met her before she had a chance to get halfway across the room. They embraced and kissed, one that spoke of shared intimacy.

Watching the two, JB experienced a feeling he had never felt before, something akin to the time when he was younger and the lab assistant had raised his voice at him, telling him he was stupid and lazy for not understanding what the man wanted him to do. He didn't know what those words meant at the time, but the way they were said hurt. His first reaction had been to want to yell back or lash out at something, but he didn't and instead kept it to himself, wanting to understand why he felt like he did.

Seeing Ruth and Gordon in warm embrace brought back some of the same emotions, but now it was Gordon that he wanted to lash out at. He frowned at his reaction, quickly realizing it was because of Ruth's attention to Gordon. But why did her attention warrant his response? It was then that he admitted he wanted Ruth for himself. Now that they were free, he was unwilling to share.

Hand in hand, Ruth and Gordon walked up. "This is Gordon," Ruth excitedly explained. "He likes to draw too."

JB felt an immediate twinge of dislike. "How do you two know each other," he stonily asked, knowing the answer.

"He came to my room before I went to your room," she blithely replied.

"The same day?" JB blinked in surprise.

"Of course not." She flipped her hand at his silliness. "It was, I don't know how many days before then, but it was a long time ago. But when he came, he saw my drawings and we spent the rest of the time drawing."

"Until the lab assistant came in and told us to get busy doing what we were supposed to do," Gordon chuckled. "We said 'sure' and then went back to drawing. He came back later and took me back to my room."

JB's irritation dissipated when he understood that nothing physical had occurred between them. "How long have you been here?" he asked, wanting to appear friendly.

"Almost four months. I was being transferred to another place when I was liberated and brought here." Letting go of Ruth's hand, he cast a quick glance around the room. Raising his voice, he said, "If I can have everyone's attention, please?" He walked to the center edge of the cot formation. "Please wake up any who are asleep." As he counted all the new arrivals, another man entered from the same door and quietly approached. Gordon turned to the man who smiled warmly at him. Giving him a nod that all was ready, Gordon stepped to the man's side.

"My name is Lowell. Along with my friends and companions in Social Injustice, we are responsible for bringing you here. I'm sure you have many questions as to why you are here and what's going to happen. I've asked Gordon, who was once just like you are now, to fill you in. What he is about to tell you will shock you. Once he has finished, we will do our best to answer your questions. Gordon."

Pausing for effect, Gordon spoke with a clear voice. "My name is Gordon. I'm a clone. What that means is that an older man decided that he wanted to make copies of himself so that when he was old, he could use one of these bodies to become young again. The way they do that is, when the time came, they would remove my brain and replace it with his. Some of you may not know what a brain is. It's inside here," he tapped his head. "It is the thing that controls everything in your body. It is your personality. It is who you are. When your brain is gone, so are you."

Lowell watched as the impact registered. Some immediately grasped the horror while others were still processing. He noted that Gordon was barely half finished when JB's jaw slacked wide and his eyes widened.

"That means you're dead," JB blurted as he finally grasped the concept. He twisted his head to rapidly glance at those seated with him. "All of us were supposed to be dead. They were going to take our bodies."

"That's right," Gordon calmly agreed. "But now that you are here, thanks to Lowell and his friends, you no longer have to worry about that. But think about this. There are twenty-seven of you here, right now. Free. But there are a lot more who are still in places around the world who do not know what is in store for them. You may be free, but their fate still awaits them. If someone doesn't do anything to help them, they are all going to die."

"But what can we do?" Chet spoke up. "The only thing I know who to do is play the piano."

"That's because none of us was allowed to discover all the things we're good at," Gordon replied. "They kept us from really doing what we like. You said you play the piano." He gazed directly at Chet. "Did they give you music scores?"

"Music scores?"

"Yes, music scores. They're pieces of paper with notes on them that correspond to the keys on the piano. You simply play the notes that are written on the paper and you can play more songs than you can ever imagine."

"They never gave me anything other than a keyboard," he tersely answered. "He told me I was doing great whenever I played. What a stupid person I was," he sadly stated, shaking his head.

"You didn't know any better," Gordon commiserated. "How could you when they never told you."

"But that still doesn't answer his question," JB pointed out. "What can we do when we don't know anything?"

Lowell stepped forward. "Each of you will be given a series of tests. They will show us what talents you have. Most of you will have more than one talent. Some will have many talents. For example, Gordon here is an excellent artist." When he saw a number of vacant stares, he explained, "That means he can draw really good. So, Gordon is helping us by drawing blueprints and diagrams of buildings."

"I'm also really good driving cars," he proudly added.

"That's right," Lowell benignly smiled. "We're teaching Gordon how to drive fast like a race car driver."

"I can draw," Ruth announced.

"Then perhaps you can work with Gordon," Lowell smiled at her, much to JB's annoyance.

JB shifted his gaze to give her a look of disappointment mixed with frustration. He then realized that Lowell was talking to him. "What?"

"I said, what are you good at?"

"Numbers. I'm good at math."

"Excellent. We need people who are good with numbers." His eyes then swept the room. "I know this is a lot for all of you to understand all at once. You've been purposely kept ignorant because there was no need to feed your brains with knowledge. To be brutally honest, they believed it was a waste of time to develop your brains. The fact that all of you have used your brains to understand what happened to you every day shows they couldn't stop you from learning. Now, as I said before, over the next several days you will be given tests to help us know where your abilities are. During this time, you are free to move around and ask questions. However, you will not be allowed to go too far. This is done for your protection. Remember. We freed you with the intent of giving each of you a long life. There are people looking for you right this very minute who want to take you back to where you came from. Do you want that?"

The response was unanimous and vocal.

"Good. If someone tells you not to do something or tells you that you can't go somewhere, it's because he or she wants to keep you safe. Also, don't be afraid to ask questions. You have a lot of learning to catch up on. We will have classes in some basic skills starting tomorrow. Use Gordon here as an example. He's been here for almost four months and already he's reading at a second grade level. Now, before I go, are there any questions?"

"Yes," Ruth answered. "Are we all going to be sleeping in this same room, using the same bathrooms?"

"No," Lowell grinned. "We're already making arrangements for each of you to have your own room. That should happen sometime tomorrow, so in the meantime, you'll have to put up with the inconvenience." He glanced down at his watch. "It's almost 2200 hours. Lights will go out in an hour. I suggest each of you get a good night's sleep. We have a busy day tomorrow."

The Vanishing Point, Underground, Atlanta

While Nick Warfield waited, his unease mounting with every Corporate beer the waitress placed on the table, Pieter Dwa was several levels below, alone in a darkened room, standing perfectly still. His eyes closed, he shut out everything else and went deep inside himself, traveling throughout the inner core of his body, sensing every part of himself. Raising his hand began slowly thumping on his chest, rhythmically beating the deliberate pulse of the Kalahari Kung spirit dance. His feet lifted and dropped in rhythm to his beating hand. Then the boiling came and he felt the dread and pain of entering *Kia*... and he went outside himself.

He swirled out of the room, past the guards, down the hallways, up flights of stairs and finally into the main part of the pub where the TV blared and patrons nursed their drinks. He paused briefly to see Warfield sitting in the corner table. Giving him a quick once over, he poured through the front door and out onto the street. It was weirdly quiet this time of night. Parked cars lined the opposite side of the street. It was then he saw it, an older model car of nondescript color halfway down the block. The driver's side window was rolled halfway down and cigarette smoke curled out through the gap to dissipate into the night air.

As he approached, he saw the glow from the end of the cigarette intensify as the man took a long drag. Hovering next to the car, he followed the man's gaze to the front of the Vanishing Point. Pieter heard a quiet low tone and realized the man was talking to someone. Looking in through the window, there was no one else in the car. He then saw him fidget with his earpiece.

"Ain't nuthin' happenin' since he went in. How long we gonna be out here?"

"Relax. It might be a long night."

"Suppose he don't come out?"

"Then he don't come out. Someone'll be along to take yer shift."

"At least, how 'bout gettin' me some coffee?"

"You shoulda thought about that before you got there?"

"They didn't gimme the chance. And I'm gonna have t' piss pretty soon."

"Jeez, Phil, you act like this is yer first stakeout."

"You know how I hate this, sittin' on my ass for hours on end. Y'know they say sittin' for too long is bad for your heart."

"So get outta the car and stand somewhere. Jeez Phil."

"Good idea. How 'bout that coffee?"

"I'll see what I can do."

Phil reached up and flicked the interior light switch so that the light would not activate when he opened the door. Pieter moved back as Phil emerged and swung around to stand on the sidewalk. Stretching and cracking his neck, Phil quickly scouted for a spot in the shadows that still gave him a view of the front of the pub.

Pieter began to feel his strength ebbing and he rapidly retreated back the way he came. Like rushing water through a funnel, he returned to himself, let out a stifled cry, and crumpled into a heap.

An hour later, a refreshed Pieter watched as Nick Warfield walked in, hood over his head. One of the two men who escorted him pulled the hood off. "He's clean," he announced.

Nick was not what Pieter expected. He studied Warfield as the man blinked to adjust his eyes. *Average height... average weight... brown hair... You'd blend into a crowd real well.*

Pieter stood up and motioned to the chair. "Please sit Mr. Warfield. Would you like something to drink?"

94

He watched in amazement as Pieter extended upwards. "Damn, you're big." The response came out before he thought about it, and he blushed slightly when he realized what he had said. "Sorry. You probably get that all the time."

He politely smiled and motioned for him to sit. "No problem. I do get it all the time."

Warfield sat uncomfortably in the chair opposite Pieter then looked back to the two men lounging in the shadows by the door he had just come through. "Friends of yours?"

Pieter slowly inhaled with a slight shrug. "You're not the only one with someone looking to make you a statistic."

He nodded appreciatively. "Wish I had the same protection." He paused and looked intently at Pieter. "Did you really blow up the Eastside Village?"

"Hardly," he calmly replied. "It's all a question of physics. I was here when the village was destroyed."

"Sure. Of course not," he lamely smiled. "By the way, one helluva trip to get down here." He looked around the half-lit room. "Guess that's why they call it the underground."

Instead of answering, Pieter leaned forward. "Tell me Mr. Warfield, why do you think I can help you?"

Warfield exhaled loudly. "Listen, all I know is that someone is trying to kill me, and I think it's because of that damn letter that jerk Dennett sent me. By the way, when do I get my phone back?"

"Your phone?"

"Yeah, the one the cabbie took from me when he told me to get lost and take another cab."

Pieter blinked as he sifted the news. "What did this cabbie look like?"

"Don't remember too much since he was pointing a gun at me. What I do remember was that he was a middle aged guy who hadn't shaved in a while. Why?" Warfield tilted his head and cocked an eyebrow.

Pieter unfolded to standing. "I'll be right back. Stay put." Leaving a speechless Warfield to worry whether he had made a mistake coming here, Pieter breezed past the two guards. "Keep him here," he commanded.

Pieter negotiated the labyrinth of corridors until he came to a thick metal door. Spinning the door handle, he pulled open the door to reveal a cacophony of activity.

95

The room was large, with work desks packed against each other, each occupied by a man or woman intently focused on their respective tasks. Office runners wove their way around desks and past other runners, carrying spread sheets, maps, analyses, and other data. On the wall opposite the door was a large wall screen filled with the streets and alleyways of Atlanta. Standing with two women, an older man with thinning white hair turned when one of the women motioned that Pieter had entered.

Making his way past the maze of desks and workers, Pieter approached the man. "There's a stakeout outside."

"How many?" the man frowned.

"One in a car not far from the front door. There's at least one more, but he's not visible."

Uttering a soft 'damn,' he turned to one of the women, a blond with a butterfly tattoo on her neck. "Emily, send someone outside to recon the area. We've got visitors." Turning back to Pieter he asked, "What's your take on the man?"

"Don't know yet. We'd just started when I learned a cabbie had taken his phone and told him to take another cab."

"Lowell's on the line," a young man called out.

"Wait here." Jason walked over to the monitor and began fussing at Lowell.

Though Pieter couldn't hear the conversation, he could tell by Jason's animated behavior that he wasn't happy. After several minutes of give and take, Jason returned.

"The cabbie got picked up a little bit ago. He's still at the interrogation center. Hope his story holds up. Lowell says not to trust Warfield. We're still checking him out."

"What does he want me to do?"

"String him a long and see what you can find out."

"What if he wants to stay here?"

"Can't do that. Send him to one of the decoy houses. Use the one in North Druid Hills."

"Off Lavista?"

"Yes."

Nodding assent, Pieter turned to leave as Jason raised his voice. "OK folks, we've got visitors outside, so look alive. How we doing on police scanner traffic? Give me some ears there."

Pieter closed the door behind him and retraced his steps, emerging back into his lair, as he liked to call it, with Warfield heaving a sigh of relief that he as back.

"We're still checking on the cabbie," Pieter evasively explained. "We'll see what we can do about returning your phone."

"So what do I do?" he lamely shrugged. "Someone's out to kill me and now I've got no phone."

"Do you have the letter?"

"Yeah." Nick reached inside his shirt and retrieved the folded and creased letter. Handing it to Pieter, he waited as he read the contents.

The letter was verbatim to the one Pieter received. Slowly refolding the letter, he was about to hand it back to him when he said, "Mind if I keep this?"

"Not at all. I don't want the damned thing."

Setting the letter to the side, Pieter said, "Tell me Mr. Warfield. If it is true that Corporate is trying to kill you, why do you think I can help you, especially now that I too am a wanted man?"

Nick chewed on his lip. "Billy Fish said that if anyone could save my ass, it was you."

Pieter calmly absorbed the compliment. *I haven't seen Billy Fish in over a year... didn't know he got out of jail...If he did, he'd be in a cordoned are...* Pieter tilted his head slightly to the left. "How do you know Billy Fish?"

"Just acquaintances. We've played pool together on occasion."

"When's the last time you saw him?"

He paused as though in thought. "It's been a month or two."

"And he told you then that I could help you?" Pieter's doubt was evident.

"No," Warfield quickly replied. "When all this stuff with Dennett happened, I called a friend who got in touch with him. He said to find you."

Though unconvinced with the answer, Pieter asked, "Why do you think Dennett's letter is so important to Corporate?"

"Damn. You read it. Isn't it obvious?"

Pieter smiled again. "I'm not sure. Frankly, I'm still trying to figure out why I'm a wanted man."

Warfield studied him for a moment before furrowing his brows in concentration. "Come to think of it, if you haven't done anything they said you did, why *are* you a wanted man?"

"I have my suspicions, but I'll deal with those. Again, Mister Warfield, how do you expect me to help you?"

Warfield looked helplessly around. "At least you got somewhere to hide. And from what little I've seen, someone's got your back. You got protection. I need protection, for a little while at least, until I can figure out where to go."

"What about your job? Will you return to work?"

"Would you?" he sourly retorted. "They trashed my place, sent people to tail me, setting me up to get killed. For what? For something I had nothing to do with."

"And where again is it that you work?"

"The aircraft plant in Hapeville. I'm a quality control specialist."

Pieter stroked his chin as he listened. "Max," he called to one of the guards lounging by the door. "Do me a favor and see what the employment status of Nicholas Warfield is. He works at the Joint Airline facility in Hapeville."

After Max left, Pieter looked at the other one. "Ed. How about getting some beers for all of us? Private."

"Great idea," he grinned, wasting no time heading out to retrieve the bottles of brew.

"Private..." Warfield sighed with pleasure. "I haven't had a private beer in so long, that I've just about forgotten what it tastes like. I'm surprised the government hasn't all but squashed private brewers out of existence."

Pieter leaned forward, quietly intoning, "I get mine from the cordoned zones. They make the best beer around."

Warfield's eyes widened. "Isn't that illegal?"

"Of course," Pieter smiled. "But which would you rather drink?"

He paused to ask the pressing question. "Is it hard to get?"

"Not if you know the right people."

Ed returned with two dark and frosty bottles with flip caps in each hand. With one hand he delivered a beer to Pieter and Warfield before returning to his place. Choosing not to wait for Max, he opened his bottle.

Warfield flipped back the top and lifted his bottle in appreciation. "Thank you." Taking a slow draught, he closed his eyes and savored the taste.

Max entered and handed a single page of paper to Pieter then settled across from Ed who lifted his beer in toast.

"It says here that you no longer have a position at the Joint Airline facility," Pieter read aloud.

Warfield's shoulders slumped. "Why am I not surprised. What else does it say?"

"It says you were terminated for failure to meet standards and moral rectitude."

"Those bastards," he snarled. "That's a damned lie, and they know it. I've been framed. Why? Why did Dennett have to send that damned letter to me? My life was going fine until a couple of days ago. Now I got no life left." He gazed plaintively at Pieter. "Can you help me?"

"Now that you're a man without a Corporation, I think you need to look at your options."

"What options?"

"The way I see it," Pieter chose his words carefully, "is that you have two options. The first is that if or when you are caught, you will be sent to the cordoned areas. The second is to join a movement that will keep your identify secret."

"And how do I go about finding something like that?"

"I can help you there," he calmly replied. "Once you finish your beer, you'll be sent to a safe house. Stay put. There's a TV and plenty of food there, so you'll have everything you need. Someone will contact you. Above all, don't go outside the house."

"How do I know who the contact is?"

"They will come as an electrician or plumber or other interior serviceman. Let them in and they'll direct you from there."

Warfield absorbed the news with apprehensive relief. Downing the last remains of his beer, he stood up. "Thank you. I knew I could trust you."

Pieter smiled and shook his hand then watched as the hood was placed back over Warfield's head. *But can I trust you?*

Phil quickly stubbed out his cigarette when he saw the cab slow down. "A cab just pulled up," he quietly announced. The door to the pub opened and Warfield burst out and jumped in the back seat. "He's on the move." He started the car and waited. The cab stayed put for a few moments before finally pulling away from the curb. Phil let it get farther down the street before pulling out.

Phil kept up a running commentary as he tailed the cab. "He's turning right onto Edgewood... now left onto Piedmont... looks like he's getting on Freedom Parkway." A while later it was, "He's turning left onto Briarcliff."

Finally, the cab turned onto Lavista with Phil a reasonable distance behind. It was less than a mile after they crossed Clairmont that the cab slowed down. An abandoned strip mall to the left, the cab turned into the housing area to the right, a neighborhood of townhomes.

"He's turned into the neighborhood across from the old Vista Grove Shopping Center."

"Keep going," the voice informed him. "We got eyes on him now."

With a sigh of thanks, Phil motored on, ready to call it a night.

With Warfield off his hands, Pieter stretched and ordered more beer. He was contemplating returning to his own digs when Jason pushed in. "I'll take one of those," he said, glancing at the beer.

"Help yourself." Pieter slid a bottle across the coffee table.

"Lowell thinks it's too dangerous for you to stay here any longer," he said, flipping open the bottle top. "He'd like for you to head out to one of the cordoned cities."

"When?"

"Real soon. Things are going to get hot around here and it'd be good if you weren't around."

"Any one city in mind?"

"Sierra Vista, Arizona."

"Arizona?" Pieter sniffed a laugh. "I'll fit in real well there."

Jason chuckled in reply. "It's far enough away to have you lay low for a while. Besides, you'll enjoy it. It'll be a nice change from the pollen capital of the world here. And it's a dry heat," he grinned.

"Who's in charge now?"

100

"Gretchen." Jason took another satisfying gulp, smacking his lips afterwards. "Good god there's nothing like a good private beer."

"How big is the cordon zone?" Pieter finished off the bottle and flipped open another.

"Pretty much everything south of Tucson between I-19 running down past the old border wall at Nogales all the way to Hermosillo, then east along I-10 to Las Cruces. It goes south from there bypassing El Paso then all the way to Chihuahua. You can't miss it," he said rolling his eyes. "It's all surrounded by forty foot high walls."

"When do I leave?"

"Don't know. In the meantime, you need to lay low at your place."

Pieter thought of his little safe haven in Chastain Park. He had spent a lot of money and time perfecting that little hideaway. Pity he'd have to leave that all behind. "What about Warfield?"

"We'll check him out."

"And check out Billy Fish. Warfield claims Billy Fish told him to find me. I think he's lying. Last time I saw Billy Fish was over a year ago, just before he was busted for black-marketing. He got sent to the big house for a bit. My guess is that if they didn't use him for testing, they sent him to a cordon. Either way, Warfield doesn't know him."

Jason finished his beer and set the bottle on the table. "That's good to know. We'll make sure he's clean. If not, we'll use him to our advantage… at least until he's compromised. After that, we'll make an example out of him."

Remembering the letter, Pieter handed it to him. "This is the same letter I received." He watched as Jason unfolded the letter and quickly read the contents. "You still think not telling the cordon zones is a good idea?"

"It's Lowell's decision," he answered, refolding the letter and sticking it in his shirt pocket. "One I agree with. Think about it. What happens if we tell them? Mass hysteria and people turning on each other. Just what Corporate wants. You know human nature. Our first instinct is self-preservation. We'll do anything to ensure our survival, even if it means killing someone else. Right now we've got folks working together. We need to keep it that way."

"What happens when they find out we knew all along and did nothing?"

Jason paused and slowly inhaled.   "We pray they will forgive us. It is the price we must pay now if we are to win in the future."

Chapter 4

SEI Directorate – Decatur
Monday, May 8, 2102

Flipping up her desk monitor, Linda touched the screen to get to the daily Intel briefing. Touching the icon, the briefing appeared, the words 'Classified – Delta' stamped across the entire top of the page in large bold red letters. She had just begun to read the executive summary when Sharon walked in.

"Sorry for the intrusion," the Interdiction Branch Manager said, "but I thought you'd want to be brought up to speed in case you get any questions."

Linda smiled despite her best efforts to appear professional. Sharon was the perfect subordinate – obeisant almost to a fault. Even back at her place, Sharon was the submissive, yet inquiring and enjoyable friend... and now lover. She was amazed that Sharon never seemed disturbed by anything. The woman's attitude was consistently positive.

"What's the progress?"

Standing before the desk, Sharon handed her a flash drive. "Thought you might want to take a look at this."

"What is it?"

"It's the interview of the taxi driver from last night."

As Linda pressed the drive into the slot on the desk monitor, Sharon came around to stand behind her. Linda clicked on the video icon and the screen filled with a camera view of the interview room. An interdiction agent sat across the table from the cabbie.

"So tell me again how you came into possession of the phone?" the agent calmly inquired.

"Like I said before," the cabbie shrugged apathetically. "This dame flags me down, gets in the cab and hands me a C-note if I take a phone from some guy and drive it outta the city. She gives me a slip o' paper with the address on it."

"What did she look like?"

"She was a good lookin' dame with a nice set o'..." He cupped his hands in front of his chest as explanation. "Said her name was Linda Nadell."

Linda flushed with indignation at the absurdity of the claim, yet at the same time liked the physical description though knowing it wasn't her.

"Thought that was sorta weird," he continued.

"What was weird?"

"Her tellin' me her name, like she wanted to make sure I knew who she was. Said it a couple o' times. Normal folks just hop in and tell me where to go. Say, you got a cigarette on you. When they dragged me in here, I left my pack on the front seat o' the cab."

The agent pulled a pack from inside his suitcoat and handed the entire pack to the cabbie. "Besides having a nice chest, what else can you tell me about her?"

"She had long platinum blond hair. Good lookin' woman. At first I thought she was a hooker."

Linda stiffened at the analogy.

"Go on," the agent urged.

"Don't remember much more."

"Then what happened?"

"Like I said, she hands me a C-note and says take the guy's phone to this address on the paper."

"You didn't think that strange?"

"Sure I did," he cocked an eyebrow at him. "But it was a slow night and besides, she said there was another five C's at the other end."

"How did you know what guy it was?"

"I ain't even gone a block when she points him out to me standing' on the sidewalk lookin' fer a cab. She hops out, breezes past the guy like she don't know him and then the guy gets into the cab. I tell him to give me his phone and take another cab."

"So he gives you his phone, just like that?" The agent raised an eyebrow in doubt.

"Well...," he hesitated. "I had a little encourager with me."

"Yes. We found your pistol underneath the front seat. You do know it's against the law to own a gun," the agent self-importantly pointed out.

"Yeah, sure. Course you ain't never driven a cab have you? You don't know the kind of wackos I get."

"If you have a problem, you're supposed to report it to the police."

"Oh yeah, right. By the time I have a chance to report it, I'd be dead."

"OK," the agent smiled. "I'll drop that for now. Let's get back to the phone. You get the phone and then what happens?"

"The man gets out and I drive off. I take my time and when I get to the address, I gotta sinkin' feeling that I been screwed, 'cause when I pull up to the house, the lights are off. So I get outta the cab and start knockin' and ringin' the bell. That's when your guys showed up."

The agent paused as he sifted the story. "The woman who gave you the money, was there anything else you can tell me about her? Unusual features, mannerisms, anything?"

"Not that I remember?" he limply shrugged. "Like I said, she was good lookin'. Wore a tight dress that advertised what she had underneath."

"Which way did she go when she left your cab?"

"I don't know," frowned in irritation. "Once they leave the cab, I don't care where they go. Besides, she got out just as he got in."

"What did he look like?"

"Man, I don't remember," he complained. "He was average, just an average sort of guy. Can I go now?"

Sharon moved back to the front of the desk as Linda clicked to see how much of the video remained noting it was almost finished. Shutting it off, she leaned back, her brows furrowed and her lips pursed. "We have any video of the cab there at that time?"

"We're working on that as we speak. At first I was concerned that they used your name, thinking we might actually believe you'd be involved with this. But then, why use someone who doesn't look like you?"

"It's a message," she answered. "They're telling me they know about me."

"What's so hard about that?" Sharon replied. "Anyone with any slight talent can do the same thing. It's not like no one knows where you work. They just don't know what you do."

Linda slowly nodded in agreement. "Get with the other directors and find out if anyone else from SEI has experienced the same treatment. Put the word out. We need to pay more attention to our surroundings."

"Yes Mam."

"Now tell me about Warfield."

"We've tracked Warfield to a townhouse on Lavista, opposite the old Vista Grove Shopping Center. The shopping center's been boarded up for years. The 'For Sale' sign has pretty much fallen apart. We're setting up an ops center inside, close enough to watch the neighborhood."

"The owners?"

Sharon shrugged. "We'll be discreet."

Linda tucked her chin in a nod. "What else?"

"The term 'Kingfisher' is most likely just a code word Dwa used to identify Warfield when he got to the Vanishing Point. Whether Dwa was actually inside the pub is another matter. I suggest we send an individual asking for the same 'Kingfisher.' That way we can know for sure."

"You have someone in mind?"

Instead of answering, Sharon smiled with confidence.

"Oh no," Linda brusquely stated. "I will not send you out to do a field agent's job. You are far too valuable, on far too many levels. If you were compromised, we could not protect you. I'm surprised at you. You should have thought this through. Not only do you have access to intel operations, you have knowledge of classifications, missions, agents, and too much else."

Sharon snorted a laugh. "I know. I was just teasing."

Linda shook her head and laughed despite herself. "That's not funny."

Sharon did a quick glance behind her then swept around the desk to plant a firm kiss on Linda's lips before quickly returning to her place in front of the desk. "Thank you," she passionately said. "Thank you for caring so much about me. I will never disappoint you."

Startled at both the abrupt display of affection as well as her own yielding to the moment, Linda collected herself, knowing she should chastise her subordinate for taking such liberties, yet pleased with the attention. "We need to be careful here at work," she gently scolded her. "You need to save those displays of affection for when we won't be bothered."

"Yes, Mam," she impishly replied.

"Now back to your idea about sending an agent in. Don't you think that would be obvious, that they would suspect us knowing?"

"Yes, that's the point. We make them nervous. They get nervous, they either get hyper-cautious and button-up or they think they're compromised and move their operation. Either way, we can track them. Dwa has to emerge sometime, and when he does, we got him."

"I wish it were that easy," she opined. "However, you've got good gut instincts. What's your plan?"

"We send in someone expendable.   If he or she is compromised, we lose an agent who knows very little. If she or he is successful, we get info that can help us. Either way we implant a bug and track the agent."

Linda pondered the implications then shrugged. "It's your call."

"Thank you, Mam," she happily replied.

Linda held her gaze for a moment. We'll continue our other, um, discussion at my place, later."

"Of course, Mam. As you wish." With a crisp nod, Sharon breezed out of the office.

North Faring Road, Los Angeles

Leaning forward, hands on the arm rests of the plush office chair, Jefferson Beauregard Clayton did not like what he was hearing. "They took my clone?"

"Yes, Boss," Jeremy contritely answered, standing in front of the massive desk.

"Why would they take my clone?"   He was clearly mystified at this affront to his standing.

"It was taken along with a number of others."

"I don't care about the others," he snarled. "To hell with the others. That was *my* clone they stole."

"I know boss."

"I thought you said it was a safe place for my clone."

"I thought it was, Boss. They had a good record."

"Well it wasn't good enough," he snapped, "was it?"

"I guess not, Boss."

"You guess not?" Beauregard's lips tightened. "It's a good thing I have more than one. If I left it to you, I'd have nothing now. Where's that damned doctor?"

"He's on his way."

The door opened and the handsome young man with close cropped hair pushed his way into the room. He wore a dark suit with an open collar shirt.

"I just heard the news, Reverend." He walked up to stand next to Jeremy.

"And that was the one I was going to use," he grumbled. "What do I do now, Doc?"

"You still have two more, Reverend," Doc calmly pointed out.

"Yeah, but you said he was the best of the three."

"That's true, but only by a tiny amount."

"Well tiny as it was, it was enough. I'm now going to settle for second best and I don't like that." Turning to Jeremy he griped, "Why can't we get him back? What's Corporate going to do about it?"

"Corporate is looking into it –"

"I don't want them looking into it, I want some action." He slapped the desk top for emphasis.

"It's not that easy, Boss. We don't know where to look and as far as we know, he could be anywhere."

"He's right, Reverend," Doc chimed in. "Remember the last time when they found that clone of the banker? The banker lived in Chicago and they discovered his clone by accident six years later, living in Budapest."

"Damn it all."   Beauregard silently fumed for a few moments more. Casting a glance at the Doc, he visibly sighed. "So which one is the next best?"

"The one in the facility in Tucson."

"Well," he morosely said, fixing Jeremy with a sharp glance, "I suppose he'll have to do. Schedule it right away before they get any more ideas about my clones."

"Yes, Boss. I'll get on it right away."

"I want it done this week," he snapped.

108

"This week? But Boss, that's too soon." Jeremy looked to Doc for support.

"This week," he growled, fixing him with a cold stare.

Jeremy knew better than to argue. He'd have to do some horse-trading and it was going to cost more, but he'd get it done. He always did. "Yes, Boss." He tucked his head to his chin in a bow then hurried out.

"It's all good, Reverend," Doc soothed. "Once we get you transferred and healed, we can reproduce you. I say we go for five this time. You can afford it and it gives you greater options."

Liking the idea, Beauregard brightened. "Yes. Five. That's much better. Spread them out again like this last time." Gazing stonily at Jeremy, he pointedly added, "Don't put one of them at the place in Decatur. I don't like what happened this last time."

"Actually," Doc chuckled, "the Decatur facility would be the best place. Having been hit once, you know their security is going to be even better now."

"Eh, maybe you're right. I'll leave that to you." The door opened and an attractive young oriental woman stood in the doorway. Glancing at the clock, Beauregard stood up. "Time for my massage. You go help Jeremy get my appointment. I'm sure you have friends who can help me."

With that, Beauregard walked over to the woman, and arm in arm, they headed down the hallway.

Social Injustice compound – East Point

Martin stood next to JB in a very quiet room littered with shell casings. They stood in one of the firing lanes as Martin explained how the rifle worked, also demonstrating how to hold it and how to aim it.

"OK," he grinned. "Now that we got the basics down, let's see how well we do." He clipped a target up. "This is called a 'target.' The object is to aim right here in the center where the little 'X' is." He flipped the toggle and sent the target downrange. Handing JB the rifle, he added, "Now do like I told you and aim and then squeeze the trigger."

JB adjusted the weapon like Martin had shown him, tugging the butt plate firmly into his shoulder. Sighting up, he released the safety and re-sighted, then gently drew back the trigger. The rifle barely bucked as it sent the round down range towards the target.

"That's good. Put the safety back on and let's see how you did." Flicking the toggle, the target began rolling back up. "Now don't be too disappointed if it's not right in the center. You've never done this before and it's a hard thing to do even for those who know how to use the rifle." His patronizing tone turned to surprise when the pulley stopped and the target settled. The shot was dead center.

Martin unclipped the target and studied the hole where the 'X' used to be then looked up to the expectantly waiting JB. Frowning in puzzlement, he slowly bobbed his head. "Not bad for a first shot. Let's see if you can do this again."

To his growing amazement, the result was the same for the next ten targets. In fact, the result was the same even when he sent the target down to the far limits of the firing range. When he reeled in the last target, his amazement had morphed to barely contained excitement.

"You are incredible," he exclaimed. "There is no one here who can shoot like you do. Even me. Wait until I tell Lowell. You're just what we needed." He saw JB's obvious pleasure at the praise. "Did you enjoy this?"

"Yes," he readily admitted. "It was fun. And I'm good at it." It wasn't said from pride, but rather the joy of discovering something new in which he excelled. Yet he wanted to make sure Martin didn't forget there was another passion he wanted to pursue. "I'm good at numbers too."

"So I've been told. Why don't you show me?" Martin turned a target over and placed it on the firing bench.

Picking up a pencil, JB was only too happy to display his knowledge. When he got to the part about putting lines through 'X's and 'O's, Martin stopped him.

"That's all very interesting, but it's not how we do it any longer. We use different symbols to represent certain numbers. Like this." He drew lines beginning with one line then two lines close together then three lines until the last group had ten lines close together. "This is the number '1'," he explained, writing the number below the single line. He continued, writing the numbers below the respective groupings of lines. "Now when we get to eleven, which is ten plus one, we write it like this – 11."

JB's fascination grew with each demonstration and explanation. Nobody back where his old room was ever took the time to tell him this. It was a whole new world for him, even better than the new world he and Ruth had just entered. Then Martin said something that pushed his joy beyond all belief.

"You know, shooting this rifle uses math."

"It does?" JB's mouth gaped open.

"Yes." Martin picked up a round and held it up for JB to study. "This is a bullet. It's shaped this way for a reason, so that it will go as fast as possible with as little resistance as possible. Inside the casing here is some stuff called powder that explodes when you pull the trigger. When the powder explodes, it pushes out this little part of the bullet at the front. This little part is what puts the hole in the target."

Placing the bullet back down on the table, he said, "All this, the rifle, the bullet, the room here, all this is a result of something called physics, which needs math to make it work."

"You can teach me?" JB gushed.

"As much as I can," he smiled kindly. "And for what I don't know, we'll find someone who does."

JB was fairly beside himself with glee. Wait until he told Ruth about all of this. Then he thought that if someone was going to help him, then someone could help her. "Ruth's really good at drawing," he blurted. "She's the best I've ever seen. She can draw pictures of you that look like you're right here."

"I'll make sure someone gives her what she needs," he replied, unsure where that came from. "I think we're finished here. We'll practice more later. Let's get on back to the others."

Once he had deposited an excited JB back in the central room with the other clones, he chuckled as he watched him hurry over to the woman called Ruth to tell her about the experience. Leaving JB in animated conversation, Martin made his way through the labyrinth of hallways and tunnels to the operations room of Social Injustice where the activity was calm, yet busy. He spied Lowell standing before the Atlanta city grid map talking to Scott who was head of security. Lowell saw him walk up and smiled.

"How's our progress?"

"We're getting there," Martin off-handedly replied. "I've tested most of the new arrivals and I think I've found our sniper." That got their attention.

"Who?" Scott asked.

"JB." He held up the targets and peeled them off one by one, showing the single hole in the center of each target.

"Damn," Scott whistled in admiration. "He's phenomenal."

"JB?" Lowell frowned, shaking his head. "I've got something else in mind for him."

"I know what you want to do," Martin placated, "but just think about it for a moment. The man's a natural, better than anyone else we got. We can still use him like you want to, but why not take advantage of his skills in the meantime?"

"We can't afford anything happening to him. The Reverend has too much security around him. And he'll have a whole lot more now that we've taken his clone. Isn't that right, Scott."

"He is right, Martin," Scott readily agreed. "Right now we need to lay low concerning the Reverend. Give him some time so that his security becomes lax. That gives us more time to study his habits."

"I suppose," Martin reluctantly agreed, "But really, what does it matter? If we take out the Reverend, his empire is gonna crash anyway."

"It's not that simple," Lowell answered, "but I'll think about it. In the meantime, perhaps we can make use of JB's skills with another target, one that's not so difficult."

"He'll need training," Martin pointed out. "Just because he was good inside, doesn't mean he can handle the pressure outside. Let me take him to the cabin."

"Too dangerous."

Martin's face tightened in a large frown. "What's the sense of finding out who can shoot if we're never going to use them? We're supposedly building an army of clones and we have, what, maybe 300 of them spread out throughout the states? How am I supposed to train them if we keep them sequestered and scattered? We're gonna need a helluva lot more if we're even going to be more than a blip on the Corporation's radar."

"Alright, Martin," Lowell half-smiled with indulgence. "What do you want to do?"

"Let me take JB to the cabin and see what he can do."

"Fine. When do you want to go?"

"Let me take him now before they get all their security organized. We'll be back in a day or two."

"You taking the girl with you?" Scott asked.

"You mean Ruth. No. I don't need the distraction, and he doesn't either."

"What's our status in the Cordons?" Lowell asked, redirecting the discussion.

"We're making progress, but they're adding to the cordon fencing."

"They're adding to the fencing? It's already forty feet tall," Scott scoffed.

"Not that," Martin explained. "They're widening the danger zones surrounding the fence, adding more mines and tunnel sensors. We need to have folks in place to mark and locate."

"They doing that just to the Tucson Cordon?"

"No," Lowell answered for him. "They're doing that to all the cordons. Something's up and we need to find out what before it's too late." Gazing pointedly at Scott, he said, "Use your resource to find out what's going on. I need answers."

Chatsworth, Georgia

JB stood in awe of the surroundings. Never in his whole life had he experienced being outside like this. The trees, the fields, the smells, the vistas were almost too much for him, yet he reveled in the experience. Martin even let him pick some colored plants called flowers. Martin said that women love getting these as gifts, so when they got back he was going to give these to Ruth.

He looked around at the wire fenced fields that stretched all around him. Martin said they were somewhere not too far from some place called Chatsworth. When Martin told him they were going for a ride, he hadn't expected it to last so long. At first he had to hunker down in the back seat so that no one would see him. Once they were out of the city, Martin pulled over and let him move to the front.

From then on, he was enamored with the scenery. Never had he ridden, let alone been in a car for so long while getting to see what was on the other side of the life he had lived. For so long, he had been held captive in such a small world of the facility. Now living with the Family, as Lowell called them, he was experiencing more than he could ever have imagined.

His curiosity burst like a dam, with Martin patiently answering his flood of questions. It was when Martin used the word 'love' that JB paused.

"What does 'love' mean?"

Martin uttered a soft chuckle. "That's a tough one. Let's see if I can make some sense of it. What do you feel like when you are with Ruth?"

"Happy," he exclaimed.

"Do you want to be with her all the time?"

JB thought a moment, realizing he did want to always be with her. "Yes."

"And if someone was going to hurt her, you would do anything to protect her."

"Yes," he adamantly replied.

"How far would you go to protect her? Would you kill someone to make sure that person would never try to hurt her again?"

JB furrowed his brows, pondering the question. "I… I suppose I would."

"Now you're beginning to understand 'love.' But 'love' is far more than that. Love means wanting the other person to be happy, even if it might make you sad."

"I don't understand."

"For example, suppose Ruth said she liked being with Gordon better than she liked being with you. Because her happiness is more important than yours, 'Love' would mean that you would let her be with Gordon."

JB blinked at the explanation. He turned to watch the passing scenery. "I don't think I like 'love,'" he quietly replied.

"That was just an example," Martin comforted. "That kind of love is hard to do. We're coming into Chatsworth," he said, his voice abruptly guarded. "You need to hunker down. There's a lever on the right sight of your seat."

"Which is the 'right' side?" JB responded looking quickly side to side.

"By the door. Feel it?"

"Yes."

"Pull it up and lean back into the seat and it will move back."

JB did as told and pushed the seat far enough back so that his head was below the window level."

Martin reached behind him on the back seat and handed him a baseball hat. "Put this over your face and pretend you are asleep."

JB complied just as a drone swept into the middle of the street. For some reason, it decided to follow the car until they were well out of town and almost in Eton. By the time they were through Eton, the drone had focused its attention on a car heading south into Chatsworth.

"Probably the local cops," Martin explained with a sigh of relief. "You can sit back up now. Pull the lever and the seat will come back up by itself." Martin looked over to see JB sitting up, hat firmly on his head now. He looked just like any other young man out with a friend.

"We'll be turning off once we get to Cisco."

"Where are we going?"

"We're going to a place where we won't be bothered."

Silence settled as each was lost in his thoughts. After a bit, JB asked, "Why do I want to be sad if Ruth is with Gordon?"

"It's not that you want to be sad. No one wants to be sad. But because you love Ruth, you want her to be happy no matter how you feel. If Ruth is happier with Gordon than you, then you will let her be with him."

"But how do I know she's happier with him? She doesn't know him like she does me."

"That's all very true," Martin grinned, pulling off the main road. The road twisted and curved and soon became gravel and dirt. Dust kicked up behind them as they wound their way into the North Georgia mountains.

After a while, the road split and he headed further up and the road became more bumpy and rough. It was obvious no one had been here in a while as every now and then, Martin would stop the car to haul a fallen branch off the road. On two occasions, he had to have JB get out and help him. The road split again and Martin followed it until they came to a weathered log cabin.

115

"We're here," Martin announced pulling into the short driveway. "We'll be here overnight, so let's unpack our gear and set up first."

JB was a willing and obedient pupil, assisting and carrying sleeping bags, food, and drinks inside to where Martin was arranging and placing food items in the small kitchen. The last item to be carried in was a large rectangular case that Martin carried in himself.

Satisfied with the arrangements, Martin motioned to the back door. "Let's get started with your first lesson."

Pushing the back door open, they emerged onto a wide back porch containing several chairs and two small tables, one the height of the porch railing. Martin placed the large rectangular case on the lower table and opened it, revealing a rifle with a long barrel.

Withdrawing the rifle, Martin explained, "This is a model 700 Remington single-action, sniper rifle with scope. It also has bipod legs for stability. We use this rifle to hit targets that are a greater distance away than we can see clearly." Handing him the weapon he said, "Place the rifle against your shoulder just like the one you used in the indoor range."

"This is heavy," JB said, feeling the heft of the rifle.

After JB positioned the rifle, Martin reached up and uncovered the two ends of the scope. "Go ahead and look through the scope."

JB did and was surprised to see things so much closer. He switched back and forth between peering down the scope and pulling his head away to see what it looked like without the magnification. "How does it do this?"

"There are things called lenses inside the scope. What they are is clear glass that is curved on two sides." He made the shapes with his hands, touching fingers and heels of the palms. "When light comes in one side it makes it bigger on the other side. When we get back, I'll show you better and explain it. Remember what I said before, it has to do with physics and math."

That was good enough for JB as he felt the heft and balance of the weapon. "What do I shoot?"

"Slow down, cowboy," Martin laughed. "Let's learn how this thing works first. I said this was a single action rifle. That means you have to put the bullet in each time you want to fire it.

Also, and this is very important, this is not like the AR-15 you shot in the indoor range. You barely felt any pressure on your shoulder each time you fired the AR-15. You'll feel the model 700, so you need to be prepared."

JB had already twisted the bolt knob up and pulled back the bolt. "Is this where the bullet goes?" He pointed to the opening.

"Very good," Martin chuckled. "OK. I think we can dispense with some of the rifle learning for later. Let's fire this bad boy." He handed JB a .308 round and watched him slide it in and ram it home, smooth as though he already had experience. Pointing to his right through the plentiful trees of the surrounding forest, he said, "A straight line from here, in between all these trees, is a small bucket nailed to a tree. There's a red circle painted on the bucket. You'll have to look through the scope to see it."

JB tucked the rifle into his shoulder and focused through the scope, slowly scanning. "I see it."

"Good. You see the 'X' inside the scope? Place where the lines cross in the center of the red circle on the bucket."

"OK."

"Now fire."

JB squeezed the trigger and felt the rifle buck. For some reason, the feel of the jolt against his shoulder thrilled him, knowing he had just sent a tiny missile out into the forest to hit a target in the distance. Here was something else he was good at, and he liked being good at something other than math. And he would study hard so that he also learned how to read, just like Gordon.

"Here, let me see." Martin reached up for the rifle and sighted down to the bucket. "Excellent shot. A little high and to the left. We need to adjust some windage and elevation."

For the next hour, JB fired the Remington until each shot was dead center. Martin moved to different targets to where JB was using the bipod and hitting targets almost 800 meters away, through rows of trees.

"Now for one little extra attachment," Martin smiled. "We add a suppressor." He retrieved the suppressor from the case and screwed it on. "Try hitting the far target."

JB rested the bipod on the table and positioned himself behind. Once he sighted in, he squeezed the trigger. Instead of

117

the loud retort as heard from all the other shots, there was barely any noise. "Why didn't it go 'bang' like all the others?"

"That's because the suppressor here," he pointed to the end of the barrel, "takes away the noise."   Scooting JB out of the way, he peered through the scope, a smile spreading on his lips when he saw the result. "Yup. You're gonna do just fine."

Leafmore Ridge, Atlanta

Warfield jumped when he heard the front doorbell ring. Instead of opening the door, he quietly sidled to the curtains of the front window and slowly pried them aside to see who stood at the door. It was a woman in a business uniform, holding a clip-pad. He then looked to the street and saw the cable van.

With a sigh of relief, he remembered what Pieter had told him concerning the next contact. "Just a minute," he called out then unlocked the doors.

The woman before him wore a thin pale blue pinstripe short-sleeved shirt with a sewn-on name in dark blue that said 'Beckie.' Her auburn hair was pulled back into a pony-tail that protruded through the gap in the back of her baseball hat with the company logo blazoned across the front.   She was very pretty and her shorts revealed athletic legs. A tool box lay on the step next to her feet.

"May I help you?" he inquired, playing the game.

"Mister Warfeld?" she ventured, studying the name on the screen of the clip-pad.

"That's Warfield," he corrected.

"Sorry.   Mister Warfield.   "I'm from the cable company. You reported a problem with your cable."

"I did? Oh, I mean, yes, I did." He stood staring at her.

After a few awkward moments, she said, "May I come in and look at it?"

"Oh... yes, yes, of course."   He stepped to the side while she retrieved her tool box and entered, stopping in the foyer to politely wait for him.

"The TV's in the room just down the hall to the right."   He led the way and pointed to the large TV recessed into the wall. Handing her the remote, he waited and watched.

118

Placing the tool box on the floor, she stood to the front of the TV and turned it on, flipping through a number of channels. She then tested the voice control. "Search for adventure movies." An instant later the menu with the listing of all the day's adventure movies appeared. "Search for news." The same result occurred as it did with several other verbal searches. Finally she commanded, "Off." The TV shut down.

Turning to Warfield, she gave him a curious look. "There doesn't seem to be anything wrong with your cable."

"Uh… OK…" he fumbled. What was he supposed to say now?

"I'm sorry," she shrugged empathetically, "but I'm going to have to charge you for a home visit."

Warfield blinked as he sorted the statement. None of this made any sense. He watched as she took out the stylus and scribbled some notes on the clip-pad. Pressing the print command, a small piece of paper scrolled out from the end of the small machine. Tearing it off, she handed it to him.

"Here's your bill. You can pay it by phone or online. My name's Beckie and I'd appreciate a good review." Picking up her tool box, she headed for the front door.

"That's it?" he asked. "Isn't there anything else you want to tell me?"

She stopped by the door and momentarily frowned then brightened. "No. I think we're all done here. Have a good day." With that, she pushed through the door and ambled to the van, taking her time to get settled before she drove off.

Warfield stood dumbly staring at her in the door way, watching until the van drove out of the neighborhood. Slowly, but firmly, closing the door, he twisted the deadbolts home then meandered over to the couch in the front room trying to understand what had just happened.

He was still sitting there when he heard a vehicle pull up in front of the house. Leaping up, he repeated the spying process at the curtains and watched a man emerge from a white cable van that looked amazingly similar to the one that left less than ten minutes ago. He watched as the man approached, carrying the same style tool box and clip-pad. Instead of waiting for the doorbell to ring, he unlocked the deadbolts and swung the door open.

"May I help you?" He stared at the man dropping his gaze to read 'Stefan' in dark blue embroidery on his shirt.

"Mister Warfield?" the man said looking his clip-pad.

"Yes."

"You reported a problem with your cable."

"You had somebody here not more than ten minutes ago," he complained.

The man's eyes jolted wide. "We did? Who was it?"

"Some woman named Beckie."

"What did she look like?"

"A few inches shorter than me. Good looking, brown hair pulled back into a ponytail."

"Damn," he muttered, pushing past Warfield into the house. "Close the door," he commanded without looking back to see if he had been obeyed. Spinning around he waited until Warfield had finished locking the last deadbolt. "How long was she here?"

"Not more than two minutes."

"Did you leave her alone at any time?"

"No."

"Tell me exactly what happened." He folded his arms and hunched forward, listening.

"She came here just like you did. Called me by my name, except she said 'Warfeld' instead of 'Warfield.' She walked in and played with the TV for maybe a minute or two before realizing nothing was wrong. I got charged for a home visit. Then she left."

"You sure she didn't touch anything?"

"She didn't even open her toolbox. Once she saw the TV was OK, she gave me the bill and left."

"Was she driving a truck just like mine?" His eyes focused intently in him.

"Yes. Just like it."

'Stefan' started pacing. Suddenly, with half-lidded eyes and a sagacious nodding of the head, he believed he knew the answer.

"Well," he said, a little louder than normal. "It was probably nothing. We'll take care of the bill for you." He carefully and quietly opened the tool box as he spoke, retrieving a small hand-held electronic wand that he began waving around the room. Moving in the direction when the needle on wand began to indicate electronic output, he moved towards the low table by the front door, pausing to read the wand whose needle was jammed to the right side indicating activity.

Feeling with his hand on the underside of the table top, he found what he was looking for and motioned Warfield over to take a look. Placing a warning finger to his lips he bent down with Warfield to show him the tiny transmitter stuck to the wood.

Standing up, he switched off the wand. "Well then, let's take a look at that TV." Leading the way, he turned on the TV and increased the volume enough to drown out their conversation.

"That was no cable person," he explained, leaning in so close to him that Warfield instinctively pulled back. "That was someone from Corporate. They know you're here." He pursed his lips and stared at Warfield. "But if they know you're here, wonder why they didn't pick you up? You know what I think?"

"No?" a muddled Warfield replied.

"I think they wanted to eavesdrop on us. This might play out to our advantage."

"How did she do it? I was with her the entire time."

"Oh, they're good," he grinned in admiration. "The old sleight of hand trick. You watch the right hand while the left hand does its dirty work. That all doesn't matter now; you need to watch what you say. We may or may not move you to another safe-house. I'll check with the bosses. You got enough to eat?"

"Yeah, sure," he unconvincingly replied. He wasn't used to cooking so much. Most of the time he ate out. But somehow that didn't seem all that important. "Don't you think I ought to be moved to a safer place?"

"No, not yet," he answered with a clever smile. "Corporate thinks we don't know about the bug. This is perfect." With that, he turned off the TV. "Well Mister Warfield," he loudly announced, walking back to the front foyer. "I think we've solved that old connection problem. If you have any more trouble, just give us a call at this number." He handed him an imaginary business card. "Have a good day."

Warfield stood in the open doorway, blankly staring at him as he jauntily walked back to the cable van, giving him a

Pavlovian wave of the hand in response to his cavalier finger wave.

Closing the door, he scrunched his face in frustration. This wasn't working out like he thought it should. Stepping over to the low table by the front door, he bent down to study the listening device. From the design and manufacture, he knew it wasn't a Corporate device. This was a homemade job, which meant Social Injustice had planted it long before he got here. He knew something was wrong when Stefan went on blabbing about Beckie before he did the search for the listening device.

Mouthing a quiet "Damn," he stood back up. There was nothing he could do now. He knew the house was being watched.

Walking back down the hallway into the family room, he turned on the TV to normal volume then went into the kitchen, leaving the lights off, to study the tiny back yard that led directly to the garage. Fencing on both sides of the yard separating the townhouse from the neighbors ensured privacy.

The garage itself had a flat roof protected from the elements by large trees on the back street that spread their thick branches over both street and garage. He noticed the clipped ends where the branches had been cut back away from the house.

From this vantage point of gazing out the kitchen window, he could see nothing except the side fencing and rear of the garage with the single house door to the left. The yard itself was entirely paved, with a metal table and chairs off to the side. A small free-standing fire pit was pushed against the fence. One thing he did notice was that the garages all seemed to be connected, a single wall separating one garage from another, much like the townhomes were connected.

Warfield walked back into the family room and opened up the liquor cabinet. He had already noted the private stock of liquors. He had partaken of the honeyed whiskey the previous evening. Pouring himself a glass of the whiskey, he went back into the kitchen and leaned against the counter as he mulled his present situation.

That they doubted him meant it was only a matter of time before they discovered Billy Fish was dead. And if Warfield didn't do something fast, he'd end up like the ex-convict. That meant he would have to escape before they came back for him.

His cover was blown.

It was well past midnight when Warfield decided it was time. He wished he had the smarts to destroy the townhouse in one loud bang, just to let them know he could play their game. But, he wasn't trained for that and had to content himself to simply disappear.

Barely opening the back door, he slipped down the steps and silently positioned the chair and table next to the garage. Climbing the chair first, he then stepped onto the center of the table. The height was sufficient that he could climb up onto the garage roof.

Low crawling across the top, he stopped at the edge and waited scanning the line of parked cars along Lavista Drive. He spent the next almost half an hour slowly scrutinizing the cars, knowing someone was watching the back of the house. He was finally rewarded when he saw the glowing end of a cigarette as the owner inhaled, in a car three garages down. Smoke curled out the cracked window.

Knowing where his quarry was, Warfield proceeded to crawl along the garage tops, carefully and slowly sliding over the raised dividing wall between each garage until he was at the last garage. With his quarry's attention focused on the garage and back of the safe house, Warfield lowered himself over the side of the end garage, out of sight. It wasn't until he had slunk along the wall, vaulted over the wrought iron fence that surrounded the townhouse neighborhood, and raced across the street well behind the man in the car, that he caught his breath.

By the time the sun was rising, he was almost to headquarters.

Vanishing Point, Underground Atlanta

Pieter had dawdled at the Vanishing Point, content to absorb as much as possible about his new mission. For the past two days, he had quizzed and queried the analysts, studied reports, maps, and diagrams, and generally made himself a good-natured nuisance.

Jason had watched the gentle giant with both aplomb and humor. The man's intellect and understanding was amazing, as was his way with people. An analyst might be in ill humor at having to interrupt his work to explain something, and then a few minutes later would be confessing his inner most anxieties and personal emotions. For all his inquisitiveness, Pieter had the gift of making people trust him, of drawing them out beyond their inner walls.

Thus it was with some pleasure that he could relax for a bit now and actually enjoy an evening meal, with the prospect of dining one-on-one with Pieter. They sat in what passed for his office, an enclosed space within the large room still humming with activity.

Jason flipped open two private beers and passed one to Pieter. "I've always wondered about that gift of yours, that thing you do with your inner spirit thing." He took a swig and set the bottle next to his plate overflowing with a cheeseburger and sweet potato fries.

"I see you're eating healthy," Pieter teased, mixing the dressing on his salad.

"Yeah, well some of us like flavor in our food," he replied with a half-smile. "So what about that gift? When did you first discover you had it?"

"I was very young." He then went on to explain about his mother and grandmother, his healing skills, and his desire to live a normal life, or what passed for normal. "It was here that I discovered I could send myself outside myself. But the effort is exhausting and I'm worthless for a good thirty minutes afterwards. It used to be longer, but as I've grown stronger, the time lessens. Perhaps one day it will disappear."

"So what do you see when you go outside yourself?" He bit into the burger.

"I see things as they are. There's nothing mystical about it." He shrugged and plopped a fork-load of salad in his mouth.

"So how far can you go? Can you follow someone, say outside the city?"

"No. I can only go so far. It's more about the time than the distance. I have to allow sufficient time to return." He grew somber. "I once failed to heed the warnings of my elders, when I was younger. I went too far and didn't have the strength to return."

"What happened?" Jason paused mid-chew.

"It took the efforts of my grandmother and other members of the convocation to find me and bring me back."

"Suppose they hadn't found you?"

Pieter was silent for a moment then quietly stated, "I would not be here today."

"You'd be dead?"

"Not quite. My body would be alive, but without spirit. Eventually I would die for lack of food and sustenance."

"What about your spirit?"

"My spirit would continue to exist, but without anchor, without a rooting substance." He took a long sip of beer, wiped his mouth and set the bottle back down. "You see, when a person dies, his soul is released to live in another world. It is the natural course of life and death. However, when a soul is removed before the body has spent its course, the spirit cannot settle because it knows it must return. If it cannot or does not return, it becomes a tormented spirit. While it can live in the spirit world, it is shunned as unnatural."

Silence settled for a bit when Pieter said, "I have felt what it is to be shunned and have no wish to repeat the experience. That is why I always leave more time to return than the journey out."

Jason nodded in empathy. "So, suppose you sent your spirit out and someone found you and killed you. What would happen then?"

"I don't know," he slowly shook his head, "and I don't want to find out. That's why I always make sure I'm safe." Taking another bite of salad, he asked, "So tell me why Lowell really wants me in Tucson."

Jason chuckled. "Sometimes I forget who I'm dealing with. I think Lowell is grooming you to take his place."

"Where's he going?" he asked, surprised.

"Nowhere that I know of, but you never know what can happen. The organization needs a charismatic, someone who can motivate and command undying loyalty and devotion."

Pieter raised a skeptical eyebrow. "And you think I'm that man?"

"I know you are."

Pieter snorted a dismissive laugh. "I am not a messiah, and have no wish to be."

"You don't need to be a messiah. You just need to be a savior, someone the people will trust to free them."

"Again I ask, why me?"

Jason chewed on a sweet potato fry, staring at Pieter. "You have the gift. I've watched you here. Everyone loves you. If a person is in a foul mood, all it takes is for you to sit down next to him and in two minutes their foul mood evaporates. You make people feel good about themselves. The cordon people need this; they need you." Dipping a fry in mayo and then into the ketchup, he added, "And the rest of the world needs you."

"Needs what? A reluctant hero? What a cliché."

"We don't need heroes," Jason corrected. "We need leaders who actually care about the world enough to change it."

"Pardon me Jason, Pieter" a pleasantly plump young woman interrupted. "But there's someone up in the pub claiming that Kingfisher sent him."

Jason and Pieter shot each other a frown of concern. "Did he say anything else?" Jason asked.

"Not really, just that Kingfisher sent him to see Pieter."

"Corporate," Pieter and Jason said at the same time.

"What's his name?

"He says he's David Wright. What do you want us to do?"

"Leave him there for the time being," Jason answered. "Tell him that Pieter will see him in a bit."

"OK Jason," she smiled.

Waiting for her to leave, Jason turned to Pieter. "They're fishing."

"Of course they are, but they don't know what 'Kingfisher' means and they're trying to find out."

"We're going to need to move to the alternate headquarters." He stood up to issue orders when Pieter stopped him.

"Wait. Bring him down. Let him sit down here while we move."

"Then what do we do with him?"

"Take him out," he coldly replied.

Jason stared hard at him, not sure whether he should be surprised at this ruthless side of Pieter or the fact that it didn't surprise him.

"It sends a message," Pieter reminded him.

"Fine."   Jason went out and announced the decision to move. A methodical scramble ensued, with everyone starting to organize.

A little while later, the man, with a hood over his head, was brought to the same room that Pieter had conducted the interview with Warfield. Pieter sat in the same chair, and he distractedly wondered about to Warfield as the hood was removed.

Pieter tilted his head to the side as he stared at the visitor. He was a short compact man in his early thirties with short red hair and a pale complexion. Pieter studied him for a moment before saying, "I know you. You're Brandon Kelly. I did a case for you about five years back, about your wife having an affair. I didn't know you worked for the Corporation."

Brandon blanched at the accusation. "I... I don't know what you're talking about.   My name's David Wright. Kingfisher sent me."

"Ah yes," Pieter acknowledged. "Of course. Perhaps I was mistaken. So tell me about Kingfisher. How's he doing?"

"How's he doing?" he dumbly repeated.

"Yes. How is he?"

"Uh... I, uh, I guess he's fine."   Little beads of sweat formed at the top of his head.

"You seem nervous."

"I'm just, just anxious. That's all."

"Have a seat Mister Kelly. Would you like a beer?"

"Uh, yes, thank you." He was half way into the chair when he realized his mistake. "Um, but my name is Wright, David Wright."

"Sorry. My mistake," Pieter politely replied. "Max," he said, turning his attention to one of the guards. "Would you do us a favor and send for some beer?" With Max off to fetch a few brews, Pieter turned his gaze back to his guest. "So, Mister Wright, you told the folks in the pub that Kingfisher sent you here. Why did he send you here, to me?"

"He said you could help me."

Cocking an eyebrow, he said, "Kingfisher said I could help you? How?"

"He said he had this letter from some guy named Dennett and that you knew all about it and that he needed to meet with you." The words burst out in a rush as though he was afraid of forgetting them.

"Meet with me? Where? When?"

"He said you were to set it up and I was to let him know."

Pieter tilted his head to the side. "Why didn't he just come himself?"

"I asked him the same thing," he shrugged. "He said it was too dangerous."

Max returned with a tray of beer and set them down on the low table between Pieter and David Wright. Without waiting to be asked, Wright reached for the frosty bottle and flipped open the top, taking a long and satisfying swallow.

"This is private," he joyously exclaimed.

"The only kind I drink," Pieter smiled, leaning forward to claim his own bottle.

"Where do you get it?"

"I have friends," he replied, effectively saying it was none of Wright's business. Taking a swig, he smacked his lips in satisfaction. "So tell me, Mister Wright, how is it that you know Kingfisher well enough for him to entrust this mission to you?"

"Uh, I don't really know him much at all. We've had the occasional drink together, but that's about it."

"And from that, he decides to trust you with his life?" He raised a skeptical eyebrow.

"Listen, Mister Dwa, I don't know why he entrusted me," he answered, almost in a whine.

"But you accepted knowing it would place your own life in danger."

Wright had already finished his first beer and reached for another. "I could use some excitement in my life," he ruefully answered. "You don't know what it's like working in a metal fabricating plant and your job is to watch the machines do the work eight to ten hours a day and all you have to do is make sure the machines keep running properly. I've been doing that for more than ten years. How's that for the height of ambition?" He took a long sorrowful gulp.

"And you think this will give you some adventure?"

"It has so far," he grimly chuckled.

Pieter nodded sympathetically. "So how is old Kingfisher doing?" he asked as if making light conversation. "He still have that scar over his right eye? I always wondered why he didn't have that fixed. The docs could have erased that with no problem."

"I never noticed the scar," he said with a thoughtful frown. "Maybe he got it fixed."

"Good for him." Pieter lifted his bottle in salute. "So what did he tell you about me?"

"He said that you were really big," he grinned.

"I'm sure he did," he smiled in reply, noting that Kelly or Wright didn't blink an eye when he first saw him. That was because they had already met – five years before. "How did you know where to find me?"

"He sent me here and told me to say that he sent me."

"Ah" he nodded, "I see. So what do you know about Kingfisher's involvement with Social Injustice?"

"He never said it as such," he replied, "but I suspected. He'd be gone for long periods of time then show up at the bar. When he sent me here, I knew he was with them."

"So you think I'm mixed up with Social Injustice?"

"Yeah," be blinked in as though it was obvious. "Hell, it's all over the news."

Pieter gazed at him, momentarily lost in his own thoughts. That was one point he didn't understand. If they knew where he was, why hadn't they raided this place? And why send this obviously poor excuse of a plant in to find out what was here?

"So what would you like for me to do for you?" Pieter asked.

"Like I said, my life has been one long moment of sheer boredom. I'd like to join Social Injustice."

"For the excitement," Pieter deadpanned.

"Yeah, for the excitement," he vigorously nodded not realizing the jest.

"I'll see what I can do. We'll have to put you in a safe house first, while we check you out.

"Excuse me Pieter," Max interrupted, "but you're needed at the moment."

"I'll be right back," Pieter told Wright as he rose from the chair. He watched as Wright's head tilted back as he stood up, his expression still unaffected. He was halfway down the hall when he saw Jason coming to meet him.

"Warfield's escaped."

"When?"

"Sometime during the night. We have to move now."

"What do you want to do with him?" Pieter asked, thumbing over his shoulder.

"Dump his body somewhere."

"Let's not," he countered. "Though he's a plant, and a bad one at that, he could prove useful."

"How so?" Jason asked, surprised at the change of heart.

"He keeps repeating the fact that it was Kingfisher who sent him. That means Corporate is searching for a man who calls himself Kingfisher. Here's an opportunity to create a persona and blame him for all sorts of things."

Jason blinked at the revelation. "I like it. We'll need to get Lowell's approval."

"Do it. I'll work him a bit more," he said, ticking his head to where Wright sat waiting. "We'll move him to another safe house and let him escape."

Pieter reentered the room, noticing Wright had finished off a third beer. "I'm glad you like the beer."

"Who wouldn't?"

"It's all worked out," he said, sitting down. "We'll move you to a safe house once we're finished here. I just need to know some particulars."

For the next half hour, Pieter grilled him while fabricating the life and persona of the man named Kingfisher. Yet during the time, Pieter would alternately refer to his guest as 'David' and 'Brandon.' By the end of the conversation, he was calling him Brandon.

"OK," Pieter said, sitting back. "I think we've done enough here. You'll be taken to a safe house. It is very important to listen to the handler who takes you there. He or she will give you instructions as to what will happen next. Most likely you will be sent to one of the training locations. Do you have any special skills we should know about, Brandon?"

"Like what?"

"Can you fire a pistol or a rifle?"

"Never had the opportunity, especially since the Corporation made owning a weapon illegal. I suppose I could have gone to one of the Corporate ranges where they allow citizens, er... I mean, employees, the chance to fire a rifle or handgun. But that's expensive and with what I make, I couldn't afford it."

"What about computers? Do you have any experience or knowledge with them?"

"Not really," he shrugged. "I can use them like most everyone else does. But if you mean like programming or things like that, no. With my test scores in high school, I was sent to a trade school instead of college. Don't see how much it benefited me though as I watch machines do the work. What skill does that take?"

Pieter stroked his chin, as though deep in thought. "What about vision? Do you wear glasses?"

"No," he proudly replied. I got 20-15 vision. I can see at twenty feet what others see at fifteen."

"Sounds to me like you'd be a good marksman, a sniper perhaps."

Brandon suddenly perked up. "I'd like that right well. Always thought I'd be a good shot."

"Good. I'll let them know. One more thing. If at any time while you are at the safe house, you feel that you might be compromised or that something doesn't feel right, you need to get out of there. Corporate is more clever than you know."

"Where do I go?"

"You come back here. You'll be safe here until we can get you to another safe place."

"Where is 'here,' anyway?" he nonchalantly asked.

"It's called the Vanishing Point," Pieter pointedly replied. "It even says it on the sign outside. That's all you need to know for now. Once you've been vetted, then perhaps we can trust you with knowing other things."

"I understand," he answered knowingly. "When do I leave?"

They both looked up when a man and woman entered.

"Is this the man?" the woman asked Pieter.

"Yes. His name is –"

"No names please," she brusquely interrupted. She looked surreptitiously around the room. "Never know who might be listening."

Pieter fought to contain a grin. She was good. "I'll leave him in your hands then."

"We'll take good care of him," she officiously replied. "If you'll come with us, sir."

With a wave of the hand, Pieter bid him adieu. He wasn't gone more than thirty seconds when Jason came in.

"Well?"

"We need to move, like you said. I think I've inflated his perceptions enough to cause some wasted time on Corporate's part. But, we need to get out of here now. And we need the cleaning team here pronto. This place needs to be free of prints."

Chapter 5

Sierra Vista – Tucson Cordon Zone
Tuesday, May 9, 2102

A mug of coffee in hand, Kevin Gonzales languidly pushed open the screen door to stand on the front porch. Gazing up at the morning sky, he inhaled the fresh air and smiled at another clear sunny day in southern Arizona. He gazed across what once was a parade field, marveling at his good fortune. He could have been sent to any one of the cordon zones, but he ended up here. And he could have been outed like the other covert Corporate agents who were caught in Bisbee and Tombstone and summarily executed.

Instead, his cover was still intact. Taking a careful sip of the hot brew, he thought that it was rather ironic that he, a Corporate agent, was the one who gave the order to execute them. He supposed he should be bothered with killing his fellow agents, but they knew the consequences of their mission when they accepted the job. Besides, his immediate decision to execute them raised his credentials in the zone, not to mention protected his own identity.

"Good morning, Governor."

He looked to his right to see Donald Anderson, his chief of staff and neighbor down the street, walking up the sidewalk towards him. Don was a fit, middle aged man who once was an accountant. His magic with numbers eventually caught up with him and he ended up here. "You're up early, Don."

Don walked up the steps and opened the screen door. "Any coffee left?"

"Help yourself," he grinned.

A moment later, Don joined him on the porch. "They got some in last night," he said, taking a slow sip of coffee.

"How many?"

"Five is what I was told."

"How many does that make now?"

"Karyn said that with these five, they now have one hundred and thirty-seven clones."

"How do they do it?" he marveled. "How do they get them past the security and into the Zone?"

"I wish I knew. On the plus side, it's good they keep it a well-guarded secret. If everyone knew, we'd have major problems." He took another sip. "This is really good coffee. Where'd you get it?"

"Normal black market."

"Expensive?"

"Too expensive," Kevin shook his head. "We've got to come up with a way of getting basic goods so everyone can enjoy the simple things like a cup of coffee in the morning. And we can't keep hitting the shops in Tucson to get what we need. They're already moving stores further away from the wall."

"What about El Paso or Hermosillo?"

"They're sending what they can up our way, but they take what they want for their own citizens and we get the leftovers. How's the farming along the San Pedro?"

"Not too bad. We're still not producing enough, though the last epidemic did help reduce the number of mouths to feed."

"That Doc still in Agua Prieta?"

"Don't know. I'll find out."

"If he is, I want to know why he's still here. That epidemic ran its course two years ago. And I don't buy that 'I'm still here because I love mankind' crap."

"I wouldn't be too hasty sending him back. We need qualified doctors. We don't have enough as it is." Don held his mug at chest level. The warmth from the side of the cup felt good.

"Eh, you may be right," Kevin nodded. "In that case, bring him back here to Sierra Vista where it's more centrally located. And let's keep an eye on him. We don't need another Bisbee-Tombstone incident."

"That was a good call on your part."

"Not much to it," he shrugged. "They were obviously Corporate agents. I just wonder why Social Injustice dumped them off on me."

"That was rather neat of them," Don sniffed a laugh. "The two of them shackled to chairs with a note pinned on each chest."

"I probably did them a favor. They were pretty messed up by the time we got the word." Kevin paused at the memory of walking into the dilapidated house on Temby Avenue in Bisbee to find a man and a woman slumped forward in back-to-back chairs, their arms and legs shackled to the cold metal arm rests and chair legs.   The two had been severely beaten and the bruises had already turned purple. Dried blood lined their chins. The man could only open one eye. But it was the woman who startled him, because when she looked up to see him, he could see the recognition, and the mixture of anger with hope in her eyes. She was expecting him to save them.

It was when she heard him give the order that she snarled, "You bastard." Yet she didn't compromise him. She knew she was dead either way.

That part impressed him... that she would willingly die for the mission. He wasn't so sure he could. In fact, he was beginning to like the life he had here. He was the governor of a quarter of the Tucson cordon zone.   He had power and influence. Yes there were drawbacks. Everyone knew who he was and wanted him to fix things. There was only so much he could do with the resources he had. Fortunately everything was run on solar power, and they had an abundance of sun so the essential energy needs were met.   But there were still food shortages and more people were arriving in Sierra Vista because their dreams of living off the land exceeded reality. The desert was a harsh mistress.

So why did he like it here better than the other side of the wall? It was a question he asked himself more and more these days. When the time came for him to go back, would he?

"Social Injustice wants another meeting," Don interrupted his thoughts.

"Is that why you're up so early?"

"Yup."

Exhaling a long sigh, he said, "What's it this time?"

"They're complaining we're allowing too many drone flyovers."

"What do they want me to do about it?"

"Nothing, supposedly. They say they can take out the low-flying ones, but the higher up ones will require long range weapons."

Kevin cocked an eyebrow.   "And you're telling me they have these weapons?"

"I guess," he answered with a shrug.

"If they're already going to do what they want, why the meeting?"

"We'll see when we get there." Don reached for Kevin's cup and took them back to the kitchen.

Kevin stared at him for a moment. "They do realize I am the governor of this district. I do have other responsibilities than simply dropping everything and come running when they want."

"This won't take long," he answered. "I'll start the car while you put on a different shirt."

"What's wrong with what I got on?" He spread his hands and looked down at the wrinkled pacific islands themed rayon shirt.

"Other than it looks like you slept in it, nothing." Don walked down the steps and down the sidewalk to his convertible two seater electric car. Unplugging the power cord, he flipped the ignition switch and the engine turned over in a low hum.

A minute later, Kevin opened the passenger door and eased down into the seat. "When are you going to find a solar car like everyone else around here?" he teased. "I'm surprised this thing still works."

"How many solar cars have a convertible top?" He spread his hands at the openness of the view.

"Point taken," Kevin smiled. "Where we headed?"

"Apartment complex off Fry." Don pulled away from the curb and after a few turns, they were on Allison Road heading towards what used to be the main gate of what once was Fort Huachuca.

"So tell me again why they always contact you to tell me what they want?" Kevin asked.

"I haven't a clue," he shook his head. "All this cloak and dagger stuff is stupid here, if you ask me."

"I would have agreed with you before the Bisbee-Tombstone discovery. Now, I'm not so sure. I wonder if Corporate's presence here is more than just looking for Social Injustice."

"What do you mean?"

Kevin twisted his head to look out at the passing buildings and people. Though the Zonies, as they called themselves, had been ostracized and cast out from society, there was not the fatalism advertised in the mainstream literature and media propaganda. He remembered watching the various TV shows

136

growing up that took place in the cordon zones with the power struggles and non-stop violence of a depraved society cut off from civilization. Every show ended with the Corporation somehow saving the free world.

When he came here, he half expected to be fighting for survival. Instead, a rule of law had long been instituted and though there were toughs to be dealt with, they were handled with rigid force. Some things were just like the world he left behind.

"I mean," Kevin answered, occasionally waving to someone on the street who recognized him, "if Social Injustice were not here, would Corporate still be here?"

"Probably."

"That's my point. What is here that Corporate needs to be worried about?"

"That we *are* here."

"Exactly. The fact that we can live in peace without the interference or control of Corporate is anathema to them. I fear there may come a time when Corporate will no longer need us as a testing ground for viruses."

Don's head snapped to stare at him.

"C'mon Don. You don't think that the instances of epidemics here are just the nature of things. The last time a real epidemic hit Arizona was back in 1918. There was nothing after that for another 150 years. Then suddenly we get hit with not one, but two epidemics within five years of each other. And the Corporation miraculously has the cures? You believe that and I got that ocean front property in Tombstone for you."

Don snickered. "How much you asking for it?"

Kevin laughed, yet he surprised himself. He suddenly realized that he didn't trust Corporate. Just as he had no qualms eliminating the Corporate agents when they threatened his cover, when the time came, Corporate would leave him here, collateral damage. It was then he decided he wanted to stay.

They turned off into the old Sierra Pines apartment complex. Someone had rebuilt the sign, skillfully painting in the white letters against the blue sky, flanked by two pine trees. Don pulled in between two converted old gas guzzlers, the solar panels bolted to the hoods.

Don led the way between the buildings and up to a ground floor apartment, knocking on the door. A moment later, the

137

door opened and a pretty petite woman with long coal black hair let them in.

"Buenos días, Gobernador Gonzales," she sweetly welcomed him.

"Good morning to you too," he smiled back. "And before you continue, I'm still learning Spanish. My last name may be Gonzales, but my mother was red-headed Irish. So it'll save us a lot of time if we continue in the language of this poor peasant." He gave her a courteous bow.

"Of course," she charmingly replied. "It is early, Governor. Have you had your coffee yet?"

"A cup would be nice, and please call me Kevin." He inhaled the aroma of brewed coffee, noting that it smelled better than his at home.

She flashed him a glance of appreciation and interest as she went into the kitchen, returning with two cups, handing one to him and then to Don. "Please sit. They will be with you in a minute."

Kevin took a sip and smiled. "This is excellent, better than I've ever had. I'd ask where you get it, but I'll leave that alone." He received a coy smile in return.

The far bedroom door opened and a man emerged. He was tall, with short curly blond hair. "Thank you for coming, Governor. If you would follow me please?"

"May I take this with me?" He held the cup up to the woman. "It's not often one gets coffee this good."

"Of course, Kevin," she replied, pleased. "If you forget to bring the cup back, I know where you live."

Snorting a laugh, Kevin and Don followed the man into the empty bedroom. Sliding the closet door to the side, he pressed the back wall panel and it slid to the side. An open elevator with no walls waited for them. A single lamp attached to the side provided dim light.

Kevin and Don followed him onto the elevator, watching as he punched in a code on the control pad. They were shortly descending well below the foundations of the building.

As they slowly descended, Kevin noted that he could reach out his hand and touch the hard packed earth. "What did you do with all the dirt?" he nonchalantly asked.

"It's a big desert out there," came the reply.

"Suppose someone punches in the wrong code?" Don asked.

"Then the elevator doesn't move," the man replied, the answer obvious.

They were about four levels down when the elevator slowed to a halt. Facing a set of metal doors and a control pad, the man again punched in a set of numbers and the doors opened with a burst of light, revealing a long empty corridor, wide enough for maybe two single-seater electric cars to pass each other. It turned sharply to the right fifty paces later then a sharp left twenty-five paces more.

Once they made the second turn, there was an uptick in activity as a group of three women approached.

"Thank you for coming, Governor," the woman in the center pleasantly greeted him. "Sorry about the time of day, but I knew you were an early riser and thought it best not to take up your work day." She was a lithe attractive woman with long blond hair that curled in ringlets over her shoulders. "You remember Zoe and Maria," she said. Zoe was a pert young woman with fair skin, blond hair and a winning smile. In contrast, Maria was a tanned middle-aged woman, with short black hair.

"Good morning Gretchen," he replied with a smile. "Glad to see you realize I do have a job. Nice set-up you have here. How long did it take you to do all this?" He motioned to the windowed offices and work rooms that now lined the hallway.

"It was here before we all came here. Used to be part of Fort Huachuca's testing and research facilities."

"But Fort Huachuca's a good eight to ten kilometers from here," Kevin pointed out. "Where's the main entrance? Surely everyone who worked here didn't all use the same elevator we did."

Gretchen grinned at the observation. "No, they didn't. Let's walk, shall we? There are some things I believe you need to know, especially as our trusted leader in this quadrant of the zone."

Kevin felt a twinge of conscience. This is what Corporate sent him here to discover. He had worked long and hard to earn their trust, rising to the heights of political power in the Zone... only to betray them.

Walking beside her, his second thoughts about his mission reemerged. Though he half-listened to her, his attention was internally focused. His mind raced as he remembered his position in SEI. Originally he was a low-level agent, sent here to see what he could find out. But as his success progressed, they were impressed and placed their assets and efforts under him. He had been lucky so far. When he was elected to the Governor position, they became even more demanding.

Yet, for some reason, all the agents SEI sent were uncovered... except for him. That thought both worried and puzzled him. And despite the failure rate, SEI kept sending more agents and more demands. As Governor, he had been witness to several executions. The last one of the man and woman in Bisbee had rattled him. He remembered the man's icy stare of hatred. The man knew who he was, but his loyalty to the Corporation and his code of honor prevented him from outing the Governor as an agent of the Corporation.

His code... his loyalty... The man died for what? For the Corporation? Somehow that cause seemed so pathetic. What a waste of a life. Kevin had already decided what he wanted his future to be. The hard part was preventing Corporate from screwing that up.

His attention was diverted when he heard Gretchen say, "The tunnels go all the way to the post. In fact, there's an entrance close to where you live."

"There is?" His shock was obvious.

"Yes," she smiled. "Two doors down."

Kevin blinked at the revelation. "Old man Henderson?"

"Yes."

He thought about the old man who had to be close to ninety years old. He'd lived in that house for at least fifty or more years. He once was the mayor of Sierra Vista. Kevin often stopped by just to chat with him and share a shot of bourbon on occasion. "A trusted ally I assume."

"None better. He's been with Social Injustice almost from the beginning." She stopped by a room with no windows, turning her attention to the group. "If you all would remain here for a moment while the Governor and I step inside."

Curious as to the reason of exclusion, Kevin followed her into a darkened room where they viewed another room through a two-way mirror. It was an interrogation room. A bound man sat in a chair opposite the interrogator, a muscular man who was calmly asking questions. The prisoner had been severely beaten and dried blood caked his nose. A pistol with a silencer lay within easy reach on the table.

"What's going on?" Kevin asked.

"Another Corporate agent," she answered.

"Another one," he huffed. "This is getting ridiculous. What's so important here that deserves all this attention?"

"That's what we'd like to know." She opened the door and the prisoner looked up as they entered.

"He's the one," he exclaimed, looking directly at Kevin. His voice and body broken, he wearily added, "He's the Corporate agent."

Kevin instinctively turned to look behind him to see who might be standing there. The movement did not go unnoticed.

"Say that again," the interrogator prompted.

"Him," he breathed heavily. "He's the Corporate agent... the one I was supposed to contact."

"Why?"

"They think he's gone rogue."

"Why do they think that?"

"All... all our agents are compromised. Someone had to know. He's the only one left."

"Me?" Kevin said, his voice dripping with sarcasm. "This ought to be good. Tell me more." He moved to stand behind the interrogator while Gretchen remained in the doorway. "What were you supposed to tell me?"

The man twisted his battered head to stare at him. "You're a marked man. They're coming for you."

Kevin involuntarily stiffened. "Why? What have I done?"

Instead of answering, the man said, "I was sent to give you one last warning. If I don't return, they will send someone to eliminate you."

Kevin's mind raced with the implications. Either way, he was a marked man. Yet why was it he felt safer here in the Zone than on the other side of the fence? The answer was obvious – when the Corporation was finished with you, you were expendable.

"What do you want to do?" Gretchen asked.

Kevin frowned and walked back to the outer room, motioning her to follow. With the door closed, he stared through the window at the prisoner. "This doesn't make any sense. Why target me as a supposed Corporation agent, then come here and tell me they're going to send someone to kill me? When did you pick him up?"

"Last night, working his way towards your house. The gun on the table is his."

His jaw tightened. "He was going to kill me."

"Most likely."

He turned towards her. "Thank you. You saved my life."

"It was nothing," she nonchalantly replied with a sly smile.

Smiling despite himself, he turned his attention back to the prisoner. "You know what I think? I think Corporate is switching tactics, looking to mimic Social Injustice. We take out important people on the other side, and they retaliate in here."

"That was my take," she replied.

Kevin shook his head. "But that's not the way Corporate normally does things. They usually apply the sledgehammer to the fly approach. Why not just take out a section of a zone in retaliation? Infect us like they usually do."

"Good question. What do you want to do with him?" She ticked her head towards the prisoner. "We can't send him back. He's seen enough to know we are here." The implication was obvious.

Kevin sighed in understanding. "It's such a waste. What a stupid way to die for such a stupid reason."

"So you agree he has to be eliminated." She studied him closely.

"I see no other reason. Like you said, we can't send him back. We can't keep him here. What would we do with him? Can we turn him?"

Gretchen paused before saying, "I'd like to try and turn him."

"Turn him?" He cocked an eyebrow in doubt. "You do remember he has a mission – to kill me. He's also a Corporate agent. He's programmed to the mission. Do you really think you could persuade him otherwise?"

"You speak as though you have experience," she mused out loud.

142

"Experience? Yes. You've seen what's happened in the past. How many agents have we taken out? How many did you think we could turn? So why him? Why now?"

"Call it a hunch," she answered.

Kevin shook his head. "I don't like it. I'm the one who has to sleep at night knowing that at some time he'll complete his mission, no matter who much he convinces you he's safe. I'd prefer he be eliminated."

Gretchen studied him for a moment before agreeing. "You're probably right. Besides, if I think about it, I really don't have the time to deal with him." Opening the door to the interrogation room, she gave the interrogator a quick head shake and closed the door.

Kevin watched the interrogator say something. A wave of anger washed over the prisoner who turned his head to the mirror. Kevin swore he saw revenge.

"I've something else to show you," Gretchen said, leading the way out to the hallway. Rejoining the others who were amiably chatting, she led the way down several hallways then to a large warehouse sized room filled with crates and forklifts moving crates.

Walking up to one of the crates, she motioned for one of the workers to come open it. Don read the writing on the side of the crate and muttered, "XM8?" He looked up at Gretchen. "What's that?"

Instead of answering, Gretchen nodded to the workman to open the crate top. Prying open the top with a crowbar, he removed the lid to reveal neatly packaged rifles.

Kevin looked at the rifles then at the number of crates that were being unstacked and restacked. "How many do you have?"

"Thousands," she said, barely containing her glee.

"Ammunition?"

"Rooms full."

"Where'd you find it?"

"Underground bunkers." She gazed at him effectively telling him that was all she was going to tell him.

Kevin let out a slow breath. "I'm not sure I want to know what you intend to do with all this, but I'm going to ask anyway."

143

"When the time comes, we'll be ready," Maria answered for her.

"Ready for what?" Don intoned. "How old are these weapons? Do they even still work?"

"They work fine," Maria reproved him.

"But are they any sort of a match for the combined power of the Corporation? They have airplanes and drones and stuff. What do we have?"

"Here," Gretchen sly smiled. "Let me show you?" She led them back out the warehouse and down several other hallways then to a series of labs where researchers fully clothed in protective gear were conducting experiments. Directing their attention through the double paned windows, she explained, "What you see here is our counter to the Corporate virus. In fact, we've developed a few of our own."

Don was the first to react. "You mean –"

"Exactly," Maria smugly answered. "We now can experiment on the other side of the wall, just like they do here."

"But innocent men, women and children will be killed," Don blurted.

"You mean like they do here?" Maria sourly responded.

Gretchen looked at Kevin. "What do you think, Governor?"

"I think," he thickly said. "We're about to start another world war." Staring back at Gretchen, he asked, "Is that what you want?"

"What other choice do we have?" Zoe's sweet voice interrupted. "They keep sending their undesirables here. Then they send us disease. You know it's just a matter of time before they decide we're no longer needed." Silence settled as they absorbed her words, knowing she was right.

Kevin was the first to intrude on the quiet. Staring directly at Gretchen, he said, "I assume you have a plan?"

"We do."

"This is suicide," Don fumed. "We're one cordon. What chance do we have? We might infect Tucson or maybe even Phoenix, but after that, they simply wipe us out. End of rebellion, end of story."

"You make an excellent observation," Gretchen readily admitted, "one that we have already solved. Let's walk some more."

She led the way down another series of brightly lit corridors and by now, both Kevin and Don gave up any effort at trying to determine where they were. So many of the work spaces looked the same.

"I feel like a rat in a maze," Don muttered, loud enough for all to hear. "Will I get a piece of cheese at the end?"

Zoe snickered and sidled closer to him, slipping an arm around his. "It's not so bad. After you're down here for a while, it all becomes familiar and you can find your way in the dark."

Liking the touch and attention of the attractive young woman, he gave her his best smile. "Don't you miss being outside in the sunlight?"

"Oh, we take frequent breaks during the day. It's not good to spend too much time below."

Walking beside Gretchen, Kevin marveled at the environment. "Everything is so bright and clean. I'm impressed.

"It didn't happen overnight," she replied. "You should have seen this place when we first discovered it. No one had been here in over fifty years."

"So, how long have you been here?"

"About seven years."

"How large is the complex?"

"It stretches from just below your place to just before the river." She stopped before a large workroom with what looked to be people working on drones. "It's not near as wide as it is long. Not sure why they designed it that way, but it does make for a long walk."

"How much of it do you use?" Kevin asked as they pushed through the double doors into the busy room.

"Probably not even a tenth of it." Directing his attention to the activity in the room, she called to one of the workers. "TJ. We have some visitors."

Kevin bit back a smile as he watched a young lad probably no more than thirteen years old approach. He walked with the unabashed confidence of one comfortable with his surroundings.

"TJ. This is Governor Gonzales and his Chief of Staff Don Anderson. I'd like for you to explain what you're doing here."

"Sure thing, Gretchen," he replied, running a hand through his mop of dark brown hair. Waving his hand at the work tables and technicians, he explained, "This here's the main drone room. We're building different kinds of drones depending on what we're gonna use them for."

He led them to the first table of the first row where a technician was wiring a small hand size drone. "This size drone is for spying. It's fast and maneuverable, but can't stay up long 'cause the battery is so small. We're working on a solar assist to improve that."

Pointing to another table three rows back with larger drones, he said, "Those size drones are message drones."

"Message drones?" Don asked. "They look like Corporate drones to me."

TJ looked at Gretchen who nodded. "They're supposed to look like Corporate drones so that we can sneak past them and deliver messages to the other Zones."

Understanding swept through Kevin and he asked, "How long does it take for a drone to get to another Zone?"

"Depends how far the Zone is and how good the operator is. Those drones there top out at about 280 kilometers an hour. So you can figure about four hours for every thousand kilometers."

"Battery life?"

"Those are bigger so we can place more photo cells on top. But even with that, I wouldn't run it longer than a couple o' hours 'cause Corporate then gets suspicious."

Kevin turned to Gretchen. "So this is how you've been communicating with the other Zones."

Giving him a smug smile, she ticked her head for him to continue listening to TJ.

"We're also working on war-drones," TJ elaborated, "individual combat drones equipped with lasers and pyrotechnics." In the same cheerful voice, he added, "And they can deliver biological and other nerve agents, too."

"I think they've heard enough, TJ," Gretchen interrupted. "Thank you for your time."

"No problem. Nice meeting you, Governor." He stuck his hand out.

Shaking his hand, Kevin smiled his appreciation. "Where did you learn all this, TJ?"

"I learned it myself," he shrugged as though it was nothing unusual.

"TJ's a natural," Gretchen explained. "He's been teaching the others. With the lack of skilled computer and technology individuals, TJ's been invaluable."

"How old are you, son?" Don asked.

"Fourteen."

Don saw him bridle at the question. "I was going to ask why you weren't in school, but I see now it would be a waste of your time. If there's anything we can do to help you, you let me know. Gretchen knows how to get ahold of me."

TJ's demeanor immediately changed. "Thanks."

"Thank you again, TJ," Gretchen said. "If we can move back to my office, we can finish up there."

Standing outside the workshop, Kevin watched TJ walk back to give what looked like some guidance to a technician. "He seems a bit young to be in charge, don't you think? How do the older ones take having to report to a fourteen year old?"

"It has its challenges," Gretchen replied. "But it's like I said. The Corporation does its best to see that we don't get scientists or engineers or anyone else with a technological skill. We were fortunate in that one slipped in several years ago, a design engineer. TJ was born here. Between the two of them we've made some outstanding progress."

"What about the biological weapons?" Don asked. "Where'd we get that expertise?"

"We stole it," she grinned.

The walk back to the office didn't take as long as Kevin and Don expected and they were soon sitting in a large room with comfortable chairs and a couch with a blanket and a pillow indicating it doubled as a bed. Waiting until all were seated before she began, Gretchen scooted the chair around from behind her desk so that they were in a circle.

Directing her attention to Kevin, she said, "I asked you here today because we believe you and the remaining leadership need to be on board with our plans, especially as what we intend to do impacts directly on everyone living in the Zone."

"And what exactly do you intend to do?" Kevin queried, not sure he wanted to hear the answer.

"We're going to war," she simply replied.

There was a pregnant pause before Don asked the obvious question. "When?"

"September 1st."

Kevin's jaw dropped. "That's less than four months away."

"We'll be ready long before then," Maria vigorously intoned. "September 1st is the date we emerge from the cordon. Things will happen before then to help our success."

Inhaling a deep breath, Kevin's lips tightened. "OK. Instead of piecemealing it to me, give me the facts so I can make some sound decisions. I have the civilian population here to worry about. You know that once we attack, we will also be attacked. Have you thought about how we're going to care for the sick and wounded? We're short doctors as it is."

"We have," Gretchen answered. "Operation Delivery will greatly help."

"And that would be?"

"We kidnap doctors and nurses and bring them into the Zones."

Kevin sat back, astounded at the brashness of the plan. "And how do you intend on getting them in here, or any of the other Zones?"

"You let us worry about that," Maria countered. "We will make it happen. What else bothers you?"

Kevin sorted out the possible outcomes, none of them good. He gave voice to his thoughts. "We attack and they counter attack. We use bio weapons and they use bio weapons. Millions die on both sides. What's the end state?"

"The end state," Zoe gently replied, "is that we are no longer used as testing for Corporate profits. How many millions in the Zones have died so that some pharmaceutical company can make a profit? Our objective is to overthrow the Corporation, the conglomerate that rules the world. And it's not millions that will die. It's more likely billions. The world will be forever changed as we know it. But I'd rather die standing and fighting than cowering in fear that one day the Corporation will infect us all here and this Zone become one large graveyard."

As he listened, Kevin thought of other possibilities. He could simply alert Corporate and tell them what was happening here. But then he would be signing his own death warrant. They already sent someone here to kill him. Once he told them SI's plans, they would simply destroy the Zone. Either way, he was a dead man. His choice was now made for him. He had no other options but to stay the course and be the Governor he was elected to be.

"We'll need supplies," he said, his mind firmly made up, "food, water, things like that. We can store them here in this facility. We need to make plans for housing. When they attack, we need a secure place for survival. Have the other quadrants been brought up to speed?"

"They're having the same meeting right now," Gretchen answered.

His lips pursed, Kevin stood up. "We'd better get going. We've a lot of work to do. I'd like a complete briefing of your battle plan sometime this afternoon, up at my place."

"I'll come myself," Gretchen replied.

Retracing their steps, Kevin and Don were soon back in Don's car heading west on Fry Boulevard towards the old fort.

Back in the underground maze, Maria glanced up at Gretchen as they walked back to the main offices. "Why didn't you tell them we had tanks?"

"In due time," she calmly replied, "in due time."

Peachtree Road, NE, Atlanta

For two days they had waited and watched. During the day, they used small powerful mini-drones, each smaller than a hummingbird that relayed the view back to a large monitor, switching to thermovision cameras and optics in the evening. Martin taught JB how to use the joystick and control pad, managing three drones at once.

Whenever it was Martin's turn to watch, JB would sit and watch TV, spellbound, earphones jammed on his head to keep the noise and distraction down. Martin silently rued the mistake of showing JB how a TV works. The man was addicted. Once he showed him how to operate the remote, JB was nonstop channel surfing.

When JB had been told the purpose of their mission, he had initially balked. The thought of making someone dead, or 'killing' someone as Martin called it, was still difficult to process. When he asked who and why, Martin replied with a justification he could understand.

"They want to find Ruth and kill her. They want to do the same to you."

"But why do they want to kill us? We haven't done anything bad."

"That's just it," Martin countered. "It doesn't matter what you did or do. The only reason you were created was to be a body for someone else to use. You were never meant to be free, to be your own person. You were never meant to live beyond a certain time. That we rescued you has ruined their plans for you, and they will do anything and everything possible to get you back."

"So they can kill me?"

"Exactly."

JB struggled to understand why someone would go to such extremes just to kill someone who had done nothing wrong. But intrinsically, he knew he had to survive. He had to survive to protect Ruth.

Now, as he flicked through the channels, his mind was wandering as he paid scant attention to the screen. He wondered if he and Ruth could go off somewhere quiet to live, like the cabin Martin had taken him to. If they went there, no one would bother them and they could live together in peace. She could draw and he could do math or shoot the rifles.

"It's time," Martin announced.

JB turned the TV off leaving the room dark, except for the dull glow from the monitor. He strode over and pulled up a chair next to Martin. Gazing into the monitor, he saw their target, a well-dressed man walking purposefully down the sidewalk towards the granite steps of the luxurious high rise where he lived.

"Set up," Martin told him, moving out of the way so JB could position the Remington and bipod. Martin stood by the window and pulled back the curtains. "We want to take him just as he's going up the steps. Sight in and fire when you're ready... Then we get out of here as fast as we can."

JB took aim and fired just as the man lifted his leg for the first step. No sooner had he squeezed the trigger that the man lurched forward and crumpled onto the hard granite steps.

As soon as JB fired, he pulled the weapon back and Martin closed the window, quickly turning off the monitor. The room was completely dark.

"Pack it up, quickly," Martin urged, using a small pencil light to search for the spent cartridge.

They were in the waiting cab by the time the police arrived.

Pharr Court South, Atlanta

Linda had just pushed through the front door at her home when her earphone vibrated and launched into the soft office ringtone. "This is Linda," she answered, depositing the mail in the bureau in the hallway. She startled to a stop when she heard the news. Ending the call, she walked over to the kitchen bar, flicked the light on and fixed herself a stiff drink before slumping into the closest chair.

Sharon found her still seated and nursing her drink when she walked in fifteen minutes later. "What's wrong?"

"Collin Dodd's been assassinated," she stoically replied.

"O my god," Sharon blurted. "When?"

"About an hour ago."

"Where?"

"Just outside his penthouse building."

Sharon yanked a chair opposite Linda. Plopping down, she leaned forward, taking Linda's hands in hers. "Why are you sitting here still? We need to get back and take control of things."

"I was politely informed that Chuck Tilman was assuming temporary responsibility for affairs until a permanent replacement would be announced.

"Good god, not Tilman," she sputtered. "Whose stupid idea was this?"

"It doesn't matter," she sourly replied. "He was still at the office when it happened."

"Oh," Sharon gave a sigh of relief. "For a moment there you had me worried."

Linda gave her a wry smile. "It's good that he's temporarily in charge?"

"Of course. He doesn't have your organizational or management skills. I've studied him. He's one of those who surrounds himself with smart folks that make him look good. But he can't make a decision unless someone tells him what to

151

do." Then she giggled. "My guess is that if he was offered the job, he'd probably turn it down out of fear that what happened to Collin would happen to him."

Linda smirked, knowing there was some truth to what she said. "Might as well make some dinner. You pick up some wine?"

"Naturally," she smiled, pulling out an expensive red.

Linda's earphone rang again. Sharon watched as Linda's face morphed from resigned acceptance to calm self-confidence. Linda ended the call with, "Yes, sir. We're on our way."

"Well?"

"Well," she coolly replied. "You're now talking to the Executive Director of SEI.

"I knew it," Sharon clapped her hands with glee. "I knew they'd come to their senses soon enough."

"Well you can save your joy for later, Acting Director Walker. We have work to do. We'll get dinner on the way."

Sharon stared blankly at her. "Um… I'm just a branch manager."

"Not anymore," she briskly replied. "You are now the Acting Director of Interdiction Branch until I can make it official."

Her eyes blinking wide, she then pumped her fist, exclaiming, "Yes!" Seeing Linda's bemused smile, she sheepishly said, "Sorry." Rethinking her reply, she qualified it. "Actually I'm not sorry. I've wanted to follow in your footsteps ever since I came to the SEI directorate. This is better than I could ever have hoped for."

Linda reached up and gently caressed her cheek. "Me too." Part of her wished they could simply stay home and enjoy themselves, but promotion brought intensity of purpose. Corporate leadership would finally see the thoroughbred race horse they had in her… and in Sharon.

Leading the way to the front door, she began delegating. "The local police will want to interfere. They'll only muck it up. Get them out of the way so we can have clear action."

"Yes, Mam."

"You need to find your replacement, ASAP. Don't settle. Make your own choices. If you have questions about someone, talk to me."

When Linda walked into Collin Dodd's old office, Chuck Tilman jumped up from the chair behind the desk. "Thank god you're here," he sighed with relief. "While I'd love the pay raise, I don't want the headaches."

"Thanks for stepping in on such short notice, Chuck." She gave him a constrained smile, one that intimated she was in charge now.

Chuck was not slow on the recognition and he emerged from behind the desk. "The latest reports are on the desk. We're still searching likely areas of where the shooter might have been. Who's taking your spot?"

"Sharon Walker will be acting Director until I make it permanent."

"Good choice," he nodded in agreement. "She's a sharp one."

"She used to work in your branch," Linda coolly pointed out. "She'll now be your equal. You going to be OK with that?"

Chuck was no fool and he understood the implication. "Like I said, she's a sharp one. I'm sure we'll get along fine."

"Excellent, Chuck." Her shoulders settled as she relaxed. "I knew I could count on you. She's going to need help, so I'm depending on you and David to help her out."

Chuck walked out just as Sharon approached the office.

"Hullo Director Tilman." She flashed him a warm smile.

"You know you can call me Chuck, now," he said unconvincingly.

"That may take me a few days," she admitted. "I'm so glad you're still in charge of Subversion Branch," she gushed. "Not that you wouldn't have made an excellent Director," she quickly added. "But there is no one with your talents who could do the job you do."

Flattered despite the circumstances, he smiled back at her. "You are most kind. I look forward to working with you, Sharon, Director Walker."

She lightly placed a hand on his arm, an act that intimated appreciation for his words as well as kinship. Walking in to Linda's office, she closed the door behind her.

Chuck stood for a moment in the outer office, puzzling through Sharon's touch, sifting possible meaning. He already knew she and Linda had a thing going on. There was no law against that, though it did smack of being unprofessional. Still, their personal relationship outside of work didn't seem to get in the way of their conduct here. Sharon was the ever respectful subordinate. But her simple act of touching his arm connoted something more, and he wasn't quite sure of what it was. Yet there was something in the act itself that bothered him. Was it genuine, or was she playing a game?

And what was with the flattering comments? Until Linda moved her over to Induction Branch, Sharon had been a low level analyst in the Subversion Branch of SEI Division. He had had little contact with her, other than some rather excellent reports she had generated on Social Injustice. That she was a rising star was apparent, but to rise so quickly in such a short time? Was it luck or opportunity? And why Linda had chosen her was still a puzzle.

As he walked out of the outer office, down the hallways, down elevators then up elevators to his office in the other side of the vast building, he wondered if she warranted further analysis. Her personnel file had already been moved over to Interdiction Branch, so he would have to use other means to learn about his new peer.

SEI Directorate – Decatur
Wednesday, May 10, 2102

It was later that morning when the Acting Director of Interdiction Branch pushed the door open to the large office of the new Director of SEI. Sitting behind the desk, Linda Nadell looked up and smiled.

"How is the Director of Interdiction Branch doing today?"

"I'm just the acting Director," Sharon politely corrected with a wry smile.

"That will be corrected by today," she reassured her.

"I've some interesting developments in the Dodd assassination," she announced, approaching the desk. "I just sent the file."

Linda touched the monitor screen and scrolled to her inbox. The file contained a number of photos. She opened the first picture.

"The first photo shows Collin Dodd lying dead on the steps to the building of his penthouse. You'll notice that it was a head shot and that he fell forwards. Thus the shot was not from the sides, but directly behind him. The autopsy has given us the angle of entry through the head. He was shot with a rifle, a .308 caliber rifle. Interestingly, no one reported hearing anything like rifle shot."

"Whoever it was used a silencer," Linda surmised.

"We believe the same thing. The next photo gives you a view of the likely direction where the shooter was positioned."

Linda brought up the photo showing the city scene with buildings, pedestrians and traffic.

"Based on the line of sight and impact, we believe the shot was executed high up from the building, an apartment building, directly in line with the front of Dodd's penthouse complex… almost 800 meters away."

Linda's jaw dropped. "That would be one incredible shot."

"I know," Sharon agreed. "We're still searching the apartments and building, and the surrounding area. There's a vacant apartment on the tenth floor that is much too clean. That's my location of choice."

"What about street cameras and such?"

Sharon smiled knowingly. "That's where it gets interesting. The next pic shows two individuals emerging into an alley behind the apartment building, not long after Dodd was killed. Notice that one of them is carrying a long case. Though nondescript, it can hold a sniper rifle. Go to the next pic and you'll see the man carrying the case looks directly at the camera. Though it's dark we've been able to gain better clarity with the next picture."

Linda flipped to the next photo. "O my god," she exclaimed. "That's… that looks like a younger version of the Reverend Clayton." She snapped her head up to look at Sharon. "That's Clayton's clone!"

"I know.

"Who's the man with him?"

"We don't know. Shortly after they emerged from the alley, they got into a waiting taxi and sped off."

"Plates?"

"Fake."

Linda stared at the image on the screen. "Why would they expose a clone like that, especially belonging to someone like Clayton?"

"My team and I have given it some thought, and the best we can surmise is that they're training the clones for something. It's obvious that it wasn't the clone who made the shot. He's only been liberated for what, a week or so? There's no way he could learn to shoot in that short amount of time, let alone shoot like that. It's obvious the man with him is the one who took the shot."

"But that still doesn't explain why the clone was there. Why jeopardize your rescue by placing the very clone you rescued in danger?"

Sharon paused as if having an epiphany. "Unless you plan to use those same clones to mount an insurrection."

Linda furrowed her brow in doubt. "How many clones have been liberated in the past year?"

"With the twenty-seven busted out this last time, that adds up to almost 300."

"300 clones are not an insurrection," she adroitly pointed out.

"Not by themselves," she slowly replied. "There has been increased activity in the cordon zones. The areas outside the Birmingham Cordon have reported an uptick of robberies and assaults."

"Your point?"

"Connect the two somehow," she shrugged. "Use the clones as a rallying cry or something along those lines."

"Even if that were the case, it still doesn't explain exposing Clayton's clone to possible recapture."

Sharon paused a moment to ponder her words. "I've given that some thought. Of the clones so far that have been liberated, over half are clones of upper echelon Corporate employees. Now they've liberated one of Jefferson Beauregard Clayton's clones. The Reverend is extremely influential in the cloning industry. How about the scenario that they intend to substitute the clones for the real employees as well as Clayton? For example, you take Clayton's clone and drag him along with you. Expose him to the seamier side of life so when he is substituted, he can wreck the cloning industry."

"That one possibly makes more sense, though we haven't addressed the more serious question. Why take out Collin Dodd? It was obvious that he was the target. Why him?"

"And still, why was Clayton's clone there for the hit?" Sharon added. She looked back over her shoulder at the closed door. Turning around, she leaned forward. "I have another concern I think is important to raise."

"Oh?"

"Investigative Branch now has jurisdiction over Collin's assassination. Makes sense. Then why do we have to find out what happened using our own resources? When I asked them for any info on what happened, they gave me the run around."

"Territorial jealousy," Linda harrumphed.

Sharon frowned and stood back up. "You're probably right, but I just can't help thinking there's something else going on."

"You're being paranoid."

"That's what I get paid to be," she smiled.

Linda returned the smile. Her attention was diverted when a soft beep notified her of a personal message. Touching the screen to open the mail, she read through it then gave Sharon a confident smile. "You are now the permanent Director of Interdiction and Deception Branch."

"Thank you," she answered, her appreciation obvious.

"Also, we have been personally invited by the Vice-President for North America Security to a social gathering this evening at his place here in Atlanta."

"We?" she replied, startled.

"Yes, we. I'm sure he wants to meet the new Director of I & D Branch." Linda chuckled at Sharon's proverbial 'deer-in-the-headlights' stare. "You'll be fine."

"What do I wear?" she asked, almost a whine.

"We'll find something suitable," she soothed.

"What's he like?"

"Who?"

"Hans Josef, the Vice-president."

Linda thought for a moment, remembering the last time she met him. It was over a year ago at another social gathering at his home. Collin had brought her along because his wife was sick.

"He's… unique," she began. "Though he appears to be easygoing, almost casual, don't let that fool you. He's a shark.

If he feels you are not capable, he will destroy you. But at the same time, if you win his trust, he will take care of you. He's highly educated in the Renaissance sense. Knows a lot about a lot. Dresses well and is refined. Not a bad looking man either."

"Married?"

"No. And I don't know what his preferences are. Rumors have him going both ways, but that's really none of our concern. Let's just say you don't want to get on his bad side."

With a resigned sigh, Sharon slumped out of the office, much to Linda's amusement.

Linda turned her attention back to the various files in Collin's database. After several hours of reading, merging, deleting and saving various files, she was about to delete an 'Odd Junk' file when she decided to double check the contents. Perusing the numerous folders, she realized most were more than a year old. Then she discovered an 'Eyes Only' folder that had been accessed the day Collin died.

Clicking on the folder icon, the screen filled with the warning 'Access Restricted to Authorized Personnel. Need to Know Only." It then asked for login and password. Linda thought for a moment, remembering what she knew about Collin. The man lacked imagination. He did have one passion though – stamps, or 'philately' as he so often corrected those philistines too ignorant to understand the beauty of the study and collecting of those historic items.

Linda typed in 'philately' as the login. She paused for only a moment remembering the one time she had foolishly asked him which stamp he liked the best. It took her almost half an hour to extract herself from his animated and passionate, and thoroughly boring, discussion. Rolling her eyes at the memory, she typed in 'penny-red.'

The folder opened revealing several files. Starting with the oldest, which was less than a month ago, she opened the file. The bold red words 'Classified-Kilo, Restricted-B level' appeared at the top. She sucked in her breath realizing the level of classification was far beyond anything she had ever been granted. Gazing quickly around the room, she pressed the door-switch button on her desk, locking her door then flicked on the outside lighted sign stating 'Classified Briefing in Progress. Do not Enter or Disturb.'

"Blinds up," she commanded and the thin opaque sound-proof wall emerged from the floor in front of the windows. As the room darkened, ceiling lights grew in brightness.

Linda then began reading, noting that the restricted level of recipients and that Collin was not an addressee.

SUBJECT: Suspected Mole in SEI and/or Protection Services

1. *(K) The recent increased activity of Social Injustice indicates that they have gained access to privileged and restricted information only available to selected levels within the leadership of SEI and/or Protection Services. Specific instances such as the liberation during transfer of the clone for the Vice-President of Internal Affairs indicates compromise has occurred within at least one of the Branches identified.*

Stunned, Linda sat back, her mind racing as to the ramifications and possible suspects. She quickly read through the rest of the file as well as the remaining files, noting that the investigation's focus had switched to SEI alone. The final file was the most damning for it pointed to an individual in one of the leadership positions who had back-channel access to high level communication.

She blinked at the revelation. Collin Dodd had been a mole.

But the more she thought about it, the more confused she became. If Dodd was the mole, who took him out? All indications were that Social Injustice did the hit, but why would they do that and not bring him in instead? Taking out one of your own does little to instill trust and confidence in an organization.

Did the Corporation take him out? If so, why? The more she thought about it, the more she realized that it would be better for the Corporation to take him out and blame Social Injustice. Solve the problem by taking action and shifting the blame to someone else.

But there was that pesky problem of the photo of Beauregard's clone with the assassin. Did the Corporation liberate him to make the hit and then advertise his 'recapture' at a later time? Her frustration was that explanation made the most sense, and that bothered her. Her concern grew as she realized

159

she had few folks she could trust. Yet she needed someone to work through the conundrum. There was only one person she knew she could trust, but Sharon didn't have access privileges to the information.

Linda shook her head in the realization that neither did she have access privileges. Then the thought emerged that perhaps she was being tested, that this was some sort of twisted mind game to see if she was worthy. Should she report the presence of higher classified material without reading it, thus showing she was observant of law and regulations?

Or should she report it after reading it, demonstrating she was rightfully placed as the Executive Director of the Subversion, Espionage, Interdiction and Detection Division. After all, what good is a spy if one observes the rules?

Or should she leave it alone and not tell anyone?

With a sigh of frustration, she decided to wait on the course of action, leaving the folder where it was. Closing Collin's remaining files and folders, she turned off the sign outside her door and released the door locks. "Blinds down," she ordered. The room began to fill with outside light.

Rising out of her chair, she walked over to stand by the tall windows, distractedly gazing out over the skyline. She was still standing there when Sharon walked in.

"Everything OK?" Sharon asked.

Looking over her shoulder, she smiled at her protégé and confidant. "Everything's fine. What say we go find something to wear for tonight."

Social Injustice compound – East Point

JB and Ruth sat on the couch in front of the TV screen, hand-in-hand, enraptured with this amazing device.

"This is bigger than the one in the room where I was staying with Martin," he explained. "The one in the room there was much smaller."

Ruth felt the touch of his strong shoulder against hers, liking the feeling it gave her. Gazing up at him, she matter-of-factly asked, "Did you really kill a man?"

"Yes," he replied, not quite understanding why he felt like he did. Part of him was glad he killed a man who wanted to take him back just to be killed. Another part felt sad that he had to do it, especially in the way he did, far away so that the man didn't even know it was coming. But then, that was the same way they did it to all of them, the ones who they took away to take their brains out.

"Did you like doing that?" She saw the turmoil and frown on his face.

"I'm not sure." He heaved a sigh. "Part of me says that I had to do it because he was a bad man and wanted to send us all back to have our brains taken out and we'd all be dead just like him. I don't understand why anyone wants to kill someone else. Why do they make us and then kill us? It's not right."

"I don't think it's right either," she agreed. "Suppose someone came here to hurt you. I would do my best to stop them even if it meant killing them."

JB gazed affectionately at her. "And I would do the same for you. I want to be with you all the time."

"You just about are," she teased. "I like sleeping with you and doing it whenever we want. No lab assistants telling us 'no' or coming in and sending me back to my room. I've got pencils and pens of so many different colors and plenty of paper. I can draw whatever I want. I'm learning how to draw and design things they call blueprints. It's fun. This is what I've dreamed about. I will not let anyone take it away from me ever again. I will die first."

JB pondered her words. "I suppose that is why they have taught me to do what I did. Martin said we are in a war against the evil of the Corporation."

"What does that mean?"

"I'm not completely sure," he lamely shrugged. "Martin said there are lots and lots more people like us. He said they call us clones, which means we're a physical copy of someone else. But he said that was the only thing the same, because we have our own minds and will."

"What's a 'will'?"

"I don't know. He said it had something to do with getting to choose what we want to do by ourselves, with no one else making the choice for us. He said it also meant having a real life, not to be killed so someone else can use our body."

Ruth pursed her lips as she thought about her past, the time before coming here. "They wanted to give our bodies to someone else," she tersely said. "That's wrong. Someone needs to stop them from doing that."

"I think that's why we're here," he quietly answered. He toggled the remote, flicking through channels before settling on one with a group of well-dressed people.

It was the mid-afternoon Corporate channel with the panel of pundits pontificating on world affairs and events. The moderator, an attractive woman in a high collar business suit, sat in the middle of the round table with four experts surrounding the remaining portion of the table. The camera focused in on her cheery face.

"Good afternoon and welcome to another edition of 'Chatterbox,' the weekly show where we ask the viewers and TV audience to ask those questions they've always wanted answers for. I'm Wendy O'Brien. Today we are privileged to have four guests who have traveled all the way from the Corporation headquarters in Antwerp. With us are Bill Kemp, Martine Chu, Shelley Cochran and Konrad Wilder." The camera paused as each guest was introduced and smiled into the camera.

"So good of you all to be here today. Alright then panel, the first question is from Jim in Tulsa Oklahoma. Let's put it on the screen behind me." The words flashed up on a dark screen behind her while she looked down to the flat monitor in the table. "Jim asks," she read aloud, "Why doesn't the Corporation have a military?"

"That's an easy one, Jim," Shelley, a matronly, self-assured woman immediately spoke up. "Let's look at our society. First, all former international borders are now transnational. This has effectively eliminated the need for conflict as has been so prevalent in our past. Secondly, the supra-corporate model of government transcends national identity. What I mean by that is that we all belong to the Corporation. In a sense we are all employees of the government. Thus, there is no longer a need for military hardware like planes and tanks and battleships. We disbanded the military decades ago and look at the fiscal savings we've incurred."

"But what about the Cordon Zones," Wendy pointed out. "Surely we need a military for things like that."

"I think Shelley has already made the point of Corporate government and the need for a military," Konrad, an older man with short hair and a receding hairline sagaciously said. Though he spoke with the hint of a German accent, his English was erudite and academic. "The forces that monitor the Cordon Zones are nothing more than an extension of the police. They are security guards and nothing more. My esteemed colleague, Shelley, has adeptly pointed out that maintaining a military in this day and age is not only superfluous, but an unnecessary expense that would accomplish nothing."

"Besides," added Shelley, "The Cordon Zones are more than adequately fenced and controlled. Think of how long the Zones have been there. – over 50 years. And what have been the results of quarantining society's undesirables? We've have over 50 years of progress, safety, and security. So, to be more direct to Jim's question, we don't have a military because a well-regulated society like the one we have now has no need of a military."

Wendy looked at the other two and asked, "Anyone else?" When they both shook their head 'no,' she proceeded to the next question. "Abby in Winnipeg asks, 'How is the Corporation form of government any better than the other forms of government?' OK, who wants to take a shot at that first? Konrad."

"Yes, thank you. History has repeatedly and consistently shown us that government, whether socialist, democratic, or monarchal, is both inept and incapable of fiscal responsibility and management. The classic example is that of this very part of the world where this broadcast is being held, the former United States. What was once the most powerful nation in the world, essentially borrowed its way out of existence. The astronomical national debt could no longer be sustained and when China and other creditor nations called in the debts in order to pay off their own fragile economies, the result was a global meltdown."

"Some of us are old enough to remember the Global Disorder of 2037," Bill, a handsome young man barely in his twenties, interrupted. When he saw the skeptical response on Wendy's face, he explained, "I had a rebirth about a year ago."

"Ah," she smiled in understanding. "You look wonderful. So tell us, how old were you when you had your rebirth?"

"This last one was my second. I was forty-five when I had the first one, and fifty one for this last one."

"How old does that make you in terms of actual years?" she asked, marveling at the man's youth.

"Seventy-five," he sheepishly grinned. "I just had a birthday."

Smiling wisely at the camera, Wendy said, "There you have it folks, the benefit of rebirth. But let's get back to Abby from Winnipeg's question. Martine, I believe you were going to add something."

"Yes, thank you Wendy." Martine was a petite and very pretty black haired woman of mixed Vietnamese and French heritage. "What I wanted to say was that the essential problem with a system where an electorate, the majority of which is poor, is that it expects the government to provide for them. The result is that a disproportionate amount of income is diverted to providing basic living needs to an equally disproportionate population that lacks the requisite skills to be a benefit to society. Businesses can't, and don't, operate that way. A good business makes money, which in turn provides for its employees."

"But some say that a business model isn't the right form for a government," Wendy replied. "For example, many felt the former United Nations was never given the chance to succeed. What are your thoughts there, Shelley?"

"A noble, though a misguided and mismanaged cause," Shelley answered. "First, the very thought that a collective organization, effectively controlled by the five nations of the Security Council, could somehow solve the world's economic and political problems was patently absurd. Not only was it glaringly ineffective in preventing wars and famine, it was a contributing factor to the Global Disorder of '37."

"How so?"

"By the time the UN folded, there were 216 member nations, of which the overwhelming majority were third world. Though the UN was established as some sort of egalitarian group, the poorer nations demanded their fair share of the global wealth from the first tier nations, even though the poorer nations did nothing to contribute to that wealth. The first tier nations, out of some sort of liberal collective guilt decided to acquiesce and thus diverted trillions of dollars... I should say, wasted trillions of dollars, by artificially pumping up corrupt regimes who subsequently squandered the resources. The result? The only thing that changed was the number of poor, which continued to increase."

"So how is the Corporation any different?"

"There is a significant difference. Remember what Martine said a little bit ago. A good business not only makes a profit, it provides for its employees. That was the essential failing of all the other types of governments. They never considered profit a good thing and could not provide for their citizens. If we view the individual as an employee rather than a citizen, you can begin to see the difference. The government took on the responsibility of providing for the citizen when he contributed nothing for his support. In contrast, the corporation employee knows that he must contribute to the success, or profit, of the business. If he doesn't, he is let go and another fills his place."

"That's why we are all now employees of the Corporation, rather than citizens of a particular nation," Bill interrupted.

"But not everyone can be an employee. There are only so many jobs and positions available," Wendy pointed out.

"Quite true. This is the classic case of Social Darwinism. The strong, or in this case, the qualified, survive. Those without the requisite skills are eliminated."

"Some would argue that this is unfair."

"Only to those who lack the necessary skills," he countered. "Remember, all are afforded the opportunity, yet not all take advantage of those opportunities."

"Doesn't that lead to increased crime and disease?" Wendy asked. "Especially those who are disenfranchised because of their lack of skills for a job?"

"There are still jobs for those with minimum qualifications, though they are few. With the advances in technology, low skilled jobs are growing scarcer. Take the fast food industry for example. When was the last time you gave your order to an actual living person? Now, you use a touch screen to place your order, scan your bank card to pay for it, and wait for delivery via neatly packaged bag that is gently pushed out the receiving belt. You even get your own drinks. Back in the kitchen, everything is computerized, even the cooking. What used to be an operation of thirty to forty individuals is now reduced to perhaps six to seven."

"But," Wendy pointed out, "that still doesn't address the crime and disease issues."

"I think Bill makes an excellent point about Social Darwinism," Martine interjected. "Those without the requisite skills are eliminated, whether through disease or crime. And if you will indulge me for a moment, let's consider crime. Because the Corporation has been consistent in its application of the law, we have an extremely low incidence of crime. Yet the occasional crime does occur and we treat it appropriately. If you steal, your dominant hand is branded and tattooed as a warning to all. You steal again and you are executed. Violent crime is treated with violent justice. You hurt someone? You receive your just rewards."

"Executed," Wendy added.

"Exactly," Martine sagely nodded. "Now I need to point out here that those sent to the Cordon Zones are usually convicted of what was once called 'white collar' crimes, things like tax evasion, insider trading and so on. And of course there are those parents sent there for the crimes of their children. But what most people fail to realize is that the Corporation has done those in the Zones a huge favor by eliminating the depraved and reprobate from society, so they would not end up in the Zones. Of course, one must realize that being sent to the Zones in the first place is an indication of the character to the individual. Thus, we see the devolution to depravity that is the norm in the Zones. The important thing here is to ensure that society's problems are kept far away from the rest of the productive society."

"So you would agree with the cordoning off of troubled areas," Wendy calmly stated.

"Of course. The Corporation is in the business of business. We take excellent care of our employees. So much so that employees like Bill here can take advantage of rebirth. The Corporation recognizes his skill-set and provides incentive for continued success."

"How many employees would you guesstimate the Corporation has?" Wendy asked.

"While I can't give you an exact figure, I'd be safe in stating that close to two-thirds of the world's population is an employee of the Corporation."

"Leaving one-third with no means of survival," Wendy calculated. "That's around one to two billion. Some would argue that we have a responsibility to care for those unfortunate souls."

"And that would be yielding to those same fatal emotional flaws that destroyed every other governmental system," Konrad firmly replied. "No government, no matter the form, can take care of all its citizens all the time. We in the Corporation recognize that. That's why we cut potential losses before they become losses. Those unfortunate to be living in places like the mid-west States are not our concern. It is our wish that they die, and die quickly so as not to be a burden on the rest of society."

"That's rather harsh, don't you think?" Wendy cocked an eyebrow in feigned self-righteousness.

"Hardly," he shot back. "What gives them the right to demand that they be given something for nothing?"

"Surely there has to be some form of work they can do," she said. "Building roads, cleaning up trash, things like that."

"Why?" Bill objected. "We have technology that takes care of things like that. Let's face it. Those individuals or families who live in cordoned zones are there for a reason. They didn't measure up. Human nature teaches us to get rid of things that don't measure up. Natural selection also plays a part. Notice where all the diseases tend to originate. That's right, in the cordoned areas."

"But your own DMI is the acknowledged leader in disease research and management. The late bio-engineer Bernard Dennett was himself responsible for a number of cures. If that's the case, how can you say that the cordoned zones are of no concern?"

"I didn't say they were of no concern," Bill replied. "DMI's research has been most beneficial in so many zones. Disease management is but one of them. Doctor Bennett was a gifted bio-engineer, to be sure. But he was only one of many talented bio-engineers. Already his replacement is making a strong contribution to the organization. The cordoned zones provide the necessary environment to find cures for diseases, some that might never have occurred until years later. But don't forget, DMI has also been instrumental in the rebirth process, discovering processes and methodologies to make rebirth a less traumatic experience. But let's get to the root of the matter.

DMI is in the business to make a profit and they do it quite well."

"I want to return to Abby from Winnipeg's question for a moment," Martine interrupted. "She asked why the Corporation form of government is better than other forms of government. The very fact that she can ask that question tells me she is an employee of the Corporation.   As such, her benefits are outstanding. Not only does she receive a salary commensurate with her skills, she has vacation time, free medical, dental and vision services, an excellent retirement package should she ever choose to retire, and if she manages her money wisely, she can rebirth herself as many times as she wants.. Done right, she could be living the high life for hundreds and hundreds of years." She paused to gaze into the camera. "What other form of government provided this? The Corporation doesn't tell her where to live or to shop, what car or clothing to buy or whom to marry. The citizen, or employee, has more freedom under the Corporation than man has experienced under any other government."

"An excellent discussion," Wendy smiled benignly. "Let's move on to the next question."

Ruth looked at JB. "Does rebirth mean using our bodies?"

"I think so."

"So they just keep making more of us to use whenever they want."

"That's what it sounds like to me too."

Her face hardening, she turned back to the TV. "Maybe they'll teach me how to use a gun."

Resurrection Industries, Tucson Facility
Tucson, Arizona

The Reverend Jefferson Beauregard Clayton studied his younger self through the one-way window. He liked what he saw. The clone was even better than he imagined – strong, virile and obviously handsome. He chuckled as he stared at the clone's face, remembering that he at one time had light blond hair. That would change as soon as he was cleared to have the hairdresser come in and adorn him with his infamous bright orange tinged in blue coiffure. That trademark had already made an impact as numerous imitators vainly tried to copy him, down to the hairdo. But they were all amateurs, dilettantes. There could only be one top dog, and it was him.

Yet he had to admit that, even being the most admired religious leader in the world, he was still a little nervous. It wasn't every day one shuffled off the outer body to emerge as a newer younger self. It reminded him of the imagery of the butterfly. In fact, he liked the symbolism so much that the latest logo branding had merged an angel with butterfly wings.

"What do you think, Boss?" Jeremy asked.

The Reverend turned to the assembled doctors and executives from both the Clayton Crusades and Resurrection Industries, and grinned. "I say let's get this show on the road. Time's a wasting."

"You're in good hands," he lead physician reassured him.

"I'm counting on it, Doc. I'm told you Docs here in Tucson are just about the best in the world."

"We pride ourselves being on the cutting edge of the latest in medicine," the physician warmly replied. "We have the leading physicians worldwide at our facility. You'll find none better."

"That's what I like to hear," he grinned.

"If you wish," another physician said, "we can take clone samples from him now, freeze them and when you're ready, we can fertilize them."

"I thought there were problems with that procedure, something about the freezing process," he frowned.

"That was several years ago, Reverend. We've made magnificent strides since then. Besides, you can still clone yourself after your rebirth."

Beauregard titled his head at the response, nodding with a self-satisfied smug. "I like it."

"How many would you like?"

"How about ten?"

"Ten?" came the startled reply.

Beauregard quickly surveyed the group. "Is that too few?"

"No, Reverend. The normal is two to three."

"Two to three?" he sneered. "That's for poor trash, and I'm not poor trash," he pointedly emphasized.

"Certainly not, Boss," Jeremy readily agreed. "You about ready?"

"Yeah. I think so." With a sweep of the hand, he commanded, "Lead the way."

As the Reverend was escorted away to be prepped for surgery, clone D107A45B was told that his time in the facility was over and that he was now going to begin a new life. Overjoyed at the prospects of life outside the walls of the facility, D107A45B readily allowed himself to be given a final round of tests, the first of which was a vitamin shot to strengthen him for the journey. The last thing he heard was "Relax. Your next journey is about to begin."

391 West Paces Ferry Road, Atlanta

Linda and Sharon stood in the portico of the impressive home of Hans Josef, the tall Doric columns towering above them. The door opened and a liveried butler escorted them in. They could hear music and the chatter of many voices beyond the closed double doors across the foyer from them.

"May I announce your presence?" the butler politely inquired.

"Linda Nadell and Sharon Walker," Linda replied.

"Please wait here." He crisply spun around and, strode across the foyer and pushed open the doors to the large reception room that was buzzing with conversation and attention seekers. Some waiters carried trays filled with champagne, cocktails, and wine while others carried empty trays, filling them up with empty glasses. The butler disappeared but soon returned with a suavely dressed gentleman in a sport coat and open collar shirt. His wavy black hair was combed straight back and he sported a neatly trimmed Vandyke.

"Linda," he warmly greeted her, his arms wide as he approached. Giving her a light buss on both cheeks, he turned his attention to Sharon. "So this is the rising star of the SEI division," he charmingly stated.

"Hans," Linda deferentially said, "This is Sharon Walker."

"Yes, I know," he grinned, his teeth perfect. "I've heard quite a bit about you." Holding his elbow out for them each to take an arm, he charmingly continued as he led them into the noisy room. "You must tell me all about yourself. No secrets now, n'cest pas?"

"Mais oui, monsieur."

Hans brightened. "Vous parlez français?"

"Oui, monsieur."

"Ah! C'est magnifique!"

Linda felt abruptly odd man out as the two engaged in an animated conversation, all in French. As they entered the main room Chuck Tilman approached and Hans handed Linda off to him while he and Sharon continued their conversation, in French, as they made their way through the crowd, pausing to stop by a beautifully crafted gnathian skyphos set in a recessed panel in the wall.

Sharon saw it and was immediately thrilled. "That's beautiful. 4th century I'd say."

"Ah, Miss Walker, you are familiar with my little trinkets of antiquities?" Hans smiled with pleasure. He gently touched her arm.

"I'd say they were a passion of mine, and I've collected a few, but this is a stunning piece." She quickly gazed around the room to see the walls and display cases filled with antiquities from around the world. Marble statues adorned low pedestals around which guests stood imbibing their drinks, impervious to the history that surrounded them. "You have a collection here worthy of the finest museum."

"Ah, ma chère Sharon, you are most kind." He again delicately touched her arm. Turning his gaze upon her, he asked, "How is it that you have no clone yet?"

"Pardon?"

"Forgive me," he suavely replied. "I do realize that was a bit of a detour. I asked, why is it that you have no clone as of yet?"

"Oh," she smiled innocently. "I decided to wait until I was thirty-five. I think rebirthing when one is in his or her forties is too soon. Why, the forties is the prime of life. If I wait until I'm thirty-five, when I'm fifty-five I'll have the body of a twenty year old again. And then I'll decide from there what age to do it again."

"An interesting answer," he nodded appreciatively. "And you'll be thirty-five in three years."

Smiling coquettishly, she leaned closer in to him. "I see someone's been doing his homework."

Hans laughed lightheartedly and clapped his hands.

Watching the interaction, Linda felt the twinges of jealousy, wondering desperately what they were discussing and resenting the attention he was giving Sharon. Hans had never showered her with the same attention.

"She appears to have tamed the beast already," Chuck observed, much to Linda's annoyance. "I don't wonder they're talking about us probably."

"Think I'll get something to eat," she mumbled, making her way to the lavishly apportioned tables where mounds of exotic foods stretched from one end to the other.

Chuck followed along and stood before the culinary display. Most of the foods he didn't recognize. Fortunately there were little placards advertising each delicacy. "What the hell is lark's tongue in aspic?" he whispered to no one. Moving along the length of the table, he found even more delicacies of doubtful interest. Realizing there was little there to satisfy his grumbling stomach, he mumbled to himself, "When I leave here, I'm going to find me some good dead cow, ground into a fine hamburger with a slab of cheddar cheese and crispy bacon on top."

"Can I come?" a voice to his side quietly asked.

Looking guiltily to his right, he smiled when he saw Tony Barnes, the Director of Signals Intelligence Branch, with the same look of disdain.

"How's the SIGINT world these days?" Chuck amiably said.

Tony cast a quick look around before answering in a low voice, "A lot better than the food here."

Chuck snorted a laugh. "Be happy to spot you a pint at Johnny's Pub when we're through here."

"You're on," he readily answered.

While Chuck and Tony chatted, Linda moved away to absentmindedly try some of the dishes while her mind struggled to make sense of Hans' fascination with Sharon. Her foul mood increased with the more time Hans spent with Sharon. She was on her fourth glass of champagne when the two finally approached, Sharon's arm wrapped in his.

"Ah, here you are," Hans announced as though discovering Linda for the first time. Unhooking himself from Sharon, he affectionately said, "Ma chère, would you mind if I talk to your boss for a while?"

"Of course not, Hans," she politely, yet with a hint of intimacy, replied. "I haven't had the chance to try any of the food yet." Excusing herself, she approached Chuck and Tony who were still in conversation.

Chuck looked up when he saw her approach. "Finally able to extract yourself, eh? He can be a charmer."

"An absolutely wonderful man," she said. "And this house is beautiful, and so well kept, especially for being over 100 years old."

"How do you know that?" Tony asked.

"This used to be the governor's mansion until about forty years ago, when the Corporation took over. It was falling apart until Hans bought it, I think about ten years ago."

"Hans?" Chuck raised an eyebrow at the overt familiarity of someone who had been a Director for all of two days. It had been over a year before he had the nerve, and permission, to call the Vice President by his first name.

"Yes, Hans," she replied wondering what the big deal was.

Hans and Linda watched the exchange among the three directors within SEI. Hans reached for a passing glass of champagne.

"Come then, Linda. Let's walk and talk, shall we?" He motioned her to one of the side rooms. "She's a sharp woman. Very impressive."

"Yes she is," she half-heartedly agreed.

"Now, now," he soothed. "Don't worry. She didn't betray you."

"Excuse me?" she replied, startled.

Hans chuckled. "Perhaps that was a poor choice of words. What I meant to say is that she is more than a loyal subordinate, doing her best to protect you. She is, in fact, quite fiercely loyal to you. She impresses me as the type of person who would take a bullet for you, part out of devotion, but the other out of responsibility for protecting a superior. You have chosen well here, but you must watch her."

"Why is that?" she asked, somewhat relieved.

"She's ambitious, almost to a fault. However, she is not one who will step over others to get what she wants. She is a rare individual who believes in the symbiotic nature of success. Your success is hers, just as hers is yours."

Linda nodded, but remained silent, listening.

Hans noted the body language and gently touched her arm. "I know all about your shared affections. You have nothing to fear from me. She is a wonderful woman, but I fear she will break your heart."

"Why?" she creased her brows, wondering what he knew that she didn't.

"There will come a time when she will move on, perhaps even move away."

"I don't understand," she said. "I realize she has her own life and career –"

"What I mean is," he interrupted, "is that with her background and language skills, she maybe of better use in the Hague."

Linda blinked at the revelation. She had known about Sharon's language skills; they were listed in her records, but as Sharon had never made much of them, neither did she. Still, she knew that at some time, one of them would move on, and she hoped it would be her moving up to an executive director position somewhere. But she was not ready to lose Sharon, not yet. There was still so much to do, to share.

Hans watched Linda sorting the future. "Now, now," he again soothed. "You can stop worrying. It won't happen for a while. She still needs nurturing and guidance. I expect you to give her everything she needs."

The point was direct. Linda understood immediately what was expected of her. Linda was grooming her to higher levels of responsibility… which meant that Linda herself was marked for higher position.

Hans smiled when he saw her visibly relax. "I'm glad you understand. You two make an excellent team. Your challenge is to get those other dinosaurs in your division to think the same way as you two do. By the way, just between you and me, there's talk of my moving to another location, probably Caracas, as the CEO of Intel Operations for the Western Hemisphere."

"Congratulations," she politely offered.

"Yes," he mused. "Thank you. When that happens, I'll need to sell this place. Hate to leave it, but the next Vice-President for North American National Security ought to live in

174

an appropriate residence, don't you think?" He stared intently at her.

His intimation suddenly becoming clearer, Linda felt light headed. "Absolutely," she earnestly replied, wanting to ask how soon this all would happen while concomitantly going through her finances to see if she could afford the place.

"I'm so glad we understand one another. I ask that you keep our little secret between us, not even to Sharon. Understood?"

"Yes, of course, whatever you wish," she almost gushed.

Hans chuckled then said, "You'll need to begin learning all that I do. I'll start sending 'Eyes Only' material for you. Secure or destroy it appropriately."

"Yes, sir."

"And as far as Miss Walker is concerned, train her for increased responsibilities, knowing she'll most likely be sent to the Hague. Use this time to your advantage. It always helps to have friends in the global headquarters."

"That bring ups another concern," she ventured.

"Oh?"

"I came across a folder in Collin's files."

Instead of answering, Hans gave her a wry smile.

"I discovered it was classified at a higher level than I have access to."

"So what did you do?" he nonchalantly inquired.

Linda took a breath and said, "I opened it."

Hans broke out into a broad smile. "Good girl. I knew you'd do the right thing. That was Collin's problem, too by the book. A good intel chief always reads other people's mail."

"Speaking of Collin," she said, greatly relieved she had passed the test. "Did the content of those messages have anything to do with him?"

"Good heavens, no," he flipped his hand dismissively. "I sent those messages, as a test. Where he failed, you passed."

"But he did read them," she pointed out.

"Well then," he chuckled, "I guess he didn't fail. Of course, it's all rather moot now."

"So there is no mole in SEI?"

Hans grew abruptly somber. "I didn't say that."

"But you just said –"

"What I said was that Collin was not the guilty party. One must always assume there is at least one individual you must carefully watch."

"Anyone in particular?"

Oh," he airily replied, "I leave that to you. You decide. Have fun with it."

Linda carefully regarded him. The man was a puzzle. "So the hit was not a Corporation sanctioned hit?"

"No," he coyly answered with a smile. "But I like the way you think. You're going to do very well here, Linda. Be sure to remind me to tell you where all the little secret places are in the house here before you move in." He gave her a wink. "Shall we get back to the party?"

Chapter 6

SEI Directorate – Decatur
Thursday, May 11, 2102

Linda read the message for the third time, making sure she comprehended the ramifications. Titled 'Operation 40 Trucks', she vainly tried to understand the title and the mission. Still, while the title might be confusing, the mission was not. Operation 40 Trucks called for the compete annihilation and destruction of all the cordon zones in the western hemisphere on September 1. Wanting further validation she called Hans.

When his calm visage appeared on the monitor she asked, "Can you go secure?"

"Naturally." The screen temporarily scrambled then resumed its clear picture.

"I have a question concerning 'Operation 40 Trucks,'" she explained.

"Ah yes," he nodded wisely. "A rather humorous label, don't you think?"

"I don't understand the name at all," she replied, "but that wasn't why I called."

"You're wondering if it's true," he answered. "Don't feel bad. You're not the first person to have called me about this. And to answer your question, yes, it is true."

"That's only four months from now."

"I know."

"That kind of makes my efforts to infiltrate Social Injustice irrelevant, doesn't it?"

"I suppose it does," he benignly answered. "However, don't cease operations just yet. We'll make that call the closer we come to initiation day. You never know, things may change or get delayed."

"There's nothing in the order concerning my field agents or SEI operations," she repeated. "Can I alert my Branch chiefs?"

Hans' calm demeanor tightened. "Are they on the distribution?"

"No."

177

"Then you have your answer. If they were to be informed, they would have been on the distribution."

"Yes, sir," she replied, chastised. Wanting to end on a positive note, she asked, "What about the title? What does it mean?"

Hans snorted a laugh. "Don't feel bad. I had to ask too. The chief of operational titles was a former military man. He explained that whenever one came to a question of great significance, the fall back answer was always '40 Trucks.' It's supposed to be humor. Sort of ironic don't you think?"

"Ironic?"

"Yes. Our final solution is reduced to 40 trucks. In other words, the answer to our problems is a simple one."

"Yes, sir," she unconvincingly agreed.

"Anything else?"

"No. That answers my questions. Thank you."

"You're welcome. By the way, how is our favorite darling Sharon working out?"

"As expected," she answered without hesitation.

"Good, good. Well then, I leave you to it."

The screen turned blank and Linda turned off the secure mode.

An hour later, the three Directors sat in the Executive Director of SEI's office as she stonily listened to Chuck's explanation of what happened. Though listening to his commentary, with the usual 'it's not my department's fault' editorial, Linda understood why Chuck Tilman had not been selected to become the Executive Director of SEI. The man was more concerned with saving his own ass than thinking outside the box. At least Jon Veldt, the Espionage Director had that going for him.

Jon was a good looking younger man, though that wasn't quite correct. He was physically younger, having had his rebirth several years ago, but his brain was probably in his mid-fifties. A charmer, he was a natural for the world of spying. Fortunately for her, he had no aspirations greater than where he was. Espionage was his world and the last thing he wanted was to move beyond that.

While Chuck droned on, she wondered whether she had been promoted because she was a talented go-getter or because there was no one else. Not liking her assessment, she interrupted Chuck's monologue and sourly said, "Let's cut to the chase. When did Warfield come in?"

"About two days ago," Jon replied.

"Why?"

"He believed he'd been compromised."

"Why did he think that?"

"Because," Jon replied, casting a sly glance at Chuck, "someone sent the handler in too soon."

"We did just like we were supposed to," Chuck defended himself. "How were we supposed to know they would mimic our handler? Besides, you should have used one of your own agents."

"Save it," Linda snapped. "If you two boys can't get along, I'll find someone who can." Shifting her gaze to Sharon, who sat absorbing the dynamics, she asked, "What's your take on this?"

Sharon was silent for a moment then said, "I think they knew all along he was a plant."

"What makes you think that?" Jon asked, already impressed with her acumen.

"There just wasn't enough of a cover story for him and it was going to eventually fall apart, especially after they found out Billy Fish had been dead for a while. Warfield had to get in and out quickly before he was compromised. But more to the present, I think our tailing him alerted them to the possibility. After all, if we knew he was meeting Dwa in the Vanishing Point, why didn't we just go in and take them all when we had the chance? They would have reasoned the same thing, which meant Warfield was a stooge for the Corporation. My guess is that they've already moved their operations to another site."

"Very good," Jon smiled.

Returning his smile, she looked to Linda. "Director Nadell, I think there's a bigger problem here."

"Oh?" Linda raised an eyebrow.

"Yes. It's the overlapping of responsibilities and functions within the organization. For example, Chuck is in charge of Subversion while Jon here has Espionage. In this operation, Jon is responsible for counter-espionage, which means he has the assets to conduct the operation solely within Espionage. He could have sent some of his people to the safe house. It's not like there was anything extraordinary about Warfield and his insertion. Yet Chuck, for some reason, was tasked to supply assets to get inside the safe house."

"That's the way it's always been done," Chuck loftily said.

"That doesn't make it right," she pointed out. "I'm not saying it's necessarily wrong either. It's just that our response time is too slow. Warfield is back and we're no closer to finding out who and where they are."

"Don't you have someone else infiltrating?" Linda asked Jon.

"We do, but he's an obvious plant."

Linda gave him a quizzical look. "Why? Isn't that foolish?"

"It could be. Our hope is that they see him for the dupe he is and fill him with all sorts of false information."

"That doesn't make any sense," Chuck frowned.

"But it does," he countered with a smile. "Remember back in World War Two when the allies were planning the invasion of Normandy. How much effort did they put in trying to convince the Germans that the attack would come across Calais or via the south of France? There were German leaders and analysts who correctly saw the lack of supposed attention given to Normandy. When Rommel took command of the defense of northwestern Europe, he wisely began emplacing obstacles and fortifications along the Normandy coast before his, um… untimely demise. The point here is that we analyze what they give us and use to our advantage."

"Thank you for the history lesson," Chuck scoffed, "but I fear it will be a waste of time."

"Let me be the judge of that," Jon calmly replied.

"What are you going to do about Warfield?" Linda asked, regaining control of the discussion.

"He can't stay here. He's still a viable agent, so I'm thinking he may be of use in one of the cordon zones. I'll probably send him out to the one in Sierra Vista."

"Sierra Vista? Arizona?" Linda ticked her head to the side. "Why there?"

'There's been some increased activity and we've lost several agents. We need a fresh face there, someone from outside the area."

Uttering a sigh that said she'd had enough, Linda thought for a moment then said, "OK. I want individual briefs from each of you. Ten minutes to sum up what you're doing and expected outcomes." She shifted her gaze between Sharon and the two men. "I'll start with Sharon first. I'll let you know when I'm ready for you."

Taking the cue, the two men stood up and walked out of the office, Jon closing the door behind them.

"Sharon's too far up her butt for her own good," Chuck snidely observed.

"Be careful," Jon gibed. "She might be your boss someday."

"I'll retire before I let that happen," he huffed. "You'd be OK with her as a boss?"

Jon gave him an indifferent shrug. "She's a smart one and takes care of those with whom she works, both above and below. Besides, Linda's in charge and it'll be a while before that changes."

"That's not what I heard," he quietly said.

"I don't want to know," Jon replied, holding up his hands. "Rumors are bad enough when the enemy does them. We don't need them here."

Chuck flashed him a look of annoyance. "You going to hang out here?"

"Might as well. I'm sure Nina here," he smiled at Linda's secretary, a pert and pretty brunette staring at the middle of three monitors on her desk, "has some excellent coffee around here somewhere."

"Help yourself, Mister Veldt," she grinned without looking up.

Inside the office Linda confided to her closest friend. "I'm grooming you to take my place. It may happen sooner than you think."

"Where are you going?" Sharon's plaintively asked, her expression betraying her disappointment.

"It's not as bad as you think," she smiled. "What I'm about to tell you is in the strictest confidence. Can you keep a secret?"

Instead of answering, she simply shook her head and smiled.

"Hans has informed me that he has been tapped to take over as the CEO of Intel Operations for the Western Hemisphere."

"Really," she said, impressed. "He's a good ally to have."

181

"Yes," she nodded.   "When that happens, it will leave a vacancy in the Vice-President for North American National Security position."   She paused for effect.

Sharon's eyes widened in glee as her mouth gaped open. "You mean…"

"It's not official.   Nothing's official, but there's talk."

Sharon flopped back in her chair.   "This is the best news I've heard in a long time."

"Better than you being promoted to my position?"

Her eyes fluttered at the revelation.   "Me?   But Chuck and Jon are far senior to me," she pointed out the obvious.

"Yes, well, they have been promoted to their level of potential.   Chuck is not competent to take this position and Jon is where he wants to be.   With that said, I am going to begin to give you access to information and material that will allow you to transition smoothly when the time comes.   Come here."

Sharon obediently responded to stand behind Linda while she brought up a document on her monitor.   When she read the bold letters of the classification she stepped away and hurriedly said, "I'm not authorized that level of access."

"I know," Linda calmly replied.   "You will be soon.   In the meantime, go ahead and read it."

Stepping forward, she peered over Linda's shoulder and read the message.   She read it a second time to be sure she understood.   "Annihilation?" she whispered.

"Yes."

Sharon moved back around to stand in front of the desk. "What about the agents we have in place?"

"We wait until the last minute to extract them."

Slowly sitting, she creased her brow.   "What about Chuck and Jon?   Do they know?"

"No," she adamantly answered.   "And they are *not* to know until they are authorized."

"I understand."

Linda breathed a soft sigh.   "What do you think about sending Warfield to Arizona?"

"Probably for the best.   It's not like he can do anything here."

"What about Dwa?"

Sharon thought for moment before answering.   "I was initially going to say 'does it really matter?'   But then we

182

haven't killed the snake. Social Injustice operates outside the Cordon Zones.   So, even eliminating all the Zones doesn't eliminate Social Injustice. In fact, it may make them bolder."

"I agree. We need to find them; we need to find Dwa."

"I've read the file on Dwa. Other than receiving Dennett's letter, what's so important about him?   He was a Special Appointee for the Public Trust, a coveted Corporate position. Why didn't we just pick him up in the first place? Tell him to give us the letter and have a happy life?"

"That was Collin's call... from Corporate.   They got nervous and managed to screw things up. I had argued against it, but it wasn't my call. Now we're having to clean up their mess."

"And probably pushing Dwa to Social Injustice in the process, though from the pic and description of him, he's going to have a hard time hiding forever, especially with his photo plastered all over the news."

Linda stared at her friend. "We have less than four months to find and crush Social Injustice. Corporate wants a clean slate over here. The western hemisphere is being used as a test bed. Based upon how successful we are will influence their actions with the rest of the world. You know your mission."

"Yes, Mam." Standing she asked, "Who would you like to see next?"

Linda thought for just a moment. "Jon. I'll save the 'pain-in-the-ass' for last."

Grinning, Sharon opened the door and saw Jon sipping coffee and chatting with Linda's secretary. "You're next," she smiled at him.

Social Injustice Compound – East Point

Ruth came into the break area to find JB mesmerized by the television. "Why do you spend so much time watching all those shows?" She scrunched her face up in bewilderment. "They all get boring to me after a while."

"I'm trying to understand and learn all that we've missed," he answered, patting the cushion on the couch for her to sit next to him. "There are all kinds of shows. Some are funny, some are scary, others are adventure. And then some are just telling

183

us stuff. I asked Martin about them and he said all the shows are controlled by the Corporation."

"It seems to me," she replied, sitting down, "that all these shows are just a way of controlling you. I've talked to others here who tell me there are people who watch television all day, that their lives are nothing more than eating and drinking and what they see on the TV."

"They don't go outside?"

"No," she adamantly answered. "So by sitting here, you've traded one form of control for another."

JB gazed at her with affectionate appreciation. "You're really smart."

"I don't know about that," she blushed. "Anyway, what are you watching?"

"There's this show that's about to start that's called 'Where Are They Now?' They're going to talk about cloning."

Ruth's ears perked up. "Like what?"

"I don't know," he shrugged. "They're going to talk to some man named Lionel Whittaker. He's a famous conductor."

"What's that mean?"

"It means he does music, like Chet does, only he doesn't play the instruments. He leads a group of other people who play instruments. I guess he helps keep them all playing the same song."

The TV hostess, a buxom blond with a photogenic smile, came on to announce the week's show. She was a very pretty woman in her mid-thirties with flawless skin and hazel green eyes. Two men sat to her left, one dressed in an expensive European cut suit, and the other in more sober business attire

"Good afternoon. I'm Teresa Rice and this is 'Where Are They Now?' Our guest for this afternoon is Lionel Whittaker, the once child prodigy of music and now the premier conductor of the Corporate Philharmonic. We're taking a little different angle this week to look into the topic of rebirth, or 'becoming Angels' as the Reverend Jefferson Beauregard Clayton likes to say. Lionel has graciously agreed to talk with us about his thoughts for rebirth. Also with us is Rick Connor from the Resurrection Industries, headquartered in Atlanta, Georgia. Let's begin with Lionel." She turned to the handsome man in the European suit. He had thick wavy black hair along with the overt self-assurance that came from adulation and success.

"I see that you've just completed another immensely successful tour with the Corporate Philharmonic. Your most recent performance was in the Tiergarten concert hall in Berlin, Germany. I assume you ended with Beethoven's *Ode to Joy*."

"Of course," he smiled suavely. "The Germans know and appreciate good music."

"And now you're back to America for some well-deserved rest."

"That's right Teresa. I've some things to settle here and of course there's the needed break for the rebirth."

"And that's what we want to talk about today. So, Lionel, tell me, when did you first decide to have a rebirth?"

"Actually, Teresa, it's something I've considered all along. Once I knew the benefits of the procedure, it was, as they say, a no-brainer." He leaned comfortably back in his thick chair, one leg crossed over the other.

"Have you already had your clone genetics taken?"

"Not yet," he answered. "My plan all along was to clone myself when I was in my prime. I consider the prime of a man's life to be in his late thirties. I've arrived at that time and am now ready. The only question is, where?"

"And what do you say to that, Rick? With the recent attack on the facility in Decatur, are folks second-guessing certain locations?"

"Absolutely not," he countered. Rick was a slender man with curly red hair, tightly cropped. "The attack on the Decatur facility was a carefully planned assault carried out by Social Injustice. They were able to breach the security because the facility protocols were not followed. We've already investigated and made the necessary reassignments and instituted tighter security. I'd say the Decatur facility is now probably the safest in the world. I'm fully confident that Mister Whittaker would receive the best support and attention there. Not only is security enhanced, we have some of the best medical professionals in the world."

"I understand that you lost some staff during the attack," she commiserated

"Yes, we did, some of the most gifted and caring individuals in the rebirth industry. We've been fortunate to find some qualified and exemplary replacements."

"That brings up an interesting question," Teresa pondered. "The attack by Social Injustice was supposedly to free as many clones as possible. Let's say for the sake of discussion that one of the clone owners was present during the attack, and that this same owner was one of those killed. What happens to the man's clone if the owner is killed or dies?"

"An excellent question, Teresa," he calmly replied. "First, there are legal restraints put in place as to the disposition of clones whose owners either chose not to claim them, or are unable to claim them, as in the example you just gave. The law requires all owners to establish disposition prior to the actual harvesting of DNA. In other words, the status of the clone or clones is already provided for should an owner die."

"Can you give us an example?" she asked.

"Certainly. Let's take Mister Whittaker here. He decides he wishes to clone himself. Based upon his income and desires, he can choose to clone himself several times. Let's say he chooses to have three clones. When the time comes, he chooses which of the clones he wishes to conduct his rebirth in. What happens to the other two? Obviously he's not going to use them, and the costs of continuing their support and welfare when they are of no use is not only prohibitive, it's foolish. So Mister Whittaker has a choice. He can continue to provide for their support, or he can donate the clones to medical research, which is the most beneficial decision as it releases him from unnecessary expense while providing bodies for medical study."

"Don't most people only have one though," she pointed out.

"That's correct. The average employee has sufficient funding to afford one clone. And that brings us back to your question. The owner dies and the clone still lives. What happens? In this instance, there are essentially three choices. First, the family can elect to retain the clone with the desire that the clone will replace the lost loved one. The second possibility is that, should there be no family, the clone will be used for medical research."

"And the last option?" she asked, curious.

"The last option is that the clone is used as a replacement or, in other words, an individual decides he or she is not satisfied with the way they are. Let's say they wish to be more athletic or more artistic. Instead of cloning themselves, they find an excess clone of an individual with the traits they desire."

"You mean they would rebirth themselves in another's body?"

"That is correct."

"Aren't there difficulties with that process?" she inquired.

"Not at all. Look at the designer genes already advertised. You want to have an Einstein or Mozart as a child? You simply chose the DNA you wish and voila, you have your child prodigy. Now it's not quite like Mister Whittaker here," he hastened to add when he saw Lionel's perturbed look. "His genius is his own."

Mollified, Lionel raised an eyebrow in doubt. "Does the genetic designing actually work?"

"For the most part, yes," Rick replied. "One has to understand that genius is also environmental. The better the environment, the better the chances of genius emerging. That's the reason there are guidelines in place, to prevent those whose heart might be in the right place, but can't reasonably hope to adequately provide for a gifted child."

"So then, not everyone can expect to have a designer baby," Teresa clarified.

"That's correct. For example, a designer baby would be a waste of DNA in the cordoned zones. The same holds true for those elements of society who provide our basic services. To be quite frank, designer children have a place only among the elite of the world. That way we know they will be properly nurtured."

Teresa nodded sagaciously then turned to Lionel. "So have you decided when to conduct your rebirth?"

"Yes, I have," he smiled. "Mister Connor and I have been in discussion for some time. I've chosen the Decatur facility and will check in sometime next week."

"And will you choose to have only one clone?"

"Heavens no. I've decided on five."

"Five?" her eyes widened in surprise.

"Yes. Does that surprise you?"

"Well frankly, yes. Why so many?"

"First," he loftily replied, "I can afford it. Second, I want to make sure I have enough clones from which to choose."

"What will you do with the others?"

"They will go for medical research," he answered without a second thought. "I see no need to keep them."

187

Both JB and Ruth sat back as if struck. "He's going to kill them all," he said, aghast. Jumping up, he exclaimed, "I got to find Martin."

"I'm coming with you," she exclaimed.

Swinging around the couch, Ruth nearly bumped in to JB as they both came to an abrupt stop. Approaching them was Martin accompanied by a woman who was obviously pregnant.

"I wanted the two of you to meet my wife, Erika." He smiled warmly at them then made the introductions. "Honey, this is JB and Ruth."

Noticing their fixation on her stomach, Erika couldn't help but chuckle. "I'm pregnant."

"What does that mean?" JB asked.

"It means I'm going to have a baby," she replied.

"What's a baby?"   Ruth furrowed her brows in concentration.

"It's a little human being."

Ruth's eyes widened. "It's inside you?"

"Yes.

"How did it get there?"

Giving her a maternal grin, Erika took her arm then looked back at Martin. "Honey, be an angel and keep JB entertained while Ruth and I have a little chat." She led Ruth away from the two men. "Here, let me explain."

As the two ladies leisurely walked towards the door, JB looked at Martin. "What's an angel?"

"Um, an angel is a being who protects someone else. They're kind and gentle and always tell the truth."

JB frowned in concentration. "Do they look different from us?"

"Well," he replied, "they look just like people except they usually have wings."

Wings?" his eyes blinked wide. "Like birds?"

"Yes," Martin smiled, "like big giant birds."

JB's frown turned to excitement. "Can they fly? Can I see one? Why did she tell you to be an angel? Are you an angel?" He looked at Martin's shoulders and automatically knew he was no angel. "But you don't have wings," he said with some disillusionment.

"Slow down," he laughed. "Angels aren't real. They're just stories."

JB's shoulders slumped in disappointment. "If they're not real, why did she tell you to be one?"

"It's what's called a figure of speech. You'll understand as time goes on. But think of it this way. An angel is a good person, someone who cares about others more than himself. An angel is a person who makes others feel good about themselves, someone who cares for those who can't take care of themselves, someone who protects others who are unable to protect themselves." He studied JB as he puzzled out the explanation then changed the topic. "You seemed to be in a hurry when we got here."

Suddenly remembering, JB whirled around and pointed at the TV. "The man on the TV said he was going to have five of us and after he chooses which one he wants, he's going to kill the rest."

"What's his name?" Martin looked at the screen, but a commercial advertising a local restaurant was on.

JB waited until the show returned, then pointed again. "Him."

"Lionel Whittaker," Martin intoned when he saw him. "Did he say when he was going to do it?"

"Very soon. That other man is the one who is going to help him."

"Rick Connor. Yes, we know the man."

"We must stop him."

"We must stop *them*," he gently corrected.

"Will you kill them?"

"Most likely," he replied, recognizing the struggle inside JB. "Remember what I told you. We do not kill innocent people. We only target those who wish to hurt and destroy other people."

"And the only way to stop them is to kill them?"

"You have a lot to learn about human nature, my friend," Martin patiently explained. "There are some people who get pleasure out of other people's pain." Seeing JB's confused look, he said, "Some people like to hurt other people. It gives them pleasure."

JB's frown intensified. "How can hurting someone bring pleasure?"

"That's just it," he nodded. "You and I, we, don't understand why someone would do this. That is why we have to

189

stop them. Directing JB's attention back to the TV, specifically Lionel Whittaker, he asked, "When that man said what he was going to do with those like you, how did feel?"

JB thought for a moment. "I was angry. I was worried."

Martin nodded at the expansion of JB's vocabulary. "Good. You're learning well. Think about your first reaction when he said what he was going to do with those like you."

JB paused only for a moment. "I wanted to hurt him."

"Now you're beginning to understand why we must stop him, and people like him and the man helping him. As long as people like them are allowed to exist, people like you will die."

JB ruminated Martin's words. The fact that he was here was because people like Martin rescued him. Otherwise he would be dead. He would never again enjoy the company and pleasure of being with Ruth. In fact, he would never enjoy anything ever again. It was at that moment he realized he had to do something so others like him could have the same pleasures.

"What can I do?" he asked.

With a sympathetic smile, Martin gave him a gentle pat on the shoulder. "You just keep doing what you're doing. You keep learning and growing. You have a special talent with a gun that few people possess. We'll keep taking advantage of that talent. In the meantime, you have a lot of catching up to do."

Martin looked over to see Erika and Ruth reenter the room. Ruth's eyes were a mixture of excitement and wonder. Ruth walked fast, with Erika doing her best to keep up.

"Erika showed me how babies are made," she exclaimed, "on the computer."

"Babies are made on the computer?" JB puzzled.

"No, silly. She used the computer to show me. Babies are made when we do it." She pressed her body against his for emphasis.

JB stared blankly at her.

"Babies are made when two people do it," she repeated.

Understanding swept through him, but he raised an eyebrow in doubt. "We've never made a baby."

"That's because they gave us stuff to make us not have babies," she wisely replied. "Erika showed me. C'mon on," she said, grabbing his hand. "I'll show you on the computer."

JB allowed himself to be led away, his happiness obvious, for he and Ruth were always together now.

"You sure that was wise," Martin wondered, watching them walk away. He studied JB and the interaction with Ruth. It was obvious he was smitten. Martin hoped Ruth felt the same way.

"It's bound to happen sometime," Erika sagaciously answered, "unless you want to continue using birth control here."

"But it would be children raising children. They know nothing of what it means to be an adult."

"So we still use birth control then," she quietly stated.

"For now," he answered with a shrug. "It's hard enough keeping them safe without having to worry about babies."

Erika nodded in understanding. "Some will want to try." She indicated the open doorway through which JB and Ruth passed.

"Those two might be good candidates when the time comes."

"What will you tell them when they discover they've been given birth control just like Corporate did?"

"We tell them the truth. Their safety comes first." Martin mulled a bit then said, "It's interesting. Once we free them and bring them here, most of them will find one other person and cling to that one as a mate. It's as though all the years of never being able to form a bond with another human are suddenly over and they're making up for all that time alone. And there are a few who go from partner to partner, searching for some form of fulfillment, never satisfied, as though there might be something or someone better the next time. They're the ones I worry most about."

He looked at his wife and rubbed her protruding belly. "You doing OK?"

"I'll be fine. We have everything we need, even a qualified midwife." She stared into his eyes, noticing his distraction. "Where are you?"

"We've another mission, a short notice one. It may cause some problems here. I'll need to clear it with Lowell first."

"So I need to have this baby as soon as possible?" she teased.

"That would help," he grinned back, "though I wonder if we shouldn't get you to one of the cordons first."

"I'm not going without you," she firmly stated.

191

"I never said you were. Lowell said he's sending Pieter to the Tucson cordon. I was thinking of asking him to send us too."

Slipping an arm around his, she brightened as they walked out the room. "I've never been to Arizona. A change would be nice."

Pieter looked askance at the transportation, a semi with a double trailer. "You expect me to ride in that?"

"It'll be fun," Lowell clapped him on the shoulder. "Just think of all the free time you'll have reading and relaxing while someone else does the driving."

Pieter stared at the very large open crate inside the front trailer. Tucked against one side was a couch and small table with a battery powered lamp. Against the opposite wall was a small frig stocked with plenty of beer. Surrounding the frig were several smaller crates with food.

"Suppose I got to go to the bathroom?" he complained.

"We've taken care of that too." He motioned him to step up into the trailer. "See?" he pointed to the portable camping potty by the front. "You're all set."

"How long am I going to be in there?"

"Just a couple of days. Four at the most."

"Four days?" he huffed.

"Quite whining," Lowell grinned. "You're as bad as my kids. 'Are we there yet? Are we there yet?' "

Pieter smiled despite himself. "I know it's the best way, but you know how I hate being cooped up. I need to be outside, and being cooped up these past days has been hard enough."

"It'll be better when you're in Arizona, all that clean air and sunshine."

"They know I'm coming?"

"Already sent a drone letting them know."

Pieter gazed around the outside of the warehouse. The night was warm and the trailers were just about loaded. "Gretchen's not going to be happy when she finds out."

"Gretchen's got more on her hands than she can handle," he reminded him. "I need you there to give spiritual authority to the whole endeavor."

192

"Ah yes," he sighed, "spiritual authority. "I'm not so sure how much that's going to play once we begin the offensive."

"Trust me, my friend," Lowell softly replied, lightly placing a hand on Pieter's arm. "They will need someone to inspire them, a messiah, a Mahdi, a deliverer. Give them the mystical. Once this is all settled, we can worry about the truth."

"The truth? That I'm nothing more than a man?"

"You know that's not true," Lowell gently reproved him. "I don't know anyone else who can send their spirit out of their body, or who can pull disease from the sick. You have gifts. It's a good thing Corporate never found out about it, otherwise you'd be some sort of Corporate spokesman touting the latest in human capabilities."

"That is if they didn't kill me first."

"It's time, Lowell," the driver announced, walking to the cab. His assistant driver was already seated up front, getting comfortable.

"Let me know when you get there." Lowell smiled affectionately at him, sticking his hand out.

Pieter grabbed the hand and pulled him in for a hug. "You be careful here. They're getting way too close." With that, he climbed up and entered the container. He gave a last wave of the fingers as they raised the side up and nailed it shut.

Tucson Medical Center – Tucson, Arizona

Doctor Philip McBride was glad his shift was over. It had been a long day, even with the extra staff on hand. Now that shift change was complete, he could toss his scrubs in the wash bin, collect his things out of his locker, and head on home. He reminded himself there were reasons he worked a double. Now he had three days off and he could make good on that promise to Jen and the kids and take them to the zip-line park over east of Tanque Verde up towards Agua Caliente Hill.

Stepping outside the back doors to the hospital, he stretched in the late evening air before heading towards his car on the third level of the parking garage. That was the privilege of being a doctor. Most staff had to take public transportation to work. Getting in, he started the car and put it in reverse, gently pressing the accelerator. It was as he was driving out that a delivery truck blocked his way coming up the levels.   The damned thing was going the wrong way.

Leaning out the window, he flicked his hand indicating they needed to turn around.   The poor man driving it abruptly realized his error and splayed his hands as apology.   Stopping the truck, the other man sitting in the truck got out and walked around the vehicle measuring gaps and position in order to proceed.

Finally, he walked over to Philip.   "I'm awfully sorry mister, but he's a new driver.   Ya mind givin' me a hand to back this thing up so we can get ya outta here?"

With a sigh of exasperation, Philip put the car in park and shut off the engine.   Opening the door, he followed the man to the rear of the truck.

"If you could stand on that side whilst I direct him from this side, that'd be great.   By the way, I'm Gus and that's Marty in the driver's seat.   We was deliverin' med supplies."

"I can see that," Philip patronizingly replied.

"Who might you be?" Gus grinned.

"I'm *Doctor* McBride," Philip answered, making sure Gus knew the caliber and quality of man he was dealing with.

"A doctor.   My my.   Hey Marty.   This guy's a doctor."

"What's up, doc?" Marty snorted a laugh at his own humor.

Rolling his eyes, Philip pursed his lips.   "Do you mind?   It's been a long day and I'm ready to go home."

"Sure, sure," Gus amiably answered.

Midway through their efforts, another man approached.   He looked to be one of the hospital cleaning crew.   "You need any help?"

"Yeah, sure," Gus cheerfully replied. "I'm Gus and that's Marty," he pointed to the driver.   Giving him the once over, he asked, "You a doc like him?"

"Nah.   I'm just one of the guys that cleans up after them. My name's Chet."   He cast a smug grin at Philip.

With growing impatience, Philip growled, "Can we dispense with the idle chit-chat?   I'd like to get home."

"Yeah, yeah, sure," Gus smiled apologetically.   "Say, Chet, how 'bout you help the doc on that side?"

"OK."   Chet walked up to stand beside Philip who was at the rear of the truck close to one of the support pylons.

Studying the angle of the truck and the space around it, he off-handedly said, "Think he needs to move it up a bit, don't you?"

With a loud huff, Philip was half tempted to return to his car and let these fools work it out. Instead, with pursed lips, he stepped in front of Chet to get a better look. And that was the last thing he remembered.

In one smooth motion, Chet swung the blackjack with expert delivery, catching Philip on the back of his head. Philip dropped like a sack of flour.

With no further words, Gus hustled back from the front, leaped up on the rear bumper and pulled open the back swinging door. Jumping down, he helped Chet lift Philip into the empty trailer.

Taking Philip's keys and staff badge, Chet got into Philip's car while Marty and Gus expertly turned the truck around. Shortly, they were passing by the exit booths, Chet using Philip's badge to access the control pad while Marty and Gus gave an amiable wave and grin to the security guard.

A short while later, they headed towards the Tucson Country club then turned on East Miramar Drive, pulling into the driveway of Philip's house. Chet remotely opened the garage door and parked the car inside. Walking back outside, he closed the garage door and walked to the front door, ringing the doorbell. Nonchalantly waiting for someone to answer the door, he cast a quick look back at Gus and Marty parked at the curb.

Ringing the doorbell, again, he continued pressing the bell until the interior hall lights came on and the door was opened by an attractive woman in her early 30's, wrapped in a silk robe over her silk pajamas.

"Missus McBride?"

"Yes?"

"Mam, we've got your husband in the back of the truck. He's not looking too good."

Thrusting the door open, she stepped out. "What's wrong?"

"Mam, looks like he was mugged or something. We found out where he lived and brought him back here."

Gus was out of the cab and walking to the back as Jennifer McBride ran across the yard. Swinging open the rear door, he reached down to help her up. Philip still lay crumpled on the metal floor.

195

"O my god!" She dropped to her knees next to him. She felt his face and neck. He was still breathing, but there seemed to be a lump on the back of his head. "Do you know what happened?" she pleaded. Looking up, her fears grew when she saw the pistol in Gus' hand.

"Missus McBride," he calmly, yet coldly said. "You need to listen very carefully if you want to save your husband's life. Do you understand?"

"What do you want from us?" she wailed.

"Getting all emotional now is not going to help. You have children?"

"Ye... yes."

"How many?"

"Two."

"Fine. You're going to get your two children and bring them here with you. You have five minutes to collect them and whatever clothes you need. Five minutes. If you're not back in five minutes, I shoot him. Then I shoot you and your two children. Understand?"

She mutely nodded, her eyes brimming with tears.

"Chet there," he said indicating the man waiting by the open front door, "will assist you. You have five minutes, starting... now."

Jennifer scrambled out of the trailer and into the house. Five minutes later she emerged with two groggy young children and several suitcases of clothing.

"You all make yourselves comfortable," Gus politely intoned before closing the door. "It's not going to be too long a ride."

2500 Peachtree Road, Atlanta

When Lionel Whittaker heard the doorbell, his first reaction was a deep frown, immediately wondering what fool would be calling at this time of night. Wrapping the silk robe tighter around him, he tied the belt in a knot as he walked to the door. Pausing in front of the small wall screen to the side of the door, he pressed the 'on' button to activate the outside camera to see who was bothering him so late.

"What do you want?" he demanded, seeing a woman outside the door, holding a pizza delivery box.

"I got a delivery to this address," she replied, looking around to see where the outside speaker was. She was a common laborer, an unskilled worker who wore her baseball hat backwards, a trait that Lionel always found irritating. Why bother wearing something if you don't know how to properly wear it?

"I didn't order pizza," he snootily informed her. Though he wasn't averse to an occasional slice of a gourmet pizza, specially prepared, pizza was the common man's meal. And by the way this woman looked, she was more than common, especially dressed in the t-shirt and ragged jeans. She had a silver chain that went from her belt loop to a thick wallet protruding from her back pocket.

"You don't have to pay for this," she explained, finally finding the camera in the corner of the hallway. "Someone sent this to you."

"Who?"

She looked at the receipt taped to the top of the box. "It doesn't say."

"What kind is it?" he asked, his frown permanently affixed. Who would send him a pizza at this time of night? Was someone playing a practical joke?

The woman lifted the top and peeked in. "Looks like a meat lovers."

"What kind of meat?"

"Jeez, mister, the regular kind of meat," she huffed with exasperation. "Pepperoni, sausage, ham, that kind of meat."

Lionel curled a lip at the thought of some mass produced pizza adorned with mass produced meats. "I don't want it."

"Whaddaya mean you don't want it?"

"I don't want it."

The woman stood there, stunned at the brazen refusal. "I can't take it back," she stated.

"You eat it then."

"I'm a vegetarian."

"Take the meat off."

"It's got cheese on it. I don't do milk products."

"Then just throw it away," he finally snipped.

"That's against company policy. I'd lose my job," she stubbornly explained.

"Well I still don't want it."

"Then I'm gonna just leave it right on the floor in front of your door." She bent down as if to deposit the pizza."

"Hold on a minute," he snapped. He didn't need the neighbors thinking poorly of him, and a pizza box outside the front door simply advertised one as trailer trash. What was with this aggravating woman? He had to give her credit for being relentless. "Alright," he answered with a long-suffering sigh. "Just a moment." Unlatching the several door locks, he swung the door open.

The woman raised the box with one hand as if to present it to him. What Lionel saw too late was the silencer of the pistol beneath the box. Two soft pings sent him reeling backwards into the hallway of his penthouse and crashing onto the floor. The last thing he saw was the woman standing over him, the pistol pointed at his head.

Chapter 7

Sierra Vista - Tucson Cordon Zone, Arizona
Friday, May 12, 2102

The antiquated Army M36 deuce-and-a-half had been stripped down to its essentials. Gone were the external exhaust pipe and other parts of the old gas engine, replaced with solar cells that lined the fenders, engine hood, and cab hood. In the back cargo bed, Philip McBride and his family sat on wooden slat benches, forlorn and apprehensive, their suitcases beneath them.

His arm wrapped protectively around his wife's shoulders, Philip stared out over the passing desert landscape, his head still aching from last night. Both children, a cherubic boy and a pampered girl, sat at the tailgate. Their hands resting on the top, they mutely stared behind them, wondering if this was a new adventure or if they were really in trouble.

When Philip asked how they got here, Jennifer had done her best to explain what happened, to include the threats on their lives.

"Criminal bastards," he had muttered.

"Where do you think we are," she anxiously asked, already knowing the answer, but refusing to believe it.

"This has got to be the Zone," he answered. "Do you remember passing through a gate in the wall?"

"No. They put bags over our heads and we were made to walk for a while. When they took the bags off, we were standing outside in the open. You were still out of it and they had to carry you. We waited until this truck showed up. You were awake by then."

"Did they say anything to you?"

"Only that they were going to kill you if I didn't cooperate."

"Murderous bastards," he again muttered. He felt the lump on the back of his head, wishing he had some ice to reduce the swelling.

For the past hour, the truck had bumped along dirt roads, but now swung onto a paved highway and picked up speed. Philip saw the sign first – Sierra Vista, 16 km.

"We're definitely in the Zone," he bleakly said.

"Why?" Jennifer asked in bewilderment.

"Are we going to be back in time for my soccer game?" the girl asked.

"I don't know, honey," Jennifer replied. "We'll have to wait and see."

"I'm bored." The boy curled a lip in ennui.

"It won't be much longer," Jennifer reassured them.

The road dipped and they crossed over a river. A little bit later, the truck slowed and turned. Philip read the street sign out loud. "North Moson Road."

Three kilometers later, it pulled off onto a dirt road that led to an abandoned warehouse surrounded by a tall chain link fence topped with razor wire. The driver got out of the truck and unlocked the gate, reversing the process once through. As he approached the building, a wide garage door slid open and he pulled into a large bay area half filled with trucks and other old military vehicles.

Hopping out of the cab, he went to the back of the truck, unhooking and lowering the tailgate. "OK folks, we're here. Grab your things and follow me."

He led them to the rear of the room to another smaller room with windows. There were several couches and chairs in it, all severely in need of repair. In the corner was an empty antique vending machine.

"Make yourself comfortable. She'll be with you in a minute." He input a code to the access pad on the wall by the vending machine. The wall slid open wide enough for him to slip through.

When the wall closed behind him, Jennifer anxiously whispered, "What's going to happen to us?"

"I don't know," Philip answered.

"This place is filthy." The girl curled a lip in disdain.

"I gotta pee," the boy fidgeted.

Jennifer looked back out into the main room, searching for a restroom. She was about to set out to find one when the wall slid open. A lissome attractive woman with long blond hair that curled in ringlets over her shoulders walked in, followed by a tanned middle-aged woman, with short black hair, and two young men armed with holstered pistols who silently positioned themselves by the door.

"Good morning Doctor McBride," the blond warmly greeted him. "I'm Gretchen, and this is my deputy, Maria."

"Why are we here?" Philip demanded.

"Mom," the boy pleaded. "I gotta go." He tightly held his legs together.

"He needs a bathroom," Jennifer explained.

"There's one across the bay," Maria answered. "I'll take him."

"Why don't you go with her," Gretchen pointedly told Jennifer, "along with your daughter while I talk with your husband." She nodded to one of the young men who moved from the door and out into the main room then turned to wait for them.

Jennifer hesitated only for a moment before following Maria through the door and out into the main room.

Once they were gone, Gretchen focused her attention on Philip. "You're probably wondering why you are here. The Zone needs doctors and you've just volunteered to serve in the Zone."

"I did no such thing," he shot back. "How dare you? How dare you presume that you can just kidnap me, threaten my family, drag me to this god-forsaken dump and then demand that I give up my medical practice in Tucson just because you want a doctor?"

"I didn't say 'want,' I said 'need.' And yes, you are giving up your practice in Tucson to serve here."

"Or what? You going to kill me? Then what? You'd be without a doctor," he sneered.

"Oh," she calmly replied. "I wouldn't presume to threaten you. That's why your family is here."

Philip stiffened as though he had just been slapped. "You wouldn't dare." He tried to sound authoritative but failed.

"Why not?" she indifferently shrugged. "You and your kind have used the Zones as your personal labs for decades. You lived in your fancy house, living your privileged life, caring for people in state of the art hospitals while on this side of the wall you spread your diseases, discovered cures you already had, just so you could go on living in your upscale world."

"I had nothing to do with that," he sputtered.

"Of course you didn't," she blithely answered, "but you certainly made sure you used the results to your advantage. But that's all rather moot now."

"They'll come looking for me once they find out I'm gone," he defiantly stated.

"I suppose that's possible," she nonchalantly agreed. "But then, where do they start looking? And when? No one will know you're gone until you don't report for work. It will take another few days for the authorities to begin investigating, so that means it will be a least a week before they even begin to look for you."

Philip's bravura suddenly evaporated as he realized it was entirely possible that he was going to become a permanent resident of the Zone. His concern grew as he also realized that he and his family would now be victims of the Corporation's disease management.

"Why are you doing this?" he wailed.

"Like I said, we need doctors."

He heard his wife and children returning and looked over his shoulder. Jennifer's face revealed her fears, and she held tightly to the boy's hand while his daughter walked next to the woman called Maria, seemingly oblivious to their predicament.

"Everything OK?" Gretchen kindly smiled.

"The bathrooms are gross," the girl announced with a touch of condescension.

"Yes, I know," Gretchen agreed. "We don't use them that often. We'll have to work on that."

"Can we go home now, Daddy?" she said to her father. It wasn't a request.

"This is your home now," Gretchen gently replied.

"This?" she sneered. "This dump? You got to be kidding me. Do you know who my Daddy is?"

"Yes I do" Gretchen chuckled. "That's why you all are here."

She quickly looked at the defeat in her parents' faces and then at the other adults. "You can't do this," she loudly exclaimed. "It's against the law. Wait until I go to the police. You're all gonna be in big trouble."

Maria cocked an eyebrow to stare at her. "Are you really that stupid?"

202

The girl's eyes widened in shock. "You can't talk to me like that, you stupid cow. Who do you think you are? You're just some social reject who couldn't make it in real life."

Maria's reaction was instant and she backhanded the girl across the face, sending her sprawling to the floor. "Out here, we have manners," she coldly lectured her. "We respect our elders."

Jennifer was down on her knees in an instant comforting her daughter who stared at Maria with a mixture of hatred and fear, her hand at her lip.

"She's just a child," Jennifer snapped at Maria, her voice rising angrily.

"She's a brat," Maria retorted. "A spoiled brat who's been given everything she wants. Well that's about to change. Out here everyone contributes. You don't contribute, you don't eat." She shook her head and looked up to Gretchen. "Why don't we just shoot the three of them? The doc can stay, but the rest of them are just going to be a drain on us. They're worthless."

"Good god no!" Philip bellowed. "I'll do whatever you want. Just leave them alone. Please."

Gretchen paused as though considering Maria's suggestion. Turning to the two guards, she instructed, "Take them below. We'll determine what to do with them later. In the meantime," she said, directing her attention to Jennifer and the kids, "I suggest you think of ways you can be a benefit to us."

The two young men corralled the family and led them through the door by the vending machine. Waiting for the door to close, Gretchen grinned at Maria.

"That was well played."

"Thank you," Maria smiled back. "That young lady, however, will be a handful."

"She just needs a good smack every now and then," Gretchen replied. "Your smack-down was a good start."

"Think he'll cooperate?"

"As long as he fears for his family, he will. After a while, when routine settles in, we'll see." She pressed the keypad by the vending machine. As the door opened, she asked, "What have we heard from up north?"

"Calgary says they're still digging up more stuff, a lot of it at the old Air Force base near Box Elder, South Dakota. Not sure what the Corporation was thinking, but burying weapons and ammo at old military installations that were eventually absorbed into cordon zones…" She left the thought incomplete, the point obvious. "Still, it works to our advantage, though Corporate has to know we're looking for stuff."

"Perhaps that's one reason why they kill so many of us so often. Keep our focus on survival instead of fighting back."

They descended the circular stairs to the waiting elevator.

"What about gun shipments?" Gretchen queried. "Anyone need anything we have?

"Atlanta says they could use some more."

"Go ahead and get a shipment out to them."

"Will do." Maria then chuckled. "Martin says he has a prodigy sniper, one of the clones."

"Really?"

"You'll never guess who."

"Ok, who?" The elevator opened and they stepped in.

"The Reverend Clayton's clone," she answered with a grin.

SEI Directorate – Decatur

Linda leaned over Sharon's shoulder, inhaling the delicate bouquet of rose perfume. She found it distracting as she tried to focus her attention on the left monitor on Sharon's desk. Instead of listening, she found herself reliving intimate moments with her subordinate. Forcing herself to pay attention, she straightened to standing.

"The cameras on his floor were turned off," Sharon explained. "I suppose that's the privilege of being part of the upper classes, but it also complicates our investigation. We've got video of a pizza delivery girl going into the building around the time of the murder. She leaves about five minutes later without the pizza box. But he wasn't the type to eat, let alone order pizza. We're checking the local pizza places to see if they made any deliveries last night, as well as the residents to see if they had placed an order."

"Professional job?"

"Looks like it. Two shots to the chest and one to the head. You can see from this pic, the head shot was delivered when he was on the ground."

"Neighbors hear or see anything?"

"Not a peep," she sighed, "though it's not like they would."

"Your version?"

Sharon sat back, placing her hands on the armrests. "Pizza girl comes to the door. He says he didn't order any pizza. She refuses to leave, maybe even threatens to leave the pizza box outside the door. Obviously he can't have that. She takes him out as soon as the door opens. Collects the spent casings and calmly departs."

"Pizza box?"

"Incinerated. With all the recycling chutes in the building, she would have gotten rid of the evidence, making it look like a completed delivery."

Linda concentrated on the center monitor, watching the video of the delivery girl as she entered the building and the elevator. "Can we get a better picture of her face?"

"No. She kept the bill of the cap low over her eyes. She knew we'd be looking."

Linda let out a slow breath. "Why him?"

"He was on that TV show, 'Where Are They Now?' and gave his thoughts on the rebirth process. Here, I'll play the clip that probably motivated his assassination." She pulled up the short clip. The camera showed Teresa Rice asking, "What will you do with the others?"

Lionel Whittaker's callous expression displayed his complete disdain for the fate of his clones. "They will go for medical research. I see no need to keep them."

"What more motivation do they need?" Sharon said, more as observation than question. "What concerns me is what seems to be a gradual increase in the number of upper class assassinations. We had twelve all last year. As of today, we're on course to double that, if everything stays like it is." She swiveled her chair around then gazed up at her superior. "I think we may have a bigger problem."

"Oh?"

"There seem to be an unusual number of missing doctors lately. One out in Tucson, another here in Atlanta, two in Chicago, two in Kansas City, one in Denver, and three in Bogotá. And that's just off the top of my head. There are more."

Linda straightened and crossed her arms. "Your hypothesis?"

"All of the doctors are from facilities in locations close to Cordon Zones, well... except for the one here in Atlanta. I think we can assume the missing doctors are ending up in the Zones, which seems logical as the Zones are the endless recipients of the attention of disease management.   This is their way of getting medical help before the next attack. That said, with the increase in the... I'll call them abductions... or kidnappings. Anyway, with the increase in medical kidnappings, it's as though they're expecting something to happen, as though they're getting ready for the next attack."

Linda pursed her lips in thought. "My first inclination is to think that Operation 40 Trucks has been compromised. But I don't see how with the restricted distribution."

"We assume all on the distribution know how to keep secrets," Sharon pointed out. "It is curious though that all the families of those missing doctors who had families, are likewise missing."

"Meaning..."

"That whatever Zones the doctors went to, their families are with them."

"Hostages?" Linda pondered.

"More than likely."

"It won't stop the operation."

"I shouldn't think it would, but let's be realistic," Sharon replied. "We can always get more doctors."

Linda slowly nodded agreement. "Anything else unusual in the Zones?"

"We've noted an increase in the use of infrared on our drones. But they only have so many devices. We just go in someplace else. It's more an inconvenience than irritation." She stopped and focused her gaze on Linda. "This may seem stupid, but why are we bothering to spend so much effort on anything that happens in the Zones when every living human being in them is going to be killed on September first?"

"Social Injustice will still exist after the Zones are destroyed," Linda reminded her.

"I know that, and that's my point. Leave the Zones alone. They're not going anywhere and in less than four months they won't exist.   Let's focus our efforts on destroying Social Injustice in the Free Zones."

206

Tilting her head, Linda momentarily pondered the course of action. She was about to agree when Hans and other Corporate superiors invaded her thoughts. Before she made a decision like that, she would need to convince her bosses and right now she wasn't so sure it would put her in a good light. "While I like the idea, I think we need to look at the whole picture. We still need to know who and where Social Injustice is. The Zones still provide us with necessary data and information. Let's continue working them until maybe a week or two before extermination day."

"Aye, aye, Captain." Sharon grinned and saluted.

Linda simply shook her head and smiled as she walked away. It wasn't the first time she reminded herself how smart she had been to promote Sharon.

Leafmore Ridge, Atlanta

Brandon Kelly sat in the TV room of the safe house so recently vacated by Warfield. His excitement had grown with the realization that he had successfully duped Pieter into believing he was David Wright. Not only that, he had gleaned so much useful information that they would all see what a key asset he was. Why he might even get a promotion out of this and become a true deep-cover agent… with an unlimited bank account.

The ringing doorbell interrupted his thoughts and he jumped up to answer. Opening the door, he was greeted by an attractive woman wearing a light blue polo shirt with a sewn-on name in a darker blue that said 'Beckie.' Her auburn hair was pulled back into a pony-tail that protruded through the gap in the back of her baseball hat with the company logo blazoned across the front. A tool box lay on the step next to her feet.

"Mister Wright?" She smiled at him, the clip-pad under her arm.

"Yes.

"I'm from the cable company. You reported a problem with your cable."

"I did?"

After a few awkward moments of silence, she repeated, "You reported a problem with your cable." He continued to stare at her until she leaned forward and whispered "You're supposed to say, 'Yes, I did.'"

"Oh," he startled then mechanically replied, "Oh yes. I did."

He remained in the doorway staring dumbly at her until she said, "May I come in and look at it?"

"Oh… yes, yes, of course." He stepped to the side while she retrieved her tool box and entered, stopping in the foyer to politely wait for him.

"The TV's in the room just down the hall to the right." He said a little too loudly before closing the door. He led the way and pointing to the large TV recessed into the wall. Handing her the remote, he waited and watched.

Placing the tool box on the floor, she stooped down and opened it. "Is there anyone else here?"

"Huh?"

"I asked, is there anyone else here?" She lifted the upper tray out.

"Uh, no. Just me."

"Good. Do me a favor and check to see if anyone has pulled up behind me or is across the street. When you do it, don't be obvious."

Walking back to the front room, he gently pulled back the curtain and surveyed the area. Seeing nothing out of the ordinary, he returned to the room only to discover she had covered the couch with a large piece of plastic that went half way across the floor.

"What's that for?"

"You'll see. I'm very fussy about my work and I don't like leaving a mess behind." She knelt again by her tool box. "Go ahead and have a seat." He started to move to another chair. "Not there. On the couch."

"With the plastic on it?" he frowned.

"Yes. Please," she said, busying herself in the toolbox.

Looking for a suitable place, he smoothed the plastic then turned around and plopped down. It was when he had settled himself that he leaned back noticing the back cushion felt oddly more firm than he remembered. In fact, it felt downright hard. He looked over at her to find her holding a pistol with a silencer on it and it was pointing at him.

"Wha-" was all that escaped his lips before she fired one round through the heart immediately followed by the soft *thunk* of a bullet hitting metal.

As he slumped forward and flopped to the floor, she stood up and rolled him over, ensuring his body remained on the plastic. The back door opened and two men dressed in cable uniforms and blue synthetic gloves came in and methodically rolled the body in the plastic while 'Beckie' retrieved the metal plate behind the couch. She spent the next few minutes searching for the spent bullet which was wedged behind the seat cushion.

Standing, she examined the hole in the back cushion. "Unless you can match the other cushion, we need another couch."

"We'll take care of it. Where're we dumping him?"

"One of the dumpsters outside SEI." She picked up the TV remote and turned it on, flipping through a number of channels, finally settling on a comedy. "Do it late, sometime past midnight. We don't want them to discover it too soon."

Walking over to the small writing desk by the wall, she bent down and wrote a note on a small piece of paper. Ripping a bit of tape from the dispenser, she walked back over to the tightly wrapped body. Inside the layers of plastic, blood still seeped from the open wound.

Bending down, she taped the note to the plastic near his head - RETURN TO SENDER.

Resurrection Industries Facility, Tucson

The Reverend was having trouble sleeping. The drug induced lethargy was causing him to dream, awaken, and dream again in a staccato fashion that produced strange visions and jumbled memories.

When he was awake, he wanted to move, to rise up from this bed and walk. What frustrated him most was that he couldn't even turn his head to see out the window where he knew the sun had been shining earlier in the day.

What he remembered of Tucson had been years ago when he was struggling to gain an audience. He had arrived in Tucson by way of hitch-hiking across Texas and New Mexico. Even to this day he never understood why he was so set on Tucson, but he arrived wide-eyed and confident.

He found the right place in a small venue that had once been a church that had morphed to a concert venue where all the pews had been removed. As prosperity moved to the suburbs and edges of the city the place was abandoned until the city decided to revitalize the blighted area.

Beauregard had been on the cusp of that revitalization, plying his brand of inner-spirituality. He lived in the lighting booth of the venue for a while, sleeping on a mattress pad and cleaning himself up in the men's room. It was a time before he had his trademark flaming red hair tinged in blue. He smiled at the memory. He had been so young then, close to the age he was now in his new body.

But he had a flair for the dramatic and an engaging personality, and soon he began to build a following, so much so that he could finally move out of the lighting booth and rent a small studio apartment.

He had been there six months when the Corporation found him and liked what they saw. After one show, they had approached him with a deal far too lucrative to turn down. In exchange for his charismatic delivery of Corporate products, they would turn him into a superstar.

And that was what he was now – a superstar, the premier religious leader in the world. And one even better, he was now a *young* superstar with a bank account even the Corporate execs had to be jealous of.

He couldn't help but break out into a broad grin. If he could have, he would have slipped his hands behind his head, crossed his legs and ordered a drink. Instead, it was like he was in a body-cast. Sure, he could move his arms and legs, but only so much and then only under the nurse's supervision. Thank the gods, or whoever, that the restrictions would get less and less as the days went on.

He stared up at the ceiling TV directly above his head, wondering what time it was and what might be of interest on the TV.

"I thought you might be awake." An attractive nurse leaned into his vision.

"What time is it?" His voice felt dry and brittle, and he licked his lips.

"It's about two o'clock in the morning," she sweetly replied. "Would you like something to drink?"

"Bourbon."

She laughed brightly. "That will have to wait for a few days. How about some cold water instead?"

"OK."

Placing a straw into his mouth, she watched as he sucked on the cold liquid then pushed the straw out of his mouth with his tongue. "Would you like to watch TV?"

"OK."

"It's voice activated, so all you need to do is tell it what you want to watch. If sports, just say 'sports' and a listing of sports will scroll down. If a movie, just say 'movie' and then tell it what type of movie, like murder mystery or comedy. When you want to turn it off, just say 'off.' OK?"

"Thank you."

Her face disappeared and he focused his gaze on the TV. "Sports." A listing of the various sports began scrolling and he said, "Cycling. Tour de France."

Immediately the previous year's Tour came on with the panel of announcers discussing the various teams and key riders just before the first rider descended the platform and onto the road in the Stage 1 time-trial. It was as the 121st rider began furiously pumping his bike up the road that Beauregard felt heavy with sleep again and closed his eyes.

When he awoke again, they were midway in the second stage, a 185 kilometers sprinters stage. He frowned trying to determine what time it might be while trying to recall the dream he was having. What he remembered was riding a bike somewhere in Europe. The scenery had started out in some idyllic alpine backroads, but as he cycled, the scenery began to change and he ended up dodging debris on the streets from destroyed and burnt out buildings. He could see people; they were blackened apparitions moving aimlessly among the rubble. He tried to remember more but the longer he remained awake, the fainter the dream was until it finally vanished, like most dreams.

SEI Directorate – Decatur
Monday, May 15, 2102

In the glow of the mid-morning sun, Linda sat in her plush swivel chair with her back to the desk. Soft music touched the corners of the room. Gazing out over the Atlanta skyline, she felt relaxed, comfortable. In less than four months, her job would become even easier. With the cordons destroyed, all she had to do was eliminate the Social Injustice factions remaining in the free zones. Her thoughts turned to wondering if she should finally take a vacation... something she hadn't thought prudent these past four years. But that wasn't all that out of the ordinary.   There were some employees who hadn't taken vacation since their employment began, wanting to save it all for when they "retired."

She snorted a laugh. Retired. What fool believed that anyone retired these days? With cloning, or becoming angels like that bombastic Reverend Clayton liked to say, who was going to retire? She knew it was only a matter of time before the Corporation required all employees take allotted vacation time every year. No more carry-over of vacation in the hopes of selling it back when retirement came.

And why would anyone want to retire to begin with? What do you do when you retire? Sit around and watch the insipid shows on TV?   With cloning, she could have a long and fulfilling career. Besides, she had ambition. She was tapped to be Hans' replacement as Vice-President of North America Security. Who knew what the future held for her. But one thing was certain; life was good.

A low beep behind her alerted her that she had received a message. Turning back around, she sighed at the interruption of her reverie. Her first inclination was to ignore it for a bit more, but she saw that the message was encrypted. "Blinds up," she commanded. While the thin opaque sound-proof wall emerged from the floor in front of the windows and the ceiling lights brightened, she decrypted the message.

EYES ONLY
TOP SECRET – OMEGA RESTRICTED
FROM: DIRECTOR   OF   SECURITY   AND
INTELLIGENCE, THE HAGUE

1530 ZULU 6 MAY 2102
TO: ADDRESSEES ONLY, RESTRICTED
SUBJECT: OPERATION 40 TRUCKS

1. Though not marked, all paragraphs and sections in their entirety are classified OMEGA.
2. Recent increased global activity indicates a unified insurrection effort to conduct and instigate global disruption.
3. This increase of activity may be viewed as:
    a. desperation with current conditions,
    b. a belief of sufficient strength to cause appropriate disruption,
    c. a belief that the Corporation is sufficiently weakened, thus lacking ability to thwart insurrection objectives.
4. Assumptions:
    a. Insurrection forces exhibit a sophisticated command and control structure and organization.
    b. Despite Corporate successes to interdict insurrection activities, recent abductions and killings indicate a strengthening of purpose.
    c. Present medical capabilities of insurrection forces are insufficient to meet present needs.
    d. Any increased demand on insurrection medical capabilities will exceed their ability to provide medical services.
    e. Heretofore, eradication and population control efforts in the Cordon Zones have been remarkably successful.
    f. Present stock of biological weapons is sufficient to initiate a preemptive strike within less than thirty (30) days.
5. Effective immediately, OPERATION 40 TRUCKS is moved forward to 1 June.
6. REPEAT: OPERATION 40 TRUCKS IS MOVED FORWARD TO 1 JUNE.
7. All recipients are to acknowledge.

END

213

TOP SECRET – OMEGA

Stunned, Linda flopped back in her chair. Quickly realizing she needed to reply, she typed in the required response and hit 'send.' Taking a deep breath, she thought about the change in Corporate plans. Something had them spooked. Looking to see if Hans was online, she saw his icon active and pressed the video-com button. His face immediately filled the screen.

"Good morning, Linda," he smiled.

She stared at him for a moment, wondering if anything unsettled the man. He just seemed too much in control of himself.

"Yes, Linda?" his smile widened.

"Oh," she reddened slightly. "Sorry. I assume you just received the same message I did."

"That's correct."

"What do you think it means?"

"It means, my dear, that Corporate has decided to eliminate its problems much sooner than anticipated."

"But why?"

With a curious smile, Hans gazed at her. "Does it really matter? Frankly, I'm surprised they haven't done this before. It's not like we don't already have enough biological agents to take care of our little problem."

Linda thought for a moment. "I suppose you're right. Do we have any follow-on orders?"

"Not yet. I assume we should see them any moment now. Any problems?"

"No, no. I just want to make sure our people are safe."

"A commendable thought," he sagaciously nodded. "I'm sure we'll find out what happens next soon enough."

"I'm sure you're right," she replied, her self-confidence returning.

"Good. By the way," he impishly smiled, "you'll need to come over to the house sometime soon to measure for curtains."

Understanding his little joke, she smiled with gratitude. "I just might do that."

"You do. And bring that delightful Sharon with you. Anything else?"

"No sir."

"Good day to you then."

214

The video screen closed, leaving the classified message still up. Closing and saving it to the secure drive, Linda stood up. "Blinds down." As the wall descended, she blinked as sunlight penetrated the room. She took several steps to stand by the window. Staring into the distance beyond the city, she wondered what life was going to be like with no Cordons to worry about. A knock on the door caused her to look over her shoulder as Sharon came in.

"You have a moment?" her subordinate asked.

"Of course." She motioned her to come to where she stood.

"We found Kelly in the dumpster outside. He had this taped to him." Sharon handed her the note.

Linda let out a long soft sigh. "Damn." Looking back up at Sharon, she asked, "Why didn't Jon tell me this?"

"He was on his way here when Kelly was discovered. He asked that I notify you while he sorts out what happened."

"Sorts out what happened?" she shook her head. "I'll tell you what happened. We sent in an amateur to do a professional job. This whole thing was handled half-assed." She paused then said, "What a pity, though I suppose it really doesn't matter now."

Sharon looked quizzically at her. "Are you OK?"

"Yes," she reassured her. "Quite OK." She crossed the room and closed the door. Returning, she gently took Sharon by the elbow and guided her to the bar against the bookshelf wall. Lowering her voice to barely a whisper she said, "They've moved up Operation 40 Trucks."

"To when?"

"June 1st."

"My god!" she sputtered. "What about our agents?"

"No word on that yet."

"But Linda," she countered. "That gives us three weeks to notify and bring everyone in. That's not enough time."

"Don't you think I know that?" she curtly pointed out.

"I'm sorry." She tenderly touched her arm. "Of course you do. Corporate didn't say anything about our covert operations?"

"No… and that's what bothers me." She walked over to sit in one of the lounge chairs by the window. Sharon sat next to her.

"What?"

"Our agents," Linda continued. "Corporate knew that moving it up to June 1st was going to complicate our covert operations, that we would lose a lot of valuable agents... agents we could use to infiltrate after the operation."

"They're condemning them to death," Sharon stated the obvious. "But, I suppose you have to look at it from the Corporate perspective. Social Injustice is getting more brazen and activity has increased. I may not be the most gifted analyst, but even I can tell there's something going on. Moving up the date will end up saving more lives in the long run."

Linda regarded her with a bemused smile. "My, my, aren't we the cool dispassionate one. Suppose that was you out there in the Cordons. I think you'd have a much different perspective."

"That's all very true, but irrelevant," she replied. "I'm not there. I'm here. Leaders make decisions all the time that affect the lives of their men and women. We're leaders. We get paid to make the tough decisions."

Linda laughed, grinning at her. "You look so serious when you talk like that." She gave her a strong affectionate hug then held her out at arms' length. "That's one of the many things I love about you. You say what you think."

Giving her an awkward and sheepish smile, Sharon reached up to squeeze her hand. "Thank you."

A knock on the door caused them to abruptly separate. Sharon flopped down on a chair while Linda folded her arms and moved closer to the window.

"Come in," Linda called over her shoulder.

Jon Veldt walked in and hurried over to them. "I assume Sharon told you the news."

"Yes."

"It's not as bad as you think," he said, his demeanor relaxing.

"What do you mean?"

"He was going wobbly on us. When we searched his apartment we found his journal. Not really sure why anyone would want to keep a journal these days, but there it is."

"Go on," Linda urged.

"Well, apparently he was having second thoughts about working for us. He was actively contemplating working for the other side. All sorts of quotes highlighted in yellow from revolutionary leaders in history. He even quoted Che Guevara." He shook his head dismissively. "It's pathetic when someone quotes another, yet knows nothing of the real substance either of the quote or behind the quote. Anyway," he plopped down in the chair next to Sharon. "SI actually did us a favor by taking him out. Sort of ironic that they never gave him a chance. Got anything in that cupboard of yours over there that might interest a tired man?"

"Help yourself," Linda smiled patiently at him. "And while you're at it, close the door when you go by."

Tilting his head at her, he gave her a look of peaked interest. With an oomph, he pushed himself out of the chair, strolled across the room, detouring to close the door, and arrived at the bar. Opening the cabinet doors, he lifted out a diamond bejeweled bottle of Henry IV cognac.

"This will do." Pouring a healthy amount, he returned to his chair, inhaling the bouquet as he walked. "Now then," he suavely smiled, "what's all this about?" He ticked his heads at the closed door.

"How long would it take to extract our operatives in the Cordon Zones?"

"Why?" he cocked an eyebrow that settled quickly after his first sip of cognac. "This is exquisite." He lifted up his tulip glass in salute.

"Just answer the question, Jon."

Frowning in thought, he replied, "Depends. If it's a real emergency, we probably could get a majority of them out in say four weeks' time, providing we were able to get in communications with them within that first week. The problem, of course, is to get in contact with them. As you know, some we don't hear from for months because we don't know where they are. And then that brings up the problem of pulling out that many operatives all at once without seriously compromising our operations." He took another sip and closed his eyes in joyful satisfaction. Opening his eyes, he looked pointedly at Linda, giving her a knowing smile. "And all this begs the question of why would we want to pull out all our operatives in the first place, unless something was going to happen in the Zones?" He winked at Sharon. "N'est pas?"

Pursing her lips, Linda commanded, "Blinds up." Waiting for the room to be secured, she sat down and leaned forward gazing at both of them in turn. Turning her focus to Jon, she tersely said, "What I am about to tell you goes no further than this room. If it does, our careers are over. Understand?"

"Yes Mam," he replied, his smile vanishing.

Linda snapped a quick glance at Sharon, took a deep breath then said, "The Corporation will exterminate all the Cordons in the world on June 1st."

Jon nearly dropped his drink as he stiffened to sitting up straight. "June 1st? That's little more than three weeks from now. I can't get my folks out in time."

"I know," she coldly replied. "So does Corporate."

Jon was silent as he rapidly sorted and sifted the news. The words stung, but he knew she was right. He was going to lose a lot of trusted and capable men and women. "Why June 1st? Why not give us time to extract our people?"

"It's not my decision. In fact, I have violated my authority and position by telling you privileged information. Neither of you should know about this. However, I cannot allow the Corporation to so cavalierly ruin my operations without trying to save as many assets as I can. Even after the Zones are destroyed, we still have the remnants of Social Injustice and other insurgency groups to deal with. I'll need all the assets I can get to do my job."

"That means extracting our people now," he firmly replied.

"That's correct. I want you to begin extracting as many agents as you can without tipping our hand. Do it so that no one suspects what we're doing. Bring then in and send them someplace else. Put them with other agents in the Free Zones. I don't care how you do it, but save as many as you can."

Jon drained his cognac and stood up. "Thank you." He stuck out a hand. "It's about time we had a boss who cared about our people."

Surprised and pleased by this display of support, she shook his hand. "Remember. Nothing leaves this room."

"I can keep a secret," he winked. "Now if you'll lower the walls, I can get started."

Walking over to the bar, he placed his empty glass by the bottle of Cognac while Linda commanded "Blinds down."

With sunlight pouring into the room, he snapped his heels and gave her a British salute. Then with a final sober grin, he said, "I'll keep you posted as to how we're doing."

"Thank you Jon."

Once he left the room, she turned to Sharon. "You'll notice I did not include Chuck in our discussions."

"Yes, I did."

"That's because he's been promoted above his talents. Chuck Tilman needs to go. I want your input as to who should replace him. Choose someone who you know will work for you."

"Yes mam."

Linda gazed affectionately at her then reached for and squeezed her hand. "We've got a lot of work to do. We'll be putting in some long hours these next few weeks, not all of them here. You may want to bring some spare clothes."

Sharon understood her meaning and smiled. "Yes Mam."

Sierra Vista - Tucson Cordon Zone, Arizona

Pieter felt like a criminal released when he felt the truck stop and heard the subsequent banging and prying to open up the side of the survival box. As the side was pushed aside and bright sunlight filled the void, he squinted and blinked, letting his eyes get adjusted. A fit, middle-aged man stood before him, hands on his hips.

"Welcome to Arizona, Mister Dwa." He caught his breath as Pieter unfolded to standing. "Good Lord," he involuntarily uttered.

Pieter walked to the opening and stood momentarily, a hand resting on the side of the crate. Gazing beyond the man's shoulder at view outside the truck, he chuckled and said, "But it's a dry heat."

The man laughed. "I've been sent to welcome you. I'm Don Anderson, the Governor's chief of staff."

Another man, a younger tanned man with black hair, poked his head around the side. "We got to get going. We don't have much time."

"Right. Thanks Rudy. If you'll follow me," he said to Pieter, "we can continue on with our journey." He jumped down to the ground and waited for Pieter to follow.

Once on the ground, Pieter stretched and inhaled a deep breath. "Finally. It's good to be outside." He glanced quickly around. They were on a dirt road between two tall hills. On both sides of the road scattered cholla interspersed with tall ocotillo extended into the distance. "Where are we?"

"Not too far from Dragoon," Don replied. "We'll need to walk for a while, so I hope you're up for some exercise."

"After sitting on my butt for two days, I need the exercise." Pieter shook his legs and arms. "Let's go."

While the men with the truck closed it up and headed back the way they came, Rudy led the other two up the road into the mountains with Pieter easily keeping pace with his long strides. They had not walked far when the road bent and they came upon an aging building that had seen little use in the past years. Parts of the stone walls had fallen in and the brittle timbers holding up what remained of the rusted tin roof looked as though they were ready to yield their strength at any time.

Rudy led them off the road, circling around the building to come upon it from the far side. Once at the building, he turned to Pieter, sizing him up. "Listen Amigo, you need to be careful here. Do not disturb or touch anything. It needs to look like no one has been here in twenty years."

"I understand."

Rudy then carefully placed his hands on a portion of the tumbled down wall and slipped in between the wall and the broken roof, cautiously stepping to the side to allow the other two men to follow. The other two followed suit, with Pieter exercising the greatest care.

Once inside the decrepit building, Pieter watched as Rudy gingerly walked over to the stone fireplace and pressed one of the stones near the base. Pieter watched in amazement as the entire fireplace rose straight up until it was above their heads, the base supported by several stout steel bars. On one support midway between the fireplace and base, was a simple control switch with two buttons – the green for down and the red for up. When the fireplace stopped rising the empty space beneath was filled with a platform wide enough for two people.

"You'll have to scrunch down a bit, Amigo," Rudy told Pieter. "We'll send Don first then you and me."

Don stepped onto the platform and pressed the green button. Shortly, Pieter and Rudy were with him in a small room with a long tunnel with a single line of lights in the ceiling dwindling off into the darkness. It was wide enough for four people to walk abreast and tall enough so that Pieter did not have to duck his head, though his head was rather close to the ceiling.

"It's a long walk from here, so we better get started," Don said.

"Where does this go?" Pieter asked as they began the journey.

"It goes underneath the wall and comes out in Dragoon. From there, we'll get a ride to Sierra Vista."

"How far until Dragoon?"

"It's about thirteen kilometers."

"Thirteen kilometers?" Pieter blinked in surprise. "This tunnel is thirteen kilometers long?"

"Yup."

"How long did it take you to build it?" he asked, dodging an overhead light.

"Years," Don answered. "We had to be especially careful when we were near the wall. About a half mile from both sides, we went deeper to avoid the ground penetrating radar."

"What did you do with the debris?"

"We brought it over to the Zone side and used it to build homes and things like that."

They walked in silence for a bit before Pieter asked, "What's going on here that's so important that I needed to come here?"

"We have a lot going on, though I didn't see the need to send you here," Don amiably replied. "I know Gretchen wasn't too pleased to hear you were coming."

"I'm sure she's not." They walked in silence for a bit before he asked, "What happened to get her sent here?"

"Used to be a mid-level analyst for a stock company in Phoenix. Taught martial arts on the side. Got caught up in an insider trading scheme. She's innocent, of course."

"Of course," he wryly answered.

"But," Don nonchalantly said, "they needed a fall guy, or gal in this instance, and she was the one that got stung. SI saw an opportunity and the rest is as they say, history. She's one helluva woman. Brilliant and clever. Not bad on the eyes either."

"What else should I know?"

"Well," Don pondered. "Where to begin." For the next hour, he explained the organization of the Zone along with the

221

daily life and concerns. He stopped when it seemed the string of lights ended at a solid wall before descending into a wide hole.

"We're here at the stairs, Amigo," Rudy explained. "Be careful as you go down. Hold onto the railing. It's a long hard fall with a sudden stop at the end."

Pieter looked at the circular stairs cut out of solid rock and the flimsy metal pipe cemented into the side wall, and the string of lights dangling descending in a line in the middle of the stairs casting hazy shadows on the walls and steps. "How far down does it go?"

"About fifty feet," Rudy said. "Follow me."

Pieter let him get ahead for a bit then gingerly followed. He soon realized that his size played to his advantage as he was able to stretch his arms and steady himself using the stairs and handrail as supports.

Once at the bottom, Pieter couldn't help but feel enveloped, like he was inside a great tomb. The tunnel seemed smaller and lower, though that was probably his imagination. His chest tightened and he had to force himself to relax. "How far to the other side?"

"It's about a mile to the steps," Rudy replied.

"Let's go." He led off in great strides forcing the other two to jog to keep pace. It wasn't until he was finally standing outside in Dragoon in the clean mid-day air and sunshine that Pieter heaved a breath of relief.

"I know how you feel." Don gave him an empathetic grin. "I hate going in that tunnel. C'mon." Turning to Rudy he nodded appreciatively at him. "Thanks. Anything I need to take back to Gretchen?"

"Just let her know that they're sending more drones over the wall down by the old train track loop this side of the river. We've taken out a good number, but we can't keep up."

"How far are they penetrating?"

"They seem to be staying close to the wall for the most part, but there are some that are penetrating deeper and take off before we can get to them. We've reported them, but that's about all we can do."

"Will do." He led Pieter to the waiting car and they were soon heading east around the mountains.

"My geography may not be the best," Pieter said as he took in the wide vistas, but isn't Sierra Vista the other way?"

"It is," Don nodded, "but there are no paved roads that way and it's too close to the wall to get to Benson and with the drones out more, we can't take a chance. This way may be longer, but it's safer.

Several hours later, they were pulling into Sierra Vista where Don parked the car at the Sierra Pines apartment complex. Hustling Pieter into the apartment and down the elevator, he then guided him past the startled workers and security into Gretchen's office area.

"Sit tight while I go find Gretchen."

Pieter looked around the office, finding the eight foot high ceilings were closer to his head than he'd like. Gazing around the room, he couldn't help noting it was orderly and tidy... and barren.   There were none of the usual personal touches – pictures of family, wall decorations, or anything that said 'this is my personal space.' Two of the walls were glass; one looked out into the hallway while the other looked out to the wider office spaces filled with men and women in focused concentration. He was standing watching them when Gretchen walked in.

"So you're here," she said, walking past him to sit behind her desk.

"Nice meeting you too," Pieter replied, locking his gaze on her.

She returned the stare then leaned forward, her elbows on the cushioned armrests. "Let's be honest here. I don't need you. I don't know why Lowell sent you here."

"As long as we're being honest," he said, sitting down in a chair by the corridor window. "I'm not sure why I'm here either. But here I am. The way I see it, we can either come up with a mutually satisfactory plan to work together or we can be pains in the ass to each other."

Gretchen quietly studied him for a few moments. "What did Lowell say you were to do here?"

"He said that you had your hands full and could use some assistance."

"I already have deputies."

"Not like me," he smiled.

She smiled despite herself. "No. I suppose not. Still, I don't need another deputy."

223

"I'm sure you don't." He leaned back, resting his elbows on the armrests and interlaced his fingers. "Why don't you look at me as your spiritual advisor."

"Spiritual advisor?" She cocked an eyebrow in puzzlement. "I don't need a spiritual advisor."

"You might not," he calmly replied, "but what about them?" He turned his head to look out to the main office room. "What about the rest of those down here working, or others in Sierra Vista?"

"But we have priests and preachers here already."

"Again," he smoothly replied, "not like me."

"So what makes you different?"

He paused before he quietly said, "I'm a healer and spirit walker."

"I don't know what that means," she frowned.

"It means," he patiently replied, "that I have the power to heal and the power to send my spirit outside my body."

Gretchen warily studied him while she absorbed his statements. The man was either a quack or telling the truth. Lowell wouldn't have sent him here if he was a quack. "While I can see the relevance of healing, what's the purpose or use of spirit walking?"

"It's complicated," he succinctly answered. He was about to explain further when Maria came bursting in, waving a piece of paper in her hand.

"They've moved up the date," she exclaimed. "We just got word. 40 Trucks got moved up to June 1st. We got less than three weeks to beat them to it." She looked at Pieter, gave him brisk "Hi," and turned her attention back to Gretchen. "We need to implement rescue operations ASAP."

Gretchen jammed a hand on her hip, rapidly assessing the news. "Spread the word. Get the teams in place. We hit them three days before G-day. Get Zoe in here. We need to pull back from the wall as fast and as far as we can."

"Bring 'em here?"

"Yes. We need to start now." She jerked her head to Pieter. "You can help."

"I'd be happy to," he amiably agreed, "if someone would tell me what's going on."

"Corporation is going to annihilate all the Zones, once and for all, on June 1st. The only way we can stop it is if we strike first."

Pieter's eyes blinked wide in shock. "What do you need me to do?"

"Do what you came for. Help keep control. You'll be the chief priest or high priest or whatever you want to call yourself. All religious individuals will report to you."

"Fine."

"Now if you'll excuse me, I've a war to get ready. Walk around; get a feel of the place. It's going to be very crowded soon. Get with Zoe to find accommodations and spread the word on your appointment."

Pieter stood up and both the women's heads tilted back as they followed him up. With a polite nod to them both, he walked out.

"He is one big man," Maria uttered, turning to watch him lope down the hallway. "What's he going to do?"

"Don't worry about him for now," Gretchen briskly answered. "We got more important things to worry about."

Pieter had wandered around for about thirty minutes when he heard a ruckus behind him. Turning, he stood to the side as several medical staff ran past him. "What's going on?" he asked as another ran by him.

"Child got bit by a brown recluse," the woman said over her shoulder.

Pieter hurried after her and was soon peering into the room where a frantic Jennifer McBride was urging her husband to do something, anything. Lying on the table, their son, his face red with fever, shivered under the sheet. Down at his left leg, the sheet was pulled back to revel an angry blister that was blue in the center and ringed by red inflamed skin.

"I need antibiotics," Philip commanded.

The medical staff looked amongst themselves. "We have over the counter antibiotics," one offered.

Philip glared at him. "What kind of place is this?"

"The place where you're sent to with nothing more than the clothes on your back," another retorted. "We have over the counter drugs because we've been fortunate to steal them from the other side of the wall, where people like you have everything you need."

His lip curling in anger, Philip was about to explode when Pieter chimed in.

"Perhaps I can help."

Philip turned to look at the tall man. "You? Are you a doctor?"

"No. I'm a healer."

"A healer?" he retorted. "What do you mean? Are you a doctor or not?"

"As I just said," he calmly answered. "I am not a doctor. I am a healer."

"And just what does that mean?"

"We're wasting time," Jennifer wailed.

"It means," Pieter replied, ignoring her, "that I have the power to heal."

Philip stared at him for a moment before snarling, "We don't need any of your mumbo-jumbo witch doctor stuff here. We need real medicine."

His lips tightening, Pieter stepped forward and in a firm voice, commanded, "Get everyone out of the room. Now. You may stay," he said to Jennifer.

"I'm not leaving," Philip stubbornly said. "That's my son on the table."

"Fine," Pieter coldly replied. "The rest of you – out. You two stay out of my way."

"What are you going to do?" Philip demanded, placing himself between the boy and Pieter.

"Do you want him healed?"

"Of course."

"Then get out of my way." Towering above Philip, he scowled at him, daring him to challenge him again.

Heaving a 'You-don't-scare-me' sigh, Philip reluctantly moved to the side.

Pieter stepped to the table, placing a large hand on the child's forehead, feeling the heat of the fever. Closing his eyes, he hovered his hands in a kind of fluttering manner all over the child, pulling the poison and sickness from him. He cringed as he felt the pain seeping into his own extremities, working their way into his body. He continued fluttering his hands down around the leg then up towards the boy's chest, where they lingered for a while.

At last, he could feel no more poison in the child. He returned his hands to the wound and concentrated on healing. So intense was his focus that he didn't hear the "O my god,' escape from Jennifer.

His strength weakening, he knew he was about finished. Opening his eyes, he saw the wound nearly healed, the fever gone, and the boy resting comfortably. Wavering slightly from lightheadedness, he turned to the medical staff, issuing one command.

"Water."

"My god," Philip burst. "How did you... what did you do?"

"I took his disease away," Philp simply stated.

"To where?"

"At the moment, it is inside me." One of the staff handed him a water bottle that he chugged to empty. "Thank you."

"But... but how?" Philip demanded.

Pieter shrugged. "I don't know the how or why, but I know what happens. I am a healer and a spirit walker." He looked down on the child. "Your boy will live and be strong again."

Jennifer rushed up to him. Staring compassionately at him, she hugged him. "Thank you."

Pieter smiled at her. "You are welcome."

Releasing him, she went to stand next to her son, lightly brushing the hair on his head.

Pieter stepped though the group and into the hall, Philip following. The rest of the staff went into the room to help Jennifer.

"I've never seen or studied or heard anything like what I just witnessed," Philip said, still trying to understand what occurred.

"It is what it is," Pieter answered with a tick of the head.

Lowering his voice, Philip leaned closer. "You seem an intelligent man. What's it take to escape this place and go back to the real world?"

Pieter held his gaze for a bit before answering. "If you understood all that was happening in the world you would thank them for bringing you here."

"Thank them?" he sputtered. "For bringing me here, to this... this primitive place?"

"Whether you realize it or not, they've done you a favor. They've saved your life... and your family as well. Be patient. In a little while you will be thanking them for bringing you here."

Turning, Pieter headed back the way he came, leaving Philip to digest the cryptic and unwelcome response.

Chapter 8

Social Injustice compound – East Point
Monday, May 15, 2102

Martin walked into the room where he knew he would find JB and Ruth, side by side, holding hands… and watching TV.

"You two are going to rot your brains," he said with a half-smile of concern.

Ruth looked up at him and innocently said, "We're watching the justice channel. It's the program called 'You Decide.'"

Martin was about to tell them most TV was garbage when he decided they needed to learn for themselves.

The commercial ended and the scene shifted to the inside of a courtroom. A robed woman sat behind the elevated judge's bench. To her left, in the witness stand, stood a well-dressed teenager with short hair, sporting a contrite demeanor. A uniformed bailiff stood next to him.

Before her, behind the victim's podium, was a short older man, the bruising around his left eye an angry purple. There were scratches and abrasions on the other half of his face. The courtroom bar stretched behind him separating the court proper from the audience.

While the camera spanned the interior of the courtroom, the voice-over narrator explained, "We're back with Judge Alison and the case of Claxton versus Lenzo. Earlier, evidence against Lenzo was shown to the accuser and to the audience. We now share that evidence with those of you at home."

The scene changed to a crisp picture of an outside street corner in the afternoon. A briefcase in hand, Claxton stood alone at a bus stop waiting for his ride home. While he waited, Lenzo and several friends approached. Though not attired as he presently was in the courtroom, Lenzo and his friends appeared as typical middle-class youngsters. They were boisterous and rowdy and soon directed their attention to Claxton.

Doing his best to ignore the taunts and insults, Claxton's nervousness began to show and he decided that he would walk to the next bus stop and away from the annoying group of teenagers.

Lenzo had his back to Claxton, laughing with his friends. No sooner had Claxton taken his first step that Lenzo whirled around and cold-cocked him, sending him reeling to the sidewalk where he lay unresponsive while Claxton and his friends laughed and directed an occasional kick to the man's body. After sating themselves, the group nonchalantly walked off laughing, leaving Claxton to be discovered by a passerby several minutes later, who arrived at the same time as the police and ambulance.

The scene was repeated several more times from different camera angles, all caught by security cameras and drones. During the showing, audible indignation could be heard from the audience.

The scene ending, the screen filled with the courtroom. Judge Allison directed her attention to Claxton and then to the audience. "As you have witnessed from the evidence, the defendant has already been found guilty of assault, assault with intent, disruption to civil society, and attempted murder. The very callousness of the act demonstrates an individual of no benefit to society." With each succeeding pronouncement, Lenzo's contrite demeanor morphed to one of terror as he realized his fate.

"Don't I even get a trial?" he blurted.

"The defendant will refrain from further comments. Bailiff, you are instructed to keep the defendant in line."

"But –" Lenzo began when he received a harsh cuff to the side of his head by the bailiff.

"Any further outbursts," Judge Alison threatened, "and I will administer the verdict myself." Turning her attention back to Claxton, she continued. "As the injured party, you have the right by law to determine punishment. To assist you in your decision, those in the courtroom gallery behind you and those watching at home will input their verdicts onto the screen you see before you on the podium. The results from those sitting in the courtroom gallery are on the left, while those from home are on the right."

She paused then spoke to the assembled group. "I remind each of you, as well as the victim, that a well ordered and regulated society needs to impose judgments that sometimes appear harsh. However, we must all understand and recognize that no one is above the law, that the law is what keeps us apart from being brutish animals, like those in the Zones. I will now entertain relevant questions pertaining to this case." She looked down at the screen on her desktop as those in the audience and at home sent in their questions.

She then replied to a number of questions, silently reading the question before lifting her head to speak to the audience or the camera. "The guilty individual is fifteen years old." "Was the victim hospitalized? Yes." "Will other members of the group be sentenced? Yes. Those individuals will appear next." "How old are the members of the group? While the ages of those guilty individuals have no bearing on this judgement, I will allow that the ages are between twelve and fifteen."

She continued on for several minutes before stating, "I will take no more questions. I want to now impress upon each of you who are providing input to the victim just how to proceed. As the guilty verdict has been rendered, there are two options of punishment – death or banishment. If death is selected, you are then required to determine the methodology. Presently, the following methods are available: beheading by either guillotine or ax, hanging, electrocution, or lethal injection. If banishment is selected, no further actions are required. I want to remind everyone that the parents of these malcontents have already been sentenced to live the rest of their lives in one of the Zones."

She paused then said, "Members of the audience, please submit your votes now."

The program then broke for several minutes of commercials advertising everything from makeup to toilet paper to vacation locations. When the show returned, Judge Alison was studying the results. Casting her gaze on Claxton, she said, "You see the results before you. Once your decision is made, I will announce the results to those participating. Have your made your decision?"

Claxton looked at the results on his screen, then to the judge then to Lenzo. The boy was terrified and pathetic. His whole body begged for mercy.

"Yes, your honor, I have reached a decision," Claxton said, his voice subdued.

"Please tell the court your decision."

"Death by guillotine."

231

While Lenzo sank to his knees, the audience clapped its approval.

Judge Alison turned her attention to the teenager who wobbled as he was forcibly brought to standing by the bailiff. "You have been sentenced to death by guillotine, execution of said sentence to be carried out within twenty-four hours. Bailiff, remove the condemned."

As the trembling Lenzo was led away, Judge Alison announced the results. "Almost 97% selected death as judgement, whereas a little more than 3% chose banishment. Of the 97% selecting death, more than half chose guillotine while 40% selected hanging. The remainder selected lethal injection."

"Bailiff," she directed. "Please bring in the next convicted individual."

"OK, you two," Martin interrupted. That's enough for today. Besides, I need JB for an assignment."

"How come I never get to go on an assignment?" Ruth looked at him with begging eyes.

"You're much too valuable to send on such a dangerous mission." He winked at JB who broke into a broad grin.

"I won't be long," JB reassured her, patting her hand.

"Besides," Martin said. "From what I've heard, you have an artist talent greater than Michelangelo."

"I don't know who that is?" she pouted.

"He was considered one of the greatest artists of all time. What he created 500 years ago still exists in museums, galleries, and private collections."

"What's a museum?" she asked, her mood improving.

"It's a large building where the works of the greatest artists in the world are on display for everyone to see. People come from all around to the museum just to look at the pictures and sculptures."

"And you think I'm good enough to be in a museum?" she brightened.

"That's what I've heard. So if I were you, I'd get to drawing and painting as much as you can."

Bouncing up, she pulled JB to standing. "I'll stay here and draw instead. You go have fun with Martin." She pressed herself against him kissed him deeply.

As the two remained in passionate embrace, Martin awkwardly coughed to interrupt but they paid him no mind.

"OK you two. That's enough," he finally said.

Separating, Ruth gently stroked JB's cheek. "I'll be in the art room when you get back."

"It'll probably be after dinner by the time we return," Martin advised. "We'll find you when we get back."

"OK," she merrily replied, walking off to create.

Martin watched her for a bit before saying, "You two are good together. I hope you have a long and prosperous life together."

"When do you think we'll have children?" JB asked.

"Um... I'd wait a bit before you start thinking about that," he evasively answered.

"Why? You have children and there are others here who have children. Why can't we?"

Martin wanted to say, 'Because you're still a child yourself,' but instead comforted him with, "You and Ruth have only been in the world for a short time. There are many things to learn, one of them being how to raise a child. Making a baby is easy. Raising them is a whole 'nuther matter."

"I don't understand."

"You will," Martin sagaciously nodded. "You will. C'mon. We've a job to do."

JB looked around at the pictures, decorations, and furniture while Martin slipped on synthetic gloves and cleared the area next to the window. "Somebody still lives here." He started to pick up a picture when Martin stopped him.

"Here. Wear these." He handed him a pair of synthetic gloves. "They're to keep our finger prints off of things," he explained.

JB slipped on the gloves then picked up the framed picture to stare at a photo of a happy couple with two small children. They were at an amusement park. A clown with outrageous red hair and an even redder nose was standing with them.

"Are these the people who live here?"

Martin twisted his head to look at the photo. "Probably." He cleared the end table by the sofa and positioned it by the window.

"Suppose they come back while we're here?"

"They're on vacation."

"Vacation?"

"I'll explain later."

JB focused his attention on the two children in the picture. They looked the same. He held the photo up for Martin to see. "Are they like me?"

Martin paused his preparations to glance at the photo. "No. They're twins."

"What are twins?"

"Twins are two children born from the same parents who look exactly the same." He unlocked the gun case and began assembling the parts.

JB furrowed his brow in thought. "If people can make two of the same kind of children, why do they make people like me?"

"It's not the same," Martin patiently explained. Casting a glance at the wall clock, he said, "We still got time."

"Why is it not the same?"

"Twins are born at the same time," he explained, slightly pulling the curtain aside to check the line of fire. "They are the same age. Though they look the same, they are two different people. With clones, people like you, a person wants a twin, but a much younger twin. The only way to do that is to wait until the person is older then take a genetic sampling from the person and make a baby. Both the baby and the person now age at the same time. Say, for example the person was twenty years old when the clone baby was born. You're good with numbers. When the person is twenty five, how old is the baby now?"

JB thought for just a second. "Five."

"Very good. Now, when the person is forty, how old has the baby become?"

"Twenty."

Martin smiled at him with admiration. "You really do have a math mind. You're learning very quickly."

Pleased with the compliment, JB looked back at the photo. "So when the person is forty and his... clone, is twenty, the person then takes the... clone's body for himself."

"Exactly."

"And the clone dies because the man wants his body."

"That's exactly right."

JB mused for a moment. "If a person has more than one clone, are they twins?"

234

"Well," Martin replied with a pensive smile, "'twins' means two, as in two people who look alike. If there are three, then they're called 'triplets.' There are different words depending on how many."

JB slowly nodded in understanding. He then flipped the picture around for Martin to see. "What happened to him?" He pointed to the clown standing next to the mother.

Martin looked at the photo again and laughed. "Nothing. He's a clown." Seeing JB's vacant look, he said, "I'll explain later. Let's finish getting set up." He headed off to the dining room to retrieve a chair.

JB peeked through the curtains to the building down the street. A man attired in black hat and white gloves stood on the top step just outside the ornate doors as though protecting the building. "There's a man standing outside. He doesn't seem to be going anywhere."

Martin returned with the chair, placing it in front of the end table. Peering through the curtains, he frowned. "You've got good eyes. Ah. I see him now. That's the doorman. We'll need to be mindful of him. I'll hold the curtains open while you take the shot. Once you take the shot, we move away from the window. We don't need anyone to see where the shot came from. Go ahead and get yourself positioned."

Picking up the rifle, JB sat down, resting the bipod on the end table. Concentrating on the crosshairs in the scope, he zeroed in on the doorman who was quite a bit larger than without the scope. He pulled back the bolt, slipped a bullet in then locked it home.

"Why are we killing this person?"

"It's complicated. I'll explain when we get back. Let's just say this person has served her usefulness."

Pharr Court South, Atlanta

Linda had just started up the steps to her penthouse building when her phone rang and the voice ID announced it was Sharon. She paused on the step, pressing the earpiece to answer.

"Hey babe," she happily answered. "Where are you?"

"Turn around."

Linda turned to look behind her, saw nothing, but then looked across the street to see Sharon holding up a wine bottle in a canvass shopping bag in one hand, and waving impishly at her with the other.

"You goof," Linda grinned. "What are you doing?"

"I got an absolutely wonderful bottle of wine for tonight." She shook the wine bag as evidence, looking at the traffic as though she were about to cross.

"You called me to tell me that?" She shook her head with bemusement.

"Well, there is one more thing." Sharon stared across the traffic, locking her gaze on Linda, who smiled back at her with warm affection.

"Yes?"

"Can you go secure?"

Puzzled while at the same time curious, she answered, "Yes," then tapped the encryption button on her earphone. "What's so secret that you need me to go secure in the middle of a busy sidewalk?" She half-smiled at her.

"Remember I said that I would never disappoint you?"

"Yes," Linda responded with a warm smile, immediately fantasizing about a bedroom diversion.

"I lied."

Linda frowned at first then in the instant she comprehended Sharon's words, the bullet entered her forehead and exploded out the back.

On cue, Sharon reacted with horror and dodged traffic to race to her friend's side. Dropping to her knees, she quickly surveyed the apartment building in the line of fire. Thankfully the shooter had already closed the window and curtains. By the time she tapped her earpiece and called out "Corporate officer down! Officer down," the shooter would already be out the building. Glaring at the stunned doorman, she yelled out, "Get an ambulance, you fool!"

Social Injustice compound – East Point

It was the middle of the night when Martin roused JB and Ruth. "Get your things, you two. You're going on a trip."

JB rubbed sleepy eyes as he untangled himself from Ruth and sat on the edge of the bed. Ruth scooted herself up next to him. They were both naked and unaffected by their nudity.

Ruth looked up to see Martin, holding two suitcases, had turned his back to them. She looked past him to see who or what else was there. "What are you looking at?"

"Nothing."

"Then why are you turned around?"

"Because you don't have any clothes on."

Ruth stood up and walked around to face him. "Am I that bad to look at?"

Martin's eyes dropped to her chest then up to the ceiling. "I told you before; there are some habits you are going to have to unlearn. Not wearing clothes in front of other people is one of them. Remember?"

"But they never bothered making us wear clothes before," JB pointed out. "They even used to watch us do it through the window in the door."

"That's because they were perverts," Martin huffed. He dropped his gaze to focus intently into Ruth eyes. "Go put some clothes on."

"What's a pervert?" JB asked, sliding pants on.

"Someone who gets his kicks from watching other people without them knowing it," he muttered.

JB paused and frowned. "You mean someone was kicking them when they were watching us do it?"

"That's not what I mean," Martin sighed. "I'll explain later." He turned around just as Ruth was slipping a shirt over her shoulders. "Things are getting too hot around here and they're about to get hotter. We need to move both of you to a safer location. Take only what you need with you." He gave them each a suitcase.

"What about my drawing things?" Ruth pointed to the bureau piled with paper, colored pencils, and other artist materials.

"Yes, you can take those. Otherwise, just take clothing and things like that." He watched as Ruth put her clothes in with JB so she would have room in her own suitcase for her art materials. He smiled at JB who didn't blink an eye when she carefully placed her clothing with his. He wondered how many husbands would have been so cheerfully accommodating.

237

Once packed, Martin led them out into the quiet corridors and then out into the parking deck behind the building. There were no lights to illuminate the desolate area and they carefully made their way down the steps to the street where a van waited for them.

Lowell stood next to the van. "Martin explained to you that we need to move you?"

"Yes," both JB and Ruth replied.

"We're sending you to a place called Arizona. It's a long way from here and you'll be riding in the van for a long time. It's very important that you listen and do what you are told. We do not want the Corporation to know you are not here anymore. Understand?"

"Yes."

"When you get to Arizona, they will take good care of you there. I want you to find a man called Pieter Dwa. Tell him I sent you and he will look out for you. Pieter Dwa. Can you remember that?"

"Yes," JB replied. "Pieter Dwa."

"Good. Have a safe trip." He stood back and slid the side door open.

Ruth went in first, followed by JB. Lowell started to close the door when JB leaned forward to look at Martin. "You're not coming with us?"

"No. I still have work here to do. Don't worry though; everything with be OK." Nodding at the drivers up front, he reassured them. "Cheryl and Allyson will take good care of you. Remember to listen to them. I'll come find you when this is all over. OK?"

"OK," he replied, his disappointment obvious.

Martin slid the door closed and smacked the side of the van. Watching it slowly pull away, he said, "Is the Tucson Zone the best place to send them?"

"Safer than here," Lowell answered. "Gretchen has a secure underground facility. They'll be safe there."

"Let's hope they make it in time."

"They'll be fine. What's the status on our assault teams?" he asked as they walked back up the steps. "We have less than a week before we attack."

"The assault teams are fine. I'm more concerned with having enough transportation and drivers to get everyone back here. We're still stockpiling food and water. Hopefully the walls will hold before Corporation hits us hard." He stopped and turned in time to see the brake lights bream brighter as the van slowed to turn down another alley way. "We've been left alone for a long time. Corporation knows we're in here. The only reason I can determine that they have left us alone is because we are not an official Zone and if they came hard down here, word would spread faster than melted butter. But so what? They could always claim they were rooting out Social Injustice."

"We can thank Sharon for that," he replied then cryptically added, "and others. We'll be fine. We just need to make sure we get as many clones here before the bio attack."

Social Injustice complex – Sierra Vista
Tuesday, May 16, 2102

In the mid-morning sunlight Pieter stood inside the edge of the warehouse, inhaling the sweet desert air. In the distance, the Mule Mountains rose before him. If he took just one step outside the protective walls and roof of the warehouse, he could turn to his right and see the Huachuca Mountains that seemed so much closer. He felt the long suppressed desire to go running, striking out across the desert in long satisfying strides, up the forest paths into the mountains to stand at the top, to take in the long vistas that seemed to stretch for days. He wondered what the view would be like standing at the top of Miller Peak.

He had been living in the dark for so long these past days that he now simply closed his eyes, arms dangling at his sides and let the warmth of the sun wash over him, savoring the pleasure of simply being outside. He remained standing there until he heard someone approaching. Not wanting to be distracted, he ignored whoever it was and reveled in the morning air. He felt the presence come closer to stand next to him.

"It is refreshing, isn't it," Gretchen said.

Opening his eyes, he looked down at her. Her arms folded in front of her, she inhaled deeply, letting the stress sluff away off her shoulders.

"I think we need to spend more time out here," he observed, "especially when the time comes for us to remain below is approaching so quickly."

"A lovely idea," she agreed. She gave him a warm smile. What she once thought was going to be a problem had turned into a blessing. She didn't understand the man's gifts, but one thing she could see was the serenity he exuded had an effect on all who worked in the 'Mines' as everyone down below referred to their underground accommodations. And Pieter never interfered with her authority, never sought to assert his position as a leader. He simply moved among the people and they gave him their devotion and affection. Even the children were captivated by the gentle giant. It was common to see him walking down the halls surrounded by kids and adults alike, all vying for his attention to which he unselfishly lavished on everyone.

Furrowing her brows, she wondered if she was jealous at the devotion everyone gave him, especially after all the healings. She chuckled to herself. She wouldn't be the least surprised if he raised someone from the dead. She then shook her head at herself, for now she was getting carried away. She was a pragmatist, a realist. While he may have a healing gift, she had the responsibility of saving everyone's life down here, not just the sick.

"Well," she finally said. "Enough ruminations. How'd you like to go for a drive?"

"Love to," he brightened.

"I thought now would be a good time for you to meet the Governor, Kevin Gonzales. He lives in what was once the post commander's house on what used to be Fort Huachuca, although everyone still calls it Huachuca."

"I assume he knows what's going on here?"

"Most of it," she replied. "He's been helpful in corralling the topside folks to get down below. He's been here a couple of times, but it didn't work out to get you two together. I thought it would be nice to do it now, outside, while we still can be outside."

"I appreciate that," he heartily answered.

A large sedan with tinted windows pulled up behind them. A young man popped out the driver's side and opened the back door for Gretchen. Pieter got his own door on the other side and

240

slid in next to her. The sedan was quite roomy and he was able to stretch out his legs.

"This is nice," he complimented.

"Thought you might like the extra room," she grinned then addressed the driver. "To the governor's house, Stan." Heading out of the complex, he turned left onto Moson Road, then left again on Highway 90. Soon they were heading through town towards the old post. Passing the long disused and dilapidated control gate, they soon arrived at the well maintained house on Grierson Avenue.

Stan pulled up in front and parked. He got out and opened the door for Gretchen while Pieter emerged from the other side. Gretchen led the way up the steps onto the screened front porch. Opening the door, she proceeded to knock on the main door, which was opened a few moments later.

A surprised and nonplussed Kevin stiffly said, "Gretchen. What a pleasant surprise. What brings you here?" He stepped out onto the porch, partially closing the door behind him.

"May we come in?" She cocked an eyebrow at him.

"What? Uh, yes... yes, of course." He took in the man next to her. "You must be the Pieter Dwa I've heard so much about."

"Guilty as charged," Pieter lightheartedly replied.

They stood awkwardly staring at each other until Gretchen burst past him and marched into the house. She led the way into the various rooms until she found the source of his discomfit. A man sat in a thick armchair, his back to them. He kept his back to them as they entered the room. Gretchen went around to stand in front of him.

"Who are you?" she demanded.

Before he could answer, Pieter walked up. "Mister Warfield. We meet again."

Warfield blanched as he stiffened. "Mister Dwa," he uncomfortably replied.

"You two know each other?" Gretchen cast them both a surprised look, then looked at Kevin who was equally mystified.

"Yes we do," Pieter calmly answered, "don't we Mister Warfield." It wasn't as question.

"Yes. We do know each other." Warfield replied, his prior look of fear replaced by calm resignation.

"How?" Gretchen asked.

"Mister Warfield is a Corporate agent," Pieter coolly explained. "He tried infiltrating our operations in Atlanta." He looked down at the half-finished cup of coffee. He picked up the cup and inhaled the bouquet. "The question I have is why is he here and why is he enjoying a cup of some of the finest coffee to be found in the Zone... with the governor, no less?"

Gretchen cast an accusatory look at Kevin.

"I didn't know he was a Corporate agent. I thought he was just a new arrival," he spouted.

Pieter let out a deep throated laugh. "That was one of the worst excuses I've heard in a long time. I suppose you treat every new arrival to a cup of coffee at your place?" He laughed again.

Even Warfield smiled at the pitiful attempt at exoneration. "Give it up Kevin. You're little façade is over. What a pity. Looks like you had a good thing going here."

Gretchen's face twisted into anger. "You son of a bitch." Before he had time to react, she hauled back and decked him hard across the jaw, sending him reeling backwards over the table and onto the floor. Shaking her hand at the pain, she glared at him as he nursed his pride and jaw. "We trusted you. We took you into our confidences."

It was then she realized the depth of his duplicity. "That agent was right when he said you were a traitor. You had him killed to silence him."

"You don't understand," he pleaded.

"Oh I understand plenty," she snarled. "You're a traitor, a traitor to everyone here, everyone who put their trust and faith in you."

"Listen," he begged. "It's not like that. Warfield here," he pointed at the man who was still quite calm, "was sent to kill me, because I had gone off the grid." He snapped his head to stare at Warfield. "Tell them."

"That part is true," Warfield said, picking up the cup of coffee and taking a sip. He looked up at Pieter. "When my cover was blown in Atlanta, they gave me another mission." He ticked his head at Kevin, "To take him out. They had the feeling he had gotten too comfortable here, that he was defecting to the dark side." He snorted a laugh at his own joke."

"And you had a change of heart," Pieter melodramatically announced.

"Something like that. You got any more coffee?" He raised his cup to Kevin.

"I'll take some of that too," Pieter said. "Why don't you go with him, Gretchen, while Mister Warfield and I get reacquainted?"

"He can go by himself. If he runs, he won't get far."

"Suit yourself," Pieter smiled and sat down opposite Warfield.   "Now why don't you tell us the truth, Mister Warfield. You must realize that you're a dead man unless you can convince us there's a reason to let you live."

As Kevin slunk away towards the kitchen, Gretchen positioned herself so she could see him and be part of the conversation at the same time.

"Like I said," Warfield began. "My cover was blown in Atlanta and they figured to send me far enough away to give me another mission. Kevin had been a problem for some time and the agents they sent here kept getting killed."

"So you volunteered for the job," Pieter sarcastically replied.

"It's not like I had a choice," he retorted. "It's not like Social Injustice where they actually care about what you think."

"You sound unhappy, Mister Warfield.   Certainly the Corporation provided for all your needs."

"Monetarily, yes," he shrugged. "But let's face it. The life expectancy of a Corporate agent in the Zones isn't exactly a selling point."

Leaning forward, Pieter looked him square in the face. "So what's the real reason you didn't kill him?"

Warfield paused to return Pieter's stare. "Because he's my brother."

Pieter blinked in surprise and sat back. "The Corporation sent you to take out your own brother?"

"In a manner of speaking, yes."

"That's rather harsh, even for the Corporation."

"Actually he's my half-brother.   Though we grew up together, we have different last names. Part of me would like to think the Corporation didn't know about that. However, the rational part of me accepts that the Corporation knew all along we were related and sent me here as a test, which I have apparently failed."

"When did you know he was here?" Gretchen interrupted.

"They wouldn't tell me the name, only that the man was the governor. It wasn't until I saw who it was that I knew I couldn't do the mission."

Gretchen looked back into the kitchen. "What's taking so long in there, Kevin? All you had to do was put some coffee in a pot and bring it out here."

"I'm coming," he testily answered.

"So what was your plan, once you realized you wouldn't complete your assignment?" Pieter asked Warfield.

"I obviously couldn't go back and... well, since I was here already, I figured I'd just blend in." He flashed Pieter a smile of bemusement. "Of course you being here sort of ruined that idea." He raised his voice for Kevin to hear. "You didn't tell me he was here."

"How was I supposed to know you two knew each other," Kevin shot back. He then stepped back into the room, but instead of holding a coffee pot, he held a Hellcat .380 in his right hand and pointed it at Gretchen. "You need to move over by your boyfriend there."

"He's not my boyfriend," she frowned at him before she saw the pistol. "What are you going to do?" she sneered. "Shoot me?"

"No," he calmly replied. "I'm going to shoot him." He swung the weapon towards Pieter and squeezed off a round, jerking his body to the left and sending him collapsing to the floor.

Training the pistol back on Gretchen, he gave her a half-smile. "Now I'm going to shoot you." The pistol barked and she reeled back a step before stumbling over Pieter and tumbling onto the floor.

Hearing the shots, the driver burst into the room. Seeing Kevin, gun in hand, the young man spun around to flee but wasn't quick enough before Kevin pumped two rounds into his back. He slumped down in the doorway.

"Was this really necessary?" Warfield frowned, standing up.

"You don't understand," Kevin brusquely answered. "Once word got out that I was Corporate, there'd be a lynch mob up here out to hang me from the first pole they could find." He pressed the clip released to see how many rounds remained.

244

"And here I thought you were so well loved by all," Warfield sardonically said.

"Save it," he snapped. "We got to get out of here." He hurried back into the kitchen, retrieving several boxes of shells. Hustling back in, he looked at the two bodies on the floor and the one in the doorway. "Just damn. I had a perfect setup here."

"Sorry I screwed it up for you," Warfield tartly replied.

"Can't be helped." Jamming the pistol in the back of his pants, he cast a sharp glance at Warfield, quickly sizing him up. "We're still about the same size. Grab something to pack some clothes in. We got maybe five minutes before all hell breaks loose." He headed upstairs to the bedroom.

"Where we headed?" Warfield asked, following him up the stairs.

"South, down towards Hermosillo. We're gonna have to lay low for a while. I got enough coin for us to live on for a while."

"Then what?" Warfield asked, pulling drawers open and pulling out shirts and shorts.

"Then that one little thing I haven't had time to tell you about yet is going to happen." He indiscriminately jammed clothing into two suitcases and then snapped them shut. "Let's go.

"What little thing?"

"On June 1st," he said racing down the stairs, "the world as we know it is coming to an end."

Ravinia Drive, Dunwoody

Hans Josef looked across his desk at Sharon whose somber expression told him she was still dealing with the death of her friend. "Let me express my sympathy for what you must be experiencing at this moment. I know she was a close friend."

"She was closer than a friend," Sharon softly replied.

"Yes, yes. Quite right." He gazed kindly at her. "Would you like a drink?"

Blinking at the offer, she nodded. "If you are having one, then yes. That would be very nice."

Pleased, Hans scooted back from his meticulously clean and organized desk and crossed over to the 16th-century Italian credenza by the wall. On top was a crystal decanter surrounded by six crystal snifter glasses.

"I have an excellent Napoleon brandy."

"Sounds wonderful," she replied, standing up. Folding her arms in front of her, she slowly walked to gaze out the tall windows of his office. She couldn't help but notice that where Linda's office was large, Hans' office was huge. The two solid walls were covered with bookshelves, paintings, and lithographs. The other two walls were glass that rose up to the twelve foot ceiling. His desk was positioned so that he could look out the windows and still see who came in through the door.

Hans approached and offered her the glass. Lifting his in salute, he said, "Here's to her memory. You were very fortunate to have shared your time together."

Sharon clinked her glass against his then took a sip. "That was very nice. Thank you."

Hans turned to look out over the Atlanta skyline. Sipping his brandy, he said, "I know you are grieving right now, but life must go on. I do not wish to make light of your heartache, but I need you to be focused on the here and now. There are things about to occur that will cause life as we know it to catastrophically change." He paused and turned to gaze around his office and at the expensive antiques and furnishings. "What a pity," he softly muttered. "I shall miss all this."

"Sir?"

As if reawakening to his surroundings, he refocused his attention to his guest. Studying her for a moment, he motion her to be seated while he commanded 'Blinds up."   While the wall blinds rose and the lights in the ceiling brightened to an almost romantic ambiance, he took a seat opposite her.

Once satisfied with the security measures, he slowly inhaled all the while intently staring at her face, causing her to squirm under his stare.

"Let's be realistic, shall we?" he began.

"Yes, Sir."

"Please," he suavely smiled, "not so formal."

"Yes, Sir... I mean, Hans," she politely smiled.

"That's better." He leaned back, resting one elbow on the arm of the chair while taking a slow satisfying sip of Bourbon. "The Corporation's decision to move up the time table of 40

Trucks is really of no consequence. The end state of the operation is the complete annihilation of the Zones. Whether that occurs three weeks from now or four months from now is really irrelevant as the result will be the same. Don't you agree?"

"Yes," she readily agreed.

Fixing her with a sharp eye, he said, "But suppose those in the Zones discover Corporate's intent. What would happen then?"

"Pardon?" she blanched.

"I said, what do you think would happen if the Zones uncovered the plot for their destruction?"

Sharon paused as if in thought. "There's really not a lot they can do about it. They're essentially caged as it is. What resources do they have that could stop the Corporation?"

Hans smiled slyly. "I notice you said 'Corporation' and not 'us.' It's almost as though you're hesitant about the relationship you have as an employee of the Corporation."

"I think you may be reading way too much into my response," she calmly said. "When I use the term 'us,' I'm usually referring to 'us' here at SEI, my immediate Corporate family."

Grinning broadly, he nodded in defeat. "An excellent answer. I see now why Linda was so keen on you." He placed the bourbon glass on the side table, crossed one leg over the other and interlaced his fingers in front of him. "But let's get to the heart of the matter, the reason why I brought you here today. Lamentably, we have lost two Executive Directors of SEI in a span of less than two months. Both their sudden demises are regrettable, especially Linda's. Not that Collin's death was less of a tragedy, but to be frank, he did not measure up to the job. Linda, on the other hand, was an exceptional performer. With her passing, you will take over as the Executive Director for SEI, effective immediately."

"Thank you, Sir... Hans," she replied with heartfelt gratitude.

"Don't thank me yet," he half-smiled. "These next three weeks are going to be exceedingly busy and perhaps difficult, for you will have to balance Corporate responsibilities with you own personal welfare."

"I'm not afraid of hard work," she forthrightly replied.

247

"I'm sure you're not," he paternally answered. "But let's return to the question I asked before. What do you perceive happening if the Zones discovered what was in store for them?"

Sharon thought quickly. "Depending on when the Zones discovered the threat would determine their response. If they found out now, that would give them some time to react, most likely infiltrating into the Free Zones as quickly as possible. A mass influx would overload the capacity to remove them and send them back, probably causing a delay in the operation. If they found out just before the attack, some would escape to the Free Zone, but most would be caught and die in place."

"An excellent quick analysis." He lifted the bourbon glass for another sip. "Now let's factor in a Zone capability to counter-attack."

"With what?" she frowned. "It's not like they have an army."

"Suppose they did? Say, not an army in the traditional sense, but one that could employ drones and the use of biological agents." He looked at her over the rim of his glass.

Sharon blinked at his statement, working though his line of questioning. "Are you saying the Zones have biological weapons?" she evasively asked.

Giving her a knowing grin, Hans placed the bourbon glass on the low coffee table between them. "Take a few days to get yourself organized. At the same time, I think it would be in your best interests to find suitable lodgings, stocked with sufficient supplies, which would allow you to survive for, say, six months to a year. Preferably a place that has restricted access. I believe you might know of a place already."

"I... I don't understand," she fumbled. "Are you saying that a global war is about to occur?"

Instead of answering, he stood up. "When you're settled, don't bother looking for Linda's assassin. He's long gone. But you knew that already, didn't you?"

"I... I don't know what you mean?" she replied, struggling to keep her voice from revealing her nervousness.

Curling a finger at her, he motioned her to follow him to his desk. Once there, he pressed the button to raise the desk monitors. On the one screen was the drone image of Sharon holding the wine bottle aloft. Opposite her across the street, standing on the bottom step, Linda stood smiling contentedly.

"When I reviewed this, I wondered why the shooter should choose this time to assassinate Linda with both of you conveniently at the same place and time? Why didn't he take you out when you ran across the street?"

"I thought the same thing."

He then rotated the view so the focus was squarely on Sharon. "I'm not a very good lip reader, especially when someone doesn't move her lips when she speaks." Hans then played the entire scene with Linda jerking back from the shot and Sharon dodging traffic to get across.

"You're quite the actress," he commented.

"I don't know what you mean," she indignantly replied. "She was my friend."

"And that's what you led everyone to believe," he serenely stated. "You even had me fooled. Well done." He pointed to the screen and Sharon's reaction to the hit. "Your emotional reaction was just a little too over the top. A good performance, but a bit too overplayed, don't you think? And then there was that furtive glance back at the place where the shooter was. Yes, well done." He gazed at the screen and commanded, "Delete all copies Linda Nadell assassination." The screen window popped up asking 'Are you sure?' "Yes." The screen window announced it was deleting all the Linda Nadell assassination files then asked, 'Delete Cloud Storage?' "Yes." Glancing over at Sharon, he smiled. "There now. All incriminating evidence is gone."

"I... I don't understand," she said, flustered.

"You will, in time," he assured her. "For now, I want you to concentrate on taking care of yourself, providing for the future. As far as the job goes, I want you to focus your efforts on realigning the organization. That should take up the remaining time between now and June 1st. If you have any questions, don't hesitate to call me. Remember," his eyes narrowed to her, "You and I are in this together. Screens down."

The epiphany exploded within her and she remained rooted in her surprise.

As sunlight filled the room, Hans sat down and began reading his message traffic. Looking up, he smiled. "Anything else?"

Sharon shook herself to action. "No, Hans. It will be as you directed. I'll keep you posted of my progress."

"Thank you," he smoothly replied. "Have a good rest of the day."

The Governor's House, Sierra Vista
Tucson Cordon Zone, Sierra Vista, Arizona

The pain swirled inside him as Pieter's spirit moved away into a void of darkness that gradually began to gain substance, the edges of things first, then with the barest hints of translucent color. As shape and color grew, he saw movement and tall forms moving towards him. They gained substance as they approached. He immediately recognized his grandmother, Gao Dwa, who looked amazingly like the woman in the picture he had on the wall in the office, before it was torched by the Corporation. With her were other spirit elders of the tribe. Some he remembered, others were unfamiliar, most likely transitioning to the spirit world long before he was born, for they still wore the clothing of their time, an adaptation of western dress mixed with African sensibility of colors, vibrant and living.

"It is not your time to be here yet, Grandson," Gao Dwa spoke. Her voice was serene and comforting. "You must go back."

"I have been injured, Grandmother," he reverently said.

"We know, Grandson," she kindly replied. "That is why we are here... to send you back before your journey here takes you too far to return."

A resonating peace enveloped him, unlike anything he had ever experienced before. "But I do not want to return. I wish to stay with you, Grandmother."

"Your time will come, my grandson, but not yet. There is still much for you to do. The woman beside you still lives. You must go back and save her. It is too late for the young man. His spirit has already departed."

"Must I go back?"

"Yes. You must save this woman before it is too late. Already her spirit tugs to be free."

Pieter paused in indecision. "When will I come back?"

"That is something we do not know. You will come when it is your time. Until then, accept your fate as it is, for it was written long before you were born."

"I don't understand," he argued. "How do you know I am not supposed to be here now?"

"You will understand in time," she patiently chastised him. "Be content that for now, you are intruding. Already you have spent more time here that necessary. You must go. Will you obey me as you have always done in the past?"

"Yes Grandmother," he contritely replied.

"Good. Then we will now send you back."

The elders surrounded him, laying their fleshless hands on him, chanting in a reverberating hum that rattled and shook him from the inside out. Pain surged and he let out a cry as he jerked awake.

He still lay on his side. Gretchen lay next to him, her breathing in short staccato gasps. The pain subsiding, he forced himself up to his hands and knees, feeling light-headed as he steadied himself.

He crawled closer to her then sat back on his legs, scooting up next to her. Closing his eyes, he hovered his hands in a kind of fluttering manner over the wound, pulling death and the leaded bullet from her body. He cringed as he felt the pain of death seeping into his own extremities, working their way throughout his body.

The pain continued to grow until he could stand it no more and he cried out, "Grandmother, help me!" before toppling backwards in a cold faint.

Voices broke through his consciousness and Pieter realized they were talking about him. Yet what they said made little sense and he paid little attention to it as he struggled to waken. Finally blinking in the bright lights of the clinic room, he slowly turned his head and took bearing of his surroundings.

To his right, Gretchen lay in a bed, her face calm in restful slumber. He felt heavy, yet he wanted to sit up. He started to position his hands to help, when he felt hands press him back into bed.

"Not so fast, Mister Dwa."

He twisted his head and saw Doctor Philip McBride standing before him. Pieter then noticed something attached to his hand and saw an IV taped to it. "How'd I get here?"

"Don Anderson brought you in," he answered. "I'll let him tell you all about it. But how about we rest for a bit more? You could use some extra sleep."

Pieter felt even more lethargic and settled back against the pillow and was soon asleep. When he woke up hours later, he was hungry. Pushing himself up on his elbows, he looked over and saw Gretchen sitting up in bed, eating a sandwich.

"The hero awakens," she teased, smiling with more than heartfelt gratitude.

"How long have I been out?" He looked down at his hand and the IV had already been removed. He was about to toss the covers off when he noticed that he was quite naked beneath them. Pulling them around him, he managed to sit up.

"Don said they found us before noon and it's now about 1900, so I'd say around six or seven hours, give or take."

His stomach growling, he looked around the room for another food tray.

"They'll be back in a minute. I told them you wanted your steak well done."

"Steak?" His eyes brightened.

"Just kidding," she grinned, "though maybe they might be able to rustle up a burger or something."

Pieter studied her for a bit. She seemed rather nonchalant about her near-death experience. He then saw her twist and cringe.

"Doc said it's gonna hurt for a while. He doesn't know or understand how the bullet managed to extract itself out of my body, let alone heal so well with just a little scar, but I said he'd have to talk with you about that." She held his gaze with hers. "Won't he." It wasn't a question.

Instead of an answer, he gave her an awkward shrug.

Still staring intently at him, she inhaled a slow breath. "Thank you for saving my life."

His first inclination was to flippantly say 'Aw it was nothing,' but he knew better, for just as it wasn't his time to go, neither was it hers. "We both have been given a gift of a renewed life. I pray we won't have to do that again." He smiled at her.

"I'd almost forgotten that you had been shot too, until I saw you in the bed next to me. I was so focused on living that I neglected to take care of you."

"There was nothing you could have done," he told her. "I was in another's hands." Changing the subject, he asked, "What about Kevin and Warfield?"

"Don't know where they've gone. Our land lines only go to Aqua Prieta. They could be anywhere in the Zone and even out of the Zone for all we know. We've got drones out looking for them, but we really can't waste the time on them. Don's stepped up to be the acting governor until we can do a proper election, but that's gonna have to wait until the dust settles." Gretchen suddenly felt awkward. "I feel like I'm rambling."

"You have a lot to worry about," he reassured her.

Doctor McBride came in holding a tray of food that he set down next to Pieter. Giving him a friendly yet reserved smile, he said, "I won't pretend to understand what happened topside, but when you've time, I'd like to discuss your healing abilities."

Pieter looked down at the meat and cheese sandwich on the tray then up to McBride.

"This is a clinic, not a restaurant," McBride gently chided. "If you want a good meal, I suggest you go to the dining hall."

"And when can I leave?" Pieter looked around for his clothes.

"There's no reason for either of you to stay here. Once you are ready, you are, unlike me and my family, free to leave." He was about to leave when Gretchen stopped him.

"Doctor McBride. I'll make a deal with you. You stay here until June 1st. If after that, you still want to leave, no one will stop you."

McBride stood and stared at her, gauging the truth in the offer.

"That's only two weeks from now," she added. "Just a little more time, then you are free to go where you will."

"I have your word?"

'You have my word."

"You're witness to this," he said to Pieter.

With a muted sigh, Pieter shook his head. "You still don't get it. First, you don't need me as a witness, because her word is good enough by itself. Second, by June 1st, you'll be thanking everyone here for saving your life."   Looking over to her, he said, "Ready to get back to work?"

"I've just been waiting for you," she teased. She gave both the men a mischievous glance and said, "Are you two going to watch me dress or can I have some privacy?"

Chapter 9

Pharr Court South, Atlanta
Wednesday, May 17, 2102

Sharon stood by the door while the real estate agent pressed his palm against the entry scanner.

"This is an absolutely stunning home," he gushed. "A little under 500 square meters. It comes with all the upgrades, including a built-in wine cooler with space for over 300 bottles." He opened the door and they stepped into what once was Linda Nadell's home.

Sharon stopped and took in the place, remembering the times she had spent here. The agent misinterpreted her pause.

"I see you've noticed the home is still furnished. Sad to say, the former owner met with an unfortunate accident and will not be reclaiming the possessions. Not wishing to be indelicate, these furnishings you see here come with the home."

"I understand," she nodded.

"You certainly may do with them as you wish, but I must tell you, the former owner spared no expense in apportioning this lovely home."

"I'll certainly take that into consideration," she politely replied. She motioned with her hand for him to continue the tour. "Please."

The agent led her through all the rooms, nooks, and crannies she already intimately knew. By the time they returned to the front door, Sharon had relived moments in each of the rooms.

"As I've already mentioned, this is a stunning home and the price is certainly manageable, especially with someone as young as yourself in such a position of responsibility. I see no problem getting an extended loan for fifty or more years."

Sharon silently and slowly nodded. Then holding his gaze with hers, she said, "I'll take it."

Social Injustice complex – Sierra Vista

Gretchen gazed out over the assembled group in the auditorium. Before her were the leaders and managers of the operations underground. On the platform with her were Maria, Zoe, Pieter, Don, and several other key leaders.

"I have asked you all to be here today in order to make an important announcement. You all know by now that the Corporation intends to destroy all the Zones throughout the world on June 1st." There was a rising hubbub of indignation and grim determination.

"Initially," she continued, "we had thought to preempt the Corporation by launching a strike well in advance of their anticipated attack. We had thought that a week would be sufficient to disrupt their plans. However, upon further review, we have determined it would be to our advantage to take the attack to the Free world as soon as we are ready. Therefore, it is our intention that we will strike one week from today."

The hubbub broke out it raucous applause and cheers. Patting her hands in the air to silence them, she loudly announced, "We have much work to do between now and then. Rescue teams must work hard to bring in as many as possible without alerting possible spies or agents of the Corporation. As many of you know, our former Governor, Kevin Gonzales, turned out to be a Corporate agent."

There was shock and consternation at the man's duplicity as those who knew him wondered how much they might have compromised.

"Where is he?" a voice shouted out.

"We're still looking for him, but to be truthful, we can't afford to spend time and assets searching for him. He is one of the reasons for us moving up our time-table. We have drones working the known tunnels, but it's very possible he's gone south towards Hermosillo or maybe even Chihuahua. We've sent word to Hermosillo, but we don't have time to send someone to Chihuahua. But rest assured, if he survives this, he will be dealt with."

She paused for the group to settle. "But he is the last of our worries right now. We need to focus on our future. That means we all need to be prepared for what happens after our attack, for without a doubt, the Corporation will retaliate. Everyone in here

256

is vitally important to our success, as is everyone below you, from the cooks and pot cleaners to the teachers who care for our children to the maintenance men and women who care for our temporary home.   Be sure you tell them how important and necessary they are.   While they might be on the front lines, they are vital to our success."

She began pacing the stage.   "And that brings me to our main focus – the attack on Corporation.   This will be a two-fold operation, an attack and rescue.   There are two Resurrection facilities in Tucson and we will rescue as many clones as possible.   As the attacking forces are retreating back to the Zone, the drone force will immediately launch their attack.   This is a globally coordinated attack.   Once the drone attack is finished, we hunker down and wait for the retaliatory strike.   As the Corporation has no military-grade weapons, their weapon of choice will one of mass destruction – biological agents.   You will impress upon all your people that under no circumstances are they to leave the facility during the next year.   Anyone exiting the facility will not be allowed back in.

She folded her arms and stood defiantly before them.   "I repeat.   Anyone leaving the facility, regardless of the reason, will be left to fend for themselves – outside.   Does everyone understand?"   She was greeted with nods of heads and a few who audibly said, 'Yes.'

"Good.   You will all receive the operations order later today.   If you have any questions, come see me afterwards."   With that, she marched off the stage, leaving the others to answer immediate concerns.

SEI Directorate – Decatur
Thursday, May 18, 2102

Sharon was startled when the video screen in her office beeped and Hans Josef appeared.

"Am I interrupting?" he smoothly asked.

"No, sir."

"Good.   Go secure.   I'll wait."

257

Sharon commanded the screens to raise while the bolts to the office door slid home and the outside light flashed "Security Briefing in Progress."

"I'm ready."

"Excellent. So how are things going so far?"

Sharon frowned, wondering why she had to go secure just for him to make small talk. "Um... fine."

"Good, good. I was wondering how your cough was coming along."

"My cough?" She tilted her head vainly trying to understand what made him think she had a cough.

"Yes. Your cough. I understand you're experiencing some chest problems, possibly a cold or perhaps even a flu bug."

"I am?" she numbly replied, mystified.

"Yes," he replied, staring hard at her. "In fact, I'm feeling a bit off myself. I'm thinking I may need to visit the doctor in the next day or two. You should too. My guess is that she'll tell you to stay home for a few days to rest. In fact, you're going to be out all next week, aren't you?"

His meaning finally penetrating through her confusion, she blinked at the realization there had been a change in operational plans. Clearing her throat in several coughs, she nodded. "Now that you mention it, I have been feeling a bit run down. I was just ignoring it, hoping it would go away and I would feel better. So much has happened these past several days, I just haven't had time to focus on my health."

Hans visibly relaxed as he saw she understood. "Yes, that does sometimes happen. In my experience, I've discovered that one feels the worse at about the seven day mark before one begins to feel better."

"I know," she readily agreed. "One wonders with all the medical advancements we have that it takes so long to get better."

"So true," he chuckled in agreement. "I do hope you get to feeling better, and let me know if there is anything I can do for you."

"Yes Sir, I will. Thank you for thinking of me."

Giving her a paternal smile, he gave her a friendly nod and clicked off.

Sharon sat for just a moment before she tapped her earphone. Social Injustice's moving up the attack meant she now had to scramble to get everything in place, and she only had seven days to do it.

Pharr Court South, Atlanta

The doorman raised an eyebrow as the large delivery van pulled up and parked in front of the building. The driver, a very muscular young man, got out and bounded up the steps. Smiling at the doorman, he held up a hand-pad and glanced down at the name.

"I've got a delivery for a Sharon Walker at this address."

"Is she expecting you?" the doorman loftily asked.

"Yeah. We called ahead and she's waiting right now."

"All deliveries are in the rear of the building," he informed him. "Make two right turns and you'll see the freight delivery area."

"Thanks friend." The man bounded down the steps and hopped in, leaving the doorman wondering what Miss Walker had ordered.

Fifteen minutes later, the two men were hauling a large crate out of the elevator and into Sharon's penthouse. The driver glanced approvingly at the accommodation.

"Nice place ya got here."

"Thank you," she replied with a polite smile.

"Where would you like us to put this?" He ticked his head at the crate.

"In the first bedroom to the left at the top of the stairs. It might be easier if you unpack it here first."

With a quick bob of the head, he and his assistant placed the crate on its side and untwisted the securing bars long the sides then pried open the top. Inside were eight large water containers.

Leaning in to whisper, she asked, "How many more do you have?"

He driver splayed his hands indicating ten more.

"Stack them in as tightly as you can."

While the assistant hauled one of the bottles onto his shoulder and moved up the stairs, the driver whispered, "We'll have more deliveries over the next few days."

Handing him an elevator key, she said, "Leave this on the table by the door here after your last delivery. If anyone asks –"

"We're delivering furniture," he knowingly added.

With a soft smile, Sharon said, "Tell Lowell thanks. Also, tell him I'll be calling out sick all next week. I'll have the radio, but wait at least a week before making contact. We need to know the virus is running its course first."

"I understand."

"And you all are secure?"

"We're fine. We finished sealing and boarding up the last of the buildings yesterday, so we're good to go.

Inhaling a deep breath, she smiled at him. "See you tomorrow?"

"Absolutely."

La Agostura, Mexico

In the early evening, with the sun just beginning to settle behind the mountains, Warfield stood in the doorway of what was once a caretaker's house in La Agostura, Mexico. He gazed out over the slender finger of the lake that had been created long ago by damming up the river. To his right, the dam seemed to be working fine for the moment, but how long that was going to last was another matter. Neither he nor Kevin knew anything about operating the release valves to let the lake water out. What would happen if they stopped working? He looked to see how much higher they were than the top of the dam and figured they were high enough that they'd have to have a flood of biblical proportions to force them out of the house.

"Tell me again why being here is a good idea?" he said over his shoulder.

Kevin was rummaging through the kitchen looking for what food remained. He was rewarded with a pantry full of canned items. "Look where we are? We're in the middle of nowhere. We're here because no one else is. Everyone's gone to some safe place waiting for Corporate's attack on June 1st. We've got food here," he held up a can of albondigas. "And we've got plenty to drink." He held a six-pack of sangria señorial."

260

Warfield turned around and motioned for one of the sangrias. Kevin pried a bottle loose and tossed it to him.

"So what do we do when the drones come?" he asked.

"*If* the drones come," Kevin corrected. "I figure we stock up everything we can find into one house and plant ourselves here for a couple of weeks. Why don't you see what you can find in the other buildings."

Warfield twisted the cap off the bottle and tossed it in the small trash can by the door. He chugged the non-alcoholic drink, the taste reminding him that he hoped whoever had lived here before had some of the real stuff around... maybe even some private stock.

He crossed the small courtyard to the other caretaker's house, looking to his left to the other two larger buildings that looked vaguely like college dorms. On the right were two smaller windowless buildings that were probably for storage. Once at the house, he found the front door locked. Puzzled as to why someone would lock the door, unless that someone was hiding something and expecting to come back.

Before breaking a window, Warfield decided to check the back door and found it locked too. Finding a suitable rock to break a window wasn't difficult and he was soon inside, in the kitchen. The refrigerator still hummed and he opened the door. What he saw caused him to pump his arm and exclaim, "Yes!" Inside, instead of food and condiments, the refrigerator was filled to the brim with beer, private stock beer.

Quickly setting down the sangria, he yanked open drawers looking for a bottle opener, finding one in the small drawer by the sink. In one smooth motion, he uncapped the bottle and took a long and satisfying gulp, smacking his lips in satisfaction. Doing a quick calculation at the number of bottles in the frig, he chuckled thinking they should last maybe a week.

Bottle in hand, he began walking through the rest of the house. It was small, two-bedroom affair with one bathroom, a kitchen/dining room and a living room. From the looks of things it appeared that a married couple with no children had lived here, for there was a definite female touch to the décor. In the main bedroom, there was a picture of a man and a very attractive woman on the dresser, most likely the couple who lived here.

Warfield rummaged through the dresser drawers and found most of them empty save for some items of older clothing left behind. It was when he pulled the drawer out that he found a palm-pad. Curious, he set the beer down on the dresser and sat on the edge of the bed. Turning it on, he was surprised at the opening screen saver – a curvaceous brunette completely naked in a provocative pose. Snickering, he flicked past the screen saver to the main menu, which essentially contained two icons. One was labeled 'foto' and the other 'video.' Activating the 'foto' icon, he was rewarded with thumbnails of numerous pictures of nude women. The same occurred with the 'video' icon.

He snorted a laugh when he realized that this was left behind because the missus wasn't too happy with the mister and his addiction. Shutting it off and tucking it into his back pocket, he proceeded though the rest of the house, when it occurred to him that something didn't make sense. Why would a couple only have beer in their frig?

He walked back in to the kitchen and realized it was amazingly clean, as was the entire house. And why leave the frig running? To keep the beer cold? It then dawned on him that perhaps not everyone was quite so gone as Kevin believed.

He headed to the front door, remembered it was locked and went back out the back door, now with a broken window. Hustling across the courtyard, he found Kevin looking through a number of magazines.

"Look at this," Kevin said, holding up a magazine.

"I don't read Mexican."

"It's not Mexican, it's Spanish."

"Yeah, well, I don't read that either. And when did you learn Spanish?"

With a less than indulgent sigh, Kevin said "Remember? I've been in the Zone for a while. It's not hard. And this magazine? It's a magazine put out in Mexico City. It's called *El Otro Mundo*, 'The Next World' in English. It's a magazine about the benefits of cloning."

"Really?"

"And look at the date. It's this month's edition."

Warfield gave him a blank look.

"This month's edition," Kevin repeated. "We're in the middle of nowhere. How did this get here?"

"I have no idea," he replied, "but I do have to admit that is rather strange. You think Corporate might be here?"

"The thought did occur to me."

"Yeah, but why here? What could they possibly want here?"

"I don't know." He gave Warfield a curious look. "You know anyone else here?"

Cocking an eyebrow, he shook his head. "It's not like they're going to tell me who all is in the Zone. I had one mission, and that was to take you out. And now here I am in the middle of nowhere trying to find a place to hide."

Ignoring him, Kevin frowned as he looked about the place. "There's something wrong here, but I can't put my finger on it."

"While you're trying to figure that out, I think someone is living here and they aren't all that far away." He then explained about the beer in the frig and the locked house. "I think someone may be returning here for whatever reason. We may want to set up a watch, after we checkout the other two buildings."

"Agreed. I'll take one and you take the other."

It was a short time later that they stood outside in the courtyard under the shade of several cottonwood trees.

"There's nothing in there," Warfield said. "It looks like it used to be a sort of classroom and workshop. There's a layer of dirt and dust that's been there for quite a while."

"Same here," Kevin replied. "Whoever lived here stayed in the cottages."

"I found a picture in the other one, but the place looks to be too clean."

"That's what was bothering me," he bobbed his head. "When we walked into the first place, it seemed much to clean. Well stocked with food, but as though no one was living there."

"So, do we move on or stay?"

Kevin thought for a moment. "I vote we stay. There's enough food to last us for a while. Let's stay and run off whoever else might show up."

Warfield gazed around the courtyard and beyond, taking in the surroundings. "You sure this is the best place to hide out?"

"Listen," he answered. "It's like I said on the way down here. All hell is going to break loose by June 1st. We don't want to be anywhere near other people until the diseases run their course. That means we may be here for a long time. If it's all the same with you, I'd just as soon hedge my bets on being solitary for a while."

"Eh, you're probably right. He looked over at the small shed We'll need to hide the car, and we still haven't checked out the storage buildings." He led the way to the two small buildings that had padlocks securing the doors. "More locks," he observed. "Someone doesn't want anyone messing with their stuff. Wonder why the one cottage was open."

"Probably to keep people like us from snooping around the rest of the place," Kevin replied. "We'll put the car behind here. You hungry?"

"Yeah. I'll bring the beer."

They spent the next two days scouting the area and setting up a night watch. It was just after the sun had set on the second night that Kevin, on his way to the hidden outpost in the clump of trees where the road made a sharp turn before coming into the housing area, heard them walking down the road. They seemed in no great hurry and talked quietly. There were two of them and they spoke English. One was a woman who offered that she looked forward to a good night's sleep finally. He let them pass, reminding himself that he was glad his brother agreed to night security – no lights. The problem was how to alert him that they had visitors.

Silently emerging from the trees, he followed in the distance as the two figures went straight to the storage building by the 'beer' house, as his brother called it. He could hear the fumbling of a key in the lock before the door opened. Stealthily racing around to the back of the cottage where his brother was, he let himself in the back door and raced to the bedroom, shaking him awake.

"Get up," he urgently whispered. "Someone's here."

Warfield needed no urging and was up and dressed in seconds, following Kevin out the back door. It was as they came around the side that they saw a dim light waving around inside the storage building. A moment later, the light flashed off and they both emerged, carrying a small satellite system and transmitter, which they set up on the ground, just outside the door.

After spending a few minutes connecting the wires and headset, the man flicked on the power and spoke into the microphone. "Sierra six-six, this is tango charlie four-niner. Sierra six-six, this is tango four-niner." He paused for a few moments then repeated the calls signs. He did this three more times before saying, "I got you sierra six-six. Be advised mass migration to the Hermosillo location is virtually complete. There are no underground facilities there. I repeat, no underground facilities." There was a lengthy pause followed by "Yes. We are alone." Another long pause was followed by, "Roger. Understood. Will reconnect at designated time. Out."

"So?" the woman asked. "What do they want us to do?"

"Stay put," he replied, unhooking the wires."

"Stay put?" she repeated with a hint of frustration. "For how long?"

"For a while still," he evasively answered.

"Gimme a break, Stephen," she snapped. "What did they say?"

"They said we're to hole up until at least the third, maybe even longer. They want to give the virus a chance to run its course before they pick us up. Here," he said handing her the headset and wiring. "Go ahead and put those away."

"And suppose someone infected comes here?" she huffed, remaining where she was. "What are we supposed to do? Did they ever think of that?"

"I don't think we have anything to worry about," he calmly replied. "No one knows were here."

"Corporate does," she pointed out.

"That's not what I mean, Carla. Obviously Corporate knows were here; they sent us, remember? But the Zonies are all gone, all huddled up together in Hermosillo... a long way from here. We're safe here." He stood up and reentered the storage shed. The dim light flashed on again as they secured their equipment.

While Stephen locked the shed, Carla looked over at the beer house. "I need a cold one."

"Me too," he readily agreed and they headed over to the house.

Once inside, it didn't take them long to discover someone had been there. Carla flicked on the kitchen lights.

"I though you said we were alone, that we were safe," she accused, pointing at the broken glass on the floor.

The front door pushed open and Kevin and Warfield came in, flipping the switch for the overhead lights. Stephen and Carla reacted instantly.

"Perhaps I can explain," Kevin amiably said. "You can put down the knives. We're Corporate agents too." He held his hands up for emphasis. "I'm Kevin Gonzales, and this is my brother, Nick."

"Tell us more, Kevin," Stephen warily stated, keeping careful grip on the kitchen knife.

"Like I said, I'm Kevin Gonzales. Perhaps you might have heard of me. I used to be the Governor of the Sierra Vista quadrant. That was, oh... until a few days ago when my cover was blown and that's why I'm down here."

"I could use a beer too," Warfield grinned, "especially as you have private stock.

Carla whipped open the refrigerator door. "Apparently you like them a whole lot," she sourly said.

"I do believe I have heard of you," Stephen said, relaxing just a bit. "So why are you here again?"

"Him," he smiled, ticking his head at Warfield.

"Your brother?"

"Yes."

"Why?"

"He was sent her to kill me."

Stephen studied him for a moment then looked at Carla. "How about getting out four beers? I want to hear this." He slid out a chair from the table and motioned Kevin and Warfield to sit.

By the time Kevin related the family story and the twin careers, there were close to a dozen empty bottles on the table, with most of those in front of Warfield who was feeling downright friendly. He gazed across the table at Carla and wondered if there was anything going on between her and Stephen. She was quite attractive, petite with black hair, dark brown eyes, and a body that more than interfered with his concentration. His mind wandered at the thought of being stranded all alone with her.

"So tell me again why Corporate sent your brother to kill you," Carla amiably asked.   She nursed her second bottle of beer.

"They believed I had gone rogue, that I had turned against the Corporation."

"Did you?"

Kevin glanced back and forth between her and Stephen. "Almost."

"Almost?"   She raised an eyebrow in doubt.   "What does that mean?"

"It means I was hedging my bets," he replied.   "For example, you just got off the horn with Corporate.   What did they tell you about what you were to do here, especially knowing that they're going to completely douse the Zones on June 1st?"

"They told us to stay put," Stephen answered, suddenly aware that his future prospects for survival had dramatically decreased.

"Stay put," Kevin repeated.   "They told you to stay here knowing they're going to gas this place, and with you in it?"

"I told you so," Carla glared at Stephen.

Pursing his lips, Stephen studied Kevin and the not quite inebriated Warfield. "If you know that, why are you still here?"

Kevin's eyes narrowed at him.   "Because we know Corporate left us here to die. I'm here because I'm a dead man either side of the wall.   He's here," he thumbed at Warfield, "because he got caught up in Corporate's grand design.   Face it. Why spend the efforts and assets getting us out?   When the final solution happens, nothing will be left in the Zones."   He paused, took a sip then added, "At least that's what they think."

"What do you mean?" Carla frowned at him.

"What I mean is this."   He leaned forward.   "Why are the people in the Zone here all running to some supposed safe place?"

"Because they know they're going to be gassed," Stephen answered.

"Correct.   How they found out is for someone else to discover, but they have.   And they also know it's going to be June 1st.   So if Corporate knows they're all huddling in specific locations anticipating being gassed, why is Corporate waiting until June 1st?"

267

Stephen blinked as he sorted out the implication. "They're probably waiting until all the Zones are in place before they start."

"Now just suppose June 1st rolls around and nothing happens?"

"What do you mean?"

"Just follow me for a minute. Suppose June 1st comes and goes and nothing happens? Then June 2nd and 3rd and a week goes by. Then what happens?"

"People will believe they were wrong," Carla answered, "and they'll start returning to the way things were before the scare."

"Exactly," Kevin triumphantly hit his hand on the table. "And that's the time to hit the Zones, just when their guard is down."

"And we'd be sitting here," she slowly said, "sitting ducks."

"That's right." Kevin glanced over to Warfield. "You gonna leave any beer for the rest of us?"

"Depends," he grinned. "How long we staying here?"

The others snickered in spite of themselves.

"Now there's one more little detail you might not be aware of," Kevin sagaciously said. "Let's suppose the Zones had a means of defending themselves in a sort of... preemptive strike."

"Like how?" Stephen asked

"Suppose the Zones had bio weapons like the Free side."

Carla's eyes widened and she sat up straight. "Are you saying some Zones have the capability to counter attack?"

"That's exactly what I'm staying."

She slumped back against the chair in stunned silence.

"I've got to notify Corporate." Stephen thrust his chair back and stood up.

"Don't be a damn fool," Kevin snapped.

"Do sit down, Stephen," Carla heaved a sigh of exasperation. "Let the man finish before you go rushing off." Seeing him hesitate, she hardened her voice. "Sit down Stephen."

Reluctantly taking a seat, he folded his arms, waiting for an explanation.

"Look at it this way," Kevin explained. "The Zones know Corporate is going to exterminate them on June 1st. So, instead of waiting for then, they launch their own attack a few days ahead of Corporate. They launch gas," he arced one hand followed by the other going the opposite direction; "the Corporation launches gas and pretty soon it's mutual annihilation. By June 1st, the entire world will have been biologically attacked. Those who remain will be those who quarantined themselves and waited out the devastation."

"You tell Corporate now," Warfield chimed in, "and they'll simply accelerate the attack, which means the Zones will do the same thing. And just how safe are you two right now? You have a place that you can wait out it out the next couple of months?"

"We have a cave," Carla volunteered. "We've been hauling food and goods up there."

"What's wrong with staying here?" Warfield asked. "Why haul all that stuff somewhere else when you have everything you need right here?" He cast an impish glance at Carla. "And I bet the beds are softer here."

""He has a point," Kevin agreed, "but with some modification. Corporate knows you are here. Do they know about the cave?"

"No," she answered. "That was my idea."

"And it's a good one," Kevin smiled at her. "We know that the Zones will launch a preemptive strike a few days ahead of Corporate, specifically May 29th."

"And how do you know that?" Stephen sniffed.

"Because I was once the Governor, remember? I was brought into the operational planning of Social Injustice's leadership. But more to the point, after the Zones attack, nothing will be evident in the Corporate side because the bio-agents they're using are delayed viruses. Ignorant of this, the Corporation will launch their own attack on June 1st to wipe out the Zones. By then, both sides will have decimated each other, but the Corporate side won't know until a week or so later when large swaths of the populations are dead or dying."

"Get to the point Kev," Warfield rolled his eyes.

"My point is, we use the cave. We go in when Corporate launches their attack and stay there until the middle or the end of the month. When the drones come by here to drop their load, and you know they will," he pointedly stared at the two across the table, "we'll be safe in the cave. With the designer airborne bio agents they have now, they have a short life span. From a warfare perspective, it's pretty smart."

"And I bet you're gonna tell us why?" Warfield said out the side of his mouth.

Carla chuckled while Kevin cast him a glace of disapproval. "I think maybe you've had enough."

"I don't think so," he jovially responded. "But I do have to pee."

He slid his chair back and stood up. "You don't have to tell me," he said to Carla. "I know where it is." He bowed gallantly and walked off.

With a bemused smile, she watched him walk away. "You were saying," she said, returning her attention to Kevin.

"What I was saying is that with the designer bio agents, their lifespan is very short and transmission is between persons. In other words, once the bio-drones go by here, the only thing we have to worry about is another human, and the infected ones will die off rather quickly."

"How do you know so much?"

"Let's just say I took an active interest in the Corporate methods when they told me I was being sent here."

"We're going to need a lot more food and supplies then," Carla said. "You two will have to help."

"No problem. I've got a car. We can load it up and speed up the process." He then looked quizzically at them. "Which reminds me… how come you two don't have a car?"

"They were all taken when everyone here cleared out," Stephen replied. "We've been hoofing it up and down ever since."

"So then," Kevin stared at them, "are we in agreement?"

"Yes," Carla replied while Stephen nodded.

"Good. Now, do either of you have any weapons?"

"We've got the pistols we were issued when we arrived here," Stephen answered.

"Ammo?"

"About 100 rounds."

"That should do us. I've got a .380 with about fifty rounds. Between us we should be able to fend off any unwanted visitors." He gave them another once over. "By the way, you really ought to be carrying. Suppose we weren't the friendly type? You two could have been jumped when you walked by me on the road."

Stephen and Carla exchanged a look. "If we were jumped," Stephen answered, "we didn't want our only means of defense to fall into the wrong hands."

"You may want to rethink that," Kevin said. "The pistols do you no good when you're dead."

"That's what I said," Carla defended herself. "That's why I still carry mine." She reached behind her and withdrew her .380 from her inside the back of her pants.

Grinning, Kevin nodded in approval. "From now on, we all carry our weapons."

"Who made you boos?" Stephen stonily asked.

"No one did," he calmly replied. "There are only four of us. However, it would be in our best interests to listen to the one who has the most experience, wouldn't you agree?" When Stephen didn't answer, he continued. "I make the assumption that both you and Carla here have expertise in areas that neither Nick nor I have. In that case, we listen to you."

"Get off your high horse, Stephen," Carla admonished. "If we're going to survive, we need to stick together."

Warfield came ambling back in. "Did I miss anything?" He opened the frig and withdrew another beer. "Anyone else want one?"

"How about that being the last one," Kevin firmly admonished.

"Yes mother," he replied with a loopy grin.

Social Injustice complex – Sierra Vista
Wednesday, May 24, 2102

Gretchen stood on the platform looking out over the group. To her rear stood Maria, Zoe, and the towering Pieter. Before her, to her left, stood the assault and extraction teams. In the middle were the drone pilots and to their left were the remaining medical and support staff.

In a clear strong voice, she said, "In a little less than an hour, the unified forces of Social Injustice will launch a coordinated attack across the globe. Our mission here in the

Tucson Zone is to rescue as many clones as possible before we launch our final solution attack. You all know what to do. You all know what is at stake. We attack to save lives as well as take lives. We have no other choice. The decision has been made for us. If we are to survive, we must strike first. We must strike hard and fast, giving them no time to react."

She then turned her gaze on the assault teams. "Once we hit zero hour, you have two hours to get in and out. We will not delay the bio attack. If you are caught falling behind, abandon in place and get yourselves to safety."

"Drone pilots," she said, facing the middle group. "You have a long assignment these next few days. Be wary and clever. Corporation will be looking for us. But we must not yield to their intimidation. That means those defending the walls must be better than good. For every drone they take out, we take out one hundred. Take the fight to them.

"For the rest of you, your mission is just as important. We have a civilization now to look after. It is up to you that we survive."

Casting one last lingering encompassing gaze, she announced, "Let's win this fight."

Without a word she spun around and descended the steps and headed off to her office, the others in tow.

An hour later, the assault teams were slipping outside the Zone walls and assembling at their predetermined rendezvous points, waiting for zero hour. Thirty minutes before the attack, assault teams moved into position while the extraction teams positioned reinforced busses and battering rams close by.

There were two cloning facilities in Tucson blissfully unaware of the impending changes about to take place in their lives. At exactly 1:45 am, the doors to both facilities were blown open and the assault teams burst in.

The Reverend Jefferson Beauregard Clayton was awake, watching a show about Roman gladiators. He was wide awake and wanted desperately to be asleep. Instead, he was still immobile from the shoulders up. He could move his arms and legs now, but with the heaviness of the head brace, he could only move his head with help. And that they were more than reluctant to do for fear of disturbing the healing of the numerous veins and nerves.

272

As the narrator droned on about the size of the gladiator sword, he could hear an elevation of noise outside the room, and the sounds of something like firecrackers. Frustrated that he couldn't see what was going on, his curiosity was partially relieved when the door slammed open and a pitiful nurse wailed,

"He's not healed. If you move him now, there's no telling what could happen."

"Take him," a cold voice commanded. "And bring her too."

"Please let me help," the nurse begged.

Beauregard saw only glimpses of the nurse and several men dressed in black. He then felt hands grabbing the sheets under him and someone, probably the nurse, holding onto the head brace. He felt a lifting motion as they raised him up. His head abruptly jerked back, and his world went blank.

Outside, dazed clones stumbled as they were herded onto busses. Frightened doctors and nurses were likewise hustled onto other busses. A firefight was still in progress between the attackers and building security. One of the nurses was hit by a stray round and crumpled to the ground, blood gushing from a head wound.

"Get 'em out of here!" the attack commander yelled to the drivers as he gathered up the remaining fighters for one final assault. In one final push, they took out the last of the security guards then quickly set about placing demolition charges. The speed in which they performed their mission had them back aboard several reinforced armored cars with plows welded to the front.

Racing through the streets, they caught up with the busses that were now illuminated by Corporate drones relaying position back to chase forces. The reinforced armored cars swept past the busses and positioned themselves in the front, speeding as fast as the treads could spin, heading towards the protected gates to the Zone. Halfway there, they were joined by the other assault team's vehicles and together formed a long line of armored cars and busses that rammed and battered anything in their way.

The defense and security forces at the Zone gates had already been alerted and were scrambling into position, some behind the concrete blocks that created a maze, which forced vehicles to slow dramatically to successfully maneuver through and around them. Others were fanning out, finding positions in

273

nearby buildings and other hidden locations. While their attention was focused on the approaching convoy, a loud explosion burst the massive iron gates wide open and the Zone army poured out, guns blazing. Leading the attack were three Miller remote stealth main battle tanks that immediately poured devastating fire into the surrounding buildings, crushing entire floors and causing buildings to collapse upon themselves.

The ferocity of the surprise attack more than startled the Corporate forces, especially with the tanks in front. The Corporate forces were quickly overwhelmed and the few still alive scuttled to safety, leaving the wounded behind.

As the Zone forces spread out to form a defensive perimeter, three tank plows rumbled up and began shoving the concrete blocks out of the way of the approaching convoy. A minute later, the convoy of armored cars and busses zoomed by, into the safety of the Zone. In one rapid smooth coordinated motion, the Zone army collected their wounded and swept back behind the walls, leaving a scattering of mines in their wake.

Once inside the Zone, the pace slowed so that the forces joined together with the tanks interspersed within the long convoy. They were a third of the way to Sierra Vista when they were alerted inbound aircraft were on the way.

The tanks wasted no time and launched a barrage of surface-to-air missiles. Those on the ground looked up in time to see numerous bursts of explosions as missiles found their targets. To their surprise, they received the 'all-clear' report when the remaining planes had fled to the other side of the wall.

The convoy's pace remained steady until they reached the outskirts of Sierra Vista, circling around the city until they were on the road headed towards Bisbee, to then disappear into the underground bunkers off Moson road.

Pharr Court South, Atlanta
Early morning, Thursday, May 25, 2102

Sharon was in deep sleep when the phone music grew louder and finally penetrated her slumber. Reaching over to the nightstand, she picked up the phone and positioned it in her ear. "This is Sharon."

"Jon here. Turn on the news."

Rubbing her eyes, she flipped off the covers and weaved her way to the TV room, pressing the 'On' button on the remote in the arm of the chair. The breaking news filled the screen.

Scenes from the cloning sites scatted throughout North America repeated and replayed. All the pictures showed the devastation and carnage from the attacks.   Then the scene shifted to the one cloning facility in Tucson where the Reverend Clayton had just received his new body. The announcer, an attractive indignant woman sat behind the news desk with the drone cameras relaying the pictures.

"And here is what happened to one of the resurrection facilities in Tucson, Arizona. This is the same facility where the Reverend Jefferson Beauregard Clayton had just received his new angelic form."

The camera slowly moved through the hallways and into the cloning and recovery rooms to reveal the dead bodies of doctors, nurses, and support staff. It appeared that some were shot down as they fled, others appeared to have been lined up against a wall and ritually executed.

"Every doctor and nurse working at the facility was brutally murdered," she announced. "Of the 76 men and women in post-operative recovery at this facility, men and women who had either had just been reborn today or in the past several days… Of these 76 men and women, these brave souls who were looking forward to a new lease on life… none were spared. Each one systematically and brutally murdered."

The camera hovered over one of the patients in a recovery room. A path of now dried blood emerged from the side of the head and trailed down onto the bed, settling in a darkened pool.

"This is all that is left of Missus Louise Janssen, the wife of industrial banker Lars Janssen IV. What remains here is the shell of a life expectant. Instead of a future with a devoted and loving husband, her beautiful life has been cut short by violence. We go now to Jesse Craven at the gates to the Zone."

Within the brightness of the construction lights set up around the entrance, the drone camera hovered in front of Jesse, a strikingly handsome man with chiseled face and meticulously coiffed hair. He stood before the open gateway to the Zone. The iron gates were splayed wide, their railings bent and twisted. Repair crews were already on the scene with large cranes and other earth moving equipment, struggling to remove the massive doors.

"Jesse," the announcer said. "What's it like there?"

"It's chaos, Lauren. What I've been able to piece together is that it was a well-orchestrated operation that began at around fifteen minutes to two, earlier this morning, when the two resurrection facilities were attacked. Timing was everything and while the insurgents at the facilities methodically murdered those reborn and waiting to be reborn, a second group destroyed the gates in time for the attacking forces to escape back into the Zone. I talked to several eye-witnesses who reported seeing tanks coming through the gates. When I asked the Corporate representative, he replied that those reports were unconfirmed."

"I understand," said Lauren, "that Corporate response forces crossed over the wall and were able to destroy much of the insurgent forces. Is that your understanding?"

"Yes, Lauren. The Corporate spokesperson said that our response force chased the insurgents into the desert where they suffered catastrophic losses."

"Thank you, Jesse." The Tucson drone camera switched off, replaced by other similar scenes. "Again, in what appears to be a massive coordinated effort, the insurgent forces of Social Injustice have carried out an attack on resurrection facilities throughout the world. Of particular interest is the fate of the well-known Reverend Jefferson Beauregard Clayton who had just recently been reborn and was recuperating at the Cortez Resurrection facility in Tucson, Arizona. While all other reborn men and women at the facility were systematically murdered, the Reverend Clayton was not among those listed as killed and is believed missing, possibly kidnapped. As of yet, there have been no demands for ransom."

Pausing momentarily to listen to the input in the earpiece, she gave a quick nod. "The Corporation was quick to condemn the attack. Here is the Corporation Spokesperson speaking to us from the Hague."

The TV screen filled with a middle-aged somber man in a business suit. His TV makeup had been hurriedly applied and his cheeks were just a bit too pinkish.

"Today, in an orchestrated effort worldwide, the insurrection forces of Social Injustice launched an attack on Resurrection facilities throughout the world, leaving in their wake an untold number of dead and injured. The attack was directed specifically against the resurrection industry and no other industry or business was affected. Our hearts go out to the families and loved ones of those who lost their lives as a result of this heinous act. To all who are watching at this moment, make no mistake.   Our response will be measured and appropriate."

The camera flashed back to Lauren who said, "When asked what the measured and appropriate response would be, we were told it would be very soon and the entire world would see it."

Sharon muted the volume. "You still there, Jon?" Her voice was tired and achy.

"Yeah."

"This couldn't have come at a worse time, for me at least. I've got this bug that is just kicking the crap out of me."

"You been to the doc?"

"Yeah. He gave me some meds. I'll probably be out only another day or two. In the meantime, I need you to take charge in my absence. Can you go secure?"

"Yeah. Hold on."

Sharon hit the secure button on her earphone and listened to the white noise when it abruptly stopped and Jon spoke.

"I'm back."

"OK," she wearily answered. "You know what Corporate is going to do already.   Their measured response is going to happen on June 1st. While I'm out, focus on getting our people out in time. I know you can handle everything, so unless you really feel the need to inform me about something really important, handle it."

"No problem, Sharon. You get some rest. I'll see you in a couple of days."

She heard the appreciation in his voice. "Thanks, Jon. I'm glad you're there."

"Anytime. G'night."

"Night." Walking back to the night table, she took out the earphone and plugged it into the charger then sat on the edge of the bed. In a sweeping epiphany, she realized that her life had just changed. She was now a sort of prisoner under house arrest. She wouldn't be able to leave her home for the next year.

Suddenly she felt very lonely.

"I should of gotten a dog or a cat or something," she mumbled. "Eh? But then I'd have to clean up after them and what would I do with all the poop when the water stops flowing?" Sighing in frustration, she shook her head. "This is pathetic. I'm already talking to myself."

Too awake to sleep now, she meandered through the rooms, upstairs to get a robe, then back downstairs to the living room and the doors to the outside deck. Knowing she had little time to relish the smell of outside air, she pulled the doors open and stepped out into the night.

Wrapping the robe tightly around her, she walked to the edge of the deck and took in the city. It was strangely quiet, despite the attacks on the cloning facilities here in the city. Except for the rare light on in an office building, which would incur a significant fine to the guilty party, the only other lights were from the street lamps and neon signs.

Inhaling the night air, she wondered what the world was going to be like a year from now.

Social Injustice complex – Sierra Vista

While the Zone forces in Sierra Vista lined up and cleaned their vehicles and equipment, the doctors and nurses were quickly hustled off in one direction and the clones were gently herded off to their new lodgings. The litter with Beauregard was sent along with the doctors and the attending nurse who refused to leave him. He still lay unconscious and the nurse upbraided the imbecility of the Zone in removing a man who had just been reborn.

It was later in the morning before the new arrivals had time to eat a good breakfast and get some rest. In a large room, the rescued clones sat on cots in neat orderly rows. With Ruth by his side, JB stood in front of them. Zoe stood off to the side, monitoring and watching.

"My name is JB, and this is Ruth, my wife," he proudly announced. "We are, or were, once like you. They call us clones. I'm here to tell you what that really means." The room grew abruptly quiet when he said, "We are all clones here, except for Zoe. What that means is that we were made to be used by someone else." For the next hour, JB told them of what fate had in store for them and how they had been rescued and that they had so much to learn.

"Each of you has a special skill, maybe even more than one, that you will need to develop and grow. For example, my wife Ruth," he waved a hand at her, "is an artist, one of the best in the world. I am good at numbers. It's called math. Each of you will take a test, just like we did. Don't worry. It's an easy test and once you're finished, it will help us know what you're good at. Ruth now has some things she wants to tell you."

Ruth stepped forward. "Everything JB told you is the truth. We weren't meant to be here, right now. We were all meant to be dead. But we're not. And that means we can now live, just like anyone else. Look around you. Do you see anyone you know?" A number of them nodded and waved to each other. "How many of you remember seeing that person more than one time?" No hands were raised. "How many of you wanted to spend another night with the same person?" At that most all the hands were raised. "Well now you can. JB and me wanted to be together more than once and once we got free, we decided we wanted to be together all the time. And now we are, in something called 'marriage,' which means he and me get to be together and no one can tell us 'no.' It's not that complicated once you understand it. You're going to have a lot of questions. That's OK. Ask anyone and, not like before where they told us we didn't need to know, now they'll answer all our questions."

"Thank you Ruth and JB," Zoe said as she stepped forward. "You will all be moved to your own private rooms. You are free to walk around the facility and talk to anyone you want. But if someone tells you they are busy, it means they have important work right now and can't take the time to talk to you. Please leave them alone and move on." She continued explaining the rules and then motioned for the helpers and assistants to begin their care. Turning to JB and Ruth, she said, "That was very good. Thank you. I think it worked better coming from you. Why don't you two go see if you can help our new friends get settled."

With a pleasant smile, Zoe left them and headed down the hallways towards the operations area. As she approached the drone command room she could see the number of interested individuals growing as the time approached to initiate Phase 2 of the operation. Weaving her way through the crowd, she saw Gretchen talking to Pieter and caught her attention, nodding that all was progressing well with the clones.

Gretchen returned the nod and looked back up at Pieter who leaned against the wall, his hands behind him as a cushion. "Looks like we have a curious crowd today," she said, directing his attention to the growing numbers both inside and outside the room.

"You may want to give them a word or warning," he replied. "Don't need anyone getting in the way, especially right now."

As more bystanders filled the edges of the room, Gretchen commanded, "No one is to interfere with any pilot. If he or she tells you to move, you move. I will not jeopardize this mission because of someone's curiosity or misplaced belief that you can do it better. Is that clear?"

Receiving the desired response, she continued. "Pilots. We have a long day ahead of us. We must strike fast and hard. You all have your assigned missions. Once your mission is complete, you may take a break unless required to assist another pilot in completing his or her assigned mission. For the rest of you, stay out of the pilot's way. You are here to observe. If anyone has any questions, Pieter and I will be here by TJ's position." She looked at the clock. "We have two minutes until zero hour. This is the start of our war. Winning is our only option."

Pieter looked out over the large room of rows and rows of pilot positions, and those sitting at the control panels. He chuckled that the average age was probably around thirteen. Then he thought about what they were doing and the sober reality hit him that they were using children to kill. TJ sat in the middle of the row of drone pilot stations closest to the hallway windows. Other pilots filled the remaining positions of the nearly 100 stations.

An expectant silence settled on the room as the seconds ticked down. When the minute and seconds hands reached twelve, Pieter commanded, "It's time."

An initial silence reigned until the pilots became singularly focused on their respective mission. Soon, grunts and exclamations pierced the quiet and the room settled into a comfortable hum.

Pieter stood next to Gretchen, watching TJ expertly maneuver the drone. Unnoticed, it blended in with the other Corporate drones circling and hovering over the Phoenix baseball stadium.

"It's a sold out crowd," TJ said, his focus on the screen in front and the controller in his hands. "It's one of the early season home games."

"What inning is it?" Pieter asked, more out of curiosity than genuine interest.

"Top of the third," TJ answered.

"Does it really matter?" Gretchen frowned.

"Not really, I suppose," Pieter shrugged, "though you'd probably want to wait until the late-comers were seated. I'd wait until the top of the fourth inning."

"Why?"

"By then everyone's settled and into the game."

"How're we doing?" Gretchen asked TJ. "Any curiosity from the other drones?"

"None so far." He swiveled the camera atop the drone in a slow 360° scanning for the nearest Corporate drones. He repeated the process with the cameras below the drone. The Corporate drones were evenly spaced around the upper bleachers while smaller drones zipped in and out of the lower levels.

The inning ended with a three-up-three-down for both sides and TJ slowly maneuvered the drone to the far right field stands. "Ready when you are," he calmly announced.

Gretchen looked at Pieter who returned her stare without emotion. She inhaled deeply the let it out in one loud breath. "Do it."

Without hesitation, TJ pressed the release button and the odorless and colorless biological organisms descended onto the crowd below. He slowly maneuvered the drone along the upper rows until he had covered the entire crowd. "I've still some left."

"Can you go lower?" she queried.

"I can," he replied followed by, "Uh-oh." I think we've been noticed." The top camera swiveled rapidly catching the rapidly approaching drones. "Well?"

"Can you outrun them?"

"Of course I can," he confidently replied. "Watch this." He swooped the drone to the lower levels, racing it along the stands, releasing more of the disease. Several of the larger Corporate drones gave chase.

"They don't have enough power or maneuverability," he chortled as he easily outdistanced them. "It's the smaller drones that'll give us the problem." True to his word, a swarm of smaller drones swept up to give chase.

TJ raced the drone out of the stadium and onto the streets and was soon heading the wrong way on West Jefferson Street. "They're gonna catch me sooner or later. Whaddaya want me to do? I still got a little bit of the stuff left." He feverishly moved the joystick on the control pad, evading the closest drones.

Pieter watched TJ's furious maneuvering, noting the boy was enjoying himself.

"Dump the rest then take it out," she commanded.

TJ skillfully maneuvered the drone lower and began releasing the rest of the disease on unsuspecting sidewalk dwellers who looked up in bemused surprise at the drones chasing each other. Abruptly sitting back, he jabbed a finger down on the self-destruct and the screen instantly went blank. Looking up at the surrounding group, he gave them a loopy grin. "That was fun."

"Maybe for you," Zoe quietly said, walking up. "Once the disease starts spreading, it won't be fun for them."

"Yeah, well," he replied. "It's either us or them."

"How long before we see results?" Pieter asked.

"A day or two" a voice from behind them, "we should begin to hear about cases. It will go exponential after that."

Gretchen turned and cast an eye on the group of physicians and research personnel who had gathered to see the results of their labors. "And you can assure me that everyone in the Zone has been inoculated?"

"If they haven't, it hasn't been for want of effort," one replied.

"We can't do anything about it now," Pieter consoled her. "Those who refused or chose not to, have no one to blame but themselves. The war has started."

Her lips pursed, Gretchen nodded then moved on to watch other pilots. Small neatly printed signs above the stations noted the mission location: Phoenix, Los Angeles, San Diego, San

Francisco, Las Vegas, Salt Lake City, Albuquerque, Denver, Guadalajara, Mexico City, and dozens of other large cities and towns.

She noted the cities and knew that at this moment, the same operation was happening in the rest of the western hemisphere. Cities like Sao Paulo and Lima and Santiago and so many others in Central and South America were being infected. And as time zones caught up around the world, the rest of the world would likewise be infected.

Looking over her shoulder, she saw Pieter in deep conversation with several of the research personnel. Retracing her steps, she drew close as one researcher explaining.

"Once the first virus is realized, Corporate will isolate it and have an antidote very quickly."

"Doesn't that sort of defeat the purpose?" Pieter said, raising an eyebrow.

"Not at all," he replied. "We've actually mixed several viruses in each batch, and no batch contains the same ratio of viruses, or the same viruses."

"And Corporate can only provide so much antiserum at any one time," another explained. "So while they may have a cure for one virus, it will take time for them to determine the second and third viruses."

"And they will be baffled at first that the antiserum isn't working, when in fact it does, but only on that one virus."

TJ walked up to listen then said, "We're making some good time. If all goes well, we should be finished within a couple of hours."

"Give me the results when you're done," Gretchen said. Stepping through the group into the hallway, she waited for Pieter to part the bodies and stand next to her. She watched him as he moved, his graceful step almost a dancer's movement. She had long since gotten over her awe at his size. Now he was just another member of SI. Well, that wasn't quite true. He was far more than simply just another member. There was something about him that set him apart, that made one notice him, and it wasn't his stature. Pieter had a peace and serenity about him that drew others to him. That he was also a handsome man didn't hurt.

As they walked down the hallway towards the main offices, Pieter said, "I heard we're almost at capacity down here. How many more do you expect before we have to close the doors. We're still getting a trickle in. Perhaps we ought to send out some drones to see what we have left out there."

"I hate to be like this, but we can't afford to send any drones out to find people. We don't have enough drones as it is, and it's not like the word hasn't spread. They've had plenty of time to get here. Those who remain outside have chosen their fate." She looked up to Pieter who said nothing, but his face expressed his concern for them. With a sigh, she rethought the problem then said, "I suppose we could spare one drone to do sweeping searches within a certain radius. But that's it. We've run out of time."

"When are we closing the doors?"

"We have maybe a day or two at the most. Once the outside world sees they've been poisoned, I doubt Corporate will wait until June 1st to retaliate."

Pharr Court South, Atlanta
Friday, May 26, 2102

Sharon reread the classified message one more time to make sure she got it right.

EYES ONLY
TOP SECRET – OMEGA
FROM: DIRECTOR   OF   SECURITY   AND
INTELLIGENCE, THE HAGUE
1530 ZULU 26 MAY 2102
TO: EXECUTIVE DIRECTOR SEI, RESTRICTED
SUBJECT: RESCUE OPERATION

1. Though not marked, all paragraphs and sections in their entirety are classified BETA.
2. Be advised that any rescue efforts on behalf of the Reverend Jefferson Beauregard Clayton are categorically discouraged.
3. Effective immediately, any operations related to the rescue of the said Clayton or any other clone or reborn individual is hereby terminated.

4.   OPERATION 40 TRUCKS will proceed as directed per DoSI message dated 1530 Zulu 6 May 2102.

5.   All recipients are to acknowledge.

END
TOP SECRET – OMEGA

Tapping her ear piece, she said, "Call Hans Josef."

A moment later, Hans came on the line. "How are you feeling, Sharon?"

"I'm still a bit under the weather." She cleared her throat in a harsh cough. "But then you already know that."

"What can I do for you?"

"Can you go secure?"

White noise filled the earpiece then stopped when Hans said, "I'm back."

"It's about this message I just received."

"About Clayton?"

"Yes," she replied, surprised. "How'd you know?"

"It's my business to know," he said with a hint of humor.

"So we just leave him, not even pretend to look for him?"

"Does it really matter? Let's look at it from the Corporate perspective. (a), the man's become expensive. He's demanding a bigger share of the profits. (b), why waste money and effort retrieving someone when the whole world is going to implode very soon. (c), he is no longer necessary for the Corporation and thus is expendable. Which leads me to remind you that – (d), both you and I are expendable. Remember what I said about taking care of yourself. Have you done so?

"Yes."

"Good. Anything else?

"No."

"Then I'll see you back at the office next week?" He snorted a laugh and hung up.

Infirmary - Social Injustice complex– Sierra Vista

Zoe stood next to JB who gazed down at the man lying in a clinic bed with a locking apparatus surrounding his head to keep it immobile. The man's eyes were closed in sleep and he looked

285

peaceful. JB frowned in the realization that he looked just like him.

"His name is Jefferson Beauregard Clayton," Zoe said.

"He was the one who was going to use my body?" he quietly asked.

"Yes."

"He was going to kill me and put his brain inside me?"

"Yes."

JB studied him silently for a while, trying to sort out how he felt. Part of him tried to understand the emotion of anger, but all he could feel was bitterness at why this man wanted to kill him and deprive him of the joy of living with Ruth. He felt the urge to reach down and hurt him. Yet there was another part that felt a sort of sadness for the man. He didn't seem to be all that threatening.

"Why is he in that thing around his head?"

"That's because he's already replaced his brain in the body," Zoe gently explained, "and that's to keep it immobile so his brain and body will heal."

"You mean he's already killed someone and taken his body?" JB felt himself getting warm. He clenched his hands into fists.

"Yes."

"He had no right to do that," he hotly replied.

"No he didn't." She turned when she heard someone walk up behind her. Giving Pieter a smile, she turned back to JB. "JB, I want you to meet someone."

He had been so focused on Beauregard that JB hadn't heard Pieter approach. Turning, he stutter stepped backwards in shock at the size and color of the big man.

"My name is Pieter." He stuck out a hand.

JB stared at it a moment, then hesitantly stretched out his hand.

"I don't bite," Pieter smiled.

"You're really big," JB said in awe. "And dark."

"Yes I am." He gently laughed with deep throated warmth.

Still holding Pieter's hand, JB began to relax as he took in the man's height and size. Yet he was fascinated by Pieter's skin and pulled himself closer to examine the smooth darkness of Africa's child.

"Why is your skin so dark?"

"I was born in Africa."

"Where is that?"

"It's very far from here."

"Is everyone in Africa dark like you?"

Pieter thought for a minute. "No. Not everyone. There are many shades of color in Africa."

"Is everyone big like you?"

Pieter laughed again at the child-like innocence. "No. We come in all sizes."

"I like your color," he said matter-of-factly. "I wish my skin was like yours."

"You should be happy with who you are. We are all different and unique," he kindly explained then looked down at Beauregard, "no matter how much others would believe otherwise. I see you have found the man who wanted to exchange your life for his."

"His name is Jefferson Beauregard Clayton," he said. "He's a famous preacher."

"Do you understand what that means?"

"No."

"I'll leave you two alone," Zoe interrupted. "Listen to what he has to say, JB." As she left, a nurse came in.

"How is he?" Pieter asked.

"We're not quite sure yet. He's regained consciousness, but he hasn't said much of anything. They said he blacked out when they moved him. There's the possibility that he may have suffered some nerve damage. We're monitoring him. Well look there, he's awake." She pointed to Beauregard whose eyes were open. Leaning over into his field of vision she sweetly asked, "How are you feeling today?"

"OK," he throatily replied, staring curiously at her. Feeling the firmness at his head, he tried turning it. "My head won't move."

"No," the nurse admonished, "and you're not supposed to, at least not for a while."

"Why not?"

"Because you've had an operation."

"A what?"

"An operation."

Beauregard furrowed his brow on concentration. He swallowed then asked, "What's that?"

287

"An operation?"

"Yes."

The nurse stood up and blinked in bewilderment. Leaning back over, she explained, "It's when you go to the hospital when you're sick and they do some things to you to make you feel better."

Beauregard digested the explanation then frowned again. "Am I sick?"

"Well, no," she answered. "You had a different kind of operation."

"I'm thirsty."

She retrieved a bottle with a bendable straw and placed the straw in his mouth. He drank a bit then pushed the straw out with his tongue. Reaching up with both hands, he felt the hardness of the brace that surrounded his head. His hands then went up and felt the bandages that wrapped around his head.

"My head hurts."

"That's where you had the operation. You've had a rebirth operation."

Beauregard stared blankly at her. "What's that?"

"Oh my," she uttered standing up straight again. "I'd better go get the doctor. Please make sure he doesn't do anything stupid," she blurted and ran off.

"What's wrong?" JB asked looking at Pieter.

"It looks like Mister Clayton here doesn't remember certain things."

JB leaned over him and stared at his face, gazing directly into his eyes.

"Who are you?" Beauregard asked, his eyes fluttering in wonder.

"I'm... uh, I'm JB." He had wanted to say, 'I'm you,' but somehow that didn't seem right. "Who are you?"

Beauregard thought hard for a bit, his face scrunched in deliberation. "I... I don't know. Do you know who I am?"

"Yes. Your name is –"

"Beauregard," Pieter's deep voice interrupted, "just Beauregard."

"Beauregard," he repeated.

The nurse returned with one of the Resurrection Industries doctor's in tow. "He doesn't know why he's had the operation," she explained.

The doctor, a young man whose future had been rocked by his kidnapping, stalked in. It was obvious he had little patience for anyone in the room. He stood by the bed and peered down at the patient. "Mister Clayton? Do you know why you're here?"

"My name's Beauregard."

"Yes, I know. Again, Mister Clayton, do you know why you're here?"

"My name's Beauregard. They said so."

His lips pursed, the doctor tried again. "OK... Beauregard. Do you know why you are here?"

"I've had an operation."

'That's right. Do you know why?"

Beauregard thought for a moment. "The nice lady said people have operations when they're sick, but she said I wasn't sick."

"No, you're not sick. You've been reborn."

Beauregard's eyes wandered as he tried to understand what that meant. "My head hurts."

"We'll get you something for your head," the doctor said then stiffly stood back up. "He's probably had brain damage in the move here," he testily announced. "What are his vitals?"

"All are normal," the nurse replied.

"Where are his charts? Get an imaging machine in here. I want a scan of the brain stem and a PET scan. There's probably damage to the hippocampus."

The nurse didn't move. "We don't have any imaging machines," she mutely answered.

"What? What kind of place is this?" he snapped. He turned his anger on all within earshot. "You people are barbaric. You snatch me from a prestigious practice, bring me here and expect me to work miracles amongst the dregs and rejects of society. I might as well be in darkest Africa."

"He's from Africa," JB pointed to Pieter.

"I don't give a tinker's damn where he's from," he fairly shouted before he blanched as a large hand wrapped around his throat and lifted his up so that he balanced on his tiptoes.

"You need to work on your bedside manner," Pieter coldly informed him. "We don't have the latest gadgets and inventions here because people like you would rather see us all dead so you can live your carefree life oblivious to the fate of people like us." Lowering him, he released his grip and brushed at the man's shirt as though straightening it. "Now, why don't you try again."

Rubbing his throat, the doctor warily regarded the big man. "Perhaps I was a bit hasty." Turning to the nurse, he politely asked, "What machines do we have here?"

"None that will be of any help," she apologetically shrugged.

With a sigh of frustration, he shifted his gaze from the nurse to Pieter to Beauregard. "Then there's nothing I can do. Perhaps in time he will heal better. In the meantime, let's make sure he doesn't turn his head or do any further damage."

"Do I have to be like this?" Beauregard called out. "I can't see. I want to see."

"When did he have his operation?" the doctor asked the nurse.

"I don't know. I think it's been at least a week or more."

"Do we have anything like a shoulder harness that will support his head if he sits up?"

"I don't know yet. I'll look."

"If not," Pieter interrupted, "ask Zoe or one of the warehouse folks. They may be able to fabricate one."

Casting him a look of impatient indulgence, the doctor turned back to the nurse. "Let me know what you find out." Without added discussion, he marched out, thankful to be out of the room yet still fuming about his circumstances.

"My head hurts," Beauregard complained again.

"Right. Sorry. He forgot to prescribe some pain meds. I'll go get you something."

Watching her leave, JB looked up at Pieter then to Beauregard. After a few moments, he said, "He's not what I thought he would be."

"What did you think he would be?"

"I don't know," he shrugged. "Someone I could be mad at. But he almost seems like us."

Pieter stepped closer to him. "What does it feel like when you are mad?"

JB thought for a bit. "It doesn't feel good. It's like it hurts inside."

"Anger and hate do more harm to those who hold it inside. Look at him now," he said ticking his head at Beauregard. "The man who wanted to kill you is right there. If you wanted to, you could kill him instead, and no one would blame you. In fact," he took several steps back towards the doorway, "I'll stand over here and stop anyone from coming in. Go ahead. Kill him if you want to. Go ahead. But remember, killing is a hard choice; it's permanent. You can't take it back. But then, you know that, for you've made that choice for someone else, before you came here."

JB twisted his head to stare quizzically at him, but Pieter just stood there, his arms folded, blocking the doorway. JB turned back to Beauregard and stepped closer to the bed to where he was almost touching it with his leg. Leaning over, he stared down at his supposed nemesis who was staring back up at him, his face in child-like expectation.

"My head hurts," Beauregard repeated.

"The nurse is getting some medicine for you," he replied.

Beauregard reached up and touched the head brace. "I don't like this."

"You only have to wear it for a little while longer."

Beauregard stared at him with a sort of fascination. "You're JB. I remember."

"Yes, I am."

"I'm Beauregard," he proudly announced.

"Yes, I know."

"I've had an operation, but I'm not sick."

JB smiled despite himself. "Yes, I know."

"Is the lady coming back soon?"

"Yes."

"Will you stay here with me until she does?"

JB stared at the hopeful eyes. "Yes."

"Thank you." He raised his hand and JB took it in his and squeezed it.

JB looked over his shoulder only to realize that Pieter had gone. Turning back to Beauregard, he said, "Do you like numbers? I've very good with numbers."

Chapter 10

Social Injustice complex – Sierra Vista
Monday, May 29, 2102

With Gretchen leaning over his shoulder, TJ pointed to the screen. "They've just gone over the wall here at Sahuarita." He swiveled the emplaced camera by the wall to scan the area back in the Zone. The large mother drone was dwindling in the distance, but they could see the small bio-drones spilling out of the belly like a swarm of bees spreading out over the countryside. "They should be in Sierra Vista in about half an hour, or less."

Standing straight up she swiveled her head and narrowed her gaze at Maria and Zoe who stood to her side. "Get the word out. I want everyone to stop whatever they're doing. I want it quiet for the next hour or more. Get someone to the nursery and let them know. Drug the little darlings if you have to, but I want it quiet."

Pieter walked in. "What's going on?"

"They're here," she tersely replied as Maria and Zoe ran off.

He looked at the small object on the screen. "Can we follow them?"

"I've got a drone coming down from Dragoon," TJ replied, switching screen view to the drone.

"Nice alliteration," Pieter chuckled.

"Nice what?" he frowned.

"Nothing," he patiently smiled.

"Can you mix in without being noticed?" Gretchen asked.

"Of course," he stated matter-of-factly.

Fixated on the screen, they watched the imaging as the drone sped its way to intercept the Corporate drones. Five minutes later, they saw their first bio-drone sweeping the countryside, looking for human life. Zooming past, they noticed the numbers of drones increasing, each one searching to fulfill its mission.

Another ten minutes and they saw the mother ship, about half the size of a football field, slowly moving towards Sierra Vista. TJ swept the drone down close to the ground as though he was searching for life. When he came close to the mother drone, he sharply angled up past the spinning propellers and brought it back down to hover directly over it, settling about a meter above the body.

"We can now keep track of when she gets here," he announced.

"How long do you think that will take?" Pieter asked.

TJ looked down at his control panel. "She's only doing around 110-120k's and hour. The drones will be here a lot sooner, but the mother ship here will be over the city in about 30 minutes."

"I've sent out word that I want it dead quiet down here," Gretchen explained. "I feel like I'm a submarine captain in one of those old World War II movies, hoping the enemy destroyer above us doesn't know where we are."

"If they did find out we were here, could they do anything?" Pieter asked, suddenly more than a little concerned.

"We do have air vents and things like that that protrude above ground," she answered. "If they sprayed their bio agents into the vents, it could possibly do some harm."

"Possibly?" His eyes blinked wide.

"We've already taken that into consideration," she mollified him. "We have measures in place that will hopefully capture and trap the agents should they be sprayed in any of the vents."

"Hopefully? I thought this was a self-contained location."

"It was, but as time went on, we felt we needed some outside air and adapted some of the air circulation systems. We'll be fine." She returned her attention to watch TJ.

"Why don't I feel reassured," Pieter mumbled to no one.

They continued watching when TJ announced, "She's picking up speed and adjusted course. She's heading straight here."

"Arrival time?" Gretchen asked.

"Ten minutes."

Without a word, she hurried out. A few moments later, her voice came over the speaker system. "The Corporate drones will be here any minute now. I ask that everyone stop whatever you are doing and remain quiet until I give the 'all clear' signal. Thank you."

She was back looking over TJ's shoulder when he informed her, "The bio-drones are already here."

From mounted cameras throughout the city, they were able to shift to different views down the streets and watch as the drones slowed down, hovered and moved on, searching for some evidence of human life. Switching from camera to camera, they saw the drones up near the Governor's house on Huachuca, or cruising down Fry Boulevard, or those drones paying particular attention to all the school buildings.

"She's almost here," TJ whispered.

From the vantage point of the small drone above the mother ship, they could see her slowing down to hover above the old Veteran's Memorial Park. The ship stayed there for a good ten minutes before TJ let out a "Whoa. She's rising."

The ship steadily rose until they could see the city and surrounding countryside. From one of the street cameras, they watched the mother ship unload another batch of bio-drones, sending one cluster off towards the Huachuca Mountains while another group headed toward the Mule Mountains and Bisbee.

"I see smoke," Pieter abruptly said. "There." He pointed to the Huachuca Mountains near Miller Peak to a tiny wisp of smoke from an obvious cooking fire.

"Damn," Gretchen moaned. "Those poor fools. Why didn't they listen? There's always someone who thinks they can do it better."

"They made their choice," Pieter soothed. "Hopefully there weren't a lot who felt the same way."

After another fifteen minutes, the mother ship began moving southeast towards Bisbee and Agua Prieta. Yet it wasn't until the drone-ship had passed the edge of the Social Injustice complex that they let out a collective breath. Waiting another twenty minutes for good measure, Gretchen gave the 'All clear.' By then, the drone-ship was passing Bisbee on its way to Aqua Prieta.

"What happens when they don't find any more folks?" Pieter asked. "They'll still have the bio-agents on the smaller drones. There's the probability that they'll be back."

Gretchen nodded agreement, lost in thought. "I wonder. TJ, do you think we could take out the mother ship after the bio-drones come back?"

TJ pondered a moment then said, "It's possible. All we'd have to do is disable the props while it's in flight. We could send in several drones and sort of do a kamikaze attack on it."

"I agree with Pieter," she said. "They'll be back. We need to take it out. Arrange it."

"With pleasure," TJ replied."

La Agostura, Mexico

With another load of food placed in the back of the car, Kevin closed the hatchback. "I'll take this up to the cave," he said to Warfield. "I think another few trips ought to do it."

"How we gonna keep the beer cold?" Warfield pretended to wonder.

"Find a real long extension cord," he chuckled.

"What a great idea. As soon as I finish up here, I'll go look for one."

"You find one and I'll help you carry that frig up to the cave."

"Spoken like a true brother." Warfield headed back to the house to continue loading up cans and boxes of food. He heard Kevin start up the car and slowly drive away. After several minutes of stacking cans and organizing boxes outside the front door, he paused to take a breather and stepped out into the morning sun. It was another beautiful sunny day in Mexico, and it was going to be a warm one. Looking out over the lake, he thought he might take a swim like he did yesterday. That had been an experience.

It had been late in the afternoon and the four of them sitting in the shade of the trees had had plenty of beer... well, at least he had. Someone had jokingly suggested they all go skinny-dipping. He hadn't hesitated a bit, but jumped up and hustled on down the hill, crossing the road and then on down to the water's edge. Peeling off his clothes, he was in the water before the rest of them were halfway down the hill.

The others were hesitant for only a moment before the two men removed their clothes and waded in. That left Carla, the gorgeous Carla. It was as though she had deliberately remained last, so that she would give them a show. And what a show it was. She slowly removed her clothes like she was doing a seductive striptease, except there was none of that feigned sensuality to it. There was almost an innocence to it that made it even more seductive.

Though daydreaming of Carla's glorious body, he turned to return to work when he saw it hovering fifty feet above him. In an instant, the drone dove straight for him and he barely had time to duck as it zoomed past and raced off.

He was startled for only a moment before he realized something was terribly wrong, for his chest suddenly felt tight and he began to get hot. Panic overtook him and he ran towards the cave, sweating as he pumped his legs as fast as he could, his chest burning and the pain increasing.

Carla saw him first. "Nick's coming up." She watched him for a bit longer. "Something's wrong. He doesn't look too good."

Kevin and Stephen stepped up beside her in the mouth of the cave. As Warfield staggered up the hill, Carla slipped away to her things in the cave.

"What's wrong?" Kevin called out.

"Drone," Warfield uttered, breathing heavily. He stopped where he was, about thirty paces away down the hill. He weaved side-to-side, light-headed, and his face was scrunched in pain. Both hands were at his chest, pressing in, vainly trying to relieve the agony.

"Stay there," Kevin somberly told him. "Tell me what happened."

"I... I," he started, the pain in his chest becoming excruciating. "O god, it hurts.

Carla walked up to stand next to Kevin. They all knew what had happened. Stephen spoke their thoughts.

"I thought they weren't going to retaliate until Wednesday, that we had another two days."

"So did we all," Kevin mutedly replied. He stared at his brother who had sunk to his knees, still clutching his chest.

"Don't let me die like this," he pleaded. "I'm done for. Put me out of this misery. O god it hurts." His body convulsed in a spasm of coughing that produced spittle heavily laced with blood.

Without a word, Carla handed Kevin her pistol then she and Stephen took a step back.

Turning it over in his hands, he stared at it as though it was some foreign object. He looked back to his brother who was on his hands and knees, grimacing and groaning in pain.

Warfield forced his head up. Sweat poured off his face and his clothes were soaked with perspiration. He said nothing, but his filmy eyes staring at Kevin begged for release.

Kevin slowly raised the gun, his hand trembling. He paused as he peered down the sights to see his brother begging for the pain to stop. The world suddenly grew quiet as he and Warfield stared at each other. Seconds seemed to stretch into minutes as though the two brothers were forever sculpted into time.

Then Warfield silently mouthed, "Do it. Please."

Kevin slowly squeezed the trigger and he felt the gun buck, yet he heard nothing. Sound returned to fill his senses when he saw blood pouring out of the hole in his brother's head.

Pharr Court South, Atlanta

Still in her pajamas, Sharon sipped her coffee and stared out the windows in the living room. It was mid-morning and she felt a malaise, a closed-in feeling that made her think that this was what cabin fever must be like. Looking down at her cup, she thought that those who got cabin fever probably ran out of coffee, which was why they went crazy. Thank god she had the foresight to stock up. She could go without food for a day or two, but not coffee.

She had been self-quarantined in the house now for more than a week, and the weather outside looked wonderful, inviting... but she knew better. Looking at the various plants and trees, she wondered what they would look like a year from now, with no one to care for them.

In the background, the TV news anchors pontificated about the latest efforts to track down the missing clones. Abruptly the volume increased causing her to turn around.

"We have breaking news," the female anchor, an attractive brunette, announced. "This morning, the Corporation launched Operation Pacify. Spokesperson Hagan Knudson stated that today's operation was conducted with the utmost care and safety for those outside the Cordon Zones."

Knudson appeared on the screen. He was a handsome middle-aged man with a thick mane of blond hair. "Today, the Corporation initialed a global effort to eradicate the possibility of any future aggressions originating from within the Cordon Zones. As many of you know, the Cordon Zones, originally designed to be a refuge for those unfit for normal society, have become a haven for all the derelicts and villains of society. As these individuals were not fit to be a part of a civilized world, they were removed to the Zones in order to keep our society safe and secure. Unfortunately, despite the best desires of the Corporation, the Zones have failed as places of refuge.

The camera angle changed and he turned with it. "Therefore, it was determined that the Zones no longer provided the means to separate the bad from the good. Further, with the burgeoning growth of our Corporate population, it was decided that the Zones could be better used for our own upright and productive employees, a sort of lebensraum for the good of the world." He paused briefly. "At eight o'clock this morning, London time, a systematic effort to eliminate the populations of the Zones was initiated and continues as I speak. By this time tomorrow, the overwhelming majority of those living in the Zones will have been eradicated. Those remaining will succumb to their fate within just a few days."

"We ask that those living near the Zones exercise caution and stay away from the walls for at least the next few weeks. Further, it is of utmost importance that anyone seen leaving out of the Zones be immediately dealt with. Do not come into contact with these people, but allow your local law enforcement to deal with them. I repeat, do not come into contact with anyone from the zones. Call your local law enforcement." Smiling, he bobbed his head with confidence. "Here's to a glorious future."

The camera returned to the news anchor, her hand at her ear piece as she intently listened. Focusing on the camera, she soberly announced, "This latest just in." A picture of Hans Josef appeared behind her. "It what appears to be a significant security breach in the upper management of the Corporation here in North America, Hans Josef, Vice-President for North America Security, has been accused of violating the Corporate Ethical Code by passing on Corporate secrets to Social Injustice. A Corporate spokesperson, speaking off the record, stated this revelation has serious repercussions at the highest levels.   An immediate investigation has been initiated.   When asked if they had Josef within their custody, they stated that his whereabouts are presently unknown. Stay tuned for continuing developments in this story and the latest in the war on the Zones."

Sharon's pulse quickened as she rapidly thought of what compromising information Hans might have unwittingly kept on her when her phone sounded and announced "Jon Veldt calling. Jon Veldt calling."

Retrieving the earpiece from the charging cradle, she placed it in her ear and pressed the answer button. "Hi Jon," she said, trying to sound nonchalant.

"Have you seen the news?"

"You mean about the Corporate attacks in the Zones?"

"No. I mean yes, but not that. I mean the news about Hans."

"Hans? They announce his promotion?"

There was a pause. "You haven't heard?"

"Heard what, Jon? You sound so mysterious."

"It was just on the news. He's under investigation for passing classified information to Social Injustice."

"What? That's impossible. Hans would never do anything like that. He has too much going for him." She relaxed as she assumed the persona of a loyal, and innocent, subordinate.

"That's what I thought, until I saw the news."

"I can't believe that.   Just because it's on TV doesn't necessarily mean it's true.   You know how the media and Corporate work."

"Yeah, I know.   We'll see.   One more thing though. How're you feeling?"

"Much better, thanks."

"You may want to stay sick for a few days more," he cryptically said.

"Pardon?"

"There's something happening, and I think it's serious. I've had an unusual number of my folks coming down sick and no one's recovering. I've talked with a number of my peers here and it's the same in each department."

"What?"

"Sharon," he heavily replied. "I think the Zones launched bio agents in their attack."

"O my god," she burst. "Are you sure?"

"Yes I'm sure. My advice to you is to stay put, watch the news and stay close to the phone. I'll call you later." With that the line went dead.

With a soft sigh of relief, Sharon went and double checked the barricaded front door then studied the camera monitor, slowly pressing the several buttons linking the strategically placed cameras out in the hallway. The hallway was empty, void of movement, and for a brief moment, she knew she was safe. A few days more and she could then finally relax.

Social Injustice complex – Sierra Vista

Gretchen stood at the operator position next to TJ's and watched the screen as Margie, a pretty teenager with long black hair, slowly maneuvered the drone up and down the streets of Sierra Vista. They were silent and empty.

"Head on out to Tombstone then down to Bisbee. Let me know if they found anyone."

"OK," Margie replied.

"Where's the mother ship?" She looked over to TJ's screen.

"Still over Agua Prieta," TJ replied. "Some of the drones are returning. Don't know how long it'll take. I wonder if they'll move it to another part of the Zone."

"Can you stay with it?"

"Depends. I only got so much battery. The mother ship can stay aloft for half a day. But she'll still need enough to return to base. I got an idea though." He skillfully lowered the drone so that it ended up resting on the mother ship. The camera angle tilted slightly. "I can turn off the props, leave the camera on and still save battery."

"Excellent. Let me know when you're ready to take it out."

"Roger Wilcox," he cheerfully replied.

Shaking her head with bemusement, she was at the door when Pieter met her.

"C'mon," he smiled. "I want to show you something."

"What?"

"Patience. You'll see."

He led her down the hallways, past the operational centers of the complex towards the infirmary. They stopped by the lounge where two men and a woman sat on a couch, watching and laughing at old cartoons on the TV. One of the men wore a rigid head brace. Pieter softly moved to the side of the couch.

JB noticed them first. "Hi Pieter," he smiled broadly at him. "We're watching these funny shows. Someone told us they're called cartoons. This one is about a bird that runs real fast and another animal that's always trying to catch him."

"I can see that." He moved around so that Beauregard could see him.

"Hi Pieter," Beauregard smiled brightly. "I'm watching TV with JB and Ruth."

"So I noticed."

"We're watching a funny show, but it's not real," he explained. "You can tell it's not real 'cause they don't look like they're real."

"No, they're not real." Pieter watched them watching the show. Where Ruth and JB laughed, Beauregard seemed fascinated, captivated by the movement and visual effects. "Beauregard?"

"Yes Pieter?" he replied, shifting his attention back to the big man.

"How does that head brace feel."

"Isn't it nice?" he blinked in happiness. "JB got them to put this on me. I can walk around now. I had an operation," he added, his face quite serious, "but I'm not sick."

"JB's nice, isn't he."

"JB's my friend," he proudly answered. "And Ruth is my friend. She's JB's wife," he confidentially added.

"So I hear." He smiled as he saw Beauregard's attention and fascination shift back to the TV. Walking behind the couch, he motioned for JB to come talk with him.

"I see you're taking good care of Beauregard."

JB looked back at Beauregard. "He's not the same like he used to be, is he."

301

"No, he's nothing like he was before."

The show ended and an excited Beauregard fairly shouted, "Pieter, Pieter."

Pieter came around to stand in front of him.

"Guess what?" he said, barely containing his excitement.

"What."

"JB and I look exactly the same, and everything," he gushed.

"I noticed that."

Pieter waited for him to continue, but he simply sat there and stared happily at him. The show resumed and his attention was snatched away to watch the bird continually outsmart the coyote.

Pieter motioned for JB to sit while he went back to where Gretchen was standing, just outside the doorway. "Well? What do you think?"

"I know this may sound awful," she replied, "but I'm sort of glad we were a little rough getting him back here. He's obviously not what he once was. I wonder if he ever will be. I still don't fully understand why you specifically wanted him saved."

"He will be a teacher," he quietly replied, listening to Beauregard's almost childish laughter.

"Him?" She turned to him, her disbelief obvious.

"He won't know it," Pieter explained. "But by being who he is, he will teach others that everyone needs to be loved. Already he is teaching JB how to forgive."

Gretchen studied him for a bit then looked back to the three on the couch. "Well, not that I want to ruin this kumbayah moment, but we do have a little thing called a 'war' going on."

Pieter narrowed his eyes to fix her with an intent gaze. In his warm deep voice, he soothed, "You've done more than is humanly possible, especially after our little experience with the former governor."

Staring back up at him, her eyes moistened briefly as she tenderly reached out to touch his arm. "I know I said 'Thank you' before, but it is still so insufficient to what I truly feel."

"It was not your time" he reminded her. "And to have you here with me, with us, is enough."

Their eyes held each other for several heartbeats before she broke the spell. "I'd better get back to see how things are progressing."

Pieter gently squeezed her hand. "I'll be up in just a minute." He ticked his head at the three on the couch.

"Take your time," she smiled at him. "You know where to find me."

"Pieter!" Beauregard called out. When he didn't get a quick enough answer, he awkwardly tried to stand and JB immediately jumped up to help him. Beauregard stiffly turned around to find Pieter watching Gretchen walk away, a warm smile curling his lips. "Pieter."

Pieter turned around, still smiling. "Yes Beauregard."

"Will you come watch the TV with us?"

"For a little bit. I've got to get back to help Gretchen shortly." He walked over to stand behind the couch.

"You don't have to stand, Pieter. We can make room on the couch, can't we JB?" He looked at JB with the eyes of innocence like a child seeking approval from his father.

"That's OK, Beauregard," Pieter chuckled. "I can't stay long. You go ahead and sit and I'll stand behind you to watch."

"OK, Pieter." Beauregard looked back to JB who held out his hands. Grasping hands, JB helped lower him to sitting next to Ruth.

"All set?" JB smiled at him.

"Yes, JB," he bobbed his head in happiness.

"What do we say?"

Beauregard thought for a moment then triumphantly announced, "Thank you!"

"Very good." JB sat on Ruth's other side. In mere minutes, the three were again laughing at the antics of the bird and coyote.

With a sigh of contentment, Pieter watched them for just a little bit more before silently backing out the room.

Gretchen walked in just as TJ loudly announced to those in the room, "They're comin' back to the mothership."

"How far do you think they sent the bio-drones?" she asked.

"Those things can do about 500k's an hour, so they probably could get to Chihuahua and back, but it doesn't account for searching time.   They probably sent in another couple of motherships to cover the whole area."

She watched in fascination as the swarms of bio-drones zoomed into view and swooped down below then up to settle within the bowels of the mothership.   Then, with the bio-drones still teeming around the open belly, the mothership began slowly turning to begin its journey back to base.

"Have you figured out a way to take it down?" she asked TJ.

"I've been thinking about that," he replied.   'The blades are free floating.   We'll need to get up into the prop motors.   She's got six props.   I think if we can take out three of them on one side, the rest won't be able to hold her up."

"Can you do it?"

"Not by myself.   Ariana and Mateo," he ticked his head side to side at the teenagers sitting on both sides of him, "are waiting until we get closer to the wall.   Then they'll come up and help me."

"About how long then?"

"I don't know," he shrugged.   "She's pickin' up speed. She's been out now for almost four hours.   She's gotta head back or otherwise she'll run outta power."

The mothership's speed increased significantly and the camera vibrated with the increased engine torque.   Bisbee came into view and was swept behind followed by Sierra Vista.

When Sierra Vista faded, TJ said to the two on either side of him, "It won't be long now.   Get ready."   He watched the progress of the ship, the tracking plot on the geo-screen directly above his drone screen.   Puzzled, he commented, "She's not slowing down."

As the mothership approached the wall, two drones shot up from the desert and tucked in behind, maneuvering up to where TJ had just reactivated his drone propellers and was matching the mothership's speed.

"She's in a hurry to get somewhere," he frowned, "and I don't think it's Tucson, not with how fast she's going."

"Let's see what's her hurry," Gretchen said, "before we take her down."

Pieter silently walked in and stood off to the side.   Gretchen felt his presence and looked back over her shoulder.   Giving him a warm smile, she shifted her attention back to the screen.

After the mothership left Tucson behind, Pieter looked at the geo-screen. "She's headed to Phoenix. What's in Phoenix?"

"Don't know," TJ responded.

Gretchen thought a moment when her jaw dropped. "DMI has a facility there. It's up in Glendale. They're going back for more bio agents."

The mother ship sped on and as the skyline of Phoenix began to draw closer, she began to slow down slightly.

"Where are they going to land it?" Pieter asked. "Certainly not at the airport. That's just about in the middle of the city. They wouldn't endanger the city like that."

"I don't know," TJ answered, "but they're gonna have to land somewhere to recharge." He looked up at Gretchen. "What do you wanna do?"

"Take it out anywhere in the city, the higher the better."

Understanding, he smiled. Glancing back and forth between Ariana and Mateo, he said, "Let's take her out when she's just above the middle of the city. That means we need to hit the motors before she gets there, in about two minutes." He leaned back and looked two positions down to his left at another teenager, a slender girl with black hair tied into two pigtails at the top rear of her head. "You ready Bianca?"

"Roger Dodger," she cheerfully replied without taking her focus from the screen.

Pieter shifted down to look at her screen. Bianca was flying a drone far to the rear of the mothership so that she could see the ship and the Phoenix skyline. He remained watching her screen as the other three pilots maneuvered their drones into position. He could see the three drones, small black spots moving just above the mothership.

"Let's do the back three engines," TJ said, "at the same time. Ready? Now."

The three black spots shot up to just below the blade and engine coupling, diving straight into the engines turbines. The screens of the three pilots immediately went blank. They jumped out of their seats and crowded behind Bianca.

The rear of the mothership shuttered as the propellers of the three rear engines coughed and sputtered. The rear of the ship began slowly sinking lower than the front. There was an attempt to increase the prop speed by the mothership pilot, but it caused the engines to overwork and smoke began to drool out

305

the rear. One after another, the rear engines locked up and the propellers stopped. The rear swung quickly down so that the ship was now vertical.   It hung there for a breath then plummeted in a descending arc, crashing into the upper stories of skyscrapers, sending debris and chunks of concrete and steel down to the streets below.

By the time the dust settled, it lay like a beached whale on its side on Monroe Street, gaping holes in the side, the rotor blades torn off or bent. In what can only be determined as a design flaw, the belly of the beast opened up and the swarms of bio-drones erupted and began delivering their lethal contents to the startled citizens of Phoenix who fled in terror.

"That worked better than I expected," TJ wryly observed.

Pharr Court South, Atlanta

Sharon maintained her pace on the treadmill, watching the news on the wall TV. She was surprised that the news was the normal pabulum of bland stories of the banal activities of noteworthy employees or other rich and famous Corporate celebrities. She had half expected the Corporation to be gloating by now of their supposedly over-dominating success in wiping out the Zones.

She also found it puzzling that Jon had not called back. She was half-tempted to call him, but decided to wait to see how things played out. Most likely he had forgotten in the whirlwind of the catastrophic news or possibly he had himself succumbed, though he hadn't sounded ill when he had called earlier. In the middle of an expose on the latest boy band, the news abruptly shifted to a reporter, an attractive blond, outside in the sunny climate of the southwest.

"This is Pinky Berg here standing in downtown Phoenix, with the latest breaking news. Behind me, you can see the smoking after effects of a Corporate drone that crashed as a result of mechanical failure. The death toll from this tragic accident is still being determined, but latest reports have at least 237 people killed. Authorities are currently investigating why the drone was flying over the city on an unregistered flight plan."

As she spoke, the chaotic scene filled with flashing blue lights and the wailing sirens of emergency vehicles. Volunteers and emergency workers were administering first aid or digging through the rubble looking for survivors. A ragged gash on the side of the drone revealed internal arcs of electricity angrily twitching across the open space. Suddenly a small cloud of bio-drones, like a swarm of bees, burst out of the gaping hole, paused for only a moment and dispersed like a silent explosion. The unseen cameraman said something in her earphone causing her to pause and look behind her. By the time she realized what it was, she instinctively ducked as it sped by them, spraying its odorless cargo upon both reporter and cameraman.

Pinky Berg quickly regained her composure. She was about to begin when she felt her chest tighten and she suddenly felt quite hot and lightheaded. Determined to carry on, she tried to stand straight only to feel excruciating pain burst throughout her chest. Her face scrunched in agony as she began to wobble. At the same time, the camera began to waver and then, without warning, fell to the ground. Yet the live feed continued as the viewing audience got to see Pinky slump to her knees, her body sweating profusely. By the time the network cut to a different story, Pinky had retched and collapsed in spasmodic convulsions.

Social Injustice complex – Sierra Vista
Sunday, June 4, 2102

It was almost a week before the morning news admitted something was happening. Safe and secure in their underground bunker, Pieter, Gretchen, Maria, Zoe and a small group of other Social Injustice leaders stood or sat in the TV room watching as the self-assured news anchor, an attractive brunette, stared calmly at the camera.

"And this just in," she said. "The Corporation has reported a virus infection spreading in a select number of locations. In a statement released by DMI, it has already isolated the virus and is now preparing sufficient supplies of the antidote to eradicate any further outbreak."

By the evening, the number of those watching increased to fill the room. The news anchor, a handsome man with coal black hair, warned viewers, "DMI, today, issued a virus alert for all locations. I repeat, the DMI has issued a virus alert for all locations. If you are experiencing any of the following symptoms, difficulty breathing, dizziness, mouth dryness, intense pain in any part of your body," he continued listing further symptoms, "seek medical attention immediately."

Despite their obvious success, no one in the room cheered or celebrated. Instead, the mood was somber, reserved. Gretchen felt the angst. Muting the sound with the remote, she walked to stand in front of the TV.

"What we have done is a terrible thing. In some respects, some would think we bear the mark of Cain. But you must not think like that. Think about what our Zone would be had we done nothing. We all would be living down here for the rest of our lives, in constant fear that those on the other side of the wall would strike again... and again... and again... until they had killed us, killed our children.

Her voice grew strong and firm as she spoke. "You must think of the Corporation as an evil bully, one so vile that he will not rest until he has inflicted more pain than you can endure. One cannot reason with a bully, and as with all bullies, he must be defeated." She paused to slowly gaze around the room. "Look around the room. Many of you were born here. What was your crime? What did you do that prevented you from enjoying life on the other side of the wall... where doctors have the latest technology and medicines... where food is plentiful and you don't have to struggle to survive... where everything you need is provided for you? What was your crime?"

She let silence settle for a moment. "Some of you may ask, 'What about all those innocent men, women and children who had nothing to do with the Corporation?' Think about it. Social Injustice is not unknown on the other side of the wall. There are many who believed as we did that not only was cloning evil, but exiling us here to the Zone was likewise evil. They joined us, became a part of us. Those who did not? They made their choice. Some may think it harsh, but those who stand to the side, who say 'It's not my problem,' are as guilty as those who inflict the pain. Though they might not administer the torment, their willingness to do nothing indicts them, for it says they approve."

Pausing to take a breath, she nodded in affirmation. "We have fought for survival. We have destroyed the enemy. In due time, we will emerge from our sanctuary here, out to a new world where we will reclaim what is rightfully ours, without fear of Corporate retribution. Think on that day when you will stand in the sunlight, breathing deep the clean air of freedom."

She stepped away from the TV, handing the remote to one of those who stood by the couch. As she pressed her way through the crowd, the clapping began followed by subtle cheers at first, soon growing to an outpouring of relief and gratitude. Many were the hands who patted her on the shoulder as she tried to make her way out. Many were the men and women who, with their eyes brimming, stopped her to give her a hug and thank her for saving their lives.

She finally made her way out the room to where Pieter was standing in the hallway. Smiling at her, he winked. "Buy you a drink, sailor?"

Grinning, she took his arm in hers. "I'd love a drink right about now. I know a quiet little place. The food's not bad either."

By the late evening, the news was bleak. The same announcer from the early evening news was still on. He looked haggard and strained. "Corporation officials have declared a state of emergency. All employees are ordered to remain where they are. Do not, I repeat, do not attempt to go to a hospital or medical facility. All medical facilities are at capacity and can no longer offer care. If you are attempting to reach a medical facility, you are to turn around and go home."

The screen filled with the gruesome picture of the cacophony of gridlocked streets with immobile cars jammed against each other, people panicking and screaming at each other, others smashing shop windows and looting, while still others hurried down sidewalks carefully avoiding crumpled bodies lying on the cold concrete of those already succumbed to the disease.

Pharr Court South, Atlanta
Wednesday, June 7, 2102

Sharon watched the news from the safety of her large penthouse, high above the maddening clamor for survival in the streets below. Occasionally she would stand in front of the tall windows overlooking the city noting the diminishing activity with each succeeding day. Today, a sunny afternoon, was an especially quiet day. Standing at the window feeling the warmth of the sun, she sipped her coffee vainly searching the streets below to find anything moving.

Yesterday the programing on TV stopped except for a few news channels, which hesitated to venture outside the safety of their studios to see the latest developments. Those few doughty news organizations that put story ahead of safety had long succumbed to the diseases and were now merely white noise on the TV screen.

The last time her phone announced a caller was when Jon had called over a week ago. He never called back. Most likely he was dead. She found it puzzling that no one had bothered to call her in the interim. But then, she reasoned, with the rapid spread of the virus, self-preservation takes control and thinking of others becomes a lesser priority.

Turning, she retraced her steps back to check the front door, a habit now that she conducted several times a day. The bolts and locks were secure as well as the crossties that spread across the breadth of the door. Thinking back, she wished she had installed the interior wall metal mesh that went on the market when the Board decided that certain employees needed greater security.

Satisfied the door was secure, she then checked the monitor on the wall by the door. She pressed the different buttons linking the various cameras out in the hallway, taking note that it was both quiet and empty.

With a deep breath, she returned to make her rounds in the penthouse. In one bedroom, toilet paper and bath supplies filled almost the entire room. She had been meticulous in planning how much she might need for a year, provided the internal plumbing stayed in good order.

The second bedroom was filled with canned goods and the latest military vacuum sealed meals stacked in boxes floor to

310

ceiling, more than enough to last the year. She knew there would come a time when those neighbors, and others, who had not perished would come looking for food. Where she had planned ahead, most didn't know what was coming.

The third bedroom was nothing but spring water containers, tightly packed floor to ceiling. She had likewise calculated the demand for water based upon a year of isolation. She would use the building water until it stopped.

The fourth bedroom was filled with weapons, ammunition, and other necessities like a solar generator, batteries, matches, and anything else she might need for survival. The rest of the penthouse was filled with books and art. If she was going to live alone for a year, she might as well be comfortable.

Walking to the bar in the dining room, she smiled at the fact that she had also stocked up on some excellent wines and cordials, more than enough to last a year. She thought about the TV show "Survive This!" where ten contestants, five men and five women, were placed on a supposedly deserted island and told to fend for themselves for a year. Of course it was an absurd show because camera crews followed them around the entire time and obviously the camera crews weren't dining on the same survival fare. In fact, when one of the contestants noted they were getting downright plump, he discovered that not only were they *not* on a deserted island, but that the supposed island was merely a peninsula leading to the mainland where civilization offered the finest in the dining experience.

That show quickly folded, replaced by a new show called "Crusoe." This show was more to reality, where individual contestants were placed on deserted Pacific islands and left alone for a year. Each contestant was allowed ten items to take with him or her.

Sharon had often wondered what ten items she would have taken. Of course, it no longer mattered now. She had taken more than ten items to survive. Knowing it was only a matter of time before the TV networks went off the air, she had invested in a good ham radio. Eschewing the cumbersome call-sign as initially allocated by the International Telecommunications Union, she chose a vanity call sign – DELILAH.

Each evening, during the TV news casts, she scoured the airwaves, listening to the ever diminishing chatter. Despite her linguistic talents, she focused on closer to home, knowing someone speaking German wasn't likely to be local.

Sharon wrapped the silk robe tighter around her, retying a knot in the belt. Though it was the afternoon, she felt little need to change out of her pajamas, though starting tomorrow, she was going to be more disciplined - get up at a reasonable time, clean up and start the day prepared... starting tomorrow.

Wandering back to the camera monitor on the wall by the door, she wished she had installed an early warning system, something that stretched across the outer hall that would alert her anytime someone was on her floor. It was too late for that now, and despite the urge to remedy the situation, she was not going to unlock the doors, for any reason.

Behind her, she could faintly hear the TV announcer declaring the latest statistics and directives. Meandering back into the TV room, she swung by the bar to pour a raspberry cordial then plopped down on the large sofa in front of the TV. It wasn't one of those grandiose large-screen TVs, the kind that took up the whole wall and made the viewer feel like she was a dwarf compared to the size of the people on the screen.

No, hers was reasonable, large, but not ostentatious. She chuckled to herself thinking 'who cared anymore? Look! I got a humongous TV, and oh yeah, I'll be dead in a day or two.' So much for bragging rights...

On the screen, a visibly tired and haggard announcer with several days of beard stubble read the news. "A state of emergency has been declared for the entire globe. Do not go out of your homes for any reason. I repeat. Do not go out of your homes for any reason. DMI is presently working at peak capacity to produce enough serum to stop the plagues. We now have the latest word from Corporation CEO Kent Santoyo."

The screen filled with a fuzzy picture of a man behind the desk. The poor quality of the image revealed it was obviously a hologram.

"Today," Kent gravely began, "we are confronted with the evil spread by Social Injustice. With our retaliation and efforts to contain their heinous acts, we are successfully waging a war of existence. SI has been pushed to the brink of extinction and it is merely a matter of time before it ceases to exist. We are now in a mopping up operation. Our own DMI is feverishly working on vaccines and it is only a matter of time before order and safety are restored. We are making superb progress. Until that time, you are asked to remain where you are. Do not venture out into public areas or outside the safety of your present location. This will all be over in a matter of days. Thank you."

By the time the evening news was supposed to be on, all programing had ceased. Sharon flicked through the channels several times, repeating the process ten and twenty minutes later with the same results.

Turning it off, she walked over and sat down by the ham radio. Slowly dialing through the frequencies, she listened for any chatter. It was quiet and she was about to give up when she heard a faint "Anyone. Anyone listening." She adjusted the dial to get the signal stronger. "Anyone. Anyone listening."

Placing her head set on, she pressed the earpiece to talk. "Yes. I hear you."

"Who are you?" came the excited reply.

"Delilah. Who are you?"

"This is echo india alpha seven lima."

"So what do I call you?"

"Eh, call me Paddy."

"Where are you?"

"Ireland. Tullamore. Where are you?"

"Atlanta, Georgia, USA."

"Are you safe?"

"Yes. And you?"

"So far. What's it like there?"

"Bad.   Both the zones and free side are pretty much nonexistent. Everyone is either dying or dead."

"Same here. How is it that you're safe?"

"I'm locked away in a tower."

Paddy laughed. "Sort of like Rapunzel."

"Yes. What about you?"

"Same here. There are four of us here, buttoned up."

"Are you with Social Injustice?"

There was a long pause before he replied, "Yes."

"Me too," she answered. "Have you had any contact with anyone else?"

"Not yet. You're the first."

The conversation continued for over an hour with each probing into the other's life and environment. By the time the

313

conversation ended, they agreed to a daily chat each day at 2000 hours.

Signing off, Sharon stood and stretched. Walking into the kitchen, she stared at the calendar stuck to the front of the refrigerator with a tacky magnet from Atlantic City. Beginning with Friday, May 19, there was a neat 'X' across each day until today. Though tempted to cross off today, she told herself that today wasn't over yet and she needed to stay consistent. Each day was marked off the following day.

With a sigh, she wondered what she was going to be like a year from now.

Chapter 11

Social Injustice complex – Sierra Vista
One year later - Thursday, May 31, 2103

Gretchen stood behind TJ sitting at the control monitor. He scratched at his face, the thin wisps of facial hair just beginning to grow. Pieter stood beside her. Behind them, it seemed like the entire community had come out to witness the day.

"I feel like Noah sending out the raven," she joked to Pieter. She looked behind her shoulder then, in a calm voice belying her excitement, she said, "Go ahead and send out the drones."

Above them in the several warehouses, batteries activated, propellers twirled and drones lifted off the ground, their cameras scanning the terrain below.

Pieter placed an arm across her shoulders, leaning down to whisper, "You were very wise to not fly the drones this past year. Otherwise everyone would have left here months ago."

"Thank you." She reached up and squeezed his hand. Yet in that instant, she was reminded of the incident almost six months ago. One of those rescued, an out-settler named Wes had stirred up trouble by deciding he was ready to leave. He had gathered a small following who were likewise beginning to exert their influence on the others. Yet Gretchen knew he had no intention of leaving but was rather challenging her authority.

Ensuring she had a large audience, she confronted him.

"So you want to leave?" she calmly asked.

"Damn right," he snorted in reply. Wes was a big burly man used to having his way.

"Fine," she loudly announced. "You and all who are willing to go with you are free to leave." She paused for effect. "But remember this, once you are on the outside, you will not be allowed to return back in here – no matter what happens to you. Once you leave here, I will bear no responsibility for what happens to you and those who go with you. If the bio-agents are still active, that is your responsibility."

The folks behind Wes began to murmur their sudden concerns when he looked over his shoulder at them and retorted,

"Eh, she's just bluffin.' There ain't nuthin out there to worry about."

"Have it your way," she shrugged. "Take them to the exit doors." She turned to Maria and began a low voiced conversation.

Several well-armed men and women, with protective face masks stepped up and motioned for him to get moving.

Startled, he quickly regained his composure while some of his less convinced followers began to trickle away. "Eh, you ain't foolin' nobody. You can't fool us. There ain't nuthin' out there. Yer just lordin' it over us to keep us here."

Gretchen paused her conversation, looked up at him and frowned. "You're still here? I told you already, you're free to leave. Go on. Leave."

Wes blinked in consternation as more of his small band of loyal followers began to quickly and silently drift away. "Wait, wait!" he harangued at them. But his efforts were of little use as in mere moments, he was left quite alone.

"Your little band of renegades seem to have fled," Gretchen wryly observed. "However, you are still free to go." She waved a dismissive hand at him. Narrowing her focus to the armed men and women, she commanded, "Toss him out."

"Wait a minute," he sputtered. "Ah… I ain't…"

"Do you want to go out or not?" she crossly demanded. "I'm not going to stand here and waste my time while you make up your mind."

"I… uh, I guess I'll stay."

"That's what I thought." Fixing him with a penetrating stare, she said, "You're a trouble-maker and I can't afford to have you stirring up more trouble." Looking back at one of the armed women, she commanded, "Take him to the holding tank until I decide what to do with him."

He was about to demand his rights when they circled him and physically escorted him away.

That was six months ago. Wes had remained in the holding tank ever since. Repeated pleas for release were met with the same response – 'I'm still deciding.' He had demanded a lawyer, which made her chuckle. Down here, she was the law. Once everyone got topside, they could put whatever government they wanted into effect. But down here, she ruled.

Her attention was diverted to the present as she focused on the screen as TJ flew the drone along Fry Boulevard. Though it was a beautiful sunny day outside, the town was empty. Layers of desert sand covered the cars and homes and businesses. Streetlights, rocking in the wind, still went through their sequences, yet there was no sign of human life. Flocks of birds swarmed from one tree to the next while high above, buzzards circled lazily in the warm air currents. An occasional coyote trotted on one of the side alleys. Tumbleweed bounced in the wind down the streets.

It was a different scene in Tucson. Instead of the orderly structure of a city like Sierra Vista where the inhabitants left in an orderly fashion, Tucson was a city of panic and devastation. Bodies littered the streets like so much flotsam, and what remained now were skeletons molded to clothing in an extricable union of flesh and fabric. Where the bodies had not been picked and sundered by carrion fowl and other animals, they remained forever in situ, some leaning forward against steering wheels, the desiccated bodies of the children in the back seat, others locked in embrace as though holding on they would escape their fate.

It was the same in every other city and town all the way up past Phoenix. The only living things were the birds and animals that moved about the streets and alleys with impervious nonchalance.

Gretchen turned around and faced the people. "We will continue monitoring today to make sure nothing is amiss. If all is clear, we will emerge tomorrow morning at ten."

A loud and raucous cheer erupted as they scattered to finalize packing. The mood was infectious and whatever arguments or disagreements among them during their time below were vanquished with the knowledge that their lives were about to begin.

Pieter smiled at the energy and excitement. In very little time, the hallway had emptied, leaving Pieter and Gretchen alone with those in the drone room.

Gretchen placed a hand on TJ's shoulder. "Let me know when you're finished. Go as far as you can today."

"Roger Dodger," he grinned, mimicking Bianca who operated the drone controls in the position next to him. She flashed him an impish knowing smile.

317

Gretchen looked up to Pieter. "Care to do a walk down memory lane here as we see how everyone's coming along?"

"Would love to," he smiled, holding out his arm for her to slide her arm around his, "though I doubt we'll see much that remains to be done. I think everyone was packed a month ago."

La Agostura, Mexico

Wiping his hands on a rag, Kevin leaned against the doorway of the house by the lake, staring up the road, watching Carla slowly amble down the hill. Her pace was unhurried and relaxed as though she hadn't a care in the world. When she saw him, she smiled and gave him a little wave. He returned the wave, flicked the rag on the small table by the door and walked out to meet her.

"You know we do have the car," he pointed out as he approached to stand before her.

"I know," she replied, "but it's not too much to carry, and I like the walk."

"And passing by him doesn't bother you?"

"He's dead and can no longer hurt us. Now, it would bother me if he suddenly came back to life," she joked.

"It will never happen," he quietly replied, remembering their abject fear when Warfield had staggered part way up to the cave only to die right there on the path. They had stayed in the cave for a few days until the smell caused them to act. Stephen suggested they bury him.

"Bury him?" Carla sputtered. "You mean like dig a grave and all?"

"No," he curtly answered. "We leave him where he is and pile rocks and dirt on top of him."

While they agreed that was a good idea, they weren't quite sure how to go about it as no one wanted to get too close. Stephen finally said they should just stand a bit away and toss rocks on Warfield from a safe distance.

Emerging from the cave, they stood upwind a distance away. Stephen was the first to toss a fist sized rock. It rolled and bounced until it hit the side of the now decaying body. Carla followed suit and soon she and Stephen were scouring the area for more rocks and tossing them at the corpse. Those that missed the mark were left where they lay, to use when the winds shifted.

Kevin remained standing, unable to bring himself to this final abuse of his brother. Yet finally, even he was forced to participate, knowing it was a matter of survival. They finally succeeded two days later, finishing off cairn with shovels of dirt.

That explained the one grave.

There was another grave a little ways off the road near the dam. Stephen was in that one.

Carla and Kevin didn't talk about that one anymore, but both knew Stephen's death was no accident. Not long after they buried Warfield, they had settled down to life in the cave, each evening venturing down to the lake to get clean and relax. Shedding their clothes they frolicked in the knowledge that they had cheated death. Carla thought it an excellent situation as she had two men who vied for her affection and she willingly shared herself with both.

Initially it seemed to work. Certain days of the week, she slept with Stephen, other days she slept with Kevin. Some days she chose to sleep alone. As time went on, Kevin perceived that his time with her was not quite so equitable. She seemed to want to sleep by herself more often when it was his turn.

One beautiful morning in October, Kevin suggested that he and Stephen fish near the dam. It was while Stephen was baiting his hook that Kevin shot him.

Carla knew what had happened and if it bothered her, she didn't express it. She merely grew more introspective. With Stephen out of the way, life settled into routine, almost like husband and wife.

Standing now in the middle of the dirt road, Kevin lifted a hand to shield his eyes from the sun, slowly surveying the lake and the surrounding hills. "I think it's about time we move on."

"Where to?"

"South. Head on down Mexico City way."

"Think anyone's still there?"

"Not likely. We'll take the satellite stuff just in case."

"Why? We haven't heard from anyone since last year."

"Better safe than sorry," he replied. "We'll load up the car with what food we can carry."

"OK."

Reaching for her hand, he felt a squeeze as they languidly made their way back to the house.

Pharr Court South, Atlanta

Sharon stood in front of the refrigerator, staring at the calendar on the door. The month displayed was May and all the dates except one had a large 'X' across them. Only the last day, today, remained unmarked. With a deep breath, she turned and walked to the doors leading to the outside patio.

Through the windows, she could see the unkempt deck, the result of a year's worth of neglect. Yet, despite a gardener's indifference, spring had been kind and all the plants flourished in the bright late morning sun. Looking at the outside thermometer attached to the wall near the door she saw it was already almost 80°.

She paused before the door, chastising herself for the delay. She had been here several times this morning, only to hesitate opening the door. Each time she reached for the handle, she had paused and looked over her shoulder at the safety and security of her home. For the past year, she had settled into this sanctuary, nestled within the strong walls, knowing she was safe from harm. Even when the storms raged outside, she knew she could fix a drink, hunker down on the sofa, put on an old movie and relax in the knowledge that she was sheltered and secure.

There had been days when she thought she might go crazy, but those faded early on, and with the ability to chat with others over the ham radio, her days were filled with news and discovery.

Her range of friends now included more than Paddy in Ireland. There was Ron in Parkersburg, Iowa and Cheryl in Pickens, West Virginia and almost a dozen others scattered throughout the United States and Canada, and a few others in Europe and South America.

Yet there was no one within 500 miles of Atlanta, not even Lowell or anyone else from Social Injustice. And that concerned her, for no one knew what was out there or who remained and survived. And if they did survive, what did they look like?

She shook her head in irritation. She had been through all this too many times, and remonstrated at herself for her wild imagination. For all she knew, there was nobody left for miles around and anyway, she would have to emerge some day from this cocoon of security.

Yet now that the day was here, she wasn't so confident anymore. Besides, she rationalized, she didn't need to do everything at once. She could start off slowly, one step at a time. The first step was to experience what it felt like to be outside again.

With another determined deep breath, she twisted the handle and opened the main door followed by the screen door. She was immediately greeted by a blast of warm air filed with the fragrance of things growing.

Stepping out through the doors and onto the garden deck, she paused to take in the broad vista of the city then raised her arms and tilted her head back. Closing her eyes, she inhaled a deep breath, letting the clean and fresh morning air flow over and inside her.

With a burgeoning smile, she crossed over to the far wall and gazed out over the silent city. Down below, traffic lights flashed their yellow warning, but nothing else moved save for the occasional bits of debris pushed along by the wind. There were still plenty of cars and trucks, most long since abandoned in place. But they were all immobile, a testament to the devastation that swept across the land.

As she gazed out, she again wondered what had happened to Hans and whether she would ever see him again. Yet that was the least of her worries. It was time to move on, to explore, to find other survivors.

She had already methodically planned her search. It would begin small, searching the surrounding area, each night returning to her base here at home. Then in the evening, she would haul out the telescope and use the vantage of the penthouse's height to scope out the surrounding buildings.

Once she was sure of the buildings around her, she would expand her search more and more until finally claiming a suitable vehicle, she would venture farther outside the city. Yet that would take time... lots of time. What she really wanted was companionship. The closest person she knew via the radio was

Cheryl in West Virginia and she had to be at least 500 miles away.

Still, she had made the first step. She was outside. The next step was to see if anyone else in the penthouse building survived.

Nodding resolutely at her decision, she absentmindedly looked down at her pale arms and frowned. She had been inside so long, she looked like a ghost, or maybe even a vampire, someone afraid of the sun. She chuckled at the comparison.

A sudden urge overwhelmed her and she went over to the small storage shed, opened it and retrieved the table umbrella. Striding across the patio, she positioned it in the table and spread it open. She then returned and with an oomph, lifted a thick cushioned patio chair and walked it over to the place by the table under the shade of the umbrella.

Satisfied with the arrangement, she headed back inside and returned shortly with a cold soda, a bowl of chips and a hardback version of *Robison Crusoe*. Settling herself in the chair, she popped open the soda and sighed with contentment. Adjusting her sunglasses, she kicked her feet up and opened the book. After all there was no need to rush. She would start her exploring tomorrow.

Besides, tomorrow was June 1st and it was always better to start something at the beginning. Today was the last day of the month, the last day of her solitary confinement. She might as well enjoy it.

Sierra Vista, Arizona
Friday, June 1, 2103

Arm in arm, Gretchen and Pieter lazily walked along Fry Boulevard, watching the burgeoning activity as those so long underground burst forth to spread out to find places to live. There was an exultant joy as so many raced and danced in the clean air of freedom.

"I'd say I was going to miss living below," she said, "but there's nothing like being outside on a day like today." She inhaled deeply, savoring the fresh air and clear sky.

"Think you can get used to it?" he chuckled.

"Oh yeah, easily."

He gazed at the flurry of bustle. Families who had grown to know one another during the year of confinement looked for homes next to each other. Others reclaimed former homes and were busily looking to reestablish businesses. What Pieter found interesting was that some immediately found a working automobile and headed out to be as far away from civilization as possible. Yet most had stayed behind, innately recognizing there was strength in unity and codependence.

"We have a society to build, schools, police, infrastructure, things like that," he commented.

"I know."

"Not everyone is going to like having rules and regulations," he pointed out, "especially if they can spread out and not have to answer to anyone."

"They will eventually," she countered. "It's up to us to institute a well-regulated society."

"They did that once," he quietly observed, "and we ended up here."

"That was then," she replied. "Hopefully we learned our lesson."

"Fortunately we do have a beginning with what you set up below. Now all we have to do is expand on it."

They stopped to watch a group of kids crawling over the playground, running and climbing and laughing.

"Wonder how long it will be before we meet other survivors," he wondered aloud.

"I don't think there's going to be a rush anytime soon. Sure, those who survived alone will probably seek out others, but I suspect it'll be some time before we see a group show up at our door."

She heard the squeal of laughter, but it was a man's laughter, of one in pure joy. Puzzled, she looked to her right at the playground where Beauregard had discovered a swing and JB was pushing him with all his might. Standing just to the side, Ruth lavished loving attention to the baby in her arms.

Made in the USA
San Bernardino, CA
20 June 2016